THE FACE TELLS THE SECRET

Jane Bernstein

Regal House Publishing

Published by
Regal House Publishing, LLC
Raleigh, NC 27612
All rights reserved

ISBN -13 (paperback): 9781947548787
ISBN -13 (epub): 9781947548794
ISBN -13 (mobi): 9781947548800
Library of Congress Control Number: 2019931629

Interior and cover design by Lafayette & Greene
lafayetteandgreene.com
Cover images © by Paradise Studio/Shutterstock

Regal House Publishing, LLC
https://regalhousepublishing.com

Printed in the United States of America

Praise for *The Face Tells the Secret*

Gorgeously written, and deeply moving, this is a book about the ways we are loved—and more importantly—the ways we let ourselves love.

- Caroline Leavitt, New York Times Bestselling Author of *Pictures of You* and *Cruel Beautiful World*

Reverberating with vivid characters, tempestuous bonds, and poignant moments, *The Face Tells the Secret* is a contemporary page-turner as haunting as it is humane.

- Rachel Simon, New York Times Bestselling Author of *Riding The Bus With My Sister* and *The Story of Beautiful Girl.*

Jane Bernstein's novel is a beautiful, almost balletic exploration of the role of repression across generations. This book asks many questions—about knowledge, forgiveness, disability, the slippery shapes of fear and love—but always through the lived life of its narrator. Her journey had me hooked.

- Elizabeth Graver, author of *The End of the Point*

A compelling novel of secrets and surprises…that makes us ask if we can really trust anyone. At the same time it makes us understand that trusting someone is the only way to be human. I have long been a fan of Jane Bernstein's work but I feel that in this novel she has brought together her considerable skills as a writer of compassion and a consummate storyteller and has told her finest story of all.

- Mary Morris, author of *Gateway to the Moon*

The characters in Jane Bernstein's expansive and beautiful novel, *The Face Tells the Secret*, are exquisite, complex, real creations. From Pittsburgh to Tel Aviv, they bring us into their lives with depth and honesty. A wonderful book."

- Karen E. Bender, author of *Refund*, a Finalist for the National Book Award

Bernstein explores with great sensitivity the complex nature of love: familial love; romantic love; love of friends; and, love of those more or less fortunate than ourselves. She asks difficult questions for which there are no easy answers: How do we lead authentic lives? How do we put back together shattered hearts? How do we recognize and embrace faith that comes unexpectedly in faraway places? Bernstein's answers are honest, surprising, and wise.

- Janice Eidus, author of *The War of the Rosens* and *The Last Jewish Virgin*

"Who should we care for?" asks Roxanne, the narrator of *The Face Tells the Secret*. "How much of our lives should we spend looking after others? When do we turn away to protect ourselves?" Jane Bernstein delivers no easy answers in this heartbreaking and, ultimately, heart-mending novel.

- Suzanne Kamata, author of *Losing Kei* and *Indigo Girl*.

For Hinda

We find out the heart only by dismantling what the heart knows.

— Jack Gilbert
"Tear It Down" from *Collected Poems*

Der ponim zogt ois dem sod

One day I would see them in a large heated pool: a man cradling a woman, swirling her in the water in dreamy figure eights, dancing, almost. The woman in his arms was so limp, neck arched and head thrown back, long legs dangling. I tried to imagine the pale man was a prince, and she was the princess he would rouse from decades of sleep with a kiss. I tried to think this unsettling sight was a dream. But the acrid smell of chlorine and the fat keys from a rental car that bulged in my pocket were of this world in a way the two of them were not.

I would see all this, but not yet.

The Nothing

ONE

I was too young to remember our journey to the U.S., so life, as I recall it, begins on a cold morning, in the back of a garden apartment in New Jersey, not far from Bell Laboratories, where my mother worked. The sun is bright overhead, and I'm wearing a new wool winter coat, double-breasted with brass buttons, and breathing, or rather, teaching myself to breathe by inhaling deeply through my nose and exhaling through my lips, practicing, as if without this practice, I would not know how to do it. Though I recall no adults nearby while I am breathing, someone has teased me for standing with my mouth open, "catching flies," which is why at four, I am trying so hard to do it the right away.

And now a year or so has passed. It's late afternoon, a raw runny-nose kind of day, and I'm alone in a playground at the back of this garden apartment complex, a dusty square with three creaky swings, a seesaw, and a small slide. I avoid all of this equipment, but the slide is what I fear most. I'm afraid of climbing the metal steps, of reaching the top and having to extend one leg and then the other, of having to loosen my grip on the railings enough to slide to the bottom. But now I've come here by myself, determined to conquer this fear. It feels as necessary as learning how to breathe. I can't say how it is I'm alone at dusk on this bristly afternoon, only that I never could have made myself go up that ladder, awkwardly reposition myself at the top, let go of the railings just enough to stutter down slowly, again and again if anyone were with me. I know this, just as I know this is not a photo I am "remembering." We had no photos. Nor was it a family story. We had no family stories. Now it seems that it makes no difference if this memory, like the one in which I teach myself to breathe, is real or manufactured. They are of me, these

1

pieces of experience, and when they return to me, I am surprised by the clarity and emotional truth of each.

My mother, Leona Garlick, was a physicist. She worked in psycho-acoustics and eventually became the first woman department head at Bell Labs.

She was different from the other mothers—*we* were different. She said this proudly, which lead me to believe that "different" was a more polite way of saying "better." Certainly she was more beautiful than the other mothers, with thick black hair, dark eyes and full lips she colored red, and she was a scientist, "not the least bit maternal," a descriptor, like "different" she used with great pride; "maternal" being something that described housewives, while she couldn't "waste her time on such nonsense."

Her words, her expressions, live in my brain.

I cannot remember her in everyday life—at the dinner table, watching a show on TV, wearing pants. Only waiting for her, knocking on the door of the office she'd set up in the house my parents bought near Bell Labs, pink from my bath, teeth brushed, dressed in pjs. Her office was a sacred room, completely different from the rest of the house, which was tidy and well-furnished and spare, with no *tchotchkes* at all. Her space was cluttered with books and journals, towers of stacked trays, and gifts she'd been given over the years: a red-tasseled scroll from China, a *netsuke* from Japan, a ceramic burro, a brass clock, inscribed with her name. Knocking softly. Daring to open the door an inch. She might swivel in her chair, might lean over, might let me put my lips to her cheek, carefully; even then I knew she did not like to be touched.

Also a treat was being allowed to sit on the edge of her bed while she dressed for an evening event, to watch the faces she made in the mirror when she dabbed on eye shadow, applied her lipstick, blotting the excess by placing a single square of toilet paper between her lips, pressing hard, then scrutinizing herself from each angle, close up, from a distance. Or sitting on the top step when the scientists came over, where I could see her in the wing chair, waving her arms languidly while she spoke, cigarette between her fingers, legs in sheer hose. The way the room went silent while she spoke; the way they waited to laugh until she did, these men. And they were all men, in those days, and she was the queen.

Once a visitor from another country wanted to say hello to me, and my mother had called warmly from the bottom of the stairs. "Roxanne, come and meet our guest." She escorted me into the living room and let me stay until nine o'clock. I know because she said, "All right, upstairs. It's nine o'clock."

On another night, I raced downstairs after the company had left, crying, "Mommy!" and was stopped by her angry visage. "Aren't you a little *old* to call me Mommy?"

How old had I been?—Six, seven? After that, I had not known what to call her and was too shy to ask. *Mommy* was too babyish. *Mom* was like a dumpling caught in my throat. *Mama* was too European. *Mother* was the name used by the scrubbed, well-mannered children in the stories I loved, when Nanny escorted them into the drawing room to say goodnight.

Because my mother had important things to do, *the girl* picked me up from school, gave me milk and cookies and sat with me until my father, a math teacher, came home. The girl was an older black woman, with shiny hair that looked to be of one solid piece, and long slender fingers. She held my hand when we walked home, brushed my hair gently, making a neat part, letting the comb tickle my scalp, and tying my hair in two pigtails. I cannot recall her face, only those beautiful hands with the long fingers and oval nails.

Then there was the Polish girl with grayish skin and moles on her cheeks; "beauty marks," she called them. She ate cookies with me, three for every one I was allowed because she was bigger, she said. After the Polish girl was a high school student with blonde eyebrows and long blonde hair. She wore pink lipstick, and one of her arms was short and hung loosely. This girl was determined to ignore me. Something about her willful lack of interest made me act in a different way with her than I had with the others. I followed her from the kitchen, and when she picked up the boxy phone and carried it as far as the extension cord would go, I trailed behind and talked at her, while she talked into the phone, traveling, phone in hand, trying to turn away from me, the cord twisting around her.

"I hate her," I told my father. Unable to explain why, I asked why her arm was like that, and he breathed heavily, which he did when he was disappointed, and said I must never be cruel. "She's a human being just like you." I was ashamed and did not know why, only that she continued to ignore me as if it was her official job, and I continued to follow her everywhere, until at last she quit.

After that, I wore a house key on a chain around my neck and let myself in through the back door.

Branches scratching the windows, voices, a stranger ringing our bell; the moan of the siren, which meant someone's house was on fire. These were the daytime sounds that made me rigid with fear. At night, I was jolted awake by crying, screaming; angry words in a language I felt but did not understand. Trembling in bed, I was unable to move. Though I could not say it was her, my body was heavy with the knowledge, and in the morning I watched, waiting from a distance, careful not to get too close. If I felt the tension abate, I might hum and twirl into the kitchen and be very cute, and sing, "Bar-rump went the little green frog one day," or "When the red red robin comes bob bob bobbing along along," or another song I'd learned in school. Sometimes I was told flatly to stop being cute, though she might pause and smile and say, "That was cute."

I loved my mother so much.

My classmates brought in ant farms and erector sets for show and tell. I asked my mother if I could bring her, and she said yes. The morning she was to come to school, she wore a tweed suit, a silk blouse, and long gold chains, one with a watch in a locket. It was all so thrilling: the heels of her pumps clicking on the old wood floor; the word "pumps"; the square briefcase she carried with its brass lock that clicked smartly, like a soldier's salute; the way she stood in front of the room. The teacher moved to the corner of the room, where she sat knock-kneed in a small chair. while my mother leaned against her desk.

The children's hands went up. I watched with pride as she pointed a polished nail to call on a boy. Her answers were so patient.

No, she was not a medical doctor. She was a scientist.

No, test tubes were not used in her lab: she had electronic equipment.

I got a hall pass so I could walk her to the front door of the school and stand with her until my father pulled up outside. After my parents drove away, I skipped back to my classroom, heels noisy on the linoleum. I felt special as I slipped into my seat.

All afternoon, I was swollen with pride. *My mother.*

At recess a boy said, "Why does she talk like that?"

"Like what?" I said.

Our teacher said, "Dr. Garlick grew up in another country and has an accent."

"No she *doesn't,*" I said.

Later, I was able to hear her as that boy had done: I could detect the subtle differences, the way she'd mastered the *w*, except when she was mad, but the *th* continued to elude her. *Den you vill go vidout dinner.*

But at the time, what the boy and teacher said felt like accusations, and they were wrong. My mother didn't have an accent or come from somewhere else.

But what were we? A year or two later, while I'm leaning against a damp brick wall at recess, picking at the mortar, a moon-faced girl walks over. She stands very close and scrutinizes me: hair, blouse, shoes. She squints, as if to see beneath my clothes, then asks, "What are you?"

I don't know what to tell her, but I think maybe my father does, since he's a teacher. When he gets home, I ask, "What am I?"

The question makes him uneasy. "Who wants to know?" he asks.

"A girl at school," I say.

"Why, is she an anti-Semite?"

"What's an anti-Semite?"

I follow him to his office, watch him open the clasp of his accordion briefcase and arrange the papers on his desk. When he goes to the bathroom, I prop myself against the door, smell the cigarette smoke that escapes from the gap near the floor, wait for the flush, then slide into a sitting position against the wall while he goes into the bedroom to change his clothes, asking, asking, until eventually I understand that "Jewish" is the answer to, "What are you?" The definition of "anti-Semite" is: "People who don't like us."

"I'm Jewish," I tell the girl the next time she approaches. She studies me in that same up-down way, hair, clothes, shoes, and says, "*I'm* Catholic," and walks away.

But what *is* Jewish? My parents considered themselves more fully evolved than our church-going neighbors with their bathtub virgins, or the typical suburban Jews with their kosher kitchens who ate spareribs and shrimp at the local Chinese restaurant. We had no Chanukah bush, like some of these families. We celebrated no holidays, had no family traditions, no siblings, cousins, uncles, aunts. It seemed, then, that "Jewish" was a category, a label for a box. But the box was empty.

When asked my religion, I learned to say, "Nothing." Later, when it puzzled friends who knew I was born in Israel and that my father taught at a Jewish school, my answer became more insistent. We were nothing. It was a milder response than the one given by my mother, who often held forth on her hatred of all religion.

For a long time, I believe that my mother's dislike of me stems from my problems with math. I love reading and drawing, the smell and texture of everything in the art room at school, the fat, waxy crayons, the jars of paste, with brushes attached to the lids, the coarse colored paper. I also love "the woods," an undeveloped triangle of land with berry bushes and scrubby trees, holes beneath the brush made by burrowing animals, and beautiful caterpillars I bring home in metal Band-Aid boxes. But numbers are as unyielding as the languages my parents spoke. In class, while everyone else's pencils glide across their pages, their erasers bobbing, I tear my paper while trying to scrub my errors, then ball up the mess I've made and throw it on the floor.

My father begins sitting with me at the dining room table every day when he gets home from school, sadness in his breathing, his stale smell, and his chalky sleeves, the annoying *kh kh* sound he makes to clear his throat. My failure, his irritation. "It's easy! Look. It's easy!"

Is this what he says to his students at Solomon Schechter?

You must finish this before I get Mother.

Looking up at him, obtuse, angry. Everything compressing, hardening inside me.

Every year it gets worse. Even now, I can't say if my failures were willful or unavoidable, only that I could not do those problems, could not disappoint my parents, yet disappointed them every day.

By middle school, I was like a bird that makes a nest with straw and tinsel, strands of audiotape and plastic bags. In my nest, along with the scary nighttime sounds and languages used to exclude me, were blue aerogrammes with Hebrew writing. A holocaust survivor who came to our school: she was part of that nest. The book with photos of living skeletons in striped pajamas: piles of bones, of shoes, of purses, the mournful girls who looked at me from the pages, as if to pull me into the picture where I belonged.

Somehow, I knew that my father had family in Israel, and my mother had been sent to live with cousins she loathed in Lyon, France. Eventually, I had enough detail to construct a Cinderella story, in which she was beautiful and smart and made to scrub the floor on hands and knees while the ugly sisters, real *miskeits*, both of them, had fancy clothes and went to balls. (I, too, was a *miskeit*, skinny and messy, with dark enough skin that the class bully, when he was done mocking me for my name, called me "jungle bunny," a slur I failed to understand, but felt as a slur.)

I must have asked before I knew not to ask, because I recall the way my mother looked at me when I came close to an unmentionable topic, her gaze so fierce I quickly averted my eyes in shame. I got that look in another situation: I was thirteen and had gone to a classmate's bar mitzvah, and when my father came to pick me up, it took a while before anyone could find me. My mother had asked where I'd been and I cheerfully confessed, "In the coat room with Richie, Neil, and Robby." I saw the look on her face and never again spoke about boys.

∾

In this time, when my mother's dislike of me weighed heavily, I met a girl in orchestra named Mindy who played the violin—I, improbably, played bass. I admired from afar her plaid mini-skirts and the color-coordinated knee socks. "Admired" is too mild: I couldn't take my eyes off her. I loved the way she wadded up her gum and placed it carefully in a tissue, the way she flipped her hair before positioning the violin on her shoulder, the way she crossed her ankles when she played. At eleven, Mindy had already "developed"; I loved the way she plucked at the hem of her sweater, pulling it away from her body to minimize the curve of her breasts, a habit she retained in middle age.

And then there was Mindy's house and her family, with an ebullient mother—a fashionable blonde dance teacher named Muriel—an older brother, and a fat beagle named Muttnik. Every day after school, Mindy and I would make ourselves a snack, curl up together in her parents' huge unmade bed, with its piled-up pillows and comforter, and watch TV. We'd kick at the dog sleeping in the bedclothes, and he'd ride the waves, groan, fart, hold his ground. The disorder was splendid, not just the messy house, with lipsticked butts in ashtrays, but the noisy relationship Mindy had with her brother, the hair-pulling and fighting in the back seat of the car, their baroque means of torture—Indian burns, noogies, half-nelsons—which did not hide their attachment to each other. Once Mindy's brother called their mother a bitch and she said, "Get out of my sight," and threw a spoon at him, and the next night, he was at the table, amusing them with the yoyo tricks he'd learned—Around the World, Walking the Dog.

The morning after my first sleepover, Mindy climbed into bed beside her mother, and I stood in the doorway until Muriel said, "Come, *tsatskelah*. I don't bite." I curled beside her and never wanted to leave.

School was like math. I tried before I gave up. By ninth grade, boys and pot and the occasional purloined bottle of booze gave me the kind of pure pleasure I'd once found in "the woods." I was bad in familiar ways: I cut classes, left a baggie of weed in my open purse, ripped up my report card when it arrived in the mail. There was so much screaming. She hated me and I hated her, and there were slammed doors and threats; once, a glass of orange juice poured over my head, and my father to the side, with his impotent, steam-engine shushing. But I was part of a community made up of other kids whose parents were unjust, so these quarrels, though vicious, did no lasting damage.

It was afterwards, when the heat had died down, that I could feel the ache of my love, and the knowledge that I could not wound her, could not, could not. Then I would knock on her door to say I was sorry. Knocked again. Twisted the knob. She would not let me in.

I wrote a letter, trying to explain how I'd felt. What did it say? *I love you, don't hate me for not being as smart as you, it's not my fault.* I put the sealed envelope on the kitchen table. Day after day it remained there unopened.

One school morning, when the unopened letter was still there, and I was standing at the stove, waiting for the water to boil, she walked past me on her way to work and said, "You ugly little worm."

That same cool tone, when I was dressed to go out with friends. "No one will ever love you."

To be hated like this made me lose my fear of her, and I fought back and then turned on myself.

Mindy was busy with extracurricular activities—choir and French club. So I went straight from school to her house, often arriving before she did. I'd follow the haze of smoke from the cigarettes that would kill Muriel, then closer, the edge of whiskey, Chanel 5, tobacco. *Come here, doll. Come, tsatskeleh, a hug for mama.* If company was over, Muriel would tell her friends, "This little beauty is my other daughter. The artistic one."

By high school, Mindy was a National Merit Scholar and in honors classes and I'd gravitated to the stoner crowd, smoked pot, ate mushrooms, spent hours designing psychedelic posters for imaginary concerts. I braided the front locks of my hair, wore Indian shirts with little mirrors sewn in the fabric and long flowing skirts. Mindy said my friends were druggies and losers and I was turning out to be like them.

I hated school, didn't give a shit about my dumpy, boring friend, stopped going to her house.

For seven years we did not speak.

Once, at the end of my senior year, I stopped to get ice cream with my friends and through the shop window saw Muriel get out of her car. I raced across the street without waiting for the light to change, and when I caught up to her, held out my ice cream and said, "Cherry vanilla." She took the cone and drew me close with her free arm. "Where have you been, *tsatskeleh?* It's been too quiet around the house."

Her blonde hair looked brittle and her skin was lined, and I felt a chill, an awareness of mortality. "I don't know," I said.

"Friends fight, *tsatskeleh.* It happens," she said. "But you could still come see me."

"*Really?*" I said.

I hugged her again and promised to visit, and didn't out of shyness. Years passed before I saw her again. She was very sick by then and would not let me apologize. "You were a *kid,*" she kept saying when I tried to explain.

That fall, at a college that admitted anyone with a beating heart, I took an intro to psych class and learned about Harry Harlow's groundbreaking studies on human attachment. Miserable, alcoholic Harry Harlow, determined to disprove an earlier theory of mother love as being dangerous, gets some rhesus monkeys, and divides the group into those who have prickly, hurtful wire mothers that can provide only nourishment, and terrycloth mothers that provide warmth but no nourishment. The monkeys with the terrycloth mothers will thrive. The warmth of these pseudo-mothers provides the comfort they need when they are frightened or left alone. The other monkeys, the ones with the wire mothers, scream and rock and pull out their hair, inconsolable, forever damaged.

I read this on the top bunk in my dorm, where I stayed instead of attending classes, taking occasional breaks from those wide-eyed, inconsolable monkeys by reading fashion magazines and getting stoned.

Take this love quiz to determine the kind of attachment you seek.

Q: Do you want to tell your romantic partner everything about you?

A: Yes, except for the monkeys.

I never wanted to speak about those monkeys, never could admit how often I saw their faces.

TWO

As if to fulfill my parents' expectations, I flunked out of school and then moved as far away as I could—for me, the West Coast. A friend in San Francisco got me a job at a dress shop in the Haight called the Chic Pea, a tiny store where a small number of pricey, badly sewn garments in crushed velvet or crepe hung on giant clotheslines. Because so few people came in to browse, I spent long afternoons sitting in an old club chair, drawing.

What was I? Men took in my dark eyes and hair and guessed Greek or Italian.

Nope.

I was elusive.

Then what was I?

A citizen of the world. It was how I thought of myself.

"Garlick is a Jewish name," said one dubious lover.

Sometimes, I told him I was from Belarus; for I knew that "Garlick" and all its variations (Gorelik, Garlick, Garelik, Gorelick, Gurlick, Horelick, Garlock) could be translated in Russian as "someone who had a house fire." There were also "Garlicks" from Lancashire, England. Sellers or eaters of garlic.

"But *you're* Jewish," he insisted.

"Some would say," I told that boyfriend, because I thought, I really did, that I had separated so completely from my parents it was as if an actual cord had been cut.

During those long afternoons at the Chic Pea, I began discharging the hated hieroglyphics of my childhood. Even when I set out to draw something realistic—the bony woman with the henna frizz looking admiringly at herself in a misshapen tunic—eights were in her hair and her nose was a seven.

Certain piquant phrases began to roll out of me during this time, complete with a slight European accent, sometimes Yiddish, other times British. *I beg to disagree. I haven't the foggiest notion.* Friends were amused by what seemed to be a shtick, particularly a boyfriend from Fairbanks, Alaska, who was fascinated by what I considered the most banal parts of my past, curious to know if we were more Phillip Roth or *Partisan Review*. I could delight him by going on about the *balabustas* in our neighborhood, the *drek* in the stores, the *miskeits* rolling in the mail carts at Bell Labs, with their bitten nails and scuffed shoes, the support staff in my mother's department. *Huh! A typical engineer! A technician!*

Even in my dreams, I felt her presence. I was always calculating. Once I worked so hard to solve a problem that had presented itself to me in a dream that I woke myself up with the question: Which is greater in number, mice or Coca Cola?

Per unit there are more mice, I decided. Per volume there is more Coke.

Then I went back to sleep.

I called home often. Something in my body demanded it. I no longer remember these exchanges, only that afterwards, raw and irritable, I quarreled with my friends, broke up with my boyfriends. Terrible PMS, I called these flare-ups.

In my second year in California, I began to put together a portfolio so I might apply to art school. On one of these phone calls, I mentioned this program to my mother. Art school was nonsense, she said. If I thought she'd waste her money paying for tuition I was out of my effing mind. I applied anyhow and was accepted. When I called home to tell my mother about the small fellowship I'd been awarded, my father said, "We'll pay the rest."

"Daddy!" I hadn't even known he was on the other line. "Daddy, wow!" Never had he shown any evidence that I was more to him than "daughter who was bad at math."

After that, I tried to talk to him when I called. I always asked how he was, and he said, "I have no complaints." Then, "I'll put your mother on the phone."

One spring, I came home for a visit. This was after I'd graduated, after I'd had my first success—designing an album cover for a record that went gold. I'd come to Bell Labs to drive my mother home from work and was standing in the lobby, looking at a display of all the scientific advancements and technology that had been developed there—the phonograph, the transistor, the laser, radio astronomy. I'd paused over a photograph and biographical sketch of William Shockley, co-inventor of the transistor, when a man came up beside me and said, "That's kind of sanitized, don't you think?"

"What is?" I said, noticing the smudges on the glass case, and then the big, handsome man with straight black hair that flopped in his eyes, and small, square teeth.

"Shockley was a racist. He spent a lot more time advancing his view that blacks were genetically inferior to whites than he did working on the transistor. Don't you think it should say that right here?" He tapped the glass.

"Maybe they should remove him from the case," I said.

"No way. He has to be here. No Shockley, no Silicon Valley. No electronic age. He was a real shit—and he changed the whole course of human history. How about 'William Shockley, co-inventor of the transistor and vocal proponent of eugenics.' What do you think? You don't work here. I can tell by your shoes."

His name was Tom. He was an electrical engineer and made me laugh. He told me he was waiting for his girlfriend to finish work, then asked for my phone number. I gave it to him, and later I married him, and much later, I'd learn that he'd come upon another young woman looking at photographs and asked for her number, and she, too, gave it to him, as did the next one and the one after.

When I explained to my San Francisco friends that I was moving, I said, "New Jersey—what you do for love!" as if I was sacrificing everything for this man. Tom had a house not far from my parents' and even closer to the split-level where Mindy lived with her husband and three kids, a fixer-upper with fat plastic children's toys in every room. The first time I visited, we fell into each other's arms, and when we parted, her blouse was wet with breast milk. We doubled over with laughter, as if we were back in junior high, and had never quarreled and hated each other. How we got together so often during that time remains a mystery, since I was commuting to New York for work, and she had her babies, and the last of her coursework, and then her clinical year.

As for my husband—he was childish and hotheaded, unfaithful, and also, in his own way, fiercely loyal. When we visited my mother and father, Tom was so protective of me it was as if he were the parent. He called my mother "Leona," so I did too, in those years. He respected her, found her maddening, and was her match, teasing her, sparring with her, sometimes heatedly. When they started talking shop—Bell Labs was then on the cusp of being split into pieces—my father and I cleared the table and made awkward conversation in the kitchen.

With Tom beside me, I could be with my mother and want nothing from her. I could laugh about her self-absorption and mimic her expressions. I pretended she was writing a memoir called *I Beg to Disagree—the Life and Times of Leona Garlick, PhD,* and on the drive to their house, proposed chapter headings. "Chapter One: You're Completely Mistaken," and "Chapter Two: Those Bastards." Chapter Ten, which had a diatribe against her support staff and a one-sentence reference to our marriage, was called, "Huh! A Typical Engineer!"

Toward the end of our marriage, Tom's sparring stopped being playful. It was as if he had to break up with my mother before he could leave with me.

One evening, after I'd won a design award, Tom boasted about it to my parents. "It's the Nobel Prize of design," he said. An exaggeration, not that it mattered: When my mother interrupted to describe her induction into the National Academy of Science, his face began to redden. "We're not talking about some award you won thirty years ago. What the fuck," he said, pushing himself from the table.

We listened to the door slam. "What's he upset about?" asked my mother after a moment of stunned silence.

I found him pacing at the side of the house. "Forget it," I said, though his pride in me had meant everything. "Please come back inside and forget it. For me, okay?"

I went into the house alone. "No one has ever spoken to me that way," said my mother when I sat at the table.

"Forget it, okay?" I begged.

My father forgot.

After he retired, he began to forget a lot of things—to turn off the flame under the tea kettle, to take his key out of the front door lock.

He's always been careless, said my mother. She had retired from Bell Labs and briefly taught, but she had no lab, no graduate students or grants, so that ended, too.

Simple tasks began to confuse my father—how to use the remote to open the garage; how to get to the dry cleaners or use the CD player.

"He's just being stubborn," my mother said.

It got worse, until even my mother could not deny it.

When I stopped at my parents' house, I helped him put on appropriate outerwear and walked with him on the quiet streets of their neighborhood, pausing to pet dogs or listen to a bird calling to its mate from a high-up branch. Then the two of us had cookies and tea.

One afternoon—this was after he'd thrown away his glasses and dentures and before he'd lost his language—he leaned across the table, studied me for a long time, and then asked, "Wasn't there another one?"

I was disheartened, though hardly surprised, that in his confused state he might imagine a more remarkable daughter, one endowed with the beauty and brilliance of his wife.

THREE

In the summer of 2000, my mother announced that she was moving to Tel Aviv. By then, my father was dead, Muriel was dead, and Tom had gone.

"You're kidding!" I said.

My mother never kidded. I'm not sure she would have been capable, had she been inclined. Still, in my shock, it was all I could manage. "Why would you do that?"

She had just turned eighty and was formidable, healthy, sharp, fashionable, still living in the house of my childhood.

I knew my father's long descent into dementia had been devastating. Though she'd never seemed to like him much, he'd been her companion, housekeeper, chauffeur, speaker of her languages, guardian of her secrets. My mother had never learned to drive, so it made sense for her to sell their house (*my* house, I still thought of it) in a town where public transportation was so poor only indigents and cleaning women took the local buses. Still, to leave the country seemed extreme when there were nearby boroughs with busy shopping areas and train service to New York.

"My mind is made up," she told me.

"Tel Aviv?" I said. "Israel?" I tried to tell myself that it was childish for a full-grown woman to feel abandoned, but I was stung, deeply hurt. "That's quite the choice for someone who doesn't like Jews."

She raised an eyebrow and scrutinized me. It was a trick she confessed to having practiced in the mirror, enamored of an English movie actor who interrogated suspects in this manner.

"Religion is what I hate. Don't twist my words."

"But *Israel?*"

Why would she relocate to a place where she had no friends or colleagues, *no interest whatsoever* in my father's niece, who lived there with her family? Then, and every other time I asked, puzzled, hurt, annoyed, she said, "No one is left in New Jersey. Everyone is dead."

"*I'm* not dead."

"You know what I mean."

Everyone you *like* is dead. That's what she meant.

I did not say this aloud, could not voice what I knew to be the case, that I brought her no comfort, no security, no companionship, no grandchild. I'd flunked out of college and failed at marriage. And now she was fleeing the country because everyone was dead.

Everyone she liked.

I moved too, fifteen months later. When I think about it now, the decision to join a design firm in a city I did not know, with its most unfortunate name—Pitts Burgh—seems petulant. Hasty, certainly. But I felt intrepid saying yes, independent, certain that this was a great move, professionally and personally.

I'd never been to Pittsburgh before Les Sheldon flew me there. What I remember from that first visit was the tall, thin railroad trestle and low-density sprawl on the way from the airport, the dark tunnel, the way the city shot out of the far end in a stunning, show-offy way, with its bridges and inclines and houses perched high on the hills. My interest was piqued by this landscape, and by Les, who'd been fat, bitter, and married when I'd known him at Cal Arts, but who had morphed in an astonishing way into a buff, tattooed single guy.

Les took me to a restaurant with tin ceilings and a busy bar, tended by middle-aged women in white shirts and black aprons who moved with the grace of dancers. In the morning, he showed me the old school house he'd bought on Smallman Street, in an area of light industry he claimed was poised for change. He'd painted the exterior lime-green, which was dreadful and not, rented out space to a yoga studio and a neighborhood redevelopment organization, and saved the whole second floor for his company, called "Intelligent Design" until the name began to take on unfortunate associations, at which point he added an orange carat and an "s" and redid the logo. I could be a partner, could co-own everything except the lime-green building, and together, we could transform Intelligent Design into the preeminent design firm and idea factory in the country. "Idea factory," as if the two of us and the comely interns Les hired walked around with hard hats and protective goggles.

Two months later, I drove across the state with a rattling U-Haul hitched to the back of my car. The truck traffic on the Pennsylvania Turnpike was thick. I found myself inhaling when I was between two semis, as if that might make my car smaller. I listened to music, but the refrain that played nonstop in my head was the warning I'd gotten at the U-Haul place. *Don't back up.* When I stopped for gas or pulled into a rest stop, I had to remember not to back up or the trailer could jackknife and I'd be stuck that way forever.

A light mist fell. Driving west, through tunnels and around s-curves, the caution grew louder. *Do not back up.* Then I saw a sign for Ohio, and in a moment of pure panic—what was I doing, heading to Ohio?—I pulled onto the shoulder and got out. Trucks barreled past, spraying grit. If there were stars, I couldn't see them in the night sky. Standing on the shoulder, I felt my mother's dislike of me. I had lived with this the way a person born without an arm knows only the experience of being one-armed. When I was with my friends or eating fabulous food or making love, when I was absorbed by a movie, designing a beautiful box, all my attention on color, texture, shape, and form, I did not feel this wound, was so detached from it that I forgot it was there. That night when I stood on the side of the road, truck tires kicking grime into my face, the sense of aloneness made me feel as if I had no skin, no cover, no protection.

I want to go home. That's what I thought as a shimmying semi thundered past, kicking grime into my face. *I don't want to be here. I want to go home.* I did not yet know that "home" was more a feeling than a place, as perhaps it had been for my mother.

I got back in the car and started the engine. I did not back up. I waited for the right lane to be clear, floored it, and continued west.

Though I kept yearning for "home," wherever that was, I stayed in Pittsburgh. I made friends, went on dates, bought a small arts and crafts house with a beamed ceiling and a "tuberculosis room," a sleeping porch with casement windows that opened onto a majestic ginkgo tree, and beyond, the city itself, twinkling at night.

I did not leave my mother behind. Her voice remained in my head, her characteristic expressions and acerbic opinions, so while shopping, I might be attracted by a leather belt with silver studs, take it from the rack, smell the leather, work it through my belt loops, see how well it fits, then hear her declare it a *shtik drek!* and whip it off my waist.

This was totally different from *thinking* about my mother, which I also did, every day. I called every Friday. These calls took such effort that I braced myself, the way one does before a dental procedure. Though I did not actually tell myself: *This will only take a minute and then you'll be fine*, I got ready as best I could while I waited for her to pick up. Then I said, "Hi, Mom!" or Ma or Mommy in a loud, false, cheerful voice.

"Who is this?" she always asked, as if there was someone else who called her "mom."

"It's me! Roxanne! I'm at my office," I added in that awful too-bright voice, because hadn't I learned that it was pointless to be alive unless one was productive? Wasn't I raised to believe that work was what distinguished us from the *balagulas* and *balabustas* and the vegetables—truck drivers, housewives, and plants—as if these three were the lowest of the low, thorny-headed worms, belonging to the same phylum. Being productive. "I'm at work!"

Years before, trying to explain what I did, I brought a souvenir for my mother. "A matchbox?" she'd said. "This is your job?" She no longer asked questions about my life and had nothing to say of hers. There were only stories I knew well, if I begged her to stay on the line. She liked to tell me about her husband Morris who'd been so devoted to her and the way he'd gone senile. "I know. I was there," I said impatiently, no longer able to be egoless, to expect nothing. "He was my father, remember?"

At the end of our phone calls, I often said, "I'd like to see you. When can I visit?" and she said, "Don't bother." I was hurt and relieved and didn't bother and knew that my reluctance to visit had nothing to do with "bother." If I saw my mother I would want something. I would not get the words I needed. I would not get reassurance. I would not get her loving gaze because there was no loving gaze, there was nothing beyond the same carefully crafted stories I knew by heart.

And so I got off the phone, turned back to my desk, and waited for Les to return from lunch and for our office to fill with the chug and hiss of the expensive espresso machine he'd lugged back from Italy and the aroma of rich, dark coffee. I waited for him to swallow his cup in a single gulp, nostrils flaring, then lower himself into his seat so we could hash over projects and hate things together—fonts, styles, trends, foods—a very comforting ritual we'd fallen into early on. If there was time, I might get him to discuss whatever woman he was seeing—my curiosity about the habits and sartorial choices of his dates was insatiable. After that, I sat at my work area and lost myself until the end of the day. Then I rose, or Les did, and one of us said, "Life," and the other, "totally overrated," and we headed out into world.

FOUR

One morning a man called at work. "My name is Harley Graeme," he said. "Edie Phillips suggested I contact you. Is this a bad time?"

Edie Phillips was the effusive chair of a committee that organized a black-tie event to raise money for kidney disease. She *loved* the invitations I had designed for the event, loved my style, my dry sense of humor. So I said, "Now is fine," and waited for the man on the phone to go on.

"It's not urgent," he said. "I can call at a time when it's more convenient. My day is completely open."

"Now is perfect," I said.

"And tomorrow, any time after ten could work. Or the day after, as long as it's before two. I know you have a lot on your plate."

"The kidney beans are gone," I said. "All that's left on my plate is a little rice."

"Excuse me?"

"Now's a good time," I said.

"Excellent. Thank you. I was wondering if we might get together. Briefly. I could swing by your office at lunch time or we could meet for coffee later in the day. Whatever your schedule permits."

I should have asked Edie to tell me something about this humble stranger, but that hadn't occurred to me until I walked into the dim, fashionable restaurant he'd suggested and a slender man rose from the bar stool—Harley T. Graeme. Oh! I thought. Then after a brief, businesslike handshake, and a lengthy decision about our booth— here, no, this one's better, what about there?—I found myself sitting across from him, thinking, what a nice-looking man!

Had so long passed since I'd seen an attractive guy that I'd become like one of those men who can't get their eyes off a woman's cleavage no matter the business at hand? It wasn't that he was gorgeous, which might have turned me off, since I was wary of men who were self-consciously handsome. It was that for a man of his age—our age—he was so clean looking, with no tufts sprouting from his nostrils or ears. Nice head of graying hair, teeth that were strong, if crowded, trim, lanky, erect.

Out of sheer nervousness I began to describe in lavish detail everything I had done for Edie, the marketing, the brochures, the invitations, the event, the band, their rendition of "My Sharona," *Ooh my little pretty one, pretty one. Ooh you make my motor run, my motor run...* I told him about the press releases, the photographer with the hair plugs, the heartbreak of polycystic kidney disease—occasionally pausing and looking up to find his soft eyes on me, his expression unreadable, yielding not a single clue.

It was only when lunch had ended and he deftly palmed the bill that I realized he hadn't said a single word about his reason for calling me. Nervousness crept upward, starting from my heels. What was my problem, blathering on the way I did, behaving like an idiot?

Harley shook my hand when we were together on the street. "Thank you for doing this." You'd think I just pulled him from a roiling river. "Thank you for taking the time."

"What business?" Edie asked when I reached her later that day. "I just couldn't stop thinking about you and Harley in different corners of the city, both of you single, how maybe you two should meet. Call me an incurable romantic."

Alone in different corners was right. Harley lived in the South Hills and worked downtown. We didn't walk the same streets or eat in the same restaurants or know a single person in common, apart from Edie, whose wealth he managed, and whose gala event I'd helped market. If Edie had asked me ahead of time whether I'd wanted to meet Harley, I would have said no. Not my type; though at that point, the only type I had was not Tom.

I called Harley to apologize. "That lunch?" I said when I reached him. "I thought I was doing a business presentation. When I think of the way I went on and on it makes me shudder."

Harley said he enjoyed listening to me.

"That's very kind, but I never asked you a single thing. Not where you live or what you do for a living. I have no idea how you spend your spare time or if you have kids or who's your favorite Steeler."

None of those things were important, Harley said.

"Don't you want your lunch date to know something about you?"

"Not particularly," Harley said.

At dinner the next week, while the tea lights flickered at our ban-quette, Harley said, "I'm not that social a guy."

He said: "I worry more than the average person, especially about my kids, and when I do, nothing else matters."

He said: "My wife wanted the marriage to be over and when I wouldn't leave, she rented an apartment and had all my possessions moved there. She'd left a note on the cartons saying, *You and your gloomy ass can go straight to hell.*"

I laughed when I heard this. That's some crazy wife, I thought, all this crucial information extinguished in the heat of my attraction.

A few nights later, he stopped at my house after work. He had a bowl of soup and gazed at me, as if this was all the sustenance he needed in life. The next night he stopped again, and the night after that, and so on.

His silence felt deep, more intimate than words. He was sad, I could tell. Though he denied it, I knew that his wife called him night-ly to berate him for his failures as a parent and human being. He worried about his sons. I was a tonic for him. Even before he said that being with me was the best thing in his life, I could feel it was true, and it was remarkable.

Soon after, after the soup and the exquisite silence was the love-making, the long nights, nestling together in my bed, the way we fit so well together, my head against his chest, leg over his leg, taking in his scent, tickle of chest hair, the beating of his heart. *Hold me*: I did not have to say it because he did.

Harley was gracious and soft-spoken, with old-fashioned manners. I was charmed when he called his childhood "perfect," with a loving mother and father, from whom he'd never heard a negative word, protective big brother, adorable baby sister, all living in harmony with their housekeeper, a collie named Laddy, and a skating rink in their backyard, where in winter they played hockey. Harley liked to shop, which amused me. I'd never been with a man who liked to shop.

"We went shopping," I told Mindy when we returned from a trip to the North Hills or South Hills. "We're looking for a chair!" You'd think I was telling her, "We went to China!" Or "We're adopting a baby!" which I also dreamed we might do. I liked Harley's seriousness of purpose and the way he sometimes detoured to pick out a new socks or a couple of shirts. "We went to Brooks Brothers! He bought some shirts!"

Mindy and I spoke nearly every night, as if we were again adolescents. My long-married friend, mother of three, licensed family therapist, was as eager to hear my breathless details as I was to relate them. "I went to Mars to meet his sister!" "His sons are really cute!" "He's so devoted to them he can't sleep unless they call to say good night!"

Mars is a suburb of Pittsburgh. Harley's sons were as handsome as their father, polite, if completely uninterested in me. His love for them was such that nearly every night he drove to his wife's house or made the three-hour trip to State College, if one or the other did not answer the phone. I had no children and was reluctant to view this as excessive. And his concern extended to me. If I went out of town, he needed to hear from me before I departed and the instant I touched down. No one had ever said, "Call me as soon as you land!" It seemed as if no one had ever loved me enough to worry about me that way.

I could wait for Harley's sons to like me. I could wait for him to relax enough to meet my friends. I could wait to go with him to the ballet or plan for a ski trip, both of which he said he loved, or spend a week in Bruges, his favorite city. He was so tender and attentive: more than anything I wanted this relationship to work.

After we'd been together for a couple of months, Harley said that a perfect chair was all that was missing from my otherwise perfect home, so we went in search of one. The perfect chair, which we found after many excursions, was the kind of chair you see in a men's club. Dark brown leather, wildly expensive, on back order. A season would pass before it was delivered; we decided Harley would move in as soon as it arrived.

Well after I met Harley's sister, we drove to meet his brother Byron, who lived with his family in Charleston, West Virginia, where he owned several fast food franchises. When Harley first took me to meet them, their Scottie would not let me enter the house. He kept skittering side to side, barking frantically, as if I were an intruder. At last, one of their girls dragged him away by the collar, and I stepped into the hall, where Byron, a ruddy-faced, beefy version of Harley, greeted me with a big hug, and said, "We all thought you had to be craz-y to take on little bro, but you look okay; you look *fine*."

It was the day after Christmas, and their little girl was wearing fuzzy antlers and a matching brown fleece. Their older daughter— leggy, pretty, with a mouthful of metal—sat at her father's feet. The fire was crackling, and the tree was decorated with delicate heirloom ornaments and ones made with cotton and popsicle sticks, and the house smelled of pine and spices from the mulled wine. I sank into the couch cushions, listened to their easy conversation, and the way they joshed with each other. Harley was of this family; he resembled them, could make small talk the way they did, and yet he was disengaged, phone on his lap. After he slipped off, his sister-in-law said, "Poor Lee-Lee's had such a hard time, with that wife who wouldn't let him sleep in the house, and now with the boys."

"He's got a house to sleep in now," I said. All that I knew about Harley took on a different shape. Maybe Byron was right and I *was* crazy.

When we left it was dark, and the heat in the car came up slowly.

"They're nice," I said, when I was warm. The bright lights from an oncoming car broke the darkness. "Welcoming."

Harley said he hated Byron, with his perfect fucking wife and his perfect fucking family.

This surprised me. In every other conversation, Harley had called his family perfect, which was different from "fucking perfect." Okay, I thought, trying to view this as an opportunity. Maybe now he'd open up.

I turned down the noisy heater fan.

"Your wife wouldn't let you sleep in the house?" I said.

Tina was as dumb as a stone, he said. The biggest mistake of his life was having married her. His mother had cried when he told her they were getting married, because Tina came from simple people and was smarmy.

Warmth radiated from the car seat. I felt as if I'd just peed on the leather. I asked what his father had thought.

Dad had just sold the family business, Harley said. Mother thought he was too young to be retired, so she made him dress in a jacket and tie and every morning go to the small office he kept in town, where he managed the family's investments, read the *Wall Street Journal* and books about the Civil War. After he died, they found file cabinets full of empty bottles of gin.

"My father would have liked you," Harley said that night in the dark. "He respected intelligence above all."

"And your mother?"

"She didn't like Jewish people," he said.

Harley dropped me off and went to search for his younger son.

"I thought your parents were without prejudice," I said the next day at dinner.

"They were," said Harley. "And they wouldn't tolerate anyone who expressed any prejudice either. Never did I hear a negative word from either of them."

"How did you know your mother didn't like Jewish people when she never said a negative word?" I asked.

"Hon!" said Harley. "Mother didn't *dislike* Jewish people."

A week later, the perfect chair arrived. It fit nicely in the living room. Harley sat on it that night. I brushed and flossed my teeth, sent off a couple of emails, and returned to the darkened room. "Are you coming to bed?" I asked.

He stayed in the chair, holding his cell phone, too worried to sleep.

At first, I absorbed his worry and fretted when he could not reach a son. Soon, though, these premonitions of disaster became nightly events that made it impossible for him to focus on anything else. He was too worried to have dinner at home and preferred noisy restaurants where conversation was impossible. Worry prevented him from socializing with my friends or going out of town. I remembered him saying on our first date that when he worried nothing else mattered. Now I felt it.

If I approached him in his chair, he could not see or hear me. I might face him, might speak in a loud voice. The emptiness of his gaze made me feel negated, blotted out.

I'd wanted to let him have his space, to sleep where he was comfortable, but one night when I stood in front of him in his chair, I was hit hard by the reality that nothing of me existed for him—my joy, my woes, the blood running through my veins—they were nothing, and I was nothing, and suddenly I was screaming, and even then he stayed motionless in his chair, nothing behind his eyes, and I began pulling at my hair, then his, then yanking him upward by the collar.

Frightened by the outburst, I grabbed my coat and left the house. It was as if all the adult layers had been stripped off and my teenaged self had emerged. I walked down the streets in my neighborhood, looking at the glowing windows in the quiet homes, and trying to settle down. That night, I knew as well as I knew anything that deciding to live with Harley had been a huge mistake.

Hours later, I fell into my empty bed and when I woke, Harley was sitting beside me. He put a mug of coffee on the night table and slipped the newspaper from its plastic bag. I took in his kind, untroubled face, his cashmere sweater, pressed trousers, shined shoes, and tried to explain how it felt to be unseen by him, that it turned me into a nonperson, and he said, "Everything is fine." No, I said. I could not turn into the person I'd become the night before. But in daylight, Harley could not remember anything from the night before.

In daylight, I was as perfect as his childhood in Sewickley, PA.

ॐ

For a year I tried to leave him.

I said we needed to part. He appeared to hear my words, said, "If that's what you want," promised to leave that day, and was home when I returned. Then we'd start to live together again until the next blowup and the next performance—my rage, his night away from home, his return, the talk, the promise, the status quo. At that point, we could hire understudies to play the parts for us. We didn't even need to be in attendance anymore.

Once, when I was extremely distraught and wept into my palms, he left for two days. On the way up to bed on the third night, someone said, "Hi, babe," and I realized that Harley had been sitting in his chair in the dark living room. "Hi, sweetheart. Why didn't you take my calls? I was so worried about you. The gas company called because no one could get in to read the meter. You look beautiful. I've missed you, babe. I'm dying inside without you."

Another time, we had a big talk before I left for a conference, and Harley vowed to be gone before I returned. He claimed he'd made arrangements to move his possessions. When I returned home, flowers and champagne were on the kitchen island, and before I could drop my bags, he'd rushed downstairs, caught me in his arms, and in a tremulous voice declared my homecoming the happiest moment of his whole g-damned life. He squeezed the breath out of me, inhaled my hair, told me that before we met he'd thought "love" was just a greeting card sentiment, no more real than Mickey Mouse, that I'd changed everything for him.

I said, "You need to leave right now," and as I struggled to free myself from his embrace, it seemed as if I was pushing away the only person who'd actually ever loved me.

"I hate myself when I'm with you," I tried to explain. "I've turned into a crazy person."

"Why do you say such things? You aren't crazy. You're beautiful," Harley said, gazing at me with a moony, wildly inappropriate look.

"I need you to be part of this breakup. Please tell me you hear what I'm saying."

I closed my eyes and waited and Harley eventually said, "I'll do whatever you want."

"Is that a promise?"

Harley promised. Then we had "the talk," in which I solemnly, calmly *yet again* set out all the reasons our relationship did not work, and he sadly agreed I was right in some of what I'd said and promised to move out by the end of the week. I thanked him for listening, quickly turning away before I began to feel as if I had thrown the puppy.

I had done this once. I'd been at a barbeque, idly gabbing, with a friend's puppy in my arms, still fluffy as a chick. I'd never had a dog, only a couple of cats that deigned to share their living quarters with me. With cats, when they squirm in your arms, you toss them to the ground. That's what I did when the puppy began to wiggle. I tossed him in an absentminded way, as if he were a cat. His scream sounded human. Over the years that scream echoed in my imagination. That's the kind of person I am, I thought, a woman who throws a puppy to the ground. It was what I felt after I said something wounding and Harley looked up at me in a stunned, defenseless way.

In my imagination I conferred with Harley's former wife. "Throw his stuff onto the lawn," said this woman, who was once my enemy and now my only ally.

Following her advice, I set a laundry basket full of his neatly folded shirts on the grass. Then I backtracked, brought it back to the front porch and topped it off with a couple of pairs of jockey shorts—tighty-whiteys.

Harley asked if I'd give him two weeks to find a place. I said no. "It's been two weeks and two weeks for a year."

So he left. The next day, when I came home from work, I went from room to room, flicking on the lights. No indentation on the leather seat, no one in the chair. In the morning, I made myself coffee, then started upstairs with the mug in my hand, feeling as still as a lake inside, just *being*. I am just being, I thought.

Soon I would feel very sad, I supposed. I would miss him, feel like an utter failure. But right then was the exquisite pleasure of just *being*.

Two weeks passed. Harley called at work and asked if I'd drive with him to Sewickley that Sunday to look at a condo he was thinking of buying.

"It's not a good idea for either of us," I said.

"Rox. Babe. We're not enemies. We've parted on good terms. How about doing me one last favor, which will take you two hours, three, max. I wouldn't ask, but no one has better aesthetic sense than yours. No one. How big a deal could it be?"

"Where are you living now?" I asked.

Harley laughed. *Heh.* I knew that "heh" well. It meant I'd get two answers or no answers. Even so, I said, "So, are you going to tell me?"

"In the Motel 6 by the airport."

"*Really?*"

Again that chuckle. *Heh.* "Yes," he said. Then, "No. Don't be silly. Look, I'll pick you up at noon and have you back by three at the latest, I promise."

"It's just my opinion and nothing else? You swear on Yanni's life?"

Yanni was Harley's younger son. His frat brothers had started calling him that because of his long black curls and his Greek mother, and the name stuck.

"I swear," said Harley.

He arrived that Sunday a few minutes before noon. I stepped outside to meet him.

It was the end of one life and the beginning of another.

FIVE

We arrived in Sewickley twenty minutes early, so Harley detoured through his old neighborhood, with its long, winding streets lined with houses built by robber barons. He parked in front of the big stone house where he had been raised, an impressive dwelling, with a slate roof, two turrets, a sunroom, and a generous yard where the ice rink had been. He got out of the car and paced in front of the house, hands in his pockets.

When I caught up with him, he said, "They painted the trim. It's supposed to be gray."

I took in the chocolate-colored trim around the small windows and door and had to agree it didn't work, given the pale gray stone façade.

"Chinese people live here," he said, as if this explained the odd choice. "My father would roll over if he knew."

I thought about our early days together, how I'd tugged on Harley for stories from his youth. I'd never questioned his perfect child-hood, never wanted to scratch beneath the veneer in search of flaws. No, I'd hungered for details so I might have a door to make my way into his history.

Now I said, "I thought your parents were completely unpreju-diced."

"My parents were perfect," he said, closing his eyes in happy remembrance. "They were wonderful people."

The condo was not far from the center of town, with its bou-tiques, faux gas lamps, manufactured charm. As we pulled into the parking lot outside the development, a green Jaguar edged beside us. A well-coiffed blonde popped out, tugged on her skirt as she approached to shake Harley's hand and then mine, saying, "Liza."

She took the lock box off the door and ushered us inside. "Aren't these ceilings incredible? And with the high-efficiency furnace, it's not at all expensive to heat, and anyhow, the winters we had as kids are gone."

With another tug on the little skirt, this amazing woman, who put a positive spin on global warming at the same time as she described the virtues of this condo, worked a manicured hand over the granite counter tops and cabinets and turned to me: "Do you cook? Personally, I nuke the takeout and say *voila*, but whatever your personal style, you have to admit this is a fabulous place to entertain."

"I'm just the friend," I said. "The second opinion."

As peppy Liza let her gaze linger on Harley, I imagined him settling into this apartment, with its wood-burning stove and Jacuzzi, buying manly leather furniture, a huge TV, and the La-Z-Boy recliner he'd confessed to wanting, to which I'd replied, "Tell me you're joking!" I imagined the two of them, strolling arm in arm, down the charming main street, window shopping, stopping for a light lunch, Liza asking for a salad instead of fries. I'd known plenty of people who'd lived together with minimal interaction and no air of quiet desperation, people who did not demand the ineffable, as I did. Harley was anxious and depressed, but I believed if I were okay, the way I imagined Liza to be, I could leave Harley in his dark room and go about my day with a clear head. I believed this. I really did.

"Is it mostly couples here?" I asked. "What if you're single?"

"*I'm* single!" She held out her ring-free hand. "There's plenty happening here for us single folks. Give me a call, Harley. You have my card."

Harley was not amused. "Why did you tell her I was single?" he asked when we were back in the car.

"She's very well-groomed," I said. "And you *are* single."

"What are you doing, babe?"

I felt as if I'd crushed a fluffy chick, ground it into the pavement with my heel. "It's a very nice place. It's spacious, and I guess it's well located. I just thought your chances of meeting someone might be greater if you lived in the city, but maybe I'm wrong."

"Listen, babe, you got me to move, but you can't stop me from wanting you to change your mind."

I tugged on the passenger door. "The condo is lovely, Harley. I need to go home."

"Can we talk about this at lunch?"

"Unlock the door," I said. "Please. I can't keep going through this."

"I'm taking it," he said.

"Really?"

As soon as Harley said yes, a pleasant feeling descended, a belief that as long as we didn't live together, we could be friends. Maybe I could remain in his sons' lives. No, that wouldn't happen, since I'd never had the chance to be in their lives to begin with.

All that mattered was that Harley had found a luxurious condo in a town he knew well, once home of industrialists, and now where their scions lived. He could golf with the men, date the women. Having lunch with him seemed like a kind gesture, and so when we were ensconced in our turquoise leatherette booth, our orders placed, I relaxed and began to tell him about clients who were opening a restaurant in Lawrenceville and wanted a different take on everything, including the oyster pail, that iconic container, best known for Chinese takeout. The oyster pail, which really had been used for shucked oysters in the early twentieth century, was a perfect object. Beautiful and functional. "You can play around with the color. You can change the shape. Use eco-friendly material. But the original is so great it's hard to figure out how to make it better. Or why. Or…"

I paused, aware of the din in the restaurant, the families squeezed into other booths, mothers, grandmothers, babies banging their high chair tables. Happy noise, family noise, playful conversation.

Harley looked up from his cell phone. "Is something wrong, hon?"

"No," I said. It was good that Harley had no interest in what I was saying. It was very good. It was, I thought, exactly what I needed.

❧

When I saw the car with West Virginia plates parked outside my house, I thought of Harley's brother, his too-tight hug and terrifying dog. What a relief I'd never have to see them again. Harley was standing on the sidewalk. I unlocked my door and waved to assure him I was safe.

Byron was the first person I saw when I opened the door. Then that Scotty, rushing toward me, barking, barking until their daughter took his collar and pulled him away. People were everywhere—squeezed onto the couch, perched in chairs and on the hassock, studying photos on the mantel. Les by the fireplace. I took in this improbable still life, these people and a dozen shadowy others, frame by frame, in a dense, slow-mo manner, stumbling for a millisecond on my mother and Byron's wife, and thinking, they *know* each other?

Then Mindy came forward, as womanly in her forties as she was when we were twelve, bosom heaving as her arms rose like a conductor's. A symphony of people called, "Surprise!" My mother was here from Tel Aviv. My mother, old and unkempt, in a suit with big, drooping shoulders and wine-colored pumps. I crossed the room, dizzied, wishing I'd washed my hair, chosen a nicer dress, hadn't wolfed an entire sandwich, laughing, covering my face, confused. It was not my birthday; Harley was not my boyfriend; my mother was not the mother of my comedy routines, who took her husband everywhere, as if he were a favorite pocketbook, but the mother I had neglected, with her dreadful history, about which I knew nothing and everything.

I kneeled beside her chair and said, "Mom!" so she might turn to me. "Ma!"

My mother regarded me in a blank, uncomprehending way that frightened and nullified me and brought to mind my father, toothless, half blind, leaning across the table. *Wasn't there another one?*

I leaned over to kiss her cheek, and she shivered, said, "Woooo," as if my lips were blocks of ice, and turned to Harley's pretty, golden-haired sister-in-law. "Her friend—why did he fly me here?"

"Harley?" said Emmy, the sister-in-law, whose real name was Martha Jane. "For Roxanne's birthday."

"Ach, who needs birthdays?" my mother said to her. "When you get to be my age, it's better to forget."

Emmy laughed and said, "Oh, I know just what you mean." The Scottie rose. She pressed him back onto her lap.

"Mom!" I said.

My mother said to Emmy, "From my world, they're all dead. Everyone who worked under me when I was at Bell Laboratories. Even the labs are gone, which is a disgrace. Nothing has come along to replace it. No institute anywhere in the world supports basic research the way we did. It's all gone. I'm the only one left. I've outlived all the others."

"Now *that's* something," said Emmy.

I touched my mother's arm, and she withdrew with a start.

Laughter at my door. More guests arriving. At least I didn't pinch her—proof I was a grown-up.

My knees hurt. I shifted my position. My mother pointed to Emmy. "Who's she?"

"How rude of me. Mom, Leona, this is Martha Jane…"

"Harley's sister-in-law. You can call me Emmy. Everyone does."

"Harley?" asked my mother. She'd let her hair go and the riot of color was disturbing—white, brown, black.

"I'll get him," I said.

I rose quickly, startling the Scottie, who stood upright on Emmy's skirt, trying to keep his balance in the hills and indentations formed by her clenched knees. He growled at me as I passed, and Emmy said, "Oh Mackie, stop," without conviction.

I worked my way through the rooms, rising on my toes to kiss each guest. What to say to Mindy when I'd claimed that Harley and I had broken up for good? When I'd told Les—"It's really over, splitsville, fini!"—he'd had that dubious *uh huh* look on his face in the office and now in my house.

Harley, who hated parties and had declined all invitations, including those to more intimate events, was alone on the deck, holding his phone. I left him there and hurried back to my mother, startling the Scottie who rose on Emmy's lap, a low rumbling in the back of his throat. "It's Rox-anne," she cooed, pressing on Mackie's back. "Stop that nonsense immediately."

I extended my hands so the dog could sniff me and know I meant no harm, then lowered myself and said, "I come in peace."

He sprang from Emmy's lap and sank his teeth into my hand, and I pulled sharply back, rising, until his front paws lifted from the floor. Byron rushed over and kicked Mackie, and when the dog relaxed his grip, a geyser of blood spurted from my hand.

Byron said, "I'm going to shoot that fucking dog!"

"I'm okay!" I cried, as shocked by the blood as by Byron's ferocity. "It's fine, everything is fine!"

The house went silent.

Byron followed me into the kitchen, where I grabbed a dishtowel to stanch the flow of blood. "Show me that hand," he said. I turned from him and kept turning, and he persisted. "Give me that hand. I want to see that hand."

Blood bloomed, coloring the cloth. "It's fine," I said, and slipped into the powder room.

"Sue me!" Byron called through the closed door, while I was wrapping a hand towel around my thumb. "You're going to need surgery on that hand! I want you to sue."

I did not yet feel the pain that would wake me in the dark, the throbbing like a message I might understand if I lay very still. All I wanted was for the bleeding to stop so I could sit with my mother and spend time with the guests who'd gathered to celebrate what they thought was my birthday, and when someone, Byron, I assumed, knocked on the bathroom door, I cried out, "Everything's fine. Don't let anyone leave!"

Harley squeezed into the tiny room and began to whisper fiercely—*honey, babe*—and pull at my arm so he could see the swaddled hand and whisk me to the emergency room. As I was begging, "Please! I'm fine," I wondered how many hours had to pass before I could remind him that he'd sworn on his son's life he was buying that condo, given that he had arranged this party and flown my mother in from Tel Aviv—on business class, I would learn.

I edged out of the powder room as soon as I could, and Mindy drew me into her soft, perfumed bosom. "I'm *so* glad things have worked out after all." She kissed my cheek. "He's *such* a sweetie."

It was the worst thing she could have said.

The guests gathered around the dining room table and filled their Styrofoam plates with pink cold cuts, potato salad, and sad, limp pickles. Harley brought Mom a plate of food, and Mindy pulled a chair beside her. I watched my mother hold court, and though her manner was familiar, she was so changed, so distressingly unkempt, with her wild hair and ill-fitting clothes, that I found myself thinking she would have been ashamed had she known. *Had she known.* I listened to the hum of conversation and felt very far away, no longer of mortal flesh, just an unseen spirit watching, thumb throbbing so regularly it was as if my heart had migrated to my hand.

I went into the dining room to get some sparkling water and heard my name broken into two syllables. "Rox-anne? Where is she? I want to go home. Tell her to take me home!" Mindy was in the kitchen, arranging candles on a huge baking sheet full of cupcakes, so I asked my mother to stay a few minutes longer. Mom walked past me to the door and rattled the doorknob, as if we'd locked her in the house. "*Someone* take me home."

Harley hurried across the room with her coat held open. After she worked her arms into the sleeves, he whisked her off to the place that she was calling "home," a downtown business hotel, identical to those in countless other cities, right down to the "art" that matched the décor and the nailed-into-the-walls headboards, as if they were a favorite of souvenir seekers now that ashtrays were hard to come by.

A few minutes later, Mindy brought out the sheet of cupcakes, each glowing from the flame of a small candle, and I made my wishes.

Even now, I cannot reveal them, since I hold onto a childlike belief that wishes can't come true if they're spoken aloud. All I can say is that they were modest as I inhaled slowly and deeply, then broadened until my wishes radiated like a pebble thrown in water, the rings widening, touching others everywhere. There was so much I wished for myself and for the people I loved, and for my struggling city (what a shock!), and for my country, misled by short-sighted politicians (who knew I was patriotic!), and for the Middle East (Arabs and Jews, Bedouin and Druse), then outward from there, until, with a great exhale, my own wind extinguished every flame. And still I wanted more—for the earth to be protected from asteroids crashing with such force that humankind is thrust into nuclear winter for all eternity. This last I can confess, since I forgot to wish that such a thing would never happen. So many wishes I forgot to make. A reason perhaps that everything got so much worse.

Six

My mother in Pittsburgh! Oh, I could not sleep, could not drive, either. Backing the car out of the garage was no problem, but to execute a three-point turn with only one hand was *looking for trouble*, something this same mother had accused me of doing. If only I could tell her: *Ma, you were right; I looked for trouble and I found it.*

Many buses went downtown. Before walking down the block to catch one, I called her hotel room.

"Who?"

"It's me. Roxanne."

"Who put me here?" She was very distressed.

"Harley," I said. "He meant well, Mom."

I couldn't believe I was using that loathsome expression, toted out to excuse someone's insensitive behavior. Harley *meant well* and thus bypassed my house and the many fine hotels nearby, including a restored Victorian bed and breakfast with lilac Jacuzzis.

I said, "Listen, Ma, I'll check you out this morning so you can come stay with me."

"Where's my ticket?" she said. "I want to go home."

"Your return flight isn't until tomorrow," I said. "How about if I come downtown now, and we'll figure out plans over lunch. There are lots of—"

"*Lunch?*" As if I'd just proposed throwing back some beers at the local strip club. "In a restaurant?"

Eventually she explained that all she ever ate midday was cottage cheese and a banana, and because I was of my mother, I had these items, which I packed in a paper bag.

On the half-empty bus to the hotel, a large unwashed man with dozens of ID tags strung around his neck sat beside me. He placed an assortment of bulging plastic bags at our feet. I edged away, patted the brown bag to make sure the bananas were not being crushed. The man smelled like a subway tunnel, of stale beer and dried urine.

40

The bus crept forward, and when we neared my stop, I imagined my mother rising when she saw me enter the hotel lobby, hurrying toward me with outstretched arms. *Tsatskeleh, look at you! So gorgeous! Your hand, my god!*

At Grant Street, my seatmate rooted around in his bags and withdrew a crushed Pirates cap. I worked my way over the shopping bags and got off. The hotel was up the block. I didn't really believe that my mother would turn and say, *Tsatskeleh, darling!* But I had the modest, if fervent wish that we might sit together with our bananas and cottage cheese, and I might have the chance to say: *It was so great that he flew you here, but living with him is killing me.*

She was sitting alone beneath an immense, hive-shaped chandelier in the massive lobby of this old hotel, the square shoulders of her burgundy suit jacket sagging, white canvas sneakers on her feet. When she saw me she said, "Hello, dear." I slid beside her and kissed her cheek, and she shivered and said, "Ooh, your nose is cold. Don't you have work?"

"I'll walk over later. It's not far from here."

Four jolly men passed, name tags clipped onto their jacket lapels. Thinning hair, all of them, freshly-shaved cheeks. Aftershave. Loafers.

"You're going like *that?*" Mom asked.

That—my jeans. "It's my place, Ma. I'm the boss, and I say no dress codes. Would you like to see where I work? We can get a taxi; it's very close. You can meet my partner Les and see some of our projects. We're doing really well, Mom."

"When are you getting married?" asked my mother.

"I tried that once," I said, deflated by the question. "It didn't work."

She pushed at the air. "At your age, you're lucky you have someone."

"Maybe I don't want *someone.*"

"Let me tell you something. It's no fun being alone. From my world, they're all gone. Dead. Everyone. My husband. Before his mind went, he did everything for me. He cooked. He paid the bills. He chauffeured me everywhere. My secretary, Dottie, when she saw him, she always said, 'Morris, you don't happen to have an unmarried brother, do you?' He was a terrible cook, but I never complained."

"Well," I said, "you did." Then I softened and put my hand on hers. She withdrew quickly. "The party was nice, wasn't it?"

"Never in my life have I been so ignored."

"No, Mom! Everyone talked to you! Mindy did, and Stu."

"*Who?*"

"Stu. Mindy's husband."

"Mindy?"

"My best friend? From New Jersey? Her mother, Muriel, had her hair done where you did. You thought she was smart. I remember you saying 'somewhere under that nest there's a brain.' Those were your words."

This was after Mindy and I had peered into the window of the beauty parlor in town one Saturday and saw them sitting side by side beneath the hair dryers. We plotted furiously to fix them up, certain our mothers, one a part-time dance instructor, the other a physicist, could also be best friends.

Now my mother said, "I haven't the foggiest idea what you're going on about. There's too much noise. Take me home. I want to go home."

Abruptly she stood, and I did too. "I brought some lunch." I opened the paper bag, showed her the separate portions of cottage cheese, napkins, plastic spoons, bananas.

"You need to fix yourself up and go to work. Take me back."

I lifted a banana from the bag. "No flecks!" I said. "Come on, Ma, please. Your flight's tomorrow. Let me show you our office. The work we do isn't rocket science, but it isn't just matchbooks either."

"Stop *pushing* at me. I'm not myself."

For the first five floors, we rode alone in the shimmying car. Then a waiter with a smooth Mayan face wheeled in a service cart with the remains of someone's dinner. Mom said, "You used to be a good-looking girl."

The waiter flashed a consoling "whatever" gesture.

I flushed, stunned. Did she not remember screaming, *You're ugly. No one will love you!* It was a judgment no lover or friend could ever erase.

"Why are you so obsessed with looks? You, of all people, who broke through every barrier. You were a feminist!"

"I was no such thing. Stop pushing and leave me be. You're late for work."

"Okay." I leaned close to kiss her cheek. "I love you, Mom."

It was not a lie, but an unpleasant fact of life, like a sore that would not heal.

My office was a mile or so from the hotel. I walked briskly, trying to shake free of the sadness. A yoga class had just let out. From a block away, I could see a group of women with rolled-up mats standing in twos and threes outside our building. The arrangement looked beautiful to me, these women in their hats and puffy jackets all part of a "we."

I paused at the corner and waited for them to disperse. Our office would be warm. Upstairs, I would find *award-winning creative solutions* for our long-standing clients. All I needed was to say "excuse me," climb a single flight of steps, and open the door to our suite. Les would turn: close-cropped bristly hair, tight black T-shirt that showed the edge of a complex tattoo, black jeans, black boots, a *show no mercy* expression on his face. He'd say something snarky—*Nice party!*—because he was not a man who wasted time with maybes. One date was enough for this single guy. One evening gave him all the information he needed. "I thought you and Harley broke up," he might say, because he'd said this before.

It was frigid, standing out here. Damp. The last of the yoga students embraced and parted. What did I want from my mother? Hello, goodbye. That was all.

It wasn't all. I wanted her to pause, let her gaze linger on my face. I wanted her to be someone she had never been, and I knew this, forgot it, knew it again, continued to forget.

I walked back to the hotel. Outside the entrance, a uniformed bellman breathed into his hands. I called my mother's room from the lobby and when she did not answer, I knocked on her door. A tray was on the floor outside the door beside hers. A white rose in a bud vase, two plates, two half-eaten croissants, two coffee cups. A story was there, and it sat like a rock in my chest.

She never answered.

Harley was sitting on the edge of the bed when I opened my eyes the next morning, holding a rolled-up newspaper and a large coffee, which I instinctively took. Creamy shirt, pressed trousers. Why was he in my bedroom? Still woozy, I tried to string together some words. Before I could speak, Harley took my wrist and set my wounded hand across the crease of his trouser leg. "I know you're worried about your mom," he said. "Don't be."

He turned my hand over, stroked the back where it was not injured, and asked if he might drive my mother to the airport. As a favor. The events of the previous days felt like scattered pieces of a jigsaw puzzle: the pink cold cuts, the lunging dog, Mom beneath the beehive chandelier in tennis shoes.

I sat upright as he stroked the back of my hand, my wrist, my arm, and tried to bring myself into the fullness of this situation, to move away from this gentle man, with his soft gaze, to our sad history together, with its silent dinners, and his nights in the dark, and the relief I felt once he was gone.

"The party was nice," I said. "Flying my mother here was extravagant. But we broke up. I need to hear that you understand that."

"What are you *doing*, babe?" Harley said, his voice tender and concerned, as if I were a toddler, still sweaty from a tantrum. "Everything is *fine*."

"Everything is *not* fine," I said, working hard to conjure up the Harley who was so deep in his own dark place most evenings that I could draw a knife across my wrist and he would not see the blood. "What's the story on that condo? Are you buying it or not?"

I waited. Asked a second time.

Harley nodded sadly. Yes, he said. They accepted his offer for ten percent below list. And now he was only asking to get the chance to spend a little more time with Mom. Quality time. He'd never met anyone like her. "She's a great lady. A truly unique individual. It's a shame she lives so far away."

He unrolled the newspaper and spread it across my lap, and when he crossed the room, elegant and loose-limbed, I flipped through the sections of the paper until a headline stopped me. "Mother of Dead Baby Charged with Murder." The mother in the photo, Amber Chatsworth, looked like a teenager. Her expression was somber or sullen—it was hard to say. She'd slapped her baby in the face "frustrated that the girl was difficult to feed," grabbed her from her high chair and "threw her against the kitchen wall and then onto the sofa." Amber was "deeply disturbed," with a long history of abuse, according to the public defender. "Truly she is not a monster."

I got out of bed and put the newspaper straight into the recycling pile, as if that might bring the baby back to life.

Mom said, "Ech, don't bother," when I called to tell her when I'd be at the hotel.

"It's not a bother. And anyhow, I'm taking you to the airport."

"No," she said. "Your friend…Harry is taking me."

"Harley," I said.

"Harry. It's right here on the notepad with his number."

She read his number to me, and I said, "Fine. Harry can take you. But I'd like to see you. It's been a really long time, you know."

"*Don't*," she said. "I need to get showered."

"You'll be in the shower all morning?" I asked. Then I gave up. "Okay, fine. Have a safe journey."

I missed Tom, who otherwise I did not miss at all. If I'd told him about this conversation, he would have laughed. He might have said, "That's a cold tit!" But Tom was somewhere, married with kids, so I called Les to tell him I could make our morning meeting.

Two hours later, while Harley and my mother were on their way to the airport, Les and I were sitting in the loft of a dreadful woman I had named "Sweetness" and her husband. There on their long,

45

smooth bark-sided Nakashima table, Les spread out colors like Tarot cards while the husband prepared ginger tea.

I'd dressed for this meeting—fitted jacket, pencil skirt, heels. This outfit seemed not to meet with the approval of Sweetness, whose real name I repressed. She fastened her eyes on me, sharing her look of frank disdain. Pursed her red lips. Flipped her hair, showed off her splendid cheekbones. I thought of the mother of my youth, with her thick black hair, the lipstick she left on cigarette butts and coffee cups, the kisses she bestowed on others' cheeks. My mother in the car with Harley. In short-term parking. Harley opening the door for her, holding out his arm. Mom taking it without hesitation.

The husband served tea in glazed mugs that had a curved lip that made it impossible to sip without dribbling. I was too old to be struggling with my mother and felt that this dilemma and my inability to solve it was a sign of a fundamental design flaw. If I'd been made properly, I'd be married with children. I'd know how to be *there* for my mother in her final years.

Sweetness said, "Nothing here is even close to my vision."

"It's a start," said her husband, as always unscathed by this harridan's acid tongue.

"Banal," Sweetness said.

Les pushed two color chips together. The husband said, "Now we're getting somewhere. Now we're making some progress."

"*Echh*," said Sweetness, turning her head as if to hawk into a spittoon.

"How can he stand her?" I asked when Les and I were back on Butler Street.

The wind had picked up, and I could feel grit between my molars as we trekked past the dark brick storefronts—tax preparer, bank, bar, luncheonette selling lottery tickets. I felt wiped out. *Done*.

When had that happened? In fear or distress, *not done* was what I'd always thought. When shown to my seat on an airplane, *not done*. When instructed to "draw my attention to the safety features of the aircraft," told to "fasten my seatbelt by inserting the metal tab into the clasp," and "lift the clasp to release," to "wear the belt low and tight across your lap." When the huge bird began its ascent—the most dangerous time, I'd been informed by Tom, who did not think it a freakish miracle that planes could fly—I had always thought, *Spare me, I'm not done yet!* Now, it was as if I'd sprung a leak and the life force was trickling out. *Done, done.*

"Dude's crazy about her," Les said.

"Please. All that pursing of the lips and flipping of the hair. She's awful."

"Don't kid yourself. She does the dirty work for them both. Dude's happy as a clam."

It was a welcome distraction to imagine the clam, with its wide, toothless smile and its inability to feel pain, or so it was said.

Les was not as happy as a clam. His list of achievements had expanded over the years—illustrator, designer, manufacturer, mentor, teacher, landlord, winner of industry awards—but he seemed no happier. His grown son thought he was a jerk. His back ached. The standing desk he'd bought had helped but not enough. His doctor had suggested yoga but Les wouldn't take a class at the studio upstairs because *yoga is for pussies.*

So when I asked, "*Could* you be as happy as a clam?" I did not believe he might say yes, and was surprised when he said, "*If* I found the right woman."

"Then how come you reject every woman you meet? What was wrong with that grant writer with the great froggy voice? She was smart and attractive. *I* thought she was great."

"She lives in Wexford."

"That's what disqualifies her? That she lives twenty minutes away?"

"Forty minutes."

"You liked her. You told me she was really nice."

"Nice isn't everything. Harley's nice, isn't he? He threw that party for you. Flew your mother in from Israel. That's pretty damn nice, if you ask me."

A burly man burst out of a pub called Hambone's. We veered without breaking stride.

"It wasn't nice, it was manipulative, and it wasn't even my birthday, which you knew. You're my friend—why didn't you say something to me?"

"Why didn't *you* tell him you don't give a shit where he lives? Or take your mother to the airport yourself?"

I stopped in the middle of the sidewalk and held out my hand. My tough-guy partner shielded his eyes so he didn't have to see the swollen thumb with its chewed-off nail. We continued our walk without speaking.

Back at our office, we drifted into separate corners, and I went to work on gift bags for an upcoming trunk show at a clothing store in Shadyside. I'd show the owners a matte paper bag, dark brown, gold logo, trim, ribbons, *frou frou*. And a second bag, metallic brown with pale blue. The brown bags would reinforce the branding we'd established for their store, though I'd throw in a glossy bag, too—cream with brown and gold. I considered sneaking in an opaque plastic bag (yellow, blue, and brown) that could be repurposed as a little lunch bag, but their clientele cared nothing about having a bag that could be reused. It was something I liked, and I knew this, because I could separate my desires from theirs, could please my clients, could satisfy all their design needs.

While I was making these decisions, everything else vanished— Sweetness, Harley, my mother, Amber Chatsworth, frustrated that her baby was difficult to feed, my throbbing hand, the jagged pieces of my past I could not seem to assemble. Kayleigh, the former intern we'd just hired, announced she was leaving. Then Les rose and said, "Life," and I said, "Do you mind taking me home?" and waved my hand.

Twenty minutes later, we pulled up in front of my house. "For instance," he said, as I was unbuckling my seatbelt. "You could have called a taxi."

I thought he meant *me* and was truly grieved. Then I got out of the car, saw my mother standing on my porch, ancient brocade suitcase at her feet, and realized he meant "taxi to the airport."

Seven

Oh, *look* at her, I will think, years later, remembering the way I'd tottered up the driveway, mincing in a tight skirt, arms flying, pointy-toed slingback shoes click-clicking, crying, "Ma! Mom! Mama!" Hopping up the steps to the porch, breathless from exertion. "How long have you been out here? What happened to your flight?"

Then trying to coerce her to step inside my house: lifting her suitcase, Mom wrenching it from my grasp, demanding I take her home. The two of us sniping and tussling over her bag like cartoon characters, as if nothing profound and unspoken boiled beneath our grievances.

The memory goes on like a flickering movie: Begging her to step inside the house, to sit. Her coat exhaled naphthalene. When I slid it off her shoulders, I saw the label was from B. Altman, a store that closed in the 1980s, and I said, "You saved this coat?" "Why not?" said Mom. "It's a perfectly good coat!"

I was hanging her coat in the closet when the backdoor lock clicked open, and the air filled with the oily, garlicky scent of takeout Chinese food. I hurried into the kitchen, just as Harley was setting out the containers. "What's going on?" I asked. "She was standing outside with her suitcase. Why isn't she on her flight?"

Mom walked unsteadily toward us, reaching from doorframe to counter.

"She is *not* okay," Harley hissed.

"Whose house is this?" Mom asked.

As Harley put out bowls and plates, he told Mom all he had done to set up the guest room for her: retrieving the space heater from storage, choosing this chair and not that one; taking the bulb from the floor lamp and putting it in the table lamp. He fretted about the room temperature and went on at length about his search for her favorite foods, all of which he'd procured, he thought, though standing in the aisle at the Giant Eagle, he'd found himself stymied, not knowing the difference between hot chocolate and cocoa. It was as if our silent evenings had been in preparation for this dinner, and he had struggled not to squander his words so he could go on and on for this special event.

I went upstairs to retrieve a sweater for Mom and Harley followed, watching as I went through my drawers.

"I know this is hard for you to accept, but she is not okay," he said, when I settled on an oversize cardigan. "No way could I have left her at the airport and let her fly alone to a foreign country, and you know what? You wouldn't have either. No matter what you say. It goes against everything I know about you. Everything. My lord."

I couldn't admit there was a kernel of truth in his words, because that kernel was wrapped in so much other stuff it was like one of those prize-winning balls I'd seen in *Ripley's Believe it or Not*; a rubber band ball as big as a house, its addled creator grinning beside it. I said, "You're the most manipulative human being I've ever met."

Harley draped the cardigan over Mom's shoulders, poured the egg drop soup into a bowl, and I followed behind with plates and utensils as if this was just another night. He unfolded a napkin and put it on my mother's lap. When the soup was in front of her she said, "I have no appetite," then finished the soup and a hearty serving of the gelatinous entrees, and when she was done told Harley about her interest in the nature of hearing. She told him about the Federal government's disastrous decision to break up AT&T in 1984, the way *those bastards* destroyed the greatest research facility in the world, *sandbox* for Shockley and Bardeen, Sessler and West, Penzias and Wilson. Harley listened to the arcane detail about the Baby Bells that formed after the monopoly was broken, and her own contribution to developing the electret microphone, occasionally checking the phone on his lap, then looking up to say, "You had a remarkable career, that's for sure."

Then, "Where am I?" Mom asked, after recounting her history with such fluency. "I'm so turned around, I haven't the foggiest notion where I am."

"You're in Pittsburgh. We thought you'd stay with us until you get your strength back. Maybe you'll decide to move here."

"Pittsburgh!" she said. "Why would I move to Pittsburgh? I don't know anyone there."

I raised my hand.

When Harley said, "Tonight we have oranges and fortune cookies," I excused myself and went upstairs. The person who looked back at me in the bathroom mirror seemed like a stranger. I reached out, touched the image, saw the arm extended. The hand, with its long, thin fingers and carelessly trimmed nails I recognized as mine, and yet seeing the familiar hand against my cheek was confusing. It was like being a dog that sees its own reflection in a mirror and thinks it's seeing another dog. I knew it wasn't another woman, of course, but could not identify the woman I saw as myself. I imagined transporting this *not me* the way one carried a small dog in a little bag, to take the yapping *not me* wherever I went, the way women toted their Chihuahuas.

Later, after my mother was set up in the guest room, I called Mindy, because she had known my mother, had known our house, was the only one in my life who did. She was a family therapist and had taken care of two ailing mothers, so I took notes when she gave me advice. *Assisted living, PGH. Gerontologist, hard to find. My own PCP okay. Book group friend w/ cousins in Israel.* "Time to be the mother of your mother."

I made an appointment for my mother with my doctor and called three local places for "senior living." She would not see my doctor, though her nose kept bleeding. She would not have lunch with some seniors at Weinberg Terrace. She would not step outside on a sunny day to see the burning bush in my garden, had *not the slightest interest* in going to a movie or shopping. A drive to the New Jersey town where we'd lived was *crazy*. She cared *not one iota* about our old house, had *no use whatsoever* for my father's cousins who also lived in New Jersey—two heavy, bosomy, lugubrious women who'd hefted themselves upright some forty years prior to emigrate to the U.S., then settled back in their club chairs, rising only to make *kneidlach*, or *p'tsha*, (*galleh*, to my mother), a garlicky gelatin made from calves' feet that was both revolting and sublime.

On the second morning my mother slept at my house, or the third, or the morning when the basement flooded after a hard rain, or the morning the maple leaves turned scarlet and the air smelled like wood smoke—on one of those morning, I shuffled outside to get the newspaper, and saw that a nest had fallen from the crab apple tree and inside was a small blue egg, empty and unbroken. When I held it, I thought of the Yiddish proverb, "He who has not tasted the bitter doesn't understand the sweet," and for an instant was lifted from all the confusion and discord. Then I heard the shrill syllables of my name, and the frantic cry of someone locked in a dark room. "Let me out! I want to go home!" I went inside and saw my mother standing in my kitchen in a thin nightgown. Bouquets of violets floated across the fabric; dried blood was smeared across her cheek.

"Why did you put me here?" she cried, freshly enraged to find herself in this alien dwelling where she did not want to be. "I want to go home."

I ran the water until it was warm, dampened a paper towel and handed it to her, taking in her multi-colored hair, yellow toenails that needed to be trimmed, my grievances so trivial it shamed me to recall them. I touched my face to show her where to wipe her cheek, and said, "Tell me what I can do to help."

"Take me home," she said.

"I'm working on it, Ma," I told her.

Seeing her in my kitchen, barefoot, in a thin nightgown, a crust of blood on her cheek, I wanted to reach out, knew I couldn't touch her, and stood, rooted at a distance, hoping at least to reassure her. "I really am," I said.

And she said, "I want to go home so I can die."

The condition of the clothing she had packed for her three-day trip made my heart ache—ripped pantyhose, underpants with stretched-out elastic, a stained blouse. Late one afternoon, I drove to a discount store to buy her something to wear while she was incarcerated in my house. As I looked through racks of unacceptable garments, the Beatles sang, "Obla-Di, Obla-Da, Life Goes on, Bra." The chorus that once had perplexed and amused me now reminded me of the days when my mother washed her silky undergarments by hand and hung them on colorful hooks from the shower rod, when her closet was packed with suits, silk blouses, and expensive pumps in cordovan and black, clip-on earrings, gold chains, expensive lapel pins, and tiny gold wristwatches with unreadable faces. My mother examining the seams of a garment to make sure that the design matched perfectly, scrutinizing the lining of pants, rejecting a jacket that had machine-made button holes. The swish of her stockings rubbing together. Her good legs. As a child, I'd liked when she stroked a calf and said, "I've always had good legs."

Standing beneath the fluorescent lighting, hearing "obla-di, obla da," I realized I had no idea what size she wore, could not guess her height or the shape of her body, because I did not know her body, had long been forbidden from touching her, could only summon up memories of the garments she chose to cover it.

A large?

Even in her present state, she seemed formidable. I examined a pair of black velour pants in a furtive way. They looked comfy, with their drawstring waist. It was dinnertime. The store was quiet. In my head she was saying, *Why don't you stop with the nagging and the burning bush and leave me be? The bloody nose is nothing. Don't you have work? Why are you pushing at me, pushing, pushing. Go!*

They were hideous, these pants. I put them back on the rack.

When I was at work I worried about her. Before I left her alone the first time, I'd written my phone number in black marker and tacked it onto the fridge. The large digits had offended her. "I'm not senile," she'd said.

"I know," I'd said. I didn't know. "Just pick up the phone when it rings. Indulge me. Okay?"

I held up another pair of pants. Black, polyester. Could anyone actually want this garment? I stretched the elastic waist. It looked as if it had been manufactured to cover the mortal flesh and nothing more.

I hung the pants back on the rack.

Sewn by a girl. A child. Who barely saw the light of day.

I checked the label. Cambodia. I dropped the pants into the rickety cart and wheeled it to another section.

It was hard to concentrate, knowing my mother was alone in my house. At work, I spent hours doodling, playing with my oyster pail, unable to think or dream. I called home. No one answered. Tried again, worried she was standing on my porch in her ancient coat, or sprawled on the floor, calling, "Help!" as she did each morning, the blood crusted on her cheek, all alone, no one to hear. I opened the flaps of the oyster pail, lifted the carton by its thin wire handle, turned it onto its side. I called and listened to the phone ring.

Mindy was right, but it was hard to be the mother of this particular mother.

"She's going to say no to everything you suggest," Mindy said. "You need to just bring her a coat, if you want her to leave the house. Help her on with it, walk her to the door. At this point, you're the one who knows what's best for her."

I recognized this strategy. It was the way Harley had "managed" me. *Humor her and do what you want.*

The Carpenters were singing, "We've Only Just Begun." Poor starved-to-death Karen Carpenter.

Lacking Harley's gifts, I'd tried and failed. Mom would not slip on the coat. Would not walk to the door. "What am I supposed to do, throw her in a sack?" I asked Mindy, when I failed to get her to have lunch with the seniors. "She wants to go home. This is not home. 'Pittsburgh? Why am I in Pittsburgh? I don't know anyone in Pittsburgh.'"

"Then you'll have to take her to Israel and get her settled there."

"Israel!" I could hardly listen. "Why did she even move there? It's not like we're Jewish."

"I hate when you do that," said Mindy. And later: "I know she's really, really hard."

In a section called Active Wear, I chose a fleece jacket (lavender, zippered) and some T-shirts.

A woman in Mindy's book group had family in Israel. I thanked Mindy for the contact information, but I could not imagine going to that fraught place, where buses, coffee shops, and market places were blowing up, or how I could actually arrange for an acceptable situation for Mom with only a stranger's name and number. I didn't know anyone there. My father's cousins were no longer alive. Their daughter, Ronit, who once spent the summer with my family, might still be in the country. I had no idea where she lived or if she still spoke English.

Israel meant sirens and the wail of anguished parents. I could not imagine it as a country where people went about their everyday lives, where they bought groceries or danced in the back of hotels. I couldn't imagine a woman in an editing room or a man in a research lab. It was true, that old proverb, "You cannot imagine what you cannot imagine." I could not imagine getting on a plane with my mother and going to this place. At the same time, this impossible trip had begun to feel inevitable.

Someone's cart had been left beside a rack of cotton cardigans on sale. Scented red pillar candles, jeweled slippers with upturned toes, tube socks, a chartreuse salad spinner, a ceramic picture frame with glazed dog bones at each corner. A woman returned, wagging a beige sweater with a huge fake fur collar and shrieking with pleasure. "Elvin will *hate* this!"

When I got home, Mom and Harley were sitting together at the dining table, picking at the remains of lo mein and chicken and cashews. I no longer protested when Harley brought Mom dinner, but did not sit with them either, which was so much better for everyone. I snipped the tags off the clothes I'd just bought and draping them over the bureau in her room, catching occasional phrases, *concert hall acoustics. Directional microphone systems. To get rid of booming. So speech sounds less hollow.* Harley spoke only to ask, "Is the soup too cold, can I warm it up for you? Here, let me get you a fresh napkin?" He did not shift in his seat, try to change the subject or say, "You told us already," as I might have. He did not wince when she boasted of her intelligence or cover his face when she talked about making a middle-aged man cry. Early in our relationship, he'd told me his only desire was to serve me. I'd been appalled. I wanted a partner, an equal. Not a slave. Now, though, I saw how relaxed he was tending to my mother. How comforting it must have been for her to have someone in the role once filled by my father—chauffer, housekeeper, tutor to the dense, ungovernable child who'd landed in their household.

I was returning the scissors to the kitchen drawer as Mom was telling Harley about her secretary, Dottie, and Morris, her husband. When she said, "He was a terrible cook, but I never complained," I fell into a familiar annoyance, as if she were fine.

Yes. You did complain, I thought, sinking into Harley's leather chair.

తి

I made another appointment with a doctor. Two hours before we had to check in, Harley arrived with tea and pastries. As soon as Mom finished breakfast, he began rushing around the house. "Hurry," he told her. "You don't want to be late!" This, as it happened, was true; even when there was no urgency, she couldn't bear being late. "Get the car!" he called to me, and I raced out, drove the car to the front of the house, returned to get my mother. When I saw her dressed in the clothes I'd left out for her—the elastic-waisted pants and zip-front top—I thought, what have I done? How could I have been so disrespectful? "Quick like a bunny!" Harley said, holding out his arm to aid her on the steps. *Quick like a bunny?* I was laughing hard, and also wishing someone would sew shut the giant hole inside me.

On the drive, I turned on the radio and was surprised to hear the opening chords of "Sympathy for the Devil." It was the intro to a story about the Rolling Stones' arrival in China. The traffic inched down Fifth Avenue toward the medical center. Stalin was poisoned after all, a reporter told us next. My mother gazed out the side window. In Haifa, the number 37 bus was blown up and fifteen people were killed, eight of them children under the age of eighteen. A Druse girl of twelve, a Christian girl of fourteen, and the rest Israeli students.

"Haifa," said my mother. "That's in Israel."

I turned the radio off and waited.

"When are you taking me home?" she asked.

"As soon as we're done here," I said.

I took a ticket at the parking garage and the gate opened.

There were so many segments to our journey, so many chances for her to balk—walking from the parking space to the garage elevator, from the elevator to hospital entrance, past the wheelchairs in the lobby, unused except for one. Helium balloons were anchored to the armrest with ribbons. Slouched in the seat was a shriveled woman with tubes in her nose, clutching a bag marked Patient Belongings.

Mom seemed not to see this woman. She walked past, saying nothing. She seemed not to notice the resident whose chest hair sprang from the V-neck of his scrubs or the nurses in their smocks, squeezed into the elevator beside us. We made our way into the waiting area for General Internal Medicine, noisy from the loud, mounted TV no one was watching. My mother was given a laptop and asked to complete a survey before she saw the doctor. We took the two vacant seats beneath the TV and when she told me she wanted to go home, I read the first question to her: "Over the last two weeks, have you felt down, depressed, or hopeless for most of the time?"

Oh yes, I thought. You have no idea.

"No," she said.

Over our heads, the chipper cohost of a morning show was chattering about therapy dogs. I entered my mother's response and went on to the next question, "Over the last two weeks, have you felt little interest or pleasure in doing things for most of the time?"

I saw myself sitting at my work area, emptied out, so distanced from what I had been or what I once made that I wondered if I too had some dementia. To look at labels or posters I'd designed and have no sense of where they came from. To find that ability, talent, is as ephemeral as love; *there*, whether you want it or not, and then *gone*.

"No," said my mother.

An obese man approached very slowly, with a wobbly, boneless gait, and a T-shirt that read, Now I Know Why Some Animals Eat Their Young.

"My current life is ideal for me," I read. "Strongly disagree, disagree, neither agree or disagree, slightly agree, strongly agree."

"Yes," said my mother.

She was full of pep.

She was never down in the dumps.

Had lots of energy.

The man lowered himself into the chair across from ours, his body like a mound of Jell-O, spilling over the sides.

"In times of trouble or difficulty, how many people do you have near that you can readily count on for help—such as offering you advice, looking after your belongings (house, pets, etc.) for a period of time, running errands for you, watching children, giving you a ride to the hospital or store, or helping out if you are sick? (O-1, 2-5, 6-9,10 or more.)"

My mother looked at me.

"I know," I said. "It's complicated. Let me read it again. In times of trouble or difficulty, how many people do you have near that you can readily count on for help…"

No matter where I was, Harley would come to my aid if I asked for help. He would pay my plane fare, retrieve me from the shoulder of a road in Saskatoon, sit in a doctor's office with me. He could not be happy with me, but if I was stricken by disease, he would wheel my chair, feed me pureed food, empty my bedpan. He would tend to my body selflessly. The other piece, the part I called *me* he could not see or understand, would never acknowledge.

I was reciting the numbers—zero to one, two to five—when I realized my mother had walked off. The obese man pointed with his thumb, and I hurried down the corridor and saw her bypass the bank of silver elevators and enter a surgical unit. I raced over and tried to edge her back to the waiting area, swearing the doctor was ready to see her.

At the elevators, she stepped between a mother and son. "I want to go home," she told them. They were the same height and heft, same blotchy skin and *tsibble* nose, same oversize black Steelers jersey. "Take me home now."

They regarded me, these two. I said, "Okay, Mom," and meant it. "We'll get you home." The relief I felt was amazing. "As soon as we can." I called the nurse from the parking garage to explain what had happened. Then I went home and booked our tickets. "We're all set," I said, then slept very deeply that night.

On the morning of our departure, I was awakened by my mother's brittle cry for help. The sun had just come up. I thought of the speckled egg that had fallen from its nest, how weightless it had felt in the palm of my hand. I thought of the mother bird expelling it, then a day or week later, the nest falling from the tree, toppled by a predator or the wind, the whole event of no consequence, unnoticed until I'd reached for the newspaper and seen it.

By the time I made it downstairs with my own packed bag, she was standing beside her suitcase at the front door. Our flight to Newark was not scheduled to depart for four hours, but my parents had always left excessively early. Years before, leaving early was lifesaving. Now, decades after the dangers had receded, the instinct remained: they'd been the guests who showed up for parties when the hosts were still in the shower, the travelers who spent all day at the airport, as if the terminal was the first fun stop on their holiday.

Harley let himself in through the back door and escorted my mother to the kitchen table, where he'd set out her tea and pastry. He took me aside while she was eating. "You need to stay until everything is settled with Mom. No matter how long it takes. She's the only one that matters. I'm fine. Don't worry about me. Everything is under control."

"Listen, Harley—" I said.

"*Don't.*" Harley threw his arms around me with such force my knees buckled. "Don't." He buried his head in my chest, pressed hard, and began to butt me. "Don't, don't, don't, don't," until the word began to feel like a rock. I struggled to get free, feeling just then that my life and all its drama was as hollow as the egg. "I know what you're going to say, and I don't want to hear it."

Harley began to cry.

"Let's go!" called my mother at the door with her suitcase.

The taxi dropped us curbside outside Departures. My mother would not let me take her suitcase, though it was from the era before wheels and she was not strong enough to carry it herself. I said, "Fine." She grabbed the handle, walked a step, rested; walked another step, rested, until in irritation, I snatched the bag and marched into the terminal. When she caught up, I saw the red ribbon snaking down to her chin.

And did I have a tissue, a napkin—something to hand my aged mother? After rooting around in my purse, all I could find was a treated cloth used for my sunglasses, soft but unabsorbent. She took the cloth and ran it across her face.

In the women's room we stood together at the sinks. With her crazy hair and bloody nose, she looked as if she'd gone through the windshield of a car. People approached—I could see their reflection in the mirror—then turned away. I wet a paper towel for my mother and when she would not take it, I tried to blot her face. She smacked me in the chest with the back of her hand.

"You need to cut that out, or I'm going to leave you here and go home," I said.

My mother started for the door.

"Fine!" I called. "It's not like I want to drop everything and go to Israel with you when you're being so mean. Because I don't. At all. Ugh," I said to the woman glaring at me at the next sink.

My mother walked out. "Have a good trip!" I called after her.

I lingered, washing my hands like a surgeon. Then I raced to catch up.

At our gate, we collapsed in molded seats beside travelers going to Orlando. The floor and seats were piled with blankies and Disney Princesses waving their wands across vinyl backpacks, limp-limbed stuffed bears, neck pillows, body pillows, chunky plastic baby paraphernalia, mothers on cell phones grinding Cheezits and Cheerios into the carpet as they paced. Hello Kitty's hydrocephalic head floated past on the side of a wheeled suitcase. What a lot of endless toil it was to take care of these little ones, what a lot of lost sleep, how unquenched my desire to have one of my own. I thought of Harley saying, "You're only as happy as your least happy child." Maybe that was the problem. Maybe, because I had no kids, I was only as happy as my least happy mother.

The Other One

EIGHT

I'm standing in front of my mother's Bauhaus building in Tel Aviv, on the corner of Rehov Nordau, a busy street with benches and palm trees in the median, waiting for her to find her keys. A Billy Crystal movie is advertised on a small billboard. Across a busy road is the beach.

"You got an apartment on the beach!" I say, puzzled, then briefly amused. My mother continues rifling through her purse.

It's late afternoon and chilly. The traffic is heavy on Ha'Yarkon, the major thoroughfare, but Nordau Street is quiet. A boy, standing to pedal a heavy bike, barefoot, rides by. Two old women, arms linked, veer toward the edge of the sidewalk as they pass. When I hear the jingle of keys I lift my mother's suitcase. She slaps my arm. I drop the bag. *I want to go home.* It's her voice, I realize, her song that's gotten stuck in my head. The desire to be home is now mine. Already I feel it. My house, my language, my work, in an office redolent with espresso, and not the fetid odor that assails me when we step inside the building.

My mother is weak and needs to rest after each step. The hall lights flicker on, casting a dim glow in the broad stairway. I move my bag. She curses these particular steps, places her palm against the wall, climbs, curses, rests. I take her bag. We climb the next step. The smell gets worse. I know *in a way* where it originates. This was the story of my life, that I was irritated by the spiny seed of knowledge inside me and yet remained clueless, oblivious.

When we reached my mother's door the rotten smell was so strong I held my breath as she worked her key into the lock, afraid of what we'd find. The stench was terrifying, as if we might find a decomposing corpse inside, instead of rotting garbage in open bags. Organic waste, left to bake in the morning sun in this closed-up apartment. My mother nudged me forward, grumbling, and I stepped inside.

Because I was like my mother, at the sight and smell of her abode, the shocked self revolted, an essential piece detaching like a helium balloon set loose. I looked at the chaos, the living quarters of someone who was disturbed, and remembered my father vacuuming, a section of the long cord folded like a lasso in his hands as he ran the upright back and forth over the flat carpet, singing a liturgical tune in a bold voice, as if certain no one could hear him over the rumble of the machine. A stab of anguish rose—who was this man I called my father?—and then my attention returned to the cascading piles, newspapers, unopened mail, equipment, clothes.

The trickle of blood etched Ma's cheek. I cleared the seat of a chair for her, found a towel that wasn't too rank and drenched a corner with warm water, wanting to clean her face but worried she would sock me. "Your nose is bleeding."

She took the towel and dabbed at her face. "It happens." She looked at the towel and then at me. "What are you doing here?"

"Helping you settle in."

"That's nice, dear," she said, suddenly tender. "Maybe another time. I'm not feeling myself."

"That's not so easy, Mom. You moved to Israel. You never said why."

"You mean the Arabs? There will never be peace. They're a primitive people who know only hatred. An eye for an eye. To them, women are shit. They take better care of their donkeys."

"Please! Don't say such racist things."

"I'll say what I damn well please."

My mother had always been harsh, but I'd never heard her speak like this. Was it something that happened with age, some hidden racism emerging like worms on a rainy day?

"Fine," I said. It wasn't fine.

She stood slowly, put her hand against the wall and went into a living room cluttered with towers of stuff, an astounding amount of it on the desk, on the bamboo-framed sofa, on the floor. Only one chair was clear, and she worked her way toward it and lowered herself into the seat.

How long had she lived this way? I thought of our weekly phone calls, all the times I'd suggested a visit. Never once when she turned me down had I imagined her alone in this chaos.

When her head began to loll, I bagged the garbage, double bagged it, my head turned away. The blood beneath her nose had begun to thicken. I dared to open the refrigerator. The white cheese had turned pink and the yellow cheese dappled and blue. Inside the jar of marmalade was a fuzzy amoeba-shaped organism, straight from a horror flick. It seemed to grow before my eyes. The pantry shelves were sticky, the lids to every jar congealed with muck. The oil was rancid. Bad smells wafted up from the drain and hovered beneath the sink, behind the fridge, inside the drawers.

I opened the window and stepped onto her small balcony. Outside was a steady buzz of motorbikes on Ha'Yarkon and across the road the Mediterranean. A market was on the corner. Surely Ma had some shekels in her wallet. If I took a few, I could get us something to eat.

The zip of the change purse roused her. "What are you doing in my bag?"

I waited without moving. A moment later, she fell back asleep, her head bobbing, as if she were a drunkard.

The market was small and well-stocked. I picked up a box of tea that was possibly chamomile (picture of a plant with small white buds), and what I assumed was goat cheese (sway-backed little creature in the field). Also rolls and garbage bags. Giant radishes bloomed from a bin, rosy and beautiful. I stopped to admire them. Once, when I still believed I could get Harley to understand the ways I'd wanted to be known by my lover, I'd cried, "I want to stand naked!" Studying the radishes, I felt as if my wish had been fulfilled, but not in the way I had intended. I was illiterate, ignorant of the native language. I had no understanding of the culture, no clear plan.

"*Heh*," Harley had said. "Be my guest!"

I handed a bill to a sullen-looking cashier with a thick black eyebrow slashed across his face and hoped it would cover my purchases.

He gave me a scornful look. I glared back: *Who are you to stare? You're a pariah! Everybody hates you. Everybody in the whole entire world!*

I took the wad of bills he returned as change, stuffed it into my pocket and left the store. It was true, this adolescent taunt. *Everyone hates you!*

Instead of going back to my mother's apartment I crossed the highway and walked out to the beach. It was dusk, and lights from the hotels to the south had begun to twinkle. A couple of boys were digging furiously, as if they had to finish their urgent job before nightfall. The waves were small and regular, with a thin line of foam that washed onto the sand. I continued down to the water's edge and listened to the lapping of waves. I knew that as long as there was a moon, the tides would change, but I did not understand why that was so, did not understand anything, really, not when my mother had gotten this apartment, why she had moved here, or if the sea across the road had been a factor.

When the boys left, I could see no one else on the beach. Though I had only been in this country for an hour, I surmised that the beach was deserted because the only fools who ventured out in these dangerous times were boys who thought themselves immortal, and me. I was wrong, of course. When the season changed, the beach would be packed, but on that evening, when I was busy surmising, this is what I believed.

❧

I heard the argument as soon as I stepped back into the building. A deep voice full of fury. An old woman's tremulous rage. The door was open. In the kitchen was a huge man in a gray tracksuit, waving papers at my mother. Shaved head, stud in one ear, Star of David the size of a dinner plate trembling against his heaving chest: this was Kotovsky, the landlord. While I was trying to unearth a word or two of the language that I had not spoken since I was a toddler, my mother smacked this giant in the belly. The futile gesture startled Kotovsky and he laughed. Then I laughed. This displeased him. The drama resumed.

I was ashamed that a stranger was seeing my mother's wrecked place and went to shut the door. I want to go home, I thought; "home" just then a state of mind, as perhaps it was for my mother, too.

Across the hall, a door opened, and a small, beautiful, bare-footed woman edged past me and walked up to Kotovsky. This was Dina. Though she was a foot shorter and half Kotovsky's weight, she was a formidable presence, standing inches from him, her arms crossed. She had a big head, blazing dark eyes, lustrous black hair that she flipped back when she began to berate him in husky, rapid Hebrew. Her chin was a whole other language, full of emotion. Kotovsky could have grabbed her by the scruff of the neck and flung her across the room. But, no, he lowered his head, then glanced upward, like a shamed boy.

Dina turned to me, said, "Leona, this is your mother?"

I nodded.

"A wonderful woman. Oh!" She clutched her chest. "We admire her so! This is so pity."

And indeed it was, I learned. My mother had neglected to pay her rent and building fees for several months. The water she'd left running had flooded the downstairs neighbor's flat. Vermin from her garbage had slithered next door. Everyone was complaining about the stench.

Dina returned to Kotovsky, hands on hips, head thrown back. The hair toss, the jutting chin. Kotovsky's shoulders drooped. Dina put her arm around my mother and speaking in that same husky voice, guided her through the crammed living room, toward her bed.

Kotovsky regarded me as if I were a thing, sexless as a chair. I have to admit it hurt my feelings. I started to speak in English, and he waved his hand and cut me off. "Lo." Now the other hand. "Lo, lo." More hand waving, as if in this interlude, a dance would begin.

After casting a spell on Kotovsky, Dina walked me to an ATM so I could get enough cash to placate him until morning. It was dark by then, and I was dopey with fatigue and felt for a moment as if I'd squeezed my eyes shut and prayed this woman into existence. The neighborhood had come alive with a multitude of young people on the street and in the cafes. Dina's admiration for my mother seemed boundless. To have as a neighbor a great intellectual was an honor, she declared. A woman who was so admired. "Such a wonderful mother, the love you have!"

Our shoulders bumped as we walked. What love? I wanted to ask, as if we were old friends who'd grown up on the same street.

"You have a husband?" she asked.

I contemplated saying yes, as if a pretend husband might protect me in this country I did not know. "Not really," I said.

"You have the JDate in America?" she asked.

I said yes, we had the JDate.

"I am having such fun on the JDate," she told me. "My English, it is no longer so good. You'll correct my errors?"

"Okay," I said. I wouldn't.

A shirtless boy biked past, his hair in dreads. His bearded dog trotted alongside him.

We paused in front of an ATM machine. "To be honored all across the world! To have so many accomplishments!"

The urge to confess rose like a wave. "She's difficult," I said, as I plucked from my wallet a card that might work here.

"Of course! You must be in charge. You must make the decisions. Oh! I am so honored to meet her daughter. We will be such good friends! You are familiar with the work of Amos Fischoff? A brilliant man, also very handsome; he is giving a lecture tomorrow night, Leona will come and you will come, also."

She saw my stunned look of sheer exhaustion and took the credit card from my hand. "This is how," she said, because I'd been trying to put my credit card into the slot where the money came out.

When at last we were back at their building, she said, "Now it is time for the daughter to take over. You will care for *Eema*." She gave a last husky, orgasmic "Oh!" and left for the night.

❧

With the windows open, the motorbikes on Ha'Yarkon seemed to zip through the rooms the next morning. I slid off the canvas cot, thinking I'd finish cleaning the kitchen before Ma woke. I'd found a stash of crumpled plastic bags and dumped old food into them, triple knotting the tops, quick, mindless, a human vacuum, sucking up the stuff. Then, drifting into the living room, I filled bags with newspapers and old magazines.

I was shoving a five-inch floppy disk into a bag when my mother appeared in the same thin nightgown she'd worn at my house, with its floating violet bouquets, screaming, "Get out!" kicking me with the side of her foot, nearly toppling from the effort. "Get out of my house or I'll call the police!"

I threw on my clothes from the day before, grabbed my bag and hurried out of the building. For a moment, I stood on the sidewalk. The small stores on the street were all open, their racks of house-wares and bins of produce set out on the sidewalk. Children were walking to school with colorful backpacks slung across their shoulders. Life on this crisp, bright morning seemed impossibly serene.

I headed south, with no destination, until I reached Gordon Street, where an internet café was open. I stopped in to check my email. An international crew, all of them skinny young men, sat at the row of computers against each wall. I took the only free computer, between a redhead with lace-up boots painted silver, and a pink-cheeked Hasid in a black hat and *tzitzit*. When I logged onto my account, I was disheartened and not surprised to see six messages from Harley.

I needed to delete these messages. I knew this in my heart and knew it because I could hear Mindy telling me not to read his email or take his calls.

I sat back, peeked to the other side. *Someone* reeked from pot.

Once when I'd told Mindy I was desperate for Harley to leave, she said, "You know what desperate women do when they really need to leave a relationship? They set the guy's car on fire. They cut his underwear in squares."

It was definitely the Hasid.

Sitting in the internet café, I thought of our silent evenings in my house, our silent dinners at the noisy sports bar Harley liked, with its huge projection TVs, the bright flickering colors, the roar of the crowd, young people squeezed close at the bar, and Harley clutching the cell phone on his lap, while I dragged my French fries through a river of ketchup. I saw myself approach him in his leather chair, his expressionless face with those dead eyes, and the words pouring out of me as I tried to extract something from him, a nod, a frown, and getting only that stony face that stripped me to the core, as if I did not exist.

"Get out of my house!" I'd screamed at Harley, throwing his wallet into the shrubs.

"Get out of my house!" my mother had screamed. "Get out or I'll call the police!"

Don't open his email, I told myself.

I deleted the first five. The sixth had an attachment. Squelch the curiosity! I thought, opening the attachment. A photo Harley had taken of himself flat on his back burst onto the computer screen. His face, as he gazed up at the camera, was as soft and helpless as a baby's. I looked furtively to either side, quickly closed the attachment and deleted everything.

When I got home, I scrambled some eggs, made a salad with tomatoes and cucumbers, and put out the fresh cheese and rolls I'd gotten across the street. When I called my mother to the table, she said, "I'm not hungry."

I said, "Show me where you sit." She took the chair that faced the window where you could almost see the sea and ate with gusto.

That night it rained heavily, which surprised me. I had not expected rain or cold nights, restaurants full of young people, dogs in jeweled collars, laughter. I had not expected that I would read dreadful news in the English edition of *Ha'aretz* that my mother picked up each day—sixteen killed in a bus bombing, thirty-four in a car—then an hour later, run down the sloping path to the beach and pass muscular men playing *mat-kot* against a hotel wall, their bare chests bronze from the sun. I had not expected that Dina would do so much for me.

Late that night, the buzzer sounded, and I hurried downstairs to meet a man named George, who'd pulled up on a motorbike with a plastic bag full of obsolete cellphones, one of which I could rent. I chose a simple gray brick of a phone.

Dina had found George for me. Dina explained the steps I needed to take so Mom could get home health care, then she put me in touch with a doctor who would examine her and start the process. His name was Dr. Barry Berenbaum, and his earliest appointment for a home visit was in two weeks. Dina found the current phone number for my cousin Ronit, who lived with her family in Ra'anana, and gave me a key to her apartment so I could use her internet when she was gone. Dina ran a program for disadvantaged children—immigrants from Ethiopia and the former Soviet Union, Israeli kids at risk—and her workday ended early. When she came home, she knocked on my mother's door to see if there was something we might need.

"To have a friend so close is fantastic," she said the first night. "You'll come over, we'll have tea and talk and I will show you the JDate and we will have a very good time."

I imagined the mother of my youth, raising an eyebrow and saying, "The *JDate?*"

"Yes," I said. "I'd like that," though having a very good time was not on my agenda. "As soon as I get this place in order."

"I'm still working on it," I said when I declined the next night.

By the third night, Dina looked so wounded that I opened the door wider to remind her of the crazy mess that filled the rooms, the lopsided stacks of magazines and journal reprints, restaurant napkins, rubber bands, twist ties, post cards, unopened mail, calculators, travel clocks with broken hinges, plant pots, baking dishes crusted with black grease, plastic containers, hangers, decorative boxes, floppy disks. I gestured to the gloves, scarves, knit hats, berets, galoshes, and sport jackets tumbling from split plastic bags.

"I've got to clear out some of this stuff before Dr. Berenbaum arrives." I waited for a sign that Dina understood.

Then I gave up. "No sane home healthcare worker would take a job in a place like this. It's gross. And also, if I can't clean up, I'll never get home."

Dina gave me a hurt look. "You don't like it here?"

"No!" I said. "I mean yes. But I have to keep on task, you know?" Dina flipped her hair. She didn't.

"I need to get Leona set up with someone who'll be able to... She's not the easiest person. I can't clean when she's awake. If she sees me touch anything, she gets upset." I rolled my eyes and said, "*Really* upset."

Should I reveal in a hushed voice just how agitated my mother became? Other people seemed to know what to tell and what to hide. Lacking this instinct, I hoped that my eye-rolling crossed cultures and communicated what I could not bring myself to say.

I quickly figured out that it was impossible to sort through my mother's stuff. It would take a lifetime if I tried to make decisions. The only way to create any order was to open an industrial garbage bag, toss in enough stuff to fill it, and bring the bag downstairs. I could only do this when she was fast asleep, or went to the market across the street—the only sojourn she willingly took and one she insisted on making alone. Even then, when I saw her handwriting on paper I was discarding or took in a whiff of naphthalene, an electric charge of despair shot through me, as if a spark of her brilliant past self had permeated each item.

How slowly she walked across the street, her shoulders hunched, shuffling. Sometimes, she rested on the bench, with her purchases in a string bag—a newspaper, a box of tea, an onion, a roll. Under the sink was a basket full of sprouted onions, and the cabinet was bursting with boxes of tea. The newspaper, she could no longer read; the roll, she ate for breakfast.

One morning, in a fury of throwing out clamps, journals, and galoshes, I threw in some onions and a small ceramic burro with a flower behind the ear and a broken hind leg that I recognized from years back. Out you go, I thought, hefting the bag and carrying it into the garbage area downstairs.

On my way back up to her apartment, I thought of the long

journey that ceramic burro had made, from New Jersey to Israel, and the long journey she had made as a child on a train to France, and my heart began to ache. I paused on the step. Don't do this, I told myself. Don't think. The ache continued to grow inside me until I thought I would burst. So I returned to the garbage area, found the heavy black bag and dug through the metal and paper, frantically, as if the burro might be asphyxiated if I didn't free it right away. When I found it, I felt no relief, so I stashed it in a desk drawer where I would not have to see it. Even out of sight, the broken burro seemed to have lodged within me.

Send work! I wrote, in an email to Les. *This is going to take time.*

Seeing these words on the screen made it real. I wasn't going anywhere soon. I had to wait for the doctor to arrive, then wait for his diagnosis. If he found that Mom had some dementia, he'd refer her to a geriatric health center for a series of tests called the "mini-mental." I had to wait for those results, and hope they backed up the doctor's assessment, so she'd get a referral from the Bituach Leumi, the National Insurance Institute, for home health care. Then I had to wait for a nurse to evaluate Mom to determine how many hours of care she would get.

Take off your shoes, I thought. Make yourself at home.

I cleared my throat and called my cousin Ronit. When someone answered, I said, "*Shalom.* Do you speak English?"

This was the awkward start of most of my interactions. It was what I said at the pharmacy and at the bank, and later, how I began my conversation with the nurse who evaluated my mother and the clerk at the employment agency where I got the names of home health care workers. It was what I would say at the Ministry of the Interior, where I ordered my birth certificate before I flew home.

"*Ken.*"

I instantly recognized Ronit's deep voice. "Ronit! This is Roxanne, your American cousin. It's been a long time. Maybe you don't remember me."

My mother barely remembered me. It didn't seem farfetched.

"Roxanne. You are in Israel on holiday? Leona and Morris are with you?"

"My father died," I said. "Awhile back."

"And Leona?"

"She lives here in Tel Aviv."

"In Tel Aviv? This I don't understand." Ronit's blunt declaration made me wonder if she was angry. Then I decided maybe not, since she invited us to lunch on Shabbat.

Later that day, while out for groceries, I bought a chartreuse orchid in a white ceramic pot. On the way back to Mom's apartment, I let myself feel how much I enjoyed walking on these streets, with their palm trees and crusty Bauhaus buildings. Ordinary life still seemed remarkable to me—the sight of children and dogs, women hanging laundry on drying racks; the two elderly women I often saw sitting together on a bench on Nordau Street, dressed in straw cloches, beige sweaters, and skirts. How do you do it? I always wondered. Even before I'd passed the bombed-out shell of a popular club for Israeli Arabs and Jews and further south the twisted remains of the Dolphinarium, where so many teenagers had been blown apart, I asked myself that question. How do you live? Those women chatting on a bench were European; they'd survived something, I knew. When I thought of them sitting in the sun together, I wondered, how? The Ethiopian cashier in the market, as lanky and elegant as a fashion model—how? The Argentinian baker, with a sign in his window, *se habla Espanol*, beneath the one in Hebrew I could not read. The Palestinians I did not see—how? The Ecuadorian house cleaner who came to Dina's with her little boy—so far from language and home and family, desperate enough to come here of all places.

Holding the orchid, I found myself thinking: I am walking in a city where everyone is wounded. Though I badly wanted to go home, I began to feel an odd kinship with this place, to feel myself an exile among exiles. Even before I knew my own story I thought: we have all lost something.

❧

When Dina opened her door, I heard a bird squawk, *Ma!* She took the orchid without a word, and put it out of view, as if it disgusted her. Then she returned and said in a cheerful way, "Roxanne! I am thinking you don't like me!"

She drew me into her cool, tidy apartment, with its olive couches and tile floor, a mirror image of my mother's but clean and well-appointed. The bandy-legged parrot followed us into a small bedroom where Dina had set up a computer desk and two wheeled chairs. The bird and the room had been her daughter's before she'd moved to Bangkok to tend bar. It was a very low-class job for a girl from their family, Dina said, pulling out a chair for me. "But now, she is having her life and I am having the JDate."

We scrutinized the photos of men on the computer and the parrot shifted side to side, squawking, "*Ma! Ma shlomkhah!*"

This is what Dina wanted. Not gratitude. Not an orchid or a bottle of wine or a scarf—gifts made her uncomfortable. She wanted me to listen as she haltingly translated notes written by potential suitors, then offer an opinion on their messages and her replies. It was a grueling task, but I hated letting Dina down, when she'd already been so disappointed. Her marriage had been loveless, her daughter devoid of ambition. Her family, wealthy merchants, who'd left Baghdad during the great exodus of Jews in the 1950s, had come to this country that had broken her heart. Peace would never happen. Too much wrong had been done on both sides.

These pasty-faced suitors, a parade of Shlomos, Shmuliks, and Shukis, seemed so vulnerable, with their public declarations of loneliness and yearning. Maybe that was why they posed with children or dogs or friends, why one embraced the wheel of a powerboat, another propped his arm on the wing of a plane, a third held a beautiful chicken with a medallion around its neck and an iridescent plume of feathers. While her beady-eyed parrot stepped side to side, squawking *Ma!* like a spoiled American kid, we discussed the significance of the time that had elapsed between her outgoing message and the man's reply and sought to interpret the silence, particularly when she could tell her present crush was online but had not written to her. Maybe she really was having fun with JDate. Who was I to contest this? All I can say is that it felt like serious business, and Dina, a Talmudic scholar, capable of endless interpretations of even the briefest responses she received.

"Now we will find someone for you," Dina said, at the end of a long night.

I'd tried to explain that I missed my house and business partner, and the steady satisfaction of work, but Dina wasn't having it, so I lied. "I have a boyfriend."

She thrust out her square chin, tossed her fabulous hair. "So where is this boyfriend?"

"He'd be here if I wanted."

It was true. Even now I could call Harley. The time difference wouldn't matter. I wouldn't even have to speak. All I needed to do was breathe into the phone and he would say, "Where are you, babe? Are you okay? Do you need anything? I was just looking at your picture and thinking how gorgeous you are and how lucky I am to have found you." Hadn't I wanted my whole life to hear this? "You've changed my life, babe. You've taught me the meaning of love." It would be like winding up a music box, watching the ballerina spin.

When I returned to Mom's apartment, I listened to her rhythmic snoring and began throwing out hanging files, accordion envelopes filled with receipts, file cards, old mail, cancelled checks. I could not start feeling sentimental. Everything had to go. I opened the desk drawer, found the ceramic burro I'd stashed a few days before, threw it in the bag.

I hefted the bag and started down. I didn't mock Dina in her search for love. It was what I'd wanted, too, what I might have had, if I'd been somebody else. The garbage area was packed. When I lowered my sack, dumping it beside the rest of the trash, I remembered the morning I'd stood on a chair and began to sing, "On Top of Spaghetti All Covered with Cheese!" The sun was shining and my father was peppering the scrambled eggs, and when I sang, "I lost my dear meatball when somebody sneezed," my mother began to laugh. As I walked back upstairs, I wondered why I'd thought of my childhood as relentlessly barren. I hadn't been whipped or molested. My parents had fed and clothed me, paid for orthodontia, eyeglasses, college tuition. Why had I expected them to understand the child in their midst, when they'd been deprived of childhood themselves? I needed to be done with this, to stop *demanding* like a baby, stomping my feet, carelessly flinging whatever was offered to me.

Was this what I had done to every man who tried to love me? By the time I pushed open the apartment door I was breathless from distress. And to my mother?

I went back down to the garbage area, untied the black bag, and sorted through sweaters that stank of mothballs and reprints from journal articles until I found the ceramic burro with its blue flower and broken leg. I placed it on the desk. Then I carried a chair beside her bed, listened to the buzzing motorbikes on Ha'Yarkon, and watched her sleep.

NINE

Dina wrote Ronit's address in Hebrew on a slip of paper. This I took to the taxi stand across the street from Mom's building on the Friday I was invited to my cousins' house. I hadn't seen Ronit since we were teenagers and she had spent the summer in New Jersey. When my father had first told me that I'd be showing my cousin a good time in America, I'd moaned and whined and threw a large rock on my bare foot, attempting to break my toe, as if this would absolve me of my responsibilities to this girl I did not know and had no wish to meet. The rock fell on my instep and rolled off, leaving me sadly able-bodied.

My life is over, I'd thought, on the drive to the airport to meet Ronit's plane. While my friends were hanging out and going to the shore, I'd be stuck with this boring stranger. I'll wait in the car, I said when we arrived.

It was a muggy day in late June. My parents, bored with my complaining, went into the terminal without me, leaving me to stew in my own outrage for the next hour. Then Ronit appeared, a big, ruddy, morose-looking blonde, her bushy hair tied in a braid. "Vered?" she asked. My mother said, "Roxanne."

She poked my shoulder when we were alone. "Vered, I have a big need for a cigarette." These were her first words to me, accompanied by her miming gesture—cigarette between her fingers, the deep inhalation.

All summer, Ronit looked morose, full of woe, though in fact she liked going to the mall and watching TV. Also cartoons, peanut butter and jelly sandwiches, individually wrapped slices of cheese, the salty French fries we got at the concession stand at the town pool, and American candy—Milk Duds and Raisinettes.

"Vered," she called me, gesturing with her chin in a forceful way that left me assuming that "Vered" meant "hey you," and was not the name on my Israeli birth certificate, a name I had never heard.

Ronit was into bubble gum music and could dance for hours at the rec center—no Bob Dylan or heavy metal or glam rock for her. She was an exotic creature who stripped to the skin at the slightest provocation, revealing her baggy cotton underpants, and lush blonde armpit hair. She sang "Sugar, Sugar" in the shower and in a year would join the army. Meanwhile, seemingly at once, she could work at the waxed bag inside the Milk Duds box, sing the chorus of "Rocketman" that played on the radio, and name the dead on her mother's side, gunned down by the *Einsatzgruppen*, nineteen people in all.

Nearly every day we went to the town swimming pool. The boys liked Ronit. She looked sexy in a swimsuit, chunky but firm in an awesome Amazonian way. The way she said "penis" instead of "peanuts" was a source of constant humor. Half the summer passed before I realized that she hung around the concession stand less for the fries than because of the boy who worked there, a tall, well-built senior named Tad, stupid and good-humored, with no self-consciousness about admitting he hadn't known that Israel was a country or teasing Ronit about her accent. He made her tell all the customers her favorite sandwich, just so he could hear her say she liked penis butter and jelly.

When I heard her husky voice on the phone, I wondered if she recalled what a hit she'd been that summer, or if she remembered the night Tad drove a group of us to a raucous Irish bar in Inwood, in Upper Manhattan, where no one was carded, and the girls got wasted on sloe gin fizzes and the boys had boilermakers. When we arrived home, miraculously intact but hours past curfew, my father was waiting on the front lawn, angrier than I had ever seen him, and frightened, it occurred to me years later, because I'd been entrusted with his niece's well-being. I listened with my arms tightly crossed, and when at last he stopped berating me and walked into the house, I said, "What a jerk," to Ronit, who two hours earlier had been dancing on the sidewalk outside the bar with boys she'd never met.

"This is the way you speak to your father who has only you in the world and worries only naturally for your safety?"

I will never forget the look of disgust on her face when she pushed past me into my parents' house. And now, all these years later, I stood on Ronit's doorstep, taking in the pale yellow stucco and tile roof, the giant spiny century plants that seemed to stand guard, white wine warm in my sweaty hands.

First impression upon seeing my cousin: she looked exactly the same as she had as a teenager. "You haven't changed at all!" I burbled.

An instant later, I realized I wasn't looking at the chunky teen with bushy blonde hair who charmed the boys with her love of *penis* but a dour, gray-haired, middle-aged woman in a loose linen shirt and pants. It was the morose expression that hadn't changed at all, as if she still held a grudge against me.

"My mother isn't so well," I said, to explain why I arrived by taxi alone. I did not add that my mother hadn't *the slightest interest* in coming with me.

Ronit walked me to a patio out back and introduced me to her small bald husband and daughter Galia—their older daughter was on holiday in Cyprus. Plates of food covered the table, and there were birds-of-paradise and banana palms, tweeting birds, purple flowers poking through a trellis, planters full of begonias and Sweet William. I was about to comment on how peaceful it all seemed when Galia, green-eyed and beautiful, said, "So what do you think of this horrible place?"

I gave an exaggerated shrug. *What right do I have to think?* It was a line from *Casablanca*.

The conversation bumped along awkwardly at first. The husband, Meir, spoke no English, and Galia, just out of the army, and eager to be with friends, was unhappy that she'd been pressed by her mother to stay at the table.

I praised the lemony chicken and roasted onions, but this did not seem to soften Ronit. She was offended that my mother had been living in Tel Aviv and never once had called and at the same time was not at all surprised. She kept returning to this and pushing it away with both hands, as if these facts were compelling and distasteful. Why hadn't we told her about my father's death? Or the Gorelicks who'd visited the year before? Why hadn't I called before now? I was too busy?

"My parents were out of touch with everyone. I don't know how it happened."

Ronit sent Meir to bring a photo album to the table. Tucked inside were a few loose snapshots in an envelope. A man with a corona of gray curls smiles in the top one. White teeth, blue shirt, slight paunch, his arm around a sleepy-looking wife. "And these are?" I asked.

Ronit was surprised. "Mark and Marilyn. The Gorelicks. They live near you in New Jersey."

"I don't live in New Jersey anymore. I live in Pennsylvania. In Pittsburgh."

"You have a husband in Pitts-boorgh?"

"Once I did," I said, as if I'd misplaced him. Then I turned back to the photos. "Is this Mark? Wow. He's a man. I guess we grew up. I haven't seen him or his brother since I was a kid."

"You didn't visit with your father?"

I had a faint childhood memory of my father bringing me to a party one summer so I could meet my cousins, two brothers who took me upstairs to their bedroom and led me out a dormer window so we could sit on the roof and shoot spitballs at the adults below. A waste, my mother had declared of my cousin Mark, who went to trade school. A nothing. And now here he is in the photo, tan from touring the Holy Land.

"Once. Maybe twice. My father almost never went anywhere without my mother. She didn't drive." I was aware just then how absurd that explanation sounded.

Ronit slid the photos back into the envelope and opened the photo album full of pictures of people I should have known and didn't. My mother set the law, I thought. Her disdain for my father's family was as much a fixture of my childhood as the oval dining room table, the breakfront filled with china, the carpet that my father often vacuumed. I never questioned it, never dared to question anything. First were old sepia-toned ones. I pointed to a stout white-haired woman whose hat was perched at an angle, and Ronit said, "That's your *savtah*, your grandmother."

In the next photo, two handsome boys, their wavy hair high off their foreheads, pose beneath spindly trees, arms around each other's shoulders. One has tiny wire-rimmed glasses. "Your father," Ronit said of the bespectacled one. "My father," of the taller one. "They loved each other very much."

Galia got up to clear the table, chided her mother in Hebrew, and left. Meir brought his chair closer. The two brothers are posed beside each other in a later photo, a glossy black-and-white. My father's hair is thinner; he holds a cigarette. They wear loose shirts tucked into baggy high-waisted trousers, and they are laughing, which stuns me. Had I ever seen my father laugh? I wanted to study each photo carefully, but Ronit flipped the pages, busy with the when and where of everyone's death. The color had faded from the next pictures, until the man on the left was the father I knew, morose and bespectacled, his thin hair combed straight back. The brother beside him on the couch is gaunt-cheeked, near death.

Ronit set the album aside and put her small, meaty hand on my wrist. "Tell me, Vered, are we so terrible?"

No!" I cried, taking in these people seated around the table in this verdant garden in Ra'anana—strangers, family members. "Not terrible! At all!"

I was wondering what had become of my ability to speak English when Ronit said, "So you'll come back. You'll see we're not so bad."

She got up from the table, and when she returned she gave me a recent photo of my father and told me her husband would drive me back to Tel Aviv. I was too weary to argue strenuously in favor of calling a taxi and simply, once again, said, "Thanks."

Meir drove reasonably until we reached the Ayalon Highway, where he floored it, weaving between the lanes, braking hard like a taxi driver, and pointing out various sites. I said "ah!" and "yes!" and took in the twinkling lights that shone from the windows of apartment buildings and tried not to think about my own mortality. When we at last pulled in front of my mother's building, I searched for a way to say good night and came up with "*bon soir.*" He squeezed my hand and laughed. I waved goodbye, happy to be alive. Also, oddly, just plain happy.

The TV was blaring when I unlocked the apartment door. I lowered the volume and pulled the bamboo-framed chair beside my mother, who was dozing on the sofa.

When Mom opened her eyes, I said, "I'm sorry you didn't come. You'd like Ronit. She's a systems programmer. Her husband drove me home. I'm going to go back again and maybe you'll come with me. She'd like to see you."

I said a few more words about the garden and family, none of which piqued her interest. Then I gave her the photo of my father and went to the kitchen to put water up for tea. On the way back into the living room, I saw her holding the picture in both hands, shaking it hard, and asking, "Why," in an angry tremulous voice. "Why did you leave me like this? Why didn't you let me die with you?"

That night, when I threw my father's vests and jackets into a trash bag along with a felt hat that smelled of hair, I thought: you just need to do it. To move on. To be like the men playing *mat-kot* behind the hotels, slamming that hard rubber ball as if they were young men living at a time of peace. You need to keep going forward, I thought, filled with such resolve to change that I retrieved the stupid little burro from the desk drawer where I'd stashed it yet again, and buried it under reams of paper, manuals, and installation instructions for long defunct appliances. As *she* had, I thought, hoisting the bag over my shoulder, recalling my mother's husky laugh of years back, her vitality. She had lost a bottom tooth. It distressed me to realize she no longer knew or cared.

The bag ripped on the way downstairs. I clenched the torn part, barely making it to the garbage area, where I lowered it carefully. By the time I was back in my mother's apartment, I was crying so hard, my knees buckled.

I went back downstairs, sat on the filthy floor and took everything out of the black bag until I found the burro. This time, I put it in my pocket—this broken burro, which I did not want and needed to keep forever.

TEN

Two days before Dr. Berenbaum arrived, Dina went away with one of her suitors—Shuki, the oral surgeon; Shlomo, the guy with the Cessna; or Shmulik, the rotund translator, whose wife had killed herself six months earlier and who stared mournfully from his photo, his sport jacket so askew it looked as if he had paused in deep thought and forgot to finish dressing. While she was gone, I fed her noisy parrot and sat at her computer to work. Now and then, when I lowered my eyes, I saw the parrot giving me a beady-eyed look. "*Ma!*" he squawked. "*Ma shlomkhah?*"

"Not much," I told him.

Everything previously drawn or assembled could now be done electronically. In an instant, I turned the oyster pail matte black, made the inside glossy red, and sent it off to Les. Then I looked at our newer projects. I read the marketing plan for an energy drink for a *mature consumer*. I hated this product. I hated the words *mature* and *consumer*. Alone, except for this noisy, bandy-legged bird, my ability to loathe something trivial wasn't much fun. I was homesick, tired of being illiterate, tired of washing my hands with shampoo and eating mayonnaise. I missed my house, missed sitting with Les, watching him lean back and cross his arms while he pondered an idea, the cotton of his T-shirt straining. I missed the epitaphs we wrote for each other. *Les Sheldon—He was short, but he was buff.*

I scrolled through some photos on Dina's dating site. The night before, to satisfy her desire that I "choose someone," I pointed to an olive-skinned man I'd thought was handsome. "Roxanne!" she gasped, as if I'd confessed to a creepy perversion. My second choice got an even more dramatic response. "Such lowlife you choose!"

How could I know their economic status in life when the text was in Hebrew? "I'm just going by their looks," I said.

After a few more choices, I realized that Dina did not like Sephardic men, whose skin was brown like hers, and it puzzled and upset me, given how proud she was of her cultured father, and her mother who'd been accepted to Oxford and ended up in a tent in Israel instead. I imagined asking her why she was so self-loathing. I imagined her asking me.

I don't know, I would say.

Dr. Barry Berenbaum was small, fortyish, with a discreet little yarmulke, neatly-trimmed beard, and a mellifluous voice with a New Zealand accent. It was early evening, a Sunday at the end of October when Dina brought him to my mother's door. I invited him into the kitchen, clean by then, and showed him to a wicker chair at the small table by a window overlooking the sea. My mother was already seated there.

Dr. Berenbaum's warm eyes fastened on my mother in such a way that she straightened, turned sideways in her chair, and glanced over her shoulder in a manner that was both flirtatious and authoritative. He spoke a few words in Hebrew to Dina, in English to me, and to my mother in some amalgam that charmed her.

It was as if she were a child and we'd set up a play date for her, because when Dina took me back to her apartment and rolled the rickety office chair beside her own, I began to worry about how they were getting along. I imagined my mother talking about her illustrious career, while he took in her stained blouse and ill-fitting slacks and the clutter in the next room. I wanted him to like her, to see something of the person she had been, and yet to understand that her bold assertions were set pieces, the embers left from the fire, and not be fooled into believing she was fine.

While I was scrolling through the JDate photos I was stopped by a face—a man with fuzzy gray hair and large, protuberant eyes that seemed to take me in. Rust-colored shirt. No kids, no props, no pets. Just a man. Standing with his arms at his sides. Behind him a stone wall. Dina noticed how closely I studied the photo and read some of the profile aloud. "He is a professor, this Baruch Geschwind, and doing *such* interesting work; Roxanne, he is so admired."

I didn't care about this man or his profession. The picture was what had drawn me in. A snapshot, it seemed, taken without much thought, yet one of those mysterious photos, where the emotion on the subject's face is as powerful and unnamable as a word on the tip of one's tongue. I touched my finger to the sharp edge of his Adam's apple. Then, fearful Dina would mock me for studying the photo, I tried to scroll past.

She grabbed the mouse, slammed it on the desktop, and returned to the photo. "He is a very great intellectual; everyone respects him so. You must write to him now; I will help you." She wheeled her chair closer. "Write to him. He is divorced a year and new to the JDate."

I wondered what had gone wrong for the man whose Adam's apple I touched, this former husband, father of two. Had he instigated the divorce or been blindsided by his spouse? I wondered if at first he'd felt furtive and lonely contacting women late at night, or if now, like Dina, he looked forward to returning home, his apartment brightened by the messages and photos, replacing the family that once filled the room with happy noise. I imagined that the man who looked straight at me had already had sex with several nubile oldsters.

Or not. I had no interest in writing to him or anyone else. "I don't live here," I said. This announcement disturbed Dina as much as my attraction to swarthy men. "Why don't you go out with him?" I said. "He's more your type."

It was true. She had a weakness for pale intellectuals, while I, apparently, liked taxi drivers and proprietors of falafel stands.

By then my thoughts had wandered. I was no longer scrutinizing the photo or thinking about Dr. Barry Berenbaum across the hall—a Jew from New Zealand, how was that possible? No, I was thinking about the mystery of attraction. A boy I had once loved because he had beautiful forearms, muscular, hairless. Another boy I could not love because I was repelled by his ears with their tightly attached lobes. The boy, the man, from whom it had been so hard to separate, with his transparent lies, his overwrought protestations of love, the crushing depression he denied, all of the energy he expended hiding whomever he was.

I tapped the photo of the man with the huge sad eyes and long neck. "Write to the guy," I said to Dina.

The man seemed to look at us both. Maybe he wasn't sad. His brow was not furrowed. He wasn't frowning. It was as if he was saying: I have seen it all and here I am, still standing. Or maybe not. Maybe he thought: Life is a vale of tears. No, that wasn't it. Life's a bitch and then you die. Not that either. I couldn't say, and for a few moments, until Dr. Berenbaum knocked on the door, I continued speculating.

"Your mother has given me permission to speak with you," he said, when I stepped into the hall.

I nodded mutely.

"She told me she'd been fine until her trip to the States. Something there made her ill, yes?" *Yis* is how he said it. "Has she been living this way for a long time?"

This way—a reminder of the clutter. "Our house wasn't like this when I was a child," I said, ashamed to admit that I didn't know.

"She was a physicist?" He seemed dubious.

"She was," I said. "Whatever she told you about her professional life was true."

"And she was depressed when you were young?"

"She was busy," I said. "She had a very demanding job, especially when she became a department head and had to manage people on top of everything else."

Just then, as if I were thousands of feet above the earth, looking down from Shlomo's Cessna, I saw fissures, rages that came without warning, terrible screaming that filled the whole house. "Getting upset" was my father's name for these episodes. What brought them on? Because I got water on the bathroom floor after a shower, because my father had bought a cheap cut of beef, because she couldn't find the stapler and was convinced I'd gone into her drawers with my sticky fingers and stolen it? That wasn't depression, though, was it? She didn't stay in bed or sit in a dark room for hours, the way Harley often did.

"I don't know," I said, remembering my father helping me glue the handle back onto a cup I'd dropped, wiping the seam with a dampened towel while I held the pieces together until the epoxy set, because we loved or feared her. "She was difficult." I was struck by the inadequacy of this word I kept using.

For a moment, I was silent, and the parrot squawked "ma!" behind Dina's door. "She had a terrible temper. Working for her must have been a nightmare. She was also extremely fearful, though only my father and I knew. No one would have believed it." It was true: My mother, who radiated confidence and never minced words, would not go out alone at night. She stiffened when a dog approached. She trusted no one. "She was isolated," I said finally.

"Yes. The situation with your sister must have been quite a strain."

A chill passed through me as if I were hollow inside. "What sister?" I said.

Dr. Berenbaum regarded me. His eyes were soft, his demeanor calm.

In the endless instant of standing outside Dina's apartment with this soft-spoken man, my thoughts blazed past my mother, past my toothless, senile father leaning across the table, asking, "Wasn't there another one?" Like a comet, further back in time, and there was no place to settle, no single incident, only the sorrowful way my father breathed, his odd, embarrassing tearful moments; the halting way he spoke in my mother's presence, his muteness when she was gone. It was as if all we had in common was our fearful love of Leona and our failure to please her.

"What did she say?"

"Families have different ways of responding to this kind of tragedy, especially years ago when the stigma was even worse. Your mother is a very proud woman."

"Can you back up, Dr. Berenbaum?" I asked. "This is new to me."

He hesitated. I could feel him trying to recall their conversation. "When I asked your mother about family, she told me everyone was dead. So I pushed a bit and asked, 'What about the woman staying with you? Is she your daughter?' She agreed. Yes, this was one of her daughters. The other was dead."

"Was she a child, the one who died, or grown up? What else did she say?"

"Something happened during childbirth. Birth asphyxia, perhaps. Lack of oxygen. She said it was the doctor's fault for letting her labor too long. That may well have been the case, since these things still happen."

"And this was in Israel? Did she say anything else?"

"She was very agitated. I saw no reason to press further."

Laugher echoed, jarring and strange, as tenants climbed the stairs, passing us as if we weren't there. I waited for the click of a lock one floor up.

"Your mother has some dementia she is working very hard to mask. You see this often. Imagine trying to admit your mind is slipping. For someone like your mother, it isn't possible. Of course she will deny it. She cannot be living on her own. I'll send a letter to the *Bituach Leumi* and recommend home health care. You're staying here in Tel Aviv?"

It wasn't a question.

I watched him walk down the steps. The lights flickered on, illuminating his path. I felt as if I were only tissue, barely anchored to the ground, and any moment might rise like a Chagall figure, float out the window and over the roof, leaving all the rooted, troubled souls behind. I touched my cheeks, felt my nose, chin, collarbones, and shoulders, as if to reassure myself of my own existence. Then Dina appeared, dressed for her date with Shmulik the translator, and I was called on to help with some weighty decisions—the necklace, yes or no, the green flats or brown ones, her hair pushed back, or let loose—and these welcome distractions brought me back down to earth.

Across the hall, my mother sat in her chair, across from the TV, in the one section of the living room I'd cleared. Her head was bowed and a journal was on her lap. As I stepped closer, the words tumbled into my mind—*the situation with your sister*—and I felt sure that I'd known about this sister. Not that I had been told and had forgotten, but that I had known without language, that the knowledge was preverbal, more a feeling than something I had put into words. I thought of a friend who was walking her two dogs off leash. One was struck by a car and the second one witnessed the death. And this second dog stood at the door waiting for her companion day after day. Not eating, not playing with her rubber bone or shaking her cloth lamb. The left-behind dog had no words, did not process the event the way humans did. The knowledge was there, the feeling of loss, of what no longer existed. Absence that has meaning, that shaped the days that followed. All that had brought the dog pleasure in the past—food, bones, toys—was no longer of interest. She's depressed, the vet had said. She misses her friend. Maybe it was this way for me, the reason an unshakable sense of loss was always within me. And for my mother, it had to be so much worse, I thought, standing beside her. I had grown up in safety and privilege and she had lost everything.

She opened her eyes, drew her journal close to her chest as if I might snatch it away. "What do you want?"

"I was wondering," I said. "Did you like Dr. Berenbaum?"

"*Who?*"

"The doctor who was just here. I thought he was nice and so I wondered."

"Why did you call him? So you could put me away?"

"Ma." There was still so much stuff piled against the walls. "I was concerned."

"I'm not senile, you know."

"No one is saying you're senile." Was there tenderness in my voice? I meant for there to be. "Your nosebleeds worried me. And even you've been saying you're not yourself. So I called Dr. Berenbaum, and now I'm wondering what you told him."

It was hard to go on. I had so completely internalized the law against asking that even now, it was hard to get the words out. "*Was there another one, Mom?*" I asked at last. "Was there another child? Daddy once asked if there was another one. Do you remember? He was still living at home with you."

She straightened. "What are you going on about? I haven't the foggiest idea."

My father's dentures were gone by the time he'd asked that question. He'd thrown away his glasses. It was as if wherever he looked, he saw a faint shape and couldn't say what it was or bring it into sharper focus.

I plowed on. "What was her name, Mom?"

"Why did you ask that man to come? So you could throw me away? Go home and leave me in peace."

"Dr. Berenbaum. You told him you had another daughter. Was she older? Could you tell me about her? All I want is to know something."

"Stop pushing at me. I'm an old lady. Leave me be."

"Please, Mom. You told a stranger about her. Please say something to me."

"Why did you come here? To blame me for your problems? The mother is always the villain. It's always her fault. Go home and leave me to die."

"How about a yes or no? Don't I deserve that?"

"You deserve *bupkis*. Go home. Go away." She grasped the journal she could no longer read. "Leave me alone so I can think."

∾

When I was in third grade, my teacher asked all the kids in class to bring in baby pictures for an art project we'd be doing. I told her we had no baby pictures and she laughed in a dubious way. *You just showed up on your parents' doorstep one day, like hello, what's for dinner?*

She was so young and pretty, with a soft voice, and an engagement ring with a tiny diamond she'd shown off to the class, holding out her hand, splaying her fingers. I'd loved this teacher and wanted so much to please her. Embarrassed by her laughter, I went back to my seat, lowered my head over my paper, and colored furiously with the fat crayons in my desk.

Later, she asked if I'd been adopted, like Chrissy, who'd come from an orphanage in Korea, then went on at great, mysterious length about how deeply Chrissy's parents loved her. My classmate, Chrissy, a cheerful girl who wore fancy barrettes and shared her pencils, went to a Korean school on Saturdays and attended potluck dinners with her family so the other children from Korea could form a community. There was no community of children born to parents who had not wanted them and were uncomfortable with one in their midst. When I'd dared to ask my mother if I was adopted, she gave me a look that curdled my curiosity. "What kind of foolish question is that?"

It was foolish. Our hands were identical, our feet odd in the same way, with oversized big toes. Lollipop toes, Mindy had named them years later.

Now, sitting on the floor of my mother's apartment, stuffing trash bags with manuscripts on dot-matrix paper and canvas-covered lab notebooks filled with my mother's elegant, familiar script, this memory came back. Why didn't we have baby pictures? Was it because of this nameless, never mentioned sister?

Over the next days, as I waited for a nurse from the National Insurance Institute to evaluate Mom, I tried asking friendly questions. How did you and Daddy meet? What was it like when you first came to the U.S.? The only stories she shared were those from her time at Bell Labs, first in Murray Hill and then in Holmdel, and they were full of color and detail, and so familiar I could repeat them verbatim.

This sister had to have been born in a different era, well before me. Maybe she wasn't an accident, as I was. Or perhaps she was the reason my parents had not wanted any more children. Perhaps, when I asked Ronit, I'd learn that *this situation* was the kind of benign family secret my friends' parents kept: that Dad had a weird uncle who lived in a hut, and Mom had been briefly married to a pothead housepainter named Roy.

I knew I wouldn't find answers in the massive amount of stuff that remained, no tiny sweaters or booties, no art work or baby pictures. But I paused now; I looked. Dried leaves fluttered from the pages of *The Age of Faith,* by Will and Ariel Durant—swamp oak, chestnut, Japanese maple, birch, the mitten, and three-fingered leaves from the sassafras tree. They triggered a dim recollection of a winter day when my father and I had walked through the woods and he'd shown me how to identify trees by their bark. I ruffled the pages until the last leaf had slipped out and waited for him to speak. He remained silent, his thin lips pursed.

What am I? I remembered the cold brick wall outside my elementary school, where I'd stood at recess, unable to answer that question. *Nothing.* How ironic that my mother was the one who tried to teach me about the limits of the naked eye. "Nothing" is what people said when the stars were not visible in the night sky. Nothing, when it was quiet. Nothing, because they lacked the language of mathematics and could not understand what they experienced every day. Remembering this lesson made me reconsider my feeling of aloneness, this sense I'd always had of being incomplete, as unfurnished as an empty apartment.

My mother had scored badly enough on the "mini-mental," to be eligible for twenty hours a week of home healthcare. On a bright morning in early November, I sat in the kitchen waiting to meet the woman who I hoped would be her companion.

Mom was dozing in the living room with the newspaper across her lap when the buzzer rang. "It's Sunny!" I said.

I saw the headline as I crossed the room: Yasser Arafat was dead, and the Israelis would not allow him to be buried in Jerusalem. I unbolted the lock, waited by the door, listening to the careful footsteps up the single flight. "Hello!" a voice echoed, and "Hello!" I called in return.

Then, Sunny, a short, square Filipino woman, dressed this morning in an olive-colored quilted jacket and red sneakers. She stepped into a kitchen that was bright and clean, craned her neck and continued past me, into a living room with a sofa and chairs upholstered in blue, and small Persian-style rugs on the tile floor. She pulled a chair close to Mom's and began talking to her in Hebrew.

I kept my distance, understanding nothing. Sunny gripped Mom's hands, listened, laughed, got Mom to show her the rest of the apartment. Later, they sat over tea while my mother held forth on the elastic constants of solid wood, on the engineering flaws in the Saarinen building in Holmdel, on her loyal secretary Dottie. She told

Sunny she hated the sun, had *no use whatsoever* for the beach, *not the slightest interest* in taking a walk. Sunny listened to all this, laughed softly, palms together, bending at the waist. Then she put a hat on my mother's head, made several admiring sounds, and helped her down the flight of stairs.

Though Mom would not admit to liking her or needing anyone's help, she did not balk when Sunny appeared. If anything, she became more compliant. I arranged for extra hours, covering the expenses from my mother's account, to which I'd gained control by steering her to the bank, having her sign *here* and *here* and *here*. I felt corrupt, exploitative, relieved. Her disdain for me felt like a gift just then. She was in good hands with Sunny. All that was left was to ask Ronit what she knew about this sister. Then I could go home.

❧

When I arrived at Ronit's on Friday afternoon, two days before my departure, Meir's family was seated at the long table on the patio—his brother, wife, and two sons. The brother was tiny and dark, like Meir. The boys, long eyelashes, hair shorn nearly to the skull, were in constant motion, even while seated. They grabbed food off each other's plates, butted each other's shoulders. One boy clocked the other on the head with a spoon; the other stabbed his brother's bicep with a fork. The adults ignored them, which seemed to work; while the quarreling was nonstop, it seemed devoid of animosity.

I had asked Ronit not to make anyone struggle to speak in English. "Being at your table is enough," I'd said. This was true: it was easy to be among this boisterous crew. Midway through the meal, Galia appeared in a tight T-shirt and khaki pants, her curly hair bundled in a charming, haphazard way. She kissed the boys and pulled a chair beside me. "So Vered," she said with great seriousness. "You've heard of the Ross Park Mall?"

This unexpected question made me laugh. "Sure. It's in the North Hills, just outside Pittsburgh."

"My friends are selling the Dead Sea products and say business is good, they have space in their apartment, and I should come. What do you think?"

I knew that after their military service, Israeli kids often traveled for six months or a year, and said, "Why Pittsburgh? Why not Peru? Or Thailand?"

"My friend says two months at the Ross Park Mall and you can backpack for a year."

"You could stay with me and save even more," I said.

"You live near the Ross Park Mall?"

"Not really. And I guess you'd need a car."

One of the boys came up behind Galia and began playing with her thick curls. Galia scolded him and he ran off. She went after him, growling like a movie monster. In a corner of the yard, she tickled him until he curled into a ball.

By then, Meir and his brother had walked off and the women had begun to clear the table. I got up to help.

Ronit was alone in the kitchen, filling a kettle. "This is so nice," I said.

She turned off the tap and looked at me with a universal "whatever" expression on her face. "You like tea?" she asked.

I liked tea, I said. Then, "I like everything here—the food, the garden, sitting with your family. Last time I was here, you asked if I thought you were terrible. I never thought that. We had fun that summer you were in New Jersey, didn't we? And we wrote to each other for a while, and then we stopped because, I don't know, that's what happens. And then there was nothing. I don't remember hearing your name or anyone else's after that. It was like a total blackout. I didn't know I had a sister until a couple of weeks ago."

Ronit looked at me and then averted her eyes. She knew something. I could tell by the expression on her face.

"You know how I found out? My mother told the doctor who examined her last month."

Ronit's sister-in-law carried a stack of dishes into the kitchen. She saw the way we stood, placed the plates on the counter, and left.

Ronit said, "And when you asked Leona?"

"Nothing. Then a blast of anger. You know how all this makes me feel? Like a book with blank pages."

"Sit with her. You're here. Maybe the time has come for her to tell. Sometimes it happens this way. People get old, they start to worry they'll die with their story inside them."

"It feels like elder abuse when I try. I don't even know this sister's name. Do you?"

Ronit squeezed her brow. "I'm sorry, Vered. I can't remember. I wish your father was here."

"So do I," I said. "Tell me what you know. Please."

"She was in a place, a—" Ronit struggled to find the right word."—home for people like her. Your father didn't speak much of her after his visits."

"My father visited her?" I recalled his open suitcase on the bed, each side neatly packed, the paper bands around the laundered shirts, each shoe in a cotton bag, but I had no memory of his absences.

"Of course. He always stayed with us when he came to see her. He was a wonderful man, your father. We miss him still."

"Really? How often did he visit?"

"Three times a year? Four? And then he didn't come, and that was it. We were very hurt that no one told us he'd died. Marilyn Gorelick called his school, and then, what can I say? The years went by. It's very sad because the two brothers could not have been closer. But after your mother broke with the family, there were very bad feelings. I thought you knew you had a sister. How would I think otherwise? But now look. After all these years, here you are, and that's something, isn't it?"

"But why the break?"

"*Why.* Because one said this and the other said that. After all they went through. Look, we are together after all this time. It's the way it should be."

Ronit's nephews thundered into the kitchen and I meandered in the garden, trying to process what she had just said. When it was time to go, Ronit linked her arm through mine and walked me to Meir's car.

"The summer in New Jersey?" she said. "Your father one

afternoon takes me into his bedroom. 'Ronit, I want to show you something.' He closes the door. Takes from his drawer a book, and inside is a picture, a photograph. 'Here,' he says. He gives me this picture of two babies, very small, wrapped up, and when I look up to ask who it is, I see that he is crying. 'Don't tell Mama.' This is what he says. I was young, and it was very upsetting to see him this way. 'Don't tell Mama.' I'll never forget."

Meir drove me home. On the silent, hair-raising ride, I kept seeing those two babies, *very small, wrapped up*. They were so vivid it was as if I'd seen the photograph myself. Just as haunting was Ronit's memory of my father, his hand on her arm, his words, "Don't tell Mama." I knew these words, knew "Mama" was his wife, my mother. I knew this hand on my arm and the way I pulled away. I knew the sadness in his breathing, his eyes when he leaned across the table to ask about the other one, nameless as an embryo. I waved goodbye to Meir and entered my mother's building. Two small, wrapped-up babies, I thought as I started upstairs. If she, nameless sister, was one, then I had to have been the other. I stopped, leaned against the cool wall, feeling like a dense, unteachable, child, so slow to process what Ronit had told me that I had never thought to ask this last question.

Oh, I wish I knew none of this, I thought. Then I found a website for the U.S. National Archives, which had databases going back to the 1800s, and with barely any effort ordered my family's immigration records. All this intimate information was just *there. Everyone knows except me!*

Later, while cleaning out a kitchen cabinet, I found a cardboard box with a label in four languages, one of which was English. "Open this kit only under clear instructions from the Home Front Command," I read. Maybe ignorance really is bliss, I thought, and opened the top flap of the box. Inside was a manual with an illustration of a man whose face was covered by a huge mask and respirator, straps hanging from all directions. The mask, to be worn only when there were instructions from the "mass media," had a drinking tube and filter. Also in the kit was a syringe, a "primary means of treatment in case of exposure to nerve gas."

I put the box back under the sink and left the apartment. I passed the elderly women on their bench, crossed the street to the beach. A couple sat in chairs at the edge of the water, holding hands. I walked past them, slipped off my shoes and put my toes in the cool, beautiful, oblivious sea.

The morning of my departure, I walked across the hall and knocked on Dina's door. How small she was in bare feet, even shorter than I, with that powerful head and lush black hair. She grabbed my hands when I told her I had come to say goodbye, and said, "*Why are you leaving us?*"

I tried to explain that I had a business and responsibilities at home.

"But we are here. Your mother, your family." Her eyes brimmed with tears.

"I know," I said. "You've been such a great friend. I can't thank you enough."

Dina let go of my hands and turned before I could finish. I'd remembered not to buy her a gift but managed to annoy her with my gratitude.

"Goodbye," I said to my mother when she and Sunny returned from a walk. "Do you remember that I'm leaving?"

Sunny had taken her for a haircut a few days earlier and now the red ends and much of the brown was gone. She looked like a different woman, with her short white hair. Less agitated. Only her dark brows and stormy dark eyes were familiar. "Where are you going?" she asked.

"Pittsburgh," I said.

"*Pittsburgh?* I don't know anyone in Pittsburgh."

I raised my hand. Then I gave her a box of Swiss chocolates, extra dark, the only kind she liked.

I remembered not to kiss her goodbye.

ELEVEN

The trees were bare when I returned to Pittsburgh, and the late afternoon sky was dark. So was my house. I walked from room to room, switching on every light. The fridge was humming and the wall clock ticked. Strange, I thought, since the clock had no gears or wheels. Contrived. I climbed on a stool to set the proper time and felt how warm my house was. I hadn't thought to lower the heat before I'd left.

Don't tell Mama. I heard my father say those words, his voice nearly inaudible, and Ronit calling him a wonderful man. It confused me, not the words, which I recognized as his, but to hear him described so fondly, when our only time together had been in the dining room after school, a workbook in front of me. His stale, unloved smell and his chalky sleeves.

Okay, careful, I thought. Don't extrapolate from noise. It was a favorite expression of my mother's. I lowered myself from the stool. What I'd learned from Ronit wasn't an artifact, like static; it was incomplete. Until the documents I ordered arrived, I needed to move on. I hefted my suitcase, dragging it upstairs, one step at a time. I did not feel it was possible, but I was old enough to understand that thinking "I can't live like this" was sentimental.

I unzipped my bag on the kitchen floor, shook the little burro out of a dirty sock and put it on the windowsill. In the corner of the floor was a laundry chute. I threw my dirty clothes down the chute and listened to them tumble into the basement. I loved this chute. Anything that got in my way went down—linens, books, shoes. Okay, I'll throw this, I thought, rapping on the side of my cocked head, so all that grieved me might drip from my brain, out my ear, down the chute, and away.

I dragged myself to bed, vowing I'd never return to Israel, and knowing I'd go back, believing I'd stop thinking about those two small babies and doubting it was possible. Such is my brain that I was able to hold onto all of these positions and still fall into the deepest slumber.

Early that evening I woke, emailed Les to let him know I'd be back at work in the morning. Then found the remote and crawled back into bed. On a nature show, a cow expelled a calf. The mother licked the amniotic fluid and muck off its face and the calf got right to its feet. I was very moved, cried briefly, wanted to watch it again. Then I decided it was a message meant for me: Get up on your wobbly legs and move on. Moooove on, I thought, and flicked the remote, as if I could find on one of the hundreds of channels another cow giving birth.

Just moooove.

I slid out of bed and made my way to the basement to do my laundry, and when I opened the door, I saw a light had been left on. Wasteful, I thought, working my way downstairs. I needed to think more about the environment.

A small living area had been set up in the corner between the workbench and furnace, with furnishings from storage. A trundle bed was neatly made. Marimekko sheets with bright little cars, a royal blue comforter that had belonged to Harley's son. A door atop two file cabinets that I'd once used as a desk. An old chair on castors.

Harley swiveling to face me. "You're home."

I covered my face, as if when I opened my eyes he might vanish, and cried, "Go *away!*"

Harley wrapped me in his trembling arms, tightening them as I tried to get free, murmuring in my hair, "I'm so happy you're home safe. So incredibly happy. Why didn't you tell me you were on your way back? I would have picked you up."

"Let me go. You're smothering me!" I jabbed him with an elbow and finally got free.

A blanket of fatigue fell over me. I looked at the klugey arrangement, made up of my stuff—the door as a desk, the file cabinets—and worried they were an early sign I'd end up a hoarder like my mother. I needed a chute to oblivion, where I could throw the clutter first, and Harley as a chaser.

"You're supposed to be in Sewickley."

"Oh, hon. Get some sleep, and we'll talk in the morning. I have so much to tell you. But first get some sleep. I'm sure you're exhausted."

"You've got to pack up and get out, Harley. I have nothing else to say." I needed clean clothes. This seemed very important. "I have to do my laundry. If you're still here tomorrow, I'm calling the police. Don't talk to me."

Get out or I'll call the police. What my mother had said to me. I threw the laundry into the washer, adding the towels and underwear left in the basket from before I'd gone away, concentrating hard on the wash cycle and temperature.

Orange juice and milk was in the fridge. Also some foodish items of Harley's—pre-cut celery and carrots on a Styrofoam tray, white around the edges; a bag of squishy, pre-sliced bagel-shaped bread; a crock of something called cheese food; a plate of glazed pastries of indeterminate age. I studied the giant raisin-studded blob and thought, who can eat this?

Mom again, which rattled me. If I went back downstairs to rout out Harley, she would break through, and I would scream and threaten, "Get out of my house!" and he would clutch me in his arms, call me *hon*, tell me I'd changed his life, and I would weaken and fold.

No, I wouldn't. There was something wrong with him. Deeply, deeply wrong.

And still, history said otherwise. History reminding me of all the past times I had approached him with such resolve and failed to seal the deal. *History.*

Two babies all wrapped up, and one of them was me.

When I returned to work, Kayleigh bounded over, tall, wholesome, ponytail swaying, nearly lifting me off my feet in her embrace, so, so, *so* happy I was home, she said, gesturing with her thumb at Les, who was lying on the floor to soothe his aching back.

Later I gave them halvah, amused by their expressions as they sampled the gritty sweet, opened the few pieces of mail addressed to me, discussed upcoming projects.

I did not go into the basement.

How do you live that way?

I knew it was twisted, closing the door and leaving Harley in the basement. My instinct for getting on with my life, no matter what, was stronger than the voice that said, this is way too weird. Don't we all make such decisions? It seems to me now that everyone closes the door on what is unbearable. Some ability to turn away allows us to live. At the heart of a good life is learning what to face head-on and what to ignore.

How many people achieve that balance? What of a man who tries to erase his marital history by throwing away every object that bears his wife's scent or carries her memory—photos, pillows, wine glasses, the plates they bought in Italy, their comforter? Not him; certainly not him.

What of this same man, whose daily life is marked by violence? The Jerusalem coffee shop he'd frequented blown up. The city bus his son took regularly until he left for graduate school in Minnesota blown up. How should he live? How should anyone live? I imagine this man brushing his teeth, making coffee, going to work, his mind on meetings and promising collaborations. The second intifada erupts; his productivity increases. He tires of sleeping in a sheet in a stripped-down apartment with shadows on the wall where art had once hung and decides it's time to date. The violence increases. His daughter helps him write a profile, not an easy task for this man, who no longer remembers who he had been before his marriage. Blood, splinters of glass, children ripped to shreds. He goes online, begins to court women. Is this oblivious, insensitive? Or is it life-affirming?

How did you keep from hearing the footsteps in the basement? How do you continue to believe in your life's work in such a fraught environment? What should this man do with his unspoken ache? Should he weigh it against the discord outside? Denigrate his own despair?

In the end, I suppose, we acknowledge what we can, what will not demolish us.

❧

On my second day home, I stopped at the yoga studio one floor above us. Nomi, the owner, was sitting at a table by the cubbies for shoes, her small face framed with short wavy hair that curled at the brow and made her look like the etching of a Roman boy. I asked if I could arrange for a private lesson for a super stubborn man, and she said, "You mean Les?"

I said, "Yes. His back has been killing me."

I was paying Nomi when a woman walked in, holding the hand of a pale, skinny girl with a mass of auburn curls and big discolored teeth. The girl grabbed my wrist with surprising force and said in an urgent way, "Going home? In a car?" Her mother pulled her away, and I took the card from Nomi and went downstairs, disturbed by the incident and the girl.

I put the card on Les's desk and went back to work. We had many beautiful boxes to design. We had "our nurses," a consortium of caregivers from various professions whose logo we'd designed a few years back, who now needed presentation items for an upcoming conference. Les and I had been asked to think beyond the daisies and ribbons and remember the men, who were twelve percent of their membership. "The men!" I'd cried out. "We will not forget the men!"

"I *love* our nurses!" I said, because Les was not so keen about this bread-and-butter work, while I liked the nurses. They were enthusiastic. Everything pleased them. If I got all agitated I'd be unable to think about the nurses! I needed to keep it together for the nurses, to be vigilant when driving. Careful on the steps. No more talking while walking. I held onto the bannister when I took the stairs; kept my eyes on the ground. Even when I was not thinking of this shadowy twin, I felt vulnerable, unsure, as if the history that had been taken from me was a rug, yanked from beneath my feet. Don't fall, I told myself when I ran in the park. With every step: *Do not fall.* This whispered caution was beneath every action. *No one will pick you up.*

When I came home from work, I heard the strains of "Bat out of Hell" while I was walking down my driveway. The vent in the basement glass block was open so I traced the source to Harley, who liked Meatloaf. When he first confessed to this, I thought he was talking about the entrée meatloaf and not the sweaty singer who went by that name, soft and white as a grub. Meatloaf was one of those American food items, like Velveeta and Marshmallow Fluff that I'd never tasted, though I'd lived in the U.S. nearly my entire life. Harley refused to believe it was possible. "You're adorable," he'd said, laughing and hugging me, then disappearing into a dark room. Now he was blaring Meatloaf as a way to fool me into thundering downstairs. My anger would be met with his delight. *Hon, I'm so happy you're here!* For so long, that delight had confused me, made me feel like a harsh, puppy-throwing woman.

I unlocked my front door. Upstairs, everything was as I'd left it. The day's mail was still scattered on the floor, my sweater draped across a dining room chair, the newspaper open on the kitchen island beside a mug half full of leftover coffee.

The silence worried me: when there were no sounds coming from the basement, I opened the door to the basement a crack and listened. Took one step down, barely breathing, sniffed, waited, sniffed again, relieved that I did not smell gas.

The email from Galia began this way: "You don't believe I'm coming to Pittsberg, well I have my ticket ha ha." Details followed: At the end of the month she'd be joining her two friends who were renting an apartment near the Ross Park Mall.

She was right, in a way. I wrote back to tell her I was *here* for anything she might need and to invite her for dinner. "Looking forward to seeing you!"

I did look forward to seeing Galia. Her email brought to mind the way she'd chided her mother in Hebrew the first time I'd visited, then gestured with her chin to me. It had made me feel she had something to tell me that her mother withheld. I was curious to know what it would be. "Curious," the word I used when I told Mindy about the photo of the two small babies, all wrapped up. "I'm kind of curious." You'd think I was talking about an episode from a mini-series on TV and not my own life.

Mindy was energized by my story and puzzled that I hadn't called Ronit to ask about the picture. She couldn't bear not knowing, even for an hour. It was impossible to explain, even to this closest friend, the body knowledge I carried, that these kinds of questions were dangerous and created rifts. I didn't want to be cast out of Ronit's garden, exiled from this family I was just now meeting.

I was easily distracted. When our client with the energy drink for mature consumers showed up for a morning meeting—a tall, hefty young man in a lavender dress shirt and jeans—I found myself more interested in the luxurious cotton and gorgeous color of his shirt than marketing strategies or competition for shelf space. In penance, I stopped in a convenience store that afternoon and studied the drinks in a smoky refrigerator case. The cans were no longer a uniform size, and the bottles, most of them plastic, had become as bloated as Americans. The contents looked radioactive. I picked up a bottle of turquoise blue water. "Who'd want to *drink* something like this?" I asked myself.

"I would," a girl piped up. She had black hair, tiny bangs that left her broad forehead bare, a ring in her septum, holey tights, biker boots.

"Can you explain why?" I asked.

"It looks good."

Years back, I'd asked my parents to have dinner at my house, and my father said, "Don't give us any of that *toe-few*."

I felt like my father when I put the turquoise water back in the case, confused by change, haunted by the other one, the one we could not see, insistent despite our efforts.

My cabinets were empty, and there was no real food in the refrigerator, so after work, I stopped at the Giant Eagle and went down every aisle, tossing napkins, toilet paper, and paper towels into my cart, and tenderly setting tomatoes and bananas in the baby seat. It took two trips to haul everything from the garage onto the kitchen floor, and when I stood to switch on the light I saw birds of paradise in a shapely glass vase with pebbles at the bottom. They were so poignant and attentive looking, with their long stalks and sharp beaks that I had to remind myself they were not sensate. Their feelings could not be hurt. They did not care if I loved them or let them wither. There was no reason why the sight of them made my heart ache, or why, knowing who'd placed them on the kitchen island, I could not pull the flowers out of the vase, snap their stems and toss them into the garbage.

Beside the vase was a ring box. When I flipped the top, I saw a diamond, nestled in its satin cushion. I turned away. Wrong! I thought. On every level. We were not together. Further, not that it should have mattered, if he'd actually known anything about me, he'd know I was the kind of person who linked diamonds with oppression. Bejeweled engagement rings were symbols of a life I'd never wanted. Harley needed a woman who wanted to be pampered and cared not a whit if he had access to her inner life or she to his.

The house was cold. I knew I shouldn't touch the ring. I turned up the heat, began to put the groceries away, then surprised myself by slipping the ring from the satin crease. It fit perfectly. I stretched out my arm the way my third-grade teacher had done when she was showing off her diamond. For a moment I felt as if the only thing that kept me from feeling loved was my own stony resistance. Say yes, I thought as I perched on the edge of a stool. The yearning welled up with unexpected ferocity. It wasn't Harley, or the diamond, or the public statement that someone loved me enough to slip it on my finger. It was the love itself I wanted.

I walked into the living room and stood in front of the leather chair so I could remember life with Harley. Then I put the ring back in the box and went downstairs.

Harley stood when he heard my footsteps and turned to face me. His gaze was blurry with affection, a sweet half smile on his handsome face.

"Enough," I said. "You need to pack up and leave right now. Tonight. This is sordid." I put the ring box on the door he was using as a desk. The knob hole had been plugged with a rolled-up takeout menu. "You can't live in someone's basement. It's too weird."

"I know," he said. "You're right."

I dared not move, lest his urge to say something authentic passed.

"Remember how you used to talk about wanting us to build something together? I took it literally. I know it's kind of dense, but I kept thinking, why do we need to buy a second home and furnish it, or whatever it is other couples do? Isn't living with each other pleasure enough? Waking beside each other? I couldn't understand that it wasn't a second home you wanted, it was substance. Depth. But as you've pointed out numerous times, for someone so good at planning other peoples' futures, I have a stunning inability to think about my own. I admit this."

"Thank you." It was flattering to be quoted directly, but I had left the milk and cottage cheese on the kitchen counter and was feeling impatient.

Harley held up a hand. "Hear me out. I know you'd like it better if I was some happy-go-lucky, life-of-the-party guy and all that, but that isn't me and never will be. So I worry a little more than the average guy, I admit it. But I'm also more caring and loyal. Everything I do, from the moment I wake up until my head reaches the pillow, is for you. Your wishes are paramount in my thoughts. And when we're apart, and I need to make a decision, I always ask myself: What would Roxanne do? And you know why? Because of your principles. Because I admire the hell out of you."

"If you loved me so much, you'd stop extolling my virtues and listen to what *I* want. But you never have. And now you're smiling. Why are you smiling? There's nothing to *smile* about."

"'Extolling my virtues.'" He gave me a moonstruck look. "I love the way you talk."

"That's nice, but you're not actually listening."

"I am listening."

"Really? Then what is it I want?"

"For me to leave."

"That's right," I said. "Immediately. Not tomorrow. Now."

"And this is truly what you want?"

"It is truly what I want."

Harley's shoulders sagged. "What are you doing, babe?" he said, as if I were a toddler with her hands in the peanut butter jar. "What're you doing?" No anger. Just the soft puzzled voice of eternal forgiveness.

"You got yourself a beautiful new condo. Many rooms, cathedral ceilings. Your mail is probably piling up. You need to pack up your stuff now and move back. Now. Are you listening to me at all?"

"It's really over for you, isn't it?" Harley lowered his face, massaged his brow for a moment. "I'm devastated. Just...just stunned."

"Do you know how many times we've had this exact same conversation? Many times. Many, many, many times. So many. I can't do this anymore. It's exhausting and bad for both of us. And the truth is you're an intruder, and you've broken into my house. If you're not out tonight, I'm calling the cops."

Harley covered his face and began to sob.

"Please, Harley. Don't."

"Do you know how I kept myself alive when you were gone? By thinking about you. Waiting for you to come home so I could get the chance to prove that I finally understood what you wanted. I booked a trip to Bermuda at a five-star hotel. I bought the ring. I believed you'd give me a chance. I'm sorry. I just don't understand why I'm being punished this way when all I've ever done was love you."

At that moment, I didn't either.

He pushed the ring box toward me. "Take it."

I pushed the box back. "I'm going out for an hour. When I come home, you better be out."

I grabbed my keys and jacket, got into my car and drove. The traffic was light when I turned onto the parkway west, heading to no particular destination. After a few minutes, I found myself on the same stretch of highway along the Monongahela River, that I had driven with Harley the day he'd asked me to look at the condo. Everything I'd let myself believe was false: It wasn't the last favor Harley would ever ask; he hadn't bought that condo; I wasn't the only offspring of Morris and Leona Garlick.

This was confirmed when my birth certificate arrived. Harley was gone by then, his basement setup so completely dismantled that the whole episode seemed like a delusion. I imagined telling someone that a man had lived in my basement. *Right. And the CIA transmits messages through the fillings in your teeth.*

The baby with my birthdate, born to Leona M. Garlick and Moritz Garlick in Tel Aviv, was named Rose. Under "number of live births" it said "two." The immigration records, which I'd gotten earlier, stated that Dr. Leona M. Garlick and Moritz Garlick entered the United States with only one child, a girl of twenty-nine months named Roxanne.

Roxanne Garlick: My name had always been something of a struggle for me. In childhood, there had been the expected taunts: "You stink, Garlick," which left me breathing into my cupped palms, never knowing if it was my name or me. Later, came The Police, with their hit single, and scores of boys sinking to one knee, wailing, "*Rox-anne!*" and begging me not to put on my red dress and take my body into the night. All grown up, I learned to say my name, and quickly add: "It's okay, you can laugh."

The trivial hardships I had endured as Roxanne Garlick were not on my mind when I studied these documents. It was the second baby, born with me, and the harshness of that x in my new name, instead of the soft, sinuous s had they chosen to call me "Rosanne." We will send you into the new world with everything in the past crossed out, it seemed to say. X you will have no religion, no culture, no holidays, no history. X to delete your sister. X to invent yourself, to mark your place on earth.

Galia was coming soon. In the meantime, I took that harsh x to work, where it joined up with other x's, first as a cross-stitch border, and then as a possible design for shoulder bags and handouts for the upcoming nursing conference. Because I remembered the men, I went beyond hand-holding, and dancing women; beyond children, ducks, flowers, butterflies, and trees seen in classic cross-stitch and made cars on a train, and elephants in a line, one trunk linked to the next, everyone connected. After I made my cross-stitch muscular, I sat with Les to show him what I'd planned for the nurses and to relax with a little hate-fest.

It was a bitter afternoon. Outside our huge windows, rattling in their frames, the sky was milky gray. We hated lilac; we hated fonts without serifs—Arial. Geneva. We hated quilted bags and *fleur de lis*, chamomile tea, P.T. Cruisers. The phone rang. We loved Kayleigh, who picked it up, saying, "Intelligent Designzzzz." She was so genuinely nice we no longer quarreled in front of her.

"I just learned my name is really Rose," I told Les.

"Rose Garlick?" His nostrils quivered from stifled laughter. "Quite the moniker."

"You think I might have changed my last name when I got married, but nope, never considered it. Not for a moment. And you know why? Because Roxanne O'Malley just wasn't me. Obviously I thought Roxanne Garlick was me, but I was wrong about that, because it's not. I'm Rose Garlick. I mean, really. It's like naming your daughter Vulva."

Les crossed his arms and leaned back in his chair. "My name is Sheldon. Sheldon Chietz, a.k.a. Sheldon Shits."

"You just made that up to take the stink out of Rose Garlick." I started to laugh until my ribs ached and it was no longer funny. I said, "Okay, we're renaming our company. We're getting rid of the whiff of fundamentalism once and for all and calling it Garlick & Chietz. How memorable is that?"

"Sheldon Leslie Chietz. Fat boy. 'Shel-don!'" he called in falsetto. "'That cake was meant for company!'" Then straightening and transforming himself into a tough guy. "'I wouldn't go in there, dude. 'Cause Sheldon Shits.'"

"Not sure I'll work that into the logo," I said.

Les held up a hand and said, "Enough," then scuffled his heels on the floor and wheeled his chair away from me. "Subject closed."

Watching him, I realized I'd known his name had been Sheldon Chietz, in the way I knew my own history, no actual facts, only an air, an awareness, a snippet of unnamable something overheard, dismissed, tucked away.

TWELVE

Galia emailed to ask if she could she bring her friends to dinner. Of course! I responded, then fell into a state of panic. What would I make them for dinner? What would I wear? In anticipation of my dinner with my young Israeli guests, I became self-conscious and stood in front of my full-length mirror for long periods of time, trying on clothes and planning menus. Grilled fish? I tucked a black shirt into jeans, pulled it out so the tails hung long. Changed out of the jeans and tried flared wool pants. Lentil salad with cumin? Roasted vegetables? I experimented with scarves—around my head, my neck, my waist. No matter how I rolled or wrapped these scarves, I ended up looking as if I'd been wounded in battle.

When the phone rang, I hopped over the heaps of clothing scattered on the floor and answered breathlessly. Dina was on the other end. She'd seen my mother standing alone on Nordau Street. "Oh, Roxanne, it was not so nice, the clothing. For such a great intellectual as your mother to be dirty that way? It is so pity."

I unwrapped the scarf still tied around my head and thanked her for telling me. "I'll talk to Sunny."

"Roxanne," said Dina in a hurried whisper.

I braced myself, waiting for her to ask when I'd return to care for my mother, to say, without words, "What kind of daughter are you, after all she's suffered. Have you no heart?"

"I met a man, the most handsome, you would not believe! I like him *very* much. Half the year, he live in Canada, and you know, already we are planning a trip to see you, the two of us. We are very excited."

"That's terrific!" I worked my way back to my bedroom, confronting the mess I'd made. I could throw on a Clash T-shirt with the sleeves ripped off, for all they'd care. "Where does he live?"

"Winnipeg. You've heard of this city?"

"Sure, of course." I lacked the heart to tell her it would be easier to meet in France. "I have a guest room. You can stay with me."

I reached Sunny on her cell phone after I cleaned up. When I told her my mother had been standing on the street alone, she was upset and promised to have a second lock installed. She did not say, "What kind of daughter are you?" Instead we talked about *Eema*, who was so strong, walked faster than Sunny, ate like a man. Sunny could increase her hours; she thought her sister, also a home healthcare worker, might be able to work on weekends. We agreed someone should be with *Eema* every day.

Two of them arrived an hour late, after a lengthy commute on two buses: Galia, big and solid like Ronit, same curly hair, though she was stormy-looking rather than morose. And Yael, with her dark, inquisitive eyes, olive skin, full lips, luscious in the way of beautiful young women. Broad shoulders, braless in her soft, loose V-neck sweater. She had an elaborate tic that involved twisting her long black hair with a finger, sweeping it onto one shoulder and then the next. I couldn't take my eyes off her, and neither could Galia, who rubbed elbows with her, scooched low in her chair so her toes reached Yael's ankle.

Galia had brought me a present from Ronit, a photo of my parents from around the time of their marriage. They're standing on a rocky ledge, no trees or greenery in the background, my mother in a blouse and shorts, ankle socks and oxfords. Her hair is in braids. She has a finger to her lips and in her free hand is a large branch, which she uses to prod my father in the rear. They're so young, in this single frozen moment, playful, in love, something I'd never imagined, certainly never seen.

Now, though, as I lit a half-dozen candles and set out an elaborate dinner for six, having expected "friends"—grilled trout, rice with chickpeas and pignolis, etc.—I was overcome by an urge to call my mother, to say, "I just saw this wonderful photo!" (As if, what? After all this time I would get a different mother?) The sadness I felt was like a pebble in my throat.

The two young women, who'd been eating at the food court in the mall since their arrival, scarfed up every morsel on the table. They were willing to answer my questions about their sales techniques at the mall—no man could resist Yael, it seemed—and their time in the army. Though they were not especially enthusiastic raconteurs, I did learn that Yael had served in southern Sinai as a radar operator and Galia had been arrested twice, once for leaving a document in a copier, another time for bringing pizza to the base on Passover.

When the serving plates were empty, I went to the kitchen to refill them and thought of my mother thousands of miles away, alone except for Sunny and her sister. Back at the table, Yael had propped her leg on Galia's lap. Galia was singing into Yael's pretty toes, as if they were a microphone.

As soon as the girls were stuffed, they grew as drowsy as puppies, leaving me to generate more polite questions, first about their travel plans—after their stint at Ross Park Mall, they planned to sell jewelry in Rio or work at a ski resort in Colorado; San Francisco and Kyoto were also possibilities. I inquired next about the wellbeing of Galia's family, and then in some desperation—for they seemed as uninterested in conversation as they were in leaving—I asked Galia if her mother had ever talked about our summer together as teenagers.

"She was very popular with the boys," I said, remembering her dancing on the sidewalk outside the Irish bar in Inwood.

Galia snorted. "She has become very small-minded. Everything with her is a scandal. A secret. I don't like secrets. They are chains." She held up her arms and rattled her invisible handcuffs.

She and Yael began to speak in Hebrew. It was as if I were a kid at my parents' table, listening to them quarrel in a language I could not understand, alert to tone and facial expression, asking, "What? What are you saying?" Getting a morsel, or a lie, which I could feel in my gut, though no one would ever confirm it.

"I hadn't realized you knew my father," I said.

"A very nice man," Galia said. "And always with the presents from America."

"Really?" I said. "What did he bring you?"

"The Walkman. So fantastic."

"What else?"

"Chess. His favorite. He loved it more than anything. And the card games." She rolled her hand to remember. "Parcheesi."

"That's crazy," I said, trying to imagine this description of my father, so unlike the man I'd known.

"No, no. Poker. That's what I meant. And the other one…"

"You knew my mother too?" I asked.

Galia picked a pine nut off her plate. "How could I? She broke from the family before I was born."

"Do you know why? I never heard the whole story."

Yael picked up a candle and let the wax drip into the center of her palm. Galia watched until Yael replaced the candle and then said, in a matter-of-fact way, "Your mother and my *savtah* were enemies. Everyone knew this. There was the fight with the baby, and *Savtah* wanting to keep her home instead of sending her to that place in the north. She was very emotional, my *savtah*. Like your father. Every birthday, every holiday, every time she sees me, every time I leave, she's a waterfall, with the crying. And babies! You know, I turn sixteen she starts asking when I'm giving her a baby to hold. I'm a kid; I'm still in school. But, *Savtah*, you know, she loved babies more than life."

Yael murmured to Galia in Hebrew. Galia said, "She has a friend who is also a twin, and this brother of hers, wherever he is, anywhere in the world, she can feel if he is hurting. Always she knows if something is wrong. She wants to know if it's this way for you."

"How could it be? She's dead."

It was very still, as if we were in a chamber beneath the earth. It was what my mother had told Dr. Berenbaum.

"Maybe," said Galia.

"Why do you say *maybe*? If she were alive, wouldn't your mother have told me?"

"My mother believes what is easiest for her to believe. She will not trouble herself with the truth if the truth is difficult. You want to know what I think?"

"Sure," I said, torn just then between wishing Galia would stop talking and wanting to shake her until every speck of information came loose.

"Your father died so they let themselves believe that she died also. But your father was old. His time had come. You are not so old."

"And? Go on."

"Why should you accept what my mother says? Maybe your sister is still in that place. Who's to say no?"

My sister. Even hearing those words was alien.

Yael looked at her watch.

"Don't leave." I felt like a baby, naked in a dark room. "I have tea and cookies."

I put the water up to boil and watched my hands as I retrieved three mugs. They were steady. I observed this with pride. Galia, I thought. Every time I'd seen her she'd been riled up about something. She and Yael were speaking softly in Hebrew when I placed the mugs on the table, neither glancing up.

I found the bakery bag, tore it open, arranged the almond macaroons and lemon squares on a plate. I thought of my mother, standing on Nordau Street, glancing around, seeing the market, the taxi stand, the hotel, recognizing these places, but no longer knowing where she was. It was what I felt just then, what I tried not to feel.

Galia leaned over and wiped a grain of rice off Yael's face with great tenderness. I set the cookies on the table and took my seat.

"I must have had a few words of Hebrew before we moved here, but all that's left are a few tourist phrases," I said. "What does 'Vered' mean?"

Galia gave me a bug-eyed look. "Vered is your name," she said.

It was late when they piled into my car with a shopping bag full of leftovers in plastic containers. The sky was clear, and across the river the tracks of the inclines were lit with small red lights. I chattered on about the days when industry was all along the river and there were eleven of these inclines to take the workers, who lived high up those craggy slopes, to the mills that lined the river's edge. Then I saw Galia's head resting against the passenger window and Yael slumped in the back, and I abruptly stopped. I was so gullible, so easy to fool. Always. Hadn't I believed the boy during hide and seek who'd said,

"Don't come out until I say so," and waited in the bushes, shivering, long after the others had run away? Hadn't I believed Harley all the times he'd promised to move? Hadn't I trusted Tom, my former husband, until the evening when his lover called me, sobbing, to say, "and now he's cheating on *me*!" So many women, so many years, every word and gesture, every plan we'd ever made, all our history a lie. Up ahead the road forked. I found the directions I'd printed out earlier and could not read them in the dim light.

"Don't go to sleep!" I said.

Galia's chin jerked up. "Ma?" She began to drift.

"I need your help," I said, changing lanes carelessly, startled by an angry horn.

Galia straightened. "Why are you so upset, with the shouting?"

"I don't know where I'm going. I've never been out this way." I gave Galia the directions.

"Okay, okay." She looked at the road signs overhead, pointed straight.

I wondered if either of them would thank me for dinner or for driving them home. It made me feel small-minded to think this. I'm not like that, I thought. Maybe there was no single self, no solid core, but an evolving way of being.

Galia told me where to exit. Two turns took us to the complex where they were staying, a series of attached units with vertical siding and slanted roofs. Even in the dark you could tell the construction was shoddy. Yael took the bag of leftovers. At the doorway, while Galia searched for the keys, Yael turned and waved.

When they were inside and the light above their door went out, I backed out of the parking area and made the two turns that got me back to the highway. I didn't like being alone with Galia's words and shook my head like a dog shedding water, as if I could unhear what she'd told me. At the traffic light, her question expanded in my empty car. I tried to list the most outrageous of Harley's lies, chronologically, and when it made me drowsy, I opened the windows to let in the wet, cold air. Outside was an auto body shop, a big new Rite Aid, a furniture rental store, a Wendy's, a tower with a tall empty frame where once there'd been a sign. I could have been driving on the outskirts of any American city. I felt the sharp edges of Galia's words in my gut, tried to hear the nurses' cheerful voices, to estimate the mileage home and the time it would take to get there, to remember all the words to "American Pie," but I was stuck, like the Chevy at the Levee.

Up ahead the road became dark in a way I did not recognize. All the lit-up detritus of urban life was gone and in its place along the road were occasional houses. In a panic, I realized I was lost.

No, not lost, I tried to tell myself. Not lost, just driving in the wrong direction. Turn around. That was all I had to do. Just turn and it'll all be fine.

My house was completely dark, except for a single candle in the dining room, flickering deep within its waxed walls. I cleared the table, arranged the plates in the dishwasher, washed the serving bowls and tall crystal wine glasses by hand. The perfect *balabusta* I'd yearned to be, I wiped up the counter and sink and ran the cloth over the faucets so they shone. My guests had eaten heartily and drank little. I corked the half bottle of remaining wine and took the empty bottle by the neck to dispose of it.

On the way to the recycling bin, I passed the powder room, where the light still burned. The switch was beside the mirror, and though I did not mean to look, I caught sight of my own face, with its dark eyes and pursed lips, and terror washed over me. This shell that held the self was not mine, not me, because there was no me, no bottom to this sea. Just these silent words—*I cannot*—before the mirror shattered and fell into itself like a building imploding. I saw the broken glass and my own arm drawn back, smashing into the space where the mirror had been, until the jagged edges around the frame, and then the bottle, broke into pieces. And only *I cannot*. I went upstairs and switched the light on in my bedroom and tried not to remember the first weeks when Harley and I were together, when I would curl beside him in this bed, the sound of his heartbeat, his arms holding me close.

I took the scissors from my desk and cut the bed sheet in half, then covered the mirrors in my bedroom and bathroom so I would not have to see my own image. I was not really Jewish, and yet I knew this was done during *shiva* so mourners could turn from their vanity and self-consciousness to the family and friends there to console them. Now, though, there was no family or friend, no body or soul, no funeral or burial, no handful of dirt thrown in the coffin, no impossibly blue sky—the sign of an uncaring world—no bitter rain as metaphor, no history. No sister. No self. Only my father leaning across the dining room table, asking me a question; my father losing his language, dying before I had an answer.

For him, no mirrors were covered, no one sat *shiva*. There'd been no funeral, only an itinerant rabbi at the gravesite, a woebegone stutterer in an ill-fitting jacket who looked as if he'd been nabbed from a residence for homeless Jews, and my mother telling the rabbi she was an atheist, with no use for his primitive incantations. The only emotion I recall was the pity I felt for the rabbi, whose services my mother had harshly rejected. I did not wonder what my father might have believed. Even in death I hardly thought of him as more than an accessory my mother toted everywhere.

And now, sitting on the edge of my stripped bed, I did not know what I was mourning or how to do it, and when I tried to unearth something that explained Galia's words, there was only the same thing as before—my father saying, "Wasn't there another one?"

Only this time I could say, "Yes, Daddy. There had been another one."

THIRTEEN

Mindy would take me in. This is how I got through the night. Mindy would say, "Come stay with us." If she was out, she'd tell me where to find the key, direct me to the frozen leftovers and the cookies she hid from her husband. And so in the morning, I stepped over the shards of glass and called. Outside, dusty-looking snow flurries were blowing, and while the phone rang, I considered going to work instead, work, where I could lose myself. I was mulling over the irony of my instinct to lose myself when at last Mindy answered the phone.

"Are you okay?" she asked when she heard my voice.

"I'm fine," I said. It was what I always said. "No," I said. "I'm not fine, but I'll be okay."

Getting to Mindy's meant driving on the Pennsylvania Turnpike, the oldest, narrowest highway system in the country, with treacherous S-curves, tunnels that had been blasted through the mountains and semis, driven by sleep-deprived, drug-addled truckers, barreling inches past my tiny car, filling me with a clanging fear that I would be sucked into one of those trucks, which my mother had explained was an actual, verifiable phenomenon known as the Venturi Effect, and not an illusion.

In this vast rural center of this seemingly endless state, the radio was full of evangelical Christians, enticing me to take Jesus Christ as my Lord and savior. No-o-o-o! I cried, switching off the radio and trying to focus on Mindy's house, her door opening, the warmth of her rooms. How full of righteous judgment I'd been in the years we didn't speak. I thought of her as clueless, couldn't understand why someone so intelligent would take up with some *zhlub* she met in her freshman year of college (granted, in comparative anatomy), at eighteen already beefy and middle-aged, the kind of local guy who'd never leave the town where we were raised and would end up working in his father's industrial lighting business. "Watch," I'd said, to the mutual friend who'd told me. "She'll get knocked up by this loser and be saddled with his babies."

And she did. She got pregnant. Instead of entering the clinical psychology program at Penn, she married Stu and they moved to a split-level a half mile from our parents, a fixer-upper with a linoleum kitchen floor that peeled at the edges, cabinets with a halo of smudge around each pull, and a dropped ceiling with fluorescent lights Stu's father installed as a gift. Another baby, then the PhD. At a backyard graduation party, Mindy schlepped her gigantic self around the yard with one kid attached to her ankle like a prison monitor, one on her hip, and the third dropping in her uterus as she ate a hot dog grilled by Stu.

Mindy was not a self-righteous person who trumpeted the "we" of the long-married couple and used this togetherness as a barricade and moral example. I knew they'd struggled. Stu let his father boss him around. His feet stank. He was a Neanderthal; his idea of a great movie was *Nightmare on Elm Street*. Mindy and Stu bickered and threatened to split up, then got older, began to accommodate, curling in each other's arms.

Max, their aged lab, greeted me at the door by jumping on me with his leash in his mouth. When at last I worked my way past, I found my friends in the kitchen, quarreling over takeout, Mindy gesturing with the phone, and Hannah pulling out menus from a junk drawer. Dark-haired last time I saw her, Hannah was now a platinum blonde who wore heavy black glasses perched low on her nose. It was an adorable new look, and they, my friends, looked plump and affluent, and once again I wondered exactly what had offended my youthful sensibilities—that Stu had no ambition greater than earning a reasonable living, enjoying his family and hanging out with his friends? A happy, angst-free man in his ancient Rutgers sweatshirt, with only one driving question on his mind just then: "What do you want? We're ordering in."

Max put his head on Mindy's lap, and I said, "Anything. I don't really care."

"We need you to care," said Stu. "We need a tiebreaker."

"Okay, Thai," I said, settling in while they haggled over choices.

I took the glass of wine Mindy offered and said, "Love the hair, Hannah."

Mindy: "It's too blonde."

"*I* think it's great," I said. "So tell me about school."

Hannah scrunched her nose, said, "It sucks," and pushed the heavy glasses higher.

"Don't listen to her. She loves her art history class," Mindy told me.

"Thank you, Mother, for once again telling me how I feel."

Dinner arrived in plastic containers. Hannah scarfed down a plateful of food and left the table. Mindy shifted in her seat, as if to call out to her, and Stu put his hand on her shoulder. *Mindeleh*, he sometimes called her in jest. *My beautiful Jewess.* She softened, sighed heavily.

Stu loaned me his ski jacket after dinner, and Mindy and I left to walk the dog in a nearby park. I pulled up the hood of Stu's jacket and listened. Hannah wanted to quit school. Mindy didn't know if it was a broken romance or something more serious that would not heal on its own. All Hannah would say was "leave me alone," and Stu was doing his Mr. Mellow thing, which was no help at all.

"Eighteen," I said, thinking of my first year of school, how lonely and disoriented I'd been. "It's a tough time for some of us. Maybe not for you."

Max squatted on the grass, his blunt snout held high.

"Oh, please," she said. "All that angst and self-loathing."

The deep, warm pockets of Stu's parka were full of small items I studied under the street light while Mindy cleaned up Max's mess. Coins, screws, PVC fittings, the fibrous pieces of peanut shells, the crimped edges of candy wrappers—ordinary domestic detritus. When I was single, I was always finding folded bills in the back pockets of my jeans. Also, single earrings, ticket stubs, subway tokens, phone numbers scribbled on cocktail napkins. Once I borrowed Mindy's robe and found Lego pieces and a doll shoe in the pocket.

I held out my hand to show her what I'd found and said, "I think the contents of a person's pockets tell you everything you need to know, and mine are empty."

"No, they're not," she said.

They are, I thought, on the way back. My pockets are empty.

By the time we returned, Hannah had gone out and Stu had drift-ed into the family room to watch basketball. Mindy made tea and we sat on stools in her kitchen, recently redone, with glass-fronted cabinets and brushed metal appliances. On the fridge were photos from Mindy's son's graduation, a shopping list, a calendar with car-toons about dieting, a magnet that had been a bagel before someone had pasted on googly eyes and embalmed it.

Our conversation jumped in time and place and tone in a way that was so comforting and familiar, it took a while before I told her about my dinner with Galia and Yael. When I got to Galia's specula-tion, "Your father died so they let themselves believe she died also," I could not figure out what to call her—baby, sister, twin? *Her*, I said when I was ready to continue.

We listened to the squeak of sneakers and the blat of horns in an arena far away. "I'm thinking your cousin has more to tell you," Mindy said.

"Why aren't you surprised by anything I've told you? Do you know some of what I've just said?"

"I feel like I heard *something*."

"What kind of something? Why wouldn't you have told me?"

"Because it's only now, listening to you, that I vaguely recall over-hearing *something* I didn't understand. It was a long time ago, when we were kids."

"Like what?" I asked. "I need you to be totally honest. What do you remember about us, Min? What were we like to you?"

"Well, *you* stole everyone's heart, you were so adorable. Even my mother liked you better than she liked me."

"No, she didn't," I said, though I was more her type of child than her serious, self-sufficient daughter.

"Us," I said, remembering what it had been like to enter a strang-er's home and feel a kind of malevolence in the air. Had our house felt like that? "My family. Our house."

"It was super neat. Nothing out of place. Compared to ours,

which was a sty. But we were never there, Rox. You practically lived at my house."

It was true. I'd walk in without knocking, follow the haze of smoke from the cigarettes that would kill Muriel, and fall into her arms. *Come here, doll. Come, tsatskeleh.*

Stu groaned loudly in the family room. Mindy said, "I was a little scared of your mother. But you know that. She didn't like me. It was kind of a shock, given what a goody-goody I was."

"She didn't *dis*like you," I said, as if this could soothe the hurt Mindy had felt all those years before.

"You really want to know what I remember, Rox? Those peach loafers you bought for yourself, and your mom being furious because they were impractical, and you wearing them until they got all gross and turned out. I mean, you were making your own dinner when you were thirteen. Buying your own school clothes. Muriel would get all bent out of shape about the way you were neglected, but if *I* said something negative, I'd get a huge lecture. How I had no right to judge after all your parents had gone through."

Unspeakable loss of such proportion there was no room for other sorrow in our house, no room for fear or desire, for failure or heartache. I didn't say this to Mindy, couldn't have explained that I had breathed this air as a child, and even now, fully grown, as I sat with my oldest friend, drinking tea, listening to a basketball game playing in the other room, I breathed this same air, lived by these same words. *You have no right...*

It was after midnight when I followed Mindy upstairs. I slid into Adam's narrow bed. Posters of well-oiled women in thongs and tattooed basketball stars still hung on the walls and stick-on stars glowed dimly on the ceiling. Staring at the stars above my head, I remembered how, as a child, I'd lose myself in screaming fits, tear posters off my bedroom walls, pound on doors until I punched holes in the thin wood, no one to calm me until I learned to calm myself. But I had learned. I hadn't been that child, that teenager, until Harley came along, his dead eyes making me as frantic as I'd ever been. I rolled over, thought about calling Ronit. Throwing my voice into the void, the awkward *shalom*, hello, asking what she might tell me about *her*.

I gave up trying to sleep and got up. My boots were by the front door. I slid into them, found Stu's parka, and went outside. Soft snow clung to the bare boughs of the sycamore trees and turned the yards into what looked like desert, with undulating waves of sand. I am Florence of Arabia, I thought, for a moment reluctant to ruin the solemn beauty of the creamy-looking drifts.

Once I'd told Harley my parents had started leaving me alone at night when I was seven, and he refused to believe me. I was misremembering, he insisted. But I wasn't. We had just moved. Everything was new—my school, our house.

The afternoons were not bad, since my father was often back from teaching an hour or two after I'd gotten home. During my short time alone, there were no flash cards to study, no arithmetic problems I could not understand, no sound of my father's heavy, disappointed breathing. I colored and drew and when I got older made maps of imaginary towns with names like Pleasantville that had pet shops, RR crossings, and penny candy stores. Ye olde swimming hole was a blue crater in the center of each one.

The evenings were different. My father set out dinner for me before he escorted my mother to a banquet or professional engagement. If there was leftover chicken or *flanken*, he put my dinner on a plate covered with waxed paper. Sometimes there was a sandwich he knew I liked—salami and mustard on rye bread; cream cheese, olive, and tomato on pumpernickel. Milk in a glass. Three Fig Newtons. A stern reminder not to answer the door for anyone.

You remember that, right? Don't answer the door.

I ate dinner right away. Then the sky would darken and I would hear someone walk toward the house. Someone knocking. Or footsteps. The screech of tires. Car lights shining on the wall. Something coming for me in the night. Fear gripped me. I became paralyzed, unable to move. My body shook as if with fever. My teeth chattered in my head. Hours could pass between the sound I heard and the purr of the car engine as my parents' car crawled up the driveway.

Hours, when I was stuck on the couch or on the floor of my room or in the closet, bones shaking, the fear never abating. Sometimes I was stuck for so long that I wet my pants and left dark stains on the rug or couch. The first moment was pleasure, a relief to release the warm urine I'd tried to hold in with the heel of my foot pressing hard. After a while, my pants became clammy and stiff, and still I could not move. It was only when l heard my parents' car pull into the driveway that I could get up, quickly change my clothes, turn over the couch cushions, throw my wet clothes in the garbage.

I never thought to push them to the bottom of the trash and was always surprised when my father confronted me with the garment between his fingers—cotton underpants. Jeans.

"You throw in the trash good clothes we buy for you?"

I said nothing.

Then I learned to say to my father, "They're ugly. I hate them."

Eventually I learned to say, "I hate you."

❧

Hannah came home while I was sitting on a bench by the back door, working off my muddy shoes. Though I'd seen her earlier that evening, I was still surprised that she was no longer the little girl who'd seen me in their family room with the comforter drawn over my head, and said to Mindy, "Mommy, she looks like a *dorf.*"

Now she gave me such a strange look that I said, "Hey, are you all right?"

"*Why* does everyone keep asking me that?" she said, with a furious unzipping of her jacket. "I don't know *what* she told you but *nothing* is wrong."

Her arrival had woken Max the dog, and when she lowered herself to the floor, he backed into her, and sat in her lap in what looked like the most uncomfortable position for both of them. Hannah put her nose in his fur, and I said, "She's your mom, and she's worried." I was struck by how inextricably "Mom" was linked with love, tenderness, and concern, no questions asked, even for me.

"Then she needs to back off and stop acting like I'll end up selling pencils on a street corner if I take some time off. Really, Mom? Like that's going to happen if I take a leave? I mean, *you* quit school."

"I am *not* a good role model," I said.

"Shut *up!* You have this fabulous business; you're doing what you want, unlike my father, stuck inside that stupid factory."

She pushed Max away, and I said, "Hannah. Your father is the most content man I've ever met."

And she said, "Uch. He's fat."

I thought I'd slip out the next morning before anyone was awake, but when I came downstairs, Mindy was already perched on a kitchen stool in a hooded gray robe, dark hair tucked behind her ears, glasses low on her nose, Sunday *Times* crossword on her lap. When she heard me, this friend, who had sheltered me without judgment, looked up from her magazine, with such affection in her gaze that I began to cry. It stunned me, the suddenness and physical ache. I was so far from understanding love in its fullest, did not yet know the satisfaction one could feel from offering comfort, in coming forward, in the laying on of hands. I kept my face hidden, ashamed of the ugliness of my grief, unable to open myself wide enough for all the comforting I needed.

"It's not what you think," I said when I could speak.

I didn't know what she thought. I didn't know what I thought either.

On the way home, I drove through the town where Mindy and I had grown up. Our street was part of a development of split-level houses constructed in the early 1960s. In recent years they'd been snapped up by Russians, as if these clapboard houses, like cars with fins, remained an image of American prosperity in the imagination of émigrés. Even bare of leaves you could see how big the trees had grown. There were additions on several of the houses and the manicured shrubs had been replaced by prairie grasses. I had forgotten how quiet these streets could be.

I knew this neighborhood better than any place I'd ever known and could still point out the house with the mother in curlers, the house with the mother who fed us any time of day, the one where the mother made her husband and his friends play poker in the garage. Then Mindy's house at the corner, with the unmade beds, the TV droning, the freezer full of frozen dinners. The mother, Muriel, was a chain-smoking blonde who talked like an airhead, embarrassed Mindy by wearing hot pants in the summer and flirting with the boys, and was as smart and big-hearted as her daughter. When company was over, she'd draw me close and tell her guests, "This is my other daughter. The artistic one."

Muriel took me to the Guggenheim and the Whitney in New York. While Mindy sulked in the gift shops, we meandered through the galleries. If my work hung at the library or local bank, Muriel would stop by and *kvell* over a favorite piece. She'd been dead for five years. Standing in front of Mindy's house, winter wind biting my cheeks, I felt as if I was just now beginning to absorb it.

At the other end of the street was the house where we'd lived from the time I was seven. What do you remember? I asked myself. The math lessons, the languages I did not know, the silence, the fear, the sense of what I could not say, the forbidden tears, the way I needed to escape so I could breathe, the way I did escape, but not fully, even now.

I walked through the snow to the back of the house, looked at their deck with its tilted-over chairs covered in green plastic, and a fierce desire came over me to see if the map I'd drawn on the closet wall was still there. I looked through the storm door, saw the cabinets, the artwork tacked haphazardly on the fridge. I could probably get in. It was something I used to do when I was in high school—cut classes and walk into peoples' houses. I looked at their clothes, opened their jewelry boxes and desk drawers, studied the contents of their medicine cabinets. I did not steal anything. Objects were sensate to me—the glass apples and soapstone ducks, the Danish bud vases and Hummel figurines—they had feelings. The Kiddush cup, bronzed baby shoe, crystal candy dishes, pewter coffee set, Christ on the cross, and the lamb in the manger—I liked to touch and examine them, as if I would absorb something of the life that went on in a house. I always left them as they were, as if they'd be unsettled, devastated if I took them from the places they belonged.

You were so alone. Mindy taking me in with that liquid gaze.

So I bought my own clothes, I answered silently, standing in the snow. So what compared to all they'd suffered.

A boy's high voice came from the distance, and the scrape of a snow shovel. I thought of the therapist I'd seen, a soft-spoken man with round cheeks, who composed himself just as I began to speak, pressing his fingers together, pursing his full lips, the room full of clocks and kachinas and tissue boxes, and I heard myself tell him: "My mother does not love me," and it seemed so ridiculous, the line a Borscht Belt comedian might utter—*her muddah didn't love her!*—that I began to laugh and could not stop. The clocks ticked. The kachina behind the therapist's head had bulging eyes, a toucan beak, feathers bursting from his crown, and the laughter hurt, though I could not make myself stop, and just as I was gaining control, I saw him clench his lips, trying mightily not to join in. Mindy was horrified when I told her this, but even then I knew that the harsh, weird noise I made was not about humor, that neither of us was amused.

Still, how could the therapy have been successful when I came to that room like a stick figure on a sheet of white paper: wavy lines for sloppy hair, a triangle for a dress that marked me as a girl, sun in the upper corner. No path to lead me out of that blankness. No true name, no sister, no history, no mother who could not love.

❧

When I got home, I swept the glass into a box and ran a damp mop over the bathroom floor and hall and continued into the kitchen. As soon as the floor was dry, I called Ronit. On the fourth ring, I got someone's disembodied voice, waited for the beep and said, "Ronit? It's Roxanne from Pittsburgh. Vered." It was the first time I'd used that odd name. "Would you please return my call?"

A splinter of glass pierced my sock, and I mopped again. I knew that no matter how many times I swept the floor, I'd keep finding slivers glinting in the corners. Broken glass like memory, seemingly swept away, but there, nonetheless, despite your efforts.

Ronit returned my call on Monday. It was nearly two o'clock, and I'd been picking at the innards of an unrolled wrap I'd gotten for lunch. "Vered," she began.

My stomach tightened when I heard her deep, blunt voice.

I knew what she was going to say. "She's alive, isn't she?"

"Yes," she said. "Please believe I did not know before now."

I looked at the mess spread out on waxed paper, smears of eggplant and half-circles of squash. "Okay," I said. "I believe you."

"I have everything you want—the name of the place where she stays, a person there who can tell you more. But, Vered, don't go. There is nothing left."

Nothing left, as if this sister had dissolved in a puddle like the Wicked Witch of the West? *I'm melting! I'm melting! Oh, what a world!*

"I don't know what that means," I said.

"She will not know who you are."

"I want to see her anyhow," I said, though I could not imagine another trip, so soon after the last one.

"It broke your father's heart going to that place. Don't go."

"You haven't told me her name," I said.

"Aviva," she said.

"Aviva." I felt my teeth against my lower lip. "Aviva," I said again.

"I did not know, Vered. This is the truth. I never thought to ask."

"I understand," I said. In a way I did. Because Aviva had been a problem, not a person. She had no identity. Her name was so seldom used, Ronit had not even known it until I had pushed her to find out.

I hung up and cleaned the mess off my desk. I listened to the hiss of the espresso machine, and The Flaming Lips, singing. *Her name is Yoshimi—she's a black belt in karate…*

Les brought me a small cup of espresso. "That was my cousin in Israel. I have a twin sister who lives in the north of the country in this place, this institution, but my cousin said I shouldn't go to see her because nothing is left. That's what she said."

Kayleigh turned from her work area. Les downed his cup, pinkie raised, then looked at me in a somber way.

"What does that mean, 'nothing is left'?" I asked.

"She's a vegetable. That's what your cousin is trying to tell you."

There was something bizarre and awful about this term. Parsnip, sister. Aviva. I bit hard on my lip. Aviva.

"I've got to see her. I don't know, I just do. Not now. Don't worry. But I do."

He punched my arm lightly and walked off, and I looked around at this space with its high ceilings and tall windows that rattled in their frames. Long ago, when this city had three times its current population, children sat in this room. An old-fashioned desk had been left behind, with a marred wooden top, a deep slot for books, a groove for pencils, a hole for an inkwell. As for the children who'd once sat here, nothing was left.

Why should I have such a sense of loss? It wasn't as if once I'd had a sister and now she was gone. I'd never known of her. Why should I feel so bereft?

I thought of an acquaintance who'd miscarried twice, as I had, bought a cemetery plot, and had a funeral for these babies that had never been born. How could you mourn what never was? I'd thought. If all of us buried our dreams this way, there'd be more cemeteries than places to live.

Sister as okra. Sister as plump peapod, and when you open it, there is nothing inside.

Later that day I called my mother's apartment, and when Sunny handed her the phone, I said, "Mama, it's me. Roxanne. I found Aviva!"

"*Whaaaat?*" Of late, my mother drew out this word when I asked her a question. It was a way to buy time, so I might not know she no longer understood much of what I asked.

"Aviva. Your other daughter. Did you know she was still alive? Aviva," I said again, needing to hear her name. "She's an Israeli citizen, so Ronit says the state takes care of the cost of her care. Daddy moved her to this place up north that was started by some Canadians whose son—"

"Canadians?" My mother cut me off. "I haven't the foggiest idea what you're talking about."

"Vered and Aviva." I waited, listening to the silence.

Sunny came on the line to tell me how strong *Eema* was and how well she was doing. "Oh, she make me laugh all ways. I am begging to disagree!"

Kayleigh approached my desk after I'd hung up, hair pulled into a ponytail. "Your *sister*! When will you meet her?"

"I've just gotten home," I said.

"Oh no, you've *got* to go; we'll be fine, really, everything will be okay, and anyways the work you did when you were gone was awesome." She crossed her hands over the Buckeyes logo on her sweatshirt. "I know it's not my place to say, but still."

Ronit suggested I sleep at her house when I arrived the next month. I could use her car, no problem. When I said I might stay in the north, she said, "Whatever is best," and assured me I could change my mind. They would always have room.

When I told Dina about my upcoming trip, she said, "I will meet you at the airport and we will drive together to Chaverim."

"This first time I need to go by myself," I said.

The next day Dina called and said, "Roxanne, I am so upset, I cannot sleep. I have talked with my friend who is a therapist and she says I must tell you what I think: I will be at the airport when you arrive."

I tried to explain why I needed to be alone, tripped over my words, tried again to thank her, which made her cry. Exhausted, I thought, this friendship is doomed.

A day later, she called to give me the name of a spa where I should stay, the most beautiful and famous and very close to Chaverim.

FOURTEEN

I picked up a small, white rental car at Ben Gurion Airport, and after studying a map the agent kept behind her desk, set off for Chaverim. It was just after ten in the morning. Unless I hit traffic, I could expect to arrive by noon. The first part of the drive was on a high-speed road, but north of Haifa were secondary roads that went past Arab towns, where the spires from mosques rose above the pastel houses, and the signs were in Hebrew, English, and Arabic.

During the trip I imagined Chaverim to be like the nursing home where my father spent his last years, the sickly smell of perfume, meant to mask the odor of urine assailing me when I reached his floor, rooms where broken people slept in beds or slouched in wheelchairs, where corpses had been dressed up and arranged around a blaring TV. I imagined a screamer, because there had been one near my father, who cried, "Help! Help me!" It was the plaintive cry of someone trapped beneath rubble. "Help!" and no one could save her. Every time I visited the screamer cried out. When my father was moved to this unit, he no longer asked if there was another one because his language was gone by then. His face was a mask; if he recognized me, I couldn't tell. He rose when I helped him to his feet and walked beside me. It brought me no comfort to remember these visits because by then, I could have been anyone.

On the way to meet Aviva, hopelessness was what I had expected. An institution, a warehouse, a place to put the bodies when technology keeps them going, or when some spark stays stubbornly lit. I imagined a dark room, the bleep of monitors, a pale form curled like a grub. Life cruelly extended by artificial means, a waste, a shame. *Nothing is left.*

I'd found the BBC on the radio and while driving through this tranquil terrain I listened to a radio report about an Israeli raid on a village and the killing of three men. I looked at the olive groves and the little goats meandering beside the road and on the radio, angry

Arabic voices, and the translator, with her plummy voice, saying, "an eye for an eye. Holy war will be raised on the Jews."

So when I arrived at Chaverim and saw the beautiful grounds, I was suspicious and felt the landscaping was fraudulent, like the perfume used at a nursing home. I parked my rental car and stepped out. Birds were singing and the sky was a cloudless blue. My knees were quaking in a furious rhythm. The buildings were stone and the gardens along the perimeter fragrant and beautiful. For *us*, the bougainvillea; to soothe *us*, the visitors; for us, jacaranda, and oleander in bloom, the lavender and mint, the century plants with tall flowering stalks. This is what I thought. To trick us into coming closer.

As I crossed the patio, laughter rang out, as unnerving as the chortling of surgeons in a hospital elevator. I could get back into the car and drive to the airport. Only Ronit would know, and she had warned me against coming. No one would think less of me. Then I reflected upon the hole in my life, the nothing, and thought, okay, you've travelled all this distance. It would be foolish to turn around now. This was how I took my first step forward.

I followed the beautiful plantings all the way to the broad doors. When they parted, I thought the birds had followed me inside until I saw in the center of the atrium a ceiling-to-floor enclosure full of bright finches, lovebirds, and cockatiels. Such lively little creatures, hopping and twittering about. While I watched them flittering from branch to branch, trilling, scattering seed, calling out, the double doors swung open, and a man pushed a wheelchair toward the enclosure. The tiniest creature was curled in the seat, head turned up, mouth in the shape of a silent scream, hands like claws—a boy, a man, a remnant of a human.

Across the room was a reception area. I asked for Mrs. Silk and moments later heard someone call, "Roxanne?"

Before me was a heavy, slow-moving woman with streaked blonde hair and the broad, pretty face of a Victorian doll.

"I'm Rochelle Silk." She took both my hands in hers. "Shelley."

"Sweaty palms!" I said. "Sorry. Sorry."

Gross, I thought, wiping them on my pants.

"You found us without too much trouble?"

Mrs. Silk wore pearls and a tan linen jacket and skirt, and close up was older than I'd thought. Later she would tell me she was from Manchester, England, and had moved here after the Six Day War, full of passion and idealism. She would sigh deeply when she said this. Now, though, she said, "Aviva and I have been here since the start; we've practically grown up together."

I followed Mrs. Silk through another set of doors into a broad corridor lined with customized wheelchairs and tall walkers with straps and handgrips and bright wheels. Music and voices and guttural sounds wafted through the hallway. "She's a lovely woman," said Mrs. Silk. "We're all very fond of her."

Lovely. I didn't see how "lovely" was possible and worried I'd be asked to feel what was not inside me.

She continued to talk about Aviva with great animation when someone in a motorized wheelchair buzzed toward us. Big grimacing face, tight pink skin, one finger on the controls. It was hard to look. Looking felt like staring, which you weren't supposed to do when someone *different* passed by, someone whose appearance threatened to ruin your perfect day. Not looking also felt rude.

Mrs. Silk said something cheerful to the man and turned back to me. "She had very little stimulation in the last place she lived, so it took some time for her to come around. It's been marvelous to see her gains. She's changed a good deal. Let me show you her room and then we'll find her."

A faint odor, alien and unpleasant, distracted me as we continued down a corridor past rooms, each decorated in a different way— posters on the walls, family photos in frames. All were vacant. It was like being in a dormitory. Then Aviva's room: a pine bureau, upon which sat a large stuffed bear, a blue elephant with curved white tusks. Two prints were on the wall—a street in the old city in Jerusalem, a Picasso bouquet of flowers. No photos. Did my father choose the prints? And the colorful quilted spread that Mrs. Silk lifted to show me the guardrails beneath? "We cover the equipment during the day," she explained. "It gives a homier feel to the rooms."

"My cousin said my father visited four times a year," I said as we continued on.

"Yes, he did, without fail, and always with food and gifts for everyone. It was such a treat to have him. When we didn't hear from him we wrote several letters and got no response. One never knows what to think when communication stops so abruptly." Mrs. Silk touched her pearls. "Your father and I had become very close over the years. He was a very special person to me, and a very nice man."

"Yes," I said. "Everyone says this."

Back in the corridor, she spoke in Hebrew to one of the aides, then turned and said, "She's in the pool with Baruch. Of course. I should have remembered."

"Wait." I leaned against the wooden railing, listening to conversations I could not understand. "I need a moment."

Mrs. Silk paused, a beatific expression on her face. Her composure made me feel worse. "Roxanne, many people are uncomfortable at first. Shall we go to my office?"

"No. I'm okay," I said, though I wasn't. "What do I do when we meet?"

"There's nothing special to do. You might start by telling Aviva who you are."

"I don't speak Hebrew."

"That doesn't matter. Once you spend time with her, you'll find other ways to relate."

"But how? She doesn't speak, she can't understand me."

"She might like it if you put lotion on her hands or sit in the swing with her. Let her show you what she likes and doesn't like. Shall we find her?"

I followed her down a long corridor that led to an annex. First there was the pungent smell of chlorine, then air that thickened from humidity. From outside the closed doors to the natatorium I could hear the echoes of conversation.

Mrs. Silk opened the door a crack and peered inside. "Shall I give the two of you some time alone?"

"Okay," I said. "Where will I find you?"

She touched my arm. "I'll be in my office all day. Stay as long as you like."

I stepped inside. It was a large pool, the size of the one at my gym. No lanes or diving boards. A hydraulic lift to lower swimmers into the water. Fiber optic tails sparkling on the tiled walls. A man was in the pool, cradling a limp woman, and he was moving, swirling, dancing with her in his arms. The woman was so skinny and pale in a stretched-out red swimsuit, broad shoulders, small breasts, long salt and pepper braid. He bounced over to the end of the pool and said, "You're Aviva's sister? Come in!"

The tile floor was wet. I took off my shoes and walked slowly toward the water. And the woman, my sister, her jaw slack, mouth hanging open as if she were asleep. Long white limbs. Hands fisted, feet turned in at the ankles. A being. The shock of seeing her breasts. A woman, the body perfectly formed, for what? The face, her face, like mine; the fluttering eyes and crowded teeth; a being, a woman, a sister, separate from me, part of me. I had yearned for a sister, but not this, not her. The air was so thick I could hardly breathe.

The man, now that I was closer, had a puff of white chest hair. His eyes, too big and blue for his narrow face, were downturned, as if in sadness, in opposition to his cheerful demeanor. An aide, I thought. A therapist who enjoyed his job, though what kind of person would do this, I could not imagine. I watched while they danced and realized there was noise in the room, like the sound in an aquarium where dolphins splashed and played; aquatic sounds that echoed as he sang and twirled in the water. I wanted to go home. Away. Anywhere else.

The man danced his way closer to me again, Aviva limp in his arms, before I realized that the echo had distorted his words, and he was speaking to me. "Come in. The water is something else."

I said, "Another time." I couldn't imagine another time. "I don't have a bathing suit."

The man called out in Hebrew to the lift operator, and a few minutes later, he handed me a blue one-piece swimsuit and pointed.

The locker room was empty. Even so, I pulled the curtain shut before I slipped into the well-worn suit. When I stepped out, I caught sight of my whole self in the mirror. At first there was a shock of recognition—I know her!—as if I was seeing a long lost relative from afar. Then, taking a step back—she's small!—another surprise, since living with Harley had given me the illusion that I was a big truck-like woman, a Hummer of a human being, driving over curbs and flattening everyone in my path. I put my arms on my hips and scrutinized my flattened image. From a distance I looked like a paper doll.

Someone needs to clothe her, I thought. A pretty tunic and flowing pants, with tabs to keep the garments in place. Someone needs to give her a name and a history and imagine a life for her.

Why don't we call her Vered? How about if we give her a career? Have her be a maker of pretty things. Beautiful containers. Nesting boxes.

I imagined myself the second doll of three nesting dolls. Vered. This time pushing the r to the back of my throat, so the name sounded as it might in Hebrew.

Aviva was the smallest doll, the one inside me.

I made my way back to the natatorium, and when I stepped close to the pool, I was again taken by the man's somber eyes and cheerful demeanor. "Welcome," he said, bobbing Aviva in his arms.

Her head lolled; her mouth hung open. Skeletal, and yet utterly slack. Boneless, dead.

"I'm Baruch. Your sister and I have become good friends."

I plucked at the stretched-out bathing suit, feeling naked and self-conscious. "Roxanne," I said.

He stayed close to the tile edge of the pool, waiting for me to join them. "Roxanne?" He did not break out into song. "This is a name I've never heard."

"Apparently I have another name. Vered."

"Come in, Vered." He extended his arms, as if to hand me Aviva. "In the water, she's very light."

I could not step closer.

"It's warm," he said. "Once you come in, you'll never want to leave."

Once, when I was married Tom had taken me scuba diving in the Caribbean. He'd hired a guide who brought us far out into the ocean in a skiff. After our equipment was adjusted—tanks, respirators, flippers—we were supposed to sit on the edge of the boat and fall backwards into the sea. Tom sat on the gunwale, lifted his knees, and fell back without pause. I could not make myself fall into the water. My heart throbbed; my breath came quickly. The guide tried to reassure me. I did not need him to tell me I'd be okay because I knew once I hit the water, I'd be fine. The language was there, the knowledge. It was my body that refused. This was fear in a way I'd never experienced, fear detached from reason or thought. That day in the Caribbean, the guide grew tired of the delay. He put his hand against my chest and pushed.

In the natatorium at Chaverim, I grasped the top of the ladder, but I could not get myself to turn. My ears throbbed from the echoing voices in the pool area. I tried to steady my breathing, worried I'd be sick. Baruch regarded me with his solemn eyes, then after a few moments silently glided away.

I stayed in the natatorium because I felt it was expected of me. I watched this man sway in the water, cradling Aviva. After a while, the lift was lowered, and a second aide sat on the edge of the pool. The two men effortlessly moved Aviva from the water to the lift, and the limp, skinny creature, this being—woman, sister, twin—was brought back onto land, wrapped in a towel and transferred into a wheelchair.

I sat in the locker room, overcome with nausea. When my stomach settled I dressed, struggling to get my shirt buttons through the buttonholes and make bunny ears with the short, waxed laces on my shoes, wishing I could unsee what I'd seen. I thought of Ronit saying, "Don't go," and was sorry I hadn't listened.

After I was dressed, I saw an aide wheeling Aviva down the corridor, and I caught up with them. Aviva was dressed in navy fleece and strapped into the seat, her wet hair in a braid, body supported by a thick black foam block. "Hi," I said. "Shalom, Aviva." She blinked, slack-jawed, displaying nothing.

The aide, a tall man with lively eyes and a missing front tooth, spoke in Hebrew to Aviva and then to me. "Hi," I said, in a high, bright voice that I hardly recognized as mine. "Here I am." Her affect did not change. "Your sister. From America."

The aide tapped Aviva's shoulder and spoke to her in Hebrew. Still nothing in her eyes. I said, "Oh well," as if my disappointment was trivial. We laughed, the aide and I, then parted.

Mrs. Silk was sitting at her desk. I sank into the soft chair meant for guests and said, "I failed." The walls of her office were crowded with photos of arid landscapes. Along her windowsill was a collection of small cacti—fuzzy, prickly, gnarled.

"You're here," Mrs. Silk said. "You've come to see your sister." She handed me a bottle of water, nudged a box of tissues close, claimed there was no such thing as failure. "There are so many ways to know another person," she said. "Once you spend time together, you'll start to understand her."

"Can I arrange to spend time with Aviva another day?"

"You can visit whenever you like. You can see her here or take her out for the afternoon. You might want to stay in one of the family houses here in the community, which your father always did. Whatever is best."

"Was my mother ever with him?" I asked.

She touched her throat, ran her hand down to the pearls, and fingered each one, as if they were rosary beads. "Your father was always alone."

"And it didn't disturb you that she never visited her daughter?"

"I try to support my families. There's no sense in judging. People do the best they can."

"What does that mean, 'people do the best they can'? I hear it all the time and never really got it."

"You don't know what your mother's life was like when Aviva was born. It was a different time. Perhaps she had severe postpartum depression; in her day, it was brushed off. Minimized. Dismissed. She might not have had the emotional or physical ability to take care of Aviva."

Mrs. Silk handed me a folder. "I made copies of her medical records as you'd asked, starting with the ones we received when she moved here. There are progress reports, notes on therapies and day programs, a copy of the sensory checklist. There's a great deal more, hundreds of pages, but I didn't want to overwhelm you, so I chose what I thought was most meaningful. Everything is in Hebrew, though. Can you get someone to help with translation?"

"I'm sure I can," I said.

When I stood to leave, I noticed what looked like pebbles in a small plant pot on her desk. "That's my *Lithops*. It's a succulent from South Africa. Some people call them 'living stones.' Aren't they marvelous?"

I agreed they were marvelous, though I didn't think so at all.

"I'll learn more about Aviva after I read this?"

"Yes," she said. "And please—you can ask whatever questions you have and meet with her therapists. We encourage family to take an active role in decision making."

"She was smaller than me at birth?"

"Yes," she said. "Roxanne. What did your cousin tell you about Aviva?"

"That I shouldn't visit. She didn't even know her name."

"Some of what you read in the medical report will be disturbing. Can someone sit with you when you go through these papers?"

"Yes," I said, though I could not imagine who.

The mountain air was cold and crisp. I took it in deeply and thought of the Man Who Likes his Job in the pool with Aviva. His big, somber eyes, and tuft of chest hair, the limp woman in his arms, the song he sang. I had never seen anything like this before, and yet this strange scene was full of familiar pieces, like a jigsaw puzzle of a monument in a distant city. As I walked to the parking lot, some of the pieces fit together: the blue sky, the ancient stones dappled with moss, the tiny flowers that found root in the crevices, and for a moment, it again seemed as if I knew every piece of what I had seen and nothing at all. The song this man sang, his big, somber eyes, my sister's hair, her feet. Had they ever touched the ground? Had anyone ever slipped shoes onto her feet? *She*—each time I heard this pronoun, a shiver went through me, a shock I did not feel when I heard her name—Aviva. *She*, there was something about it, something feminine. *She*, a girl, a woman. *Her* hair, her hands. And all that went along with it, even, or especially, in the house where I was raised, where there was no conversation about what girls could do, because girls grew up and did it. *She*, getting her period. *She*, at a party; *her* dress. *Her* kiss at twelve, the surprise of a boy's tongue in her mouth. *Her* dreams. *Her* room with two beds. *Her* sister beside her.

"Next time you come..." Mrs. Silk had said.

I had smiled and nodded and thought of my suitcase in the rental car. I could drive to Ronit's, where Galia's room had been set up for me, and fly home from there, or knock on Dina's door, sit with her while she looked at men, pretending to swoon over the plump, pale-faced ones, then cross the hall to my mother's apartment, chant, "Aviva! Aviva!" and go home.

Or I could go to the nearby spa Dina had recommended, which had a long massage menu and the most delicious food. Maybe I could get a hot stone massage. Or maybe, like Harley, I could sleep in the car.

I was standing in the parking lot when a tall, thin man in a leather jacket hurried by. His stride was long and his hair was in disarray. Someone familiar, I thought, trying to place him. Merchant, neighbor, passerby? The sky had grown dark. I watched him zip his jacket to the neck and realized it had gotten cold. Maybe that was why I was shaking.

He pulled out his keys and his car let out a yip of recognition. Its headlights winked. I thought of those Japanese pets that gave their owners comfort—toys that blinked, inflatable dolls. He got into his car, backed up and around. A whole world of people satisfied by robotic voices and soft contours.

The man pulled up in front of me and lowered his car window. "Are you okay?"

Now I saw that it was the Man Who Likes His Job, with his sad eyes and cheerful demeanor. For a moment, I was silent, afraid if I opened my mouth, an ocean of sorrow might spill out. "I'm fine," I said. "Thanks. I'm all right."

"You know where you're going?" His English was excellent.

"I have a map. I'm okay."

He pulled away.

I'm fine!

I was so lost. I hadn't turned the key in the ignition and already I was lost.

I followed the signs for Rosh Pina, where I would find the spa. The roads were narrow and curving, and the oncoming cars, with their bright headlights, seemed to be coming straight at me.

The desk clerk, finding I had no reservation, told me they were full up. I asked if she could recommend another place and she turned to make a phone call.

The guests padded around the lobby in their slippers and terry robes, as if this was a sanatorium. I hadn't tired of watching them when the clerk returned with the name of a nearby guesthouse with a vacant room. When I arrived twenty minutes later, I felt like the first person who'd stumbled onto the grounds in decades.

My room was spare—a desk, a hard-backed chair, a second chair, on which were three thin neatly folded towels. Above a chest of drawers was a watercolor of cypress trees. I walked across the cold tile floor and studied the photographs on the wall. One was a portrait of a slight man in small wire-framed glasses, with a black medical bag beside him. In the second, a large group of adults and children posed in front of a lake. The captions were in Hebrew.

I slid beneath tight sheets and fell immediately to sleep, and when I opened my eyes it was light. Does she wake of her own accord? I wondered. Was it noisy where she slept, the way it was in a hospital, where clanking carts and conversations announced the dawning day? If she was roused by activity, did she think *morning* and anticipate all that was in store for her?—nourishment, an aide with strong arms, sunlight, music. If language did not shape this anticipation, how did her body register the cycle of daily activities? How did her body signal the pleasure she felt when the metal shades were raised and daylight brightened her room? Or her impatience as she waited to be lifted from her bed and taken from her room to experience the company of others? How did she ask or signal her despair or call out if someone was hurting her? *Mama!* That sound that sprang from the lips of babies worldwide, useless for orphans whose cries went unanswered for so long they learned not to cry.

I thought of the dog waiting by the door for her friend. I thought of the baby, Roxanne, curled beside a sister in embryonic fluid. I thought of them sleeping together in a crib. To have this sister, this twin nestled beside me and then to have no one? What happens when you lack the words to explain an absence, a state of being without? Had I stopped smiling? Lost my appetite? Was this primal heartache the reason I could not work with numbers—two take away one, and no one to explain the answer? If I grieved silently, failing to thrive, who might have noticed? Would my father have been able to hold the remaining baby, knowing he'd sent the other one away? Nothing in my dim memory said yes.

The floor was icy. Some of what you read in the medical record will be disturbing, Mrs. Silk had said. More disturbing than what I'd seen? I opened the shutters, thinking I might have a view of the lake in the photo on the wall. Instead I saw a barn and a series of stalls. The old-fashioned key was on the bureau. The hotel name in English as well as Hebrew was on the plastic medallion dangling from the chain. Paradise, it said.

&

In Paradise, breakfast was served in a cold room with low ceilings and long tables. On my first morning, the only guests were a young couple in the far corner. They sat with their elbows on the table and their opposite arms clasped, as if they were about to arm wrestle. A swarthy young man with a shaved head set a plate in front of me with brown bread, soft cheeses, and a salad of tomatoes and cucumber. There was no coffee in Paradise, but there were fresh herbs for tea and halvah made with honey from local hives. Also wireless, two outdoor hot tubs, and a specialist in the Alexander Technique.

Outside, the sheep *bahhed* in their odd phlegmy voices. I wondered where Aviva was right then and what she felt or thought. What was the purpose of her life? What was the purpose of mine?

I'd found a website once that promised to lead me to that answer. Not your job or your goal, but your real purpose, it said. I was instructed to ask myself, "What is the purpose of my life" and then write whatever answer came to mind and keep writing until all the false answers got pushed aside. I would know when I got to the correct answer because it would make me cry. That was my true purpose.

What would the server say if I asked him that question? And the young woman, clasping the hand of her lover across the room? Would she say, "To get married"? When I was young, I thought marriage and children were the sad wishes made by women without ambition. I'd had no interest in babies, never held one, felt no ease with my friends' kids until they grew older. Then I'd gotten pregnant. Tom had been overjoyed. His eyes filled with tears, and he loved me more than ever and told me so, pulling me close, reassuring me. *You will be fine. You'll be a wonderful mother.* It was spring. I let those words sink into me. The cherry trees were in bloom. Everywhere daddies had babies strapped to their chests, and pairs of laughing mothers strolled with their little ones. Adorable toddlers peered from backpacks and bounced on subway seats. The desire to be a mother grew. Our baby, I thought, in a tentative, hopeful way. Then the miscarriage, these cells, this protoplasm expelled, but not the dream of the baby, not the yearning to hold, to touch, to tend. My empty arms ached.

When I visited my mother, I knew not to tell her about the miscarriage, because speaking of it would make me cry, and crying was forbidden. My crying was over nothing; it was being spoiled rotten, it gave her a headache, all that *wah wah wah*. I had everything handed to me on a silver platter, knew nothing about sorrow. But she was my mother, and when I saw her, the words came out. "I was pregnant," and though I covered my face, I could not push the crying back inside.

I felt her sit on the couch beside me, felt her breathe. "You will live through this," she said. Her voice quavered. I felt her helplessness. My crying grew wilder, until I thought something inside me would rip. For the lost baby, for me, for my mother, with her own unspeakable losses, who I could not ever seem to comfort.

Across the room, the young couple kissed.

To be productive, I'd written, after reading the website. To distinguish myself from the *balabustas* and *balagulas*.

It had not made me cry.

Paradise had been a health farm, established at the turn of the twentieth century by the German doctor whose photo was in my room. For all I knew, the spartan rooms had been part of the plan, the icy floors thought to have a salutary effect. I stayed for three nights, saying nothing more than *"boker tov"* and *"todah."* I worked in the mornings, and in the afternoons, I wandered through the pastures past the dairy cows and unlatched the gate to the cool stalls, where the goats, and sheep with tagged ears, were resting. The painful memory of those miscarriages kept returning, that my body had rebelled, that my husband had lost interest.

On my first day in Paradise, the voice that castigated me was louder than the others: Why is everything about you? it asked. Why is it *your* loss, *your* miscarriages, *your* horror upon meeting this sister? By the second day, the voices had receded. No expectations hung heavy in the air—that every mother loved her children; that every sister was bursting with joy at finding a lost sibling. There were no platitudes about love or loyalty in Paradise, no rush to stamp an experience with the expected sentiment, only the knowledge that I had become the guardian of her name—Aviva. That was all—Aviva.

In Paradise, the eggs I ate were from the chickens in the nearby coops. The cheese was from the milk of their goats and sheep, the vegetables from the garden, the flowers from their greenhouses. I liked to crouch beside the sheep in their cool stalls and let them run their fat tongues across my palms and bring carrots to the donkey, who quickly learned I had treats and began meeting me at the gate.

If I stroked her muzzle for too long she became impatient for her treat and lifted a lip, showing off her huge square teeth. The cows swished their tails and looked at me with their big wet eyes. Empty eyes, I would have said before this trip, though now I wasn't sure.

Aviva's vision was within the normal range, Mrs. Silk had told me. So was her hearing. In the packet she'd given me was a "sensory response check list" filled out by the aides and therapists who worked with Aviva, over a hundred very specific questions about her likes and dislikes, the ways she was oversensitive, the ways she needed to be stimulated.

The document was in Hebrew, so the pages of questions were as beyond my understanding as my mother's decision to move back to this country, where there were no kin except the grown child she had left behind, whose name she could not remember, whose existence she had denied. It was as if she'd been driven by some primitive instinct that she, herself, no longer recognized. I wondered if she dreamt of Aviva, if the name flittered through her consciousness like a moth.

I would bring her to Chaverim. It seemed important to do this. Maybe it would unearth something within her and she would tell me the pieces of this story that still were hidden. I tried not to hope for any great emotional release. I'd just tell Sunny we were spending the day together. Then I'd pull up in front of her building, cut the engine, wait. Sunny would bring my mother down. I'd help her into the passenger seat. I haven't the foggiest idea where I am, she would say when I fastened her seat belt.

Neither do I, I would tell her.

FIFTEEN

As soon as I reached the second floor in my mother's building, I saw the new lock Sunny had installed. Just as I had asked, it was too high for Mom to reach. But the door was ajar. I walked right in, pausing in the spotless kitchen. Magazine photos had been tacked onto the fridge with magnets, and on the small table near the window were two pomelos in a bowl and two round polka dot placemats. Sunny had a son in the Philippines she had not seen in five years; he lived in the house she still owned. I knew I needed to talk to her about the door but when I thought of all that she'd left behind and all she tolerated from my mother, I hated complaining about anything.

I called "hello?" and stepped into the living room, where the remainder of my mother's bagged possessions were piled against one wall. "Shalom?"

They were in my mother's small bedroom. Sunny was arranging a floppy-brimmed hat on Mom, pushing up the front and then experimenting with the sides. I watched my mother step closer to the mirror, turning her head to one side and then the other, regarding herself with pleasure. When Sunny noticed I was there, her eyes widened and she said, "Ohhhh," like a drowning woman.

Sunny put her hands on my mother's shoulders, turning her from the mirror to the doorway, where I stood, and I found myself facing a small happy lady in a white sweater, powder blue pants, canvas sneakers, with a silly hat on her head.

"Oh, hello, dear," she said, as if she'd seen me the day before. There was no surprise in her greeting, only a kind of ordinary pleasure. I took her hand, felt her loose skin as she withdrew from my touch.

Sunny helped get Leona dressed and into the car. Like Harley, her veneer of good cheer overrode my mother's confused resistance. *Oh, Leona! Going for a nice ride. With your daughter. Ohhh, it is so happy, the mother and the daughter together!*

Sunny waved as we drove off. As soon as we were out of the city, my mother's head drooped. I busied myself reading signs and paying attention to the road until we were north of Haifa, where small towns dotted the arid rocky land. Then I found that when I looked to one side, it was the Jewish homeland, a dream realized after thousands of years of yearning, and when I looked to the other side, there were Palestinians uprooted from their ancestral homes. I wondered idly if the best I'd ever be able to do would be to look one way and see a neglectful mother, and look the other way and see a woman who'd been a victim herself, isolated and alone at the end of her life.

After I exited the highway and began to take the series of turns up the mountain, the car began to buck, and my mother woke.

"Did I fall asleep? It's not like me to nap in the middle of the day."

"People get drowsy in the car," I said.

"Where *are* we?" She put her hand against the window. "You know, I haven't the foggiest idea…"

I wondered if she was seeing the craggy landscape, or if her perception went no farther than the glass, and I asked, "What is home to you, Mama?" A few minutes later, when I saw the first small sign for Chaverim, I asked again.

This time she said, "New Jersey."

It was a curious answer, one I would not have given myself, though most of my life I had lived there. "Why?" I asked.

"I had a wonderful career at Bell Laboratories. I was the first woman to become a department head, you know, and our group… We published many important papers. Work that is still cited. I had a wonderful career, you know…"

"I do," I said. "Even when I was a kid I knew you were special. Do you remember that I brought you into school for show and tell? Ma?"

"I was the first woman to become a department head at Bell Labs," she said.

"Do you remember where you were born?"

My mother said, "Bad things happened to me."

"I know," I said, holding my breath, waiting.

"Everyone is dead. My husband, Morris. He did everything for me…"

I let her continue, telling me about my father, until I pulled into the parking lot at Chaverim. Then I said, "Do you remember that you had twins, Ma? Vered, Roxanne, that's me. And your other daughter, Aviva. That's who we're visiting today."

"Is that so!"

"Aviva is a pretty name. Was she named after someone?"

My mother looked out the window, hearing, not hearing, ignoring me, unable to answer. "Do you remember having twins and that something was wrong with one of them?"

I reached for her hand, and she withdrew sharply. "Stop *mutchering* me."

"But if you really forgot Aviva, why did you leave me behind and move here? You hated religion, hated Zionism. I never even thought of myself as Jewish." The parking lot was nearly empty. "Mom?"

"I'm an old woman. Leave me alone," she said.

You're barking up the wrong tree, babe. This favorite expression of Harley's seemed apt just then. I was always barking, and every tree was wrong. I held out my hands and helped her step from the car. She looked up, shading her eyes with her hand. "You know, I haven't the foggiest notion where I am."

"We've come to Chaverim to visit your daughter. The other one. It's chilly outside. You might want your jacket."

She let me help her into the tan windbreaker Sunny had packed, an old "Members Only" jacket that had been my father's. It smelled of mildew and mothballs, like everything my mother owned, like my mother herself. She took my arm when we walked up the wide path to the main building, pausing every few feet, saying, "Wooo," then asking where we were. She seemed not to notice her surroundings as we entered the building, did not comment on the enclosure with the chirping birds, or turn when we passed the Orthodox family, the mother adjusting her flowing blonde tresses, the son in a wheelchair, his face blotchy with acne, limbs folded like wings, yarmulke on his small head. I realized I wasn't the only one she could not see, that she did not see anything, really. Her tormented question, "Where am I?" seemed unrelated to place.

An aide walked us to the room where Aviva's music class was about to begin. We waited in the hall while aides wheeled two residents through the broad door. Next came a boy, secured to a standing frame with blue Velcro straps. The device's swivel casters were noisy on the tile floor. In the final wheelchair was Aviva, dressed in a red cotton turtleneck. Thick pads supported her head, and a seatbelt was fastened around her waist. Her long black braid was shot through with gray as mine would have been, had I stopped coloring it. Bony face, long-lashed eyes that fastened on nothing, slack mouth. Her hands were fisted, her feet turned in.

A finger in a live socket, I thought. Pain without purpose.

The residents were arranged in a circle. I took my mother's arm so we could stand beside Aviva, because there was a second voice within my head. *Your sister.*

My mother shook me off. "These people are in wheelchairs."

"That's true," I said. "Let's say hello."

The aides began handing out instruments. Aviva got bells with straps that looped around her wrists. I was trying to get my mother to join me in the room when an aide passed, pushing the wheelchair of a woman with a small malformed face, and a tube attached to her neck. My mother called out to the aide in Hebrew, and I cried, "Ma!" and tugged on her arm. She jerked free. The aide spoke a few soft words and brought her a chair.

The room was stuffy and unpleasant smelling—saliva, peppermint, sweat. I walked beside Aviva. Her blinking eyes were almond-shaped like mine, her black eyebrows unplucked. Slack mouth, chafed chin, kerchief tied around her neck. I touched her arm, then moved beyond the fabric of her sleeve to take her hand. There was no grasp, no reciprocity. Fraud, I thought of myself, as I took Aviva's hand, because just then, this sister, this mother, I wanted to be free of both.

A CD was popped into a player and music filled the room. The drummer used the stick between his teeth to bang on his drum, and the tambourine player shook her ankle and screeched. To shake the bells meant moving or trying to move her whole body, and Aviva did this, making an odd sea mammal sound. The man beside her sang in an off-key voice, and the therapists joined in, these tenders and touchers as inscrutable to me as their charges, happy, it seemed, enjoying the familiar tunes, chatting, clapping, singing along. Then the next song. *Ein.* I heard that word. *Ein li eretz acheret.* Land—*eretz.*

A new voice joined the others—dry, tuneless, confident. It was my mother singing. My mother, softened and transformed by the music, was clapping her hands with the melody. I felt a kind of lightness in the room and had the same odd sense I'd had in the car: Look one way there was illness, heartbreak, broken beings. Look the other way, and it was a sing-along, enjoyed by all.

Another song began. A tall aide put her hands on Aviva's shoulders and moved her to the rhythm of this slower, moodier song. My mother knew this song, too, and swayed without self-consciousness. Then the music stopped, and the aides began gathering the instruments.

I walked over to Aviva and waited, as if she might glance up at me. Then I stepped behind her chair, took the grips, and wheeled it a few feet forward. It was heavier than I'd imagined. My mother got up and pushed past the wheelchairs lined up in the doorway. "Wait!" I called.

A Slavic-looking aide—tall, willowy, blonde hair in a knot—gestured *go* with her chin, and I let go of the wheelchair and hurried after my mother, waving my arms, and crying, "Hang on!"

And what did she say?

"I want to go home." Of course. "Take me *home.* I want to go home."

After my mother was settled in her apartment, I crossed the hall and knocked on Dina's door. When she saw me, she laughed with pleasure, dark eyes sparkling, glossy hair cut to chin length, a stunning look. She took my hands, kissed my cheeks, pulled me into her kitchen, all the anguish I'd caused her forgotten. While she tossed half the contents of her fridge onto the table, I said a few words about these last days. Aviva, unresponsive; the kind Shelley Silk. Her parrot marched from side to side, squawking and pecking at dust.

Our parting, which left all my emotions jangling. Aviva wheeled one way, my mother hurrying in the opposite direction; that I'd never said goodbye. In the midst of talking, I knew I would wake early and return one last time to Chaverim.

The man from Winnipeg was long gone. I sat with a cup of tea and a small container of yogurt and listened to Dina tell me about the new man, a dental surgeon who in photos had the unlined face of a child. The parrot followed us to her office, where she wheeled the wobbly chair beside her own, so we could look at her new suitors. While I helped evaluate the subtext of their messages, I thought about the long drive back to the Galilee. Was my need to return the same pathology that kept me calling my mother each week? Or maybe that wasn't pathology. Maybe it was what you did—for your mother. For your sister.

We worked on a response to the apple-cheeked Dov, who glowered at us in his photo, chest hair blooming from the top of his shirt, leather jacket. They'd spent Saturday night together, and, "Oh, you would not believe!" I thought of Dov in bed with Dina, and my little rental car, sputtering, grunting. The empty parking lot. The flittering birds. The questions I could not answer. What was the purpose of my life?

Sixteen

A week had passed since my first visit, almost to the hour, and Aviva was in the pool. Instead of standing by the door to the natatorium, I decided to wait on the patio at the back of the building.

It was chilly, and no one else was outside. I zipped my jacket high and sat on a teak bench near a cluster of century plants. The birds were louder and more raucous than the ones in the enclosure. I needed to be patient. After Aviva was done swimming (with the Man Who Likes his Job?) I had to wait until she was showered (how?), dried off (by whom?), and dressed.

I could feel my bare hands stiffen from the cold. To steady and distract myself, I took the small journal from my bag and began to doodle. At first just designs. Then the doodling changed into big-eyed, button-nosed dolls with round Victorian faces. I turned them into paper dolls with tabs above their pudgy, naked shoulders, and then drew outfits. A bonnet; a high-necked dress.

I was so deeply into drawing that the sound of the doors sliding open jolted me, and when I looked up, out he stepped, the Man Who Likes his Job, a tall, thin bird, the locks of his gray hair lifting in the breeze, tragic, playful expression, many-pocketed shorts, boyish, loping gait. First, I lowered my head so he would not see me. Then, curious about this man who took such pleasure being in the pool with Aviva, I looked up.

He passed, halted comically, then backtracked, stopping in front of me. "You're Aviva's sister."

I snapped shut my book and said, yes, here I was again, and wanting to say sorry. "You went through all that trouble of finding me a bathing suit, and I never even went into the pool."

"So the next time you'll come in. I promise you'll like it very much."

We looked at the empty chair nearby, and when I nodded, he

pulled it close and lowered himself slowly, extending his long, pale legs. A fresh thick scar ran along one knee.

"Did you know that last week was the first time I was meeting Aviva?" I asked.

"Yes, of course," he said. "Chaverim is a very small village."

"It's not such a happy story," I said.

"Should it be?"

Something in his gaze, benign but frank, his bright, sad eyes, and this gnawing sense that we'd already met in some distant life, made it possible for me to say what I felt, rather than what I was supposed to feel. "Everyone here is so cheerful and matter of fact. Maybe to you this is part of life, but to me, honestly, it's disturbing. I just couldn't make myself go into that water."

I watched him massage his scarred knee. "It *is* part of life, you know."

"Then maybe I'm a terrible person, because it's not one I'm able to face."

"I doubt you're a terrible person," he said. "You probably just need time to acclimate."

Three women in white uniforms stepped into the garden, one passing a cigarette to her friend, another pulling two chairs to a third so they could sit together. Tenders and bathers, like this man. Open-hearted people who believed all humans were loveable.

"You're a traveler, yes? Where do you come from?"

"Pittsburgh. It's in the U.S.," I said.

"And you speak Hebrew?"

"Not at all."

"So, okay, then you know what it's like to find yourself alone in a strange city very far from home. You don't speak the language; you can't find your way around. The food is terrible; the people push past you, everyone scowling. The narrow streets seem full of danger, and you want to go home; it is all you want. But then you return to this city. Perhaps you must, for professional reasons. And this next time, you recognize a landmark. You know how to ask for bottled water, *con gas*. To say thank you. You step further from your hotel and have an encounter, something trivial, but pleasant. Then slowly it begins to change. You're less fearful, less suspicious. Then without knowing it you start to enjoy. Chaverim is a different country. I didn't come to this understanding quickly. It took time. First I had to get used to the foreignness. Then I was able to enjoy."

"How much time?" I asked. "How long did it take you?"

He thought about this, massaging his knee. "Maybe three months to become accustomed to my friends here, like Aviva, longer before I began to enjoy, which at present, I do."

"How long have you worked here?" I asked.

My question amused him. "I'm a visitor. Like you."

"Oh." Had I offended him? "You have a child here—"

"A nephew. His mother—my sister—asked me to look after him when she got sick. No one else would make that promise, so I agreed. On those first visits, what I saw, what I'm thinking you see, was a kind of living hell, yes? Let these poor souls die. I'm not ashamed to tell you it was what I thought, particularly of Dan, whose life truly seems one of unrelenting misery. I've come to see this isn't the case for many of his colleagues at Chaverim, but it is for him, I fear. Seizures all day long, muscle spasms, skin ailments, fed by a g-tube, so much medication to treat the symptoms and alleviate the pain that his ability to be awake and alert is minimal."

"And you continue to come here all the time anyhow? That's pretty remarkable."

"It isn't. This is what I'm trying to explain. The first visits, after my sister died, felt like a punishment. I'd drive here, and Dan would be in pain or sleeping, unimpressed by my efforts, and I'd ask myself why I bothered to honor this promise to my sister when my presence meant nothing to him. I wrestled with this dilemma for many weeks until Shelley, Rochelle Silk, helped me find ways to make these visits enjoyable. That's how I began to swim with Aviva."

"Because she had no visitors?"

"She enjoys the water," he said.

"And no one else takes her."

"Her time with me is extra."

I pressed on my chest to push back the wild creature beneath my ribcage. "Does she know you after all the times you've gone swimming with her?"

"Are you asking if she anticipates my arrival? That I can't say. Does she in her own way know my touch? I think yes. But I'm not driven by such expectations."

The clatter of swivel casters on tile distracted me, and when I looked up I saw that several people had drifted into the garden, among them the boy from Aviva's music class, secured against his standing frame with blue pads and Velcro straps. A couple, his parents, I supposed, were rolling him into the shade.

"Do you mind me asking all these questions?" I asked.

"Why would I mind?"

"I don't know," I said. "Maybe you're in a rush and I'm straining your patience."

"If I was in a rush, I wouldn't have stopped."

This exchange amused me. "Where are you from, with that flawless English?"

"Hardly flawless," he said. Then he told me he'd lived in the U.S. for nearly ten years—in Philadelphia, San Francisco, and Minneapolis, where his son had been born, and where now he was doing a post doc in chemistry.

I shielded my eyes from the glare and the Man Who Likes his Job transformed into a man with a son in Minneapolis. Then the two of us shifted so smoothly from Chaverim, it was as if a breeze had carried my troubles over the mountains. Soon there was a daughter in Tel Aviv, a documentary film editor; a restaurant he liked in Pittsburgh, where he collaborated with a group that did work in facial expression analysis; his fondness for San Francisco, where he'd lived long enough for his wife to get a Masters in Occupational Therapy, and where they thought they'd stay. "My wife was very happy in San Francisco," he said.

"And now is she happy in Tel Aviv?"

"Now she is not my wife."

Was there a new wife? I wondered but did not ask because we'd turned to our overlapping time years back, where we'd lived, had espresso, browsed through books at City Lights, maybe even run into each other.

"I'm thinking I saw you there, checking out books in…"

"Social sciences. Philosophy…"

"I guess not," I said. His name was Baruch. In San Francisco, he'd been studying the role of maternal depression in mother-infant bonding.

"And you?" he asked.

"I was a runaway," I said.

He knew, without my explaining, that I hadn't been a teenager sleeping in the street, but rather someone trying to escape from unpleasantness. In those days, there were so many in the city who'd changed their names, donned saffron robes, imagining, as I had, that in a new place, you could invent yourself. He knew something about the necessity of space and time to dream; I could tell by the questions he asked when I told him about all the hours I'd spent doodling in the green velvet chair at the Chic Pea. Young, unencumbered, with just enough money for food and rent and so little vanity or professionalism that I pretty much gave my work away. I told him, because he asked, about the album cover I did for a local band for a couple of hundred dollars flat, that when the record went gold, the cover became a calling card, the way I began to build my career. And he told me about his early studies with mothers and infants and the kind of work he did now, with computer vision.

There was so much else we talked about in this long conversation that neither of us wanted it to end: it wasn't just the range of topics, but the intimacy of our conversation, the questions we mulled but could not answer—who should we care for? How much of our lives should we spend looking after others? When do we turn away to protect ourselves?

When the wind picked up, we got up to move into the atrium, and the journal slipped off my lap, its pages splayed. When he retrieved it for me, he asked, "May I look?" and though I felt some reluctance, I said, "Sure."

He was amused by the naked baby's face. "That's Shelley," he said.

"It didn't start out that way," I said, taking the notebook back.

"How strange. And remarkable. To be able to take in the world that way."

"We aren't calling each other remarkable, remember? I think you're going to have to stick with strange," I said.

"In a good way," he said. "As in 'not banal.' Unique."

"Not familiar?"

"The drawings aren't at all. You are, in a way."

"Yes," I said, brightening. "You too. As if we've met before."

It was an electric moment that we held then broke in synchrony as we moved inside.

We found good chairs in the atrium and continued to talk until he glanced at his watch. "I really must get going. I've arranged to hike in the Banias with a companion."

He retrieved a wallet from his back pocket and asked to borrow a pen, and I watched him position the card on his knee and write his contact information on the back in neat block letters, wondering about this companion—male, female?

"I see Aviva whenever I'm here," he said, handing me the card. "Whenever you like, I can give you a report."

I looked at his handwritten name and cell phone number then slid the card into my bag, sorry our conversation had come to an end. When he rose, I did too, following him down a corridor to a set of side doors that parted for us. "If we had met in San Francisco and you'd asked me about my background, I would have said I was nothing. No siblings. Not Christian, not Jewish."

"And now?" he asked.

"I don't know," I said. "Ask me the next time we meet."

We walked together down the long sloping drive to the parking area. His car was parked next to mine in the nearly empty lot. I said, "When I saw you swimming with Aviva, I thought of you as the Man Who Likes his Job. You looked so…joyful in the water. Thank you for swimming with her, for looking out for her. And for stopping to talk to me."

He took out his car keys, and his car made its affectionate yip and lit up. "You know, I am a man who likes my job," he said.

"I can tell," I said. "What would you do if you were me? Aviva and I have been separated our whole lives. When I think about the way my family tried to erase her existence, I feel this urge to defend her, but it's not like I can change her situation. And it's sentimental to imagine my being here means something to her, isn't it? She doesn't care one way or another."

"What about you? Did you ever think that in time you might find that Aviva means something to you?"

"No," I said.

"It might help if you didn't view Aviva as an all-or-nothing problem. You know, when you're here, you're here and it's good, and that's what it is."

I stood in the lot, knowing I should let him leave. "That day, when you were swimming with Aviva, and I walked toward the pool, what did you see? I mean, since you study faces?"

"An honest expression of sadness." Then he explained—eyelids droopy, inner corners of the brow going up, lip corners pulled down. He'd been taken by the purity of the emotion on my face.

"Could you tell I was Aviva's sister?"

"Yes, of course," he said.

"So I also looked like death?"

"That I don't see. And when you begin to spend time with Aviva, you'll experience her in a different way, too."

"I don't know. It's hard to imagine," I said.

He opened his car door and strapped himself into his seat.

"I'm sorry. I don't mean to make you late."

"Ah, sorry, sorry," he said.

I watched him drive away, then walked back up the hill to the building and thought about Baruch's early work with mothers and infants. Infants as young as two months respond to their mothers' expressions, he'd said. In one of their studies, they'd videotaped two groups of three-month-old babies. The infants in the first group faced mothers who acted in a flat, depressed way. These babies mirrored the blank gaze of their mothers, unlike the babies with cheerful, expressive mothers: these second pairs responded in symmetry. Infants could cope with a brief "still face" by attempting to get their mothers' attention, but if it continued, they became withdrawn, disorganized. In later studies, even when depressed mothers got better, the infants did not. Their behavior problems continued. They suffered socially, were clingy and anxious, did not separate from their mothers as readily as the others.

I entered the building, passing the birds in their enclosure and the visiting families.

I thought how distressing it was to try to interact with someone who would not return your gaze. My mother. Harley in his chair. Aviva.

I met up with my sister in the greenhouse, a bright space, where trays of seedlings lined the wall, and in the center of the room was a large wood table, where on this day, sprigs of fragrant herbs had been set out. When the pretty young aide sitting with Aviva saw me, she gestured for me to take her place at the table and left the two of us alone. I turned Aviva's wheelchair from the table to me. "Hello," I said.

Boneless twin, with eyes that did not seem to take me in, thick eyelashes, long hair that someone had braided. Peach-colored fleece sweater, zipped high. Slack mouth. Cool fisted hands. Turned-in feet with the toes touching, sheathed in booties. Wasn't I supposed to feel love, seeing all the ways we were alike—ears, brow, hair, chin? Shouldn't love simply rise?

What a myth I'd created by imagining I'd sprung from the soil and not from the loins of my wounded parents. Sitting woodenly beside Aviva, I felt all the ways I was of my mother.

She breathed. So did I.

The loamy, earthy smell was comforting. I touched her hand. *Does it matter to you if I don't come back?* I knew it didn't.

A group of three walked and rolled past. I waited for them to arrange themselves around a wooden workspace.

May I kiss you goodbye? Our mother does not like to be kissed. I did. I feared all the ways I was like my mother, but in this way, I was not. I loved kisses of all kinds, velvet lips and clever tongue. I loved the casual friend's peck on the cheek, Mindy's hug and double kiss, the first on the cheek, the second on my forehead.

"I'm going to kiss you goodbye." I glanced around, feeling foolish to have said this aloud.

Flawless skin untouched by the sun, fair down on her cheeks, un-plucked brows. Scented lotion. My lips against her skin. My hushed goodbye.

SEVENTEEN

This time, I returned to an empty house, no Harley hiding in the basement, only his voice on my answering machine. *How are you, babe? It's been too long!* While I let the messages play, in case someone else beside Harley tried to reach me, I scooped up the mail and magazines fanned out on the floor and threw my dirty clothes down the chute. I dashed upstairs to prop Baruch's business card against the lamp on my desk and returned to hear Harley say, "Give me a call so I know you're okay." A year had passed since we'd lived together, and still he was asking, "Where've you been hiding, hon?"

Later, while I was sitting at my desk, Mindy called, and when I tried to describe Chaverim, I said it was horrible and that I wished I'd never known about Aviva. As soon as I stopped speaking, every word seemed inadequate. Chaverim was beautiful, too, and I had known about Aviva, in a way, her name and existence made tangible what I had felt for so long.

When I got off the phone, I touched the raised letters on Baruch's card, and saw his eyes, the deep pools of sadness, his half-hearted smile. What can you do? Eyes closed, a half nod. Why argue? What's to say? An expression that sometimes seemed to suggest powerlessness and other times a rueful accommodation to life exactly as it was.

When I recalled his kindness, I let my head fall against the wooden desk. Wasn't I supposed to feel better? I did what I was supposed to do—flew to Israel, held my sister's hand, returned to say goodbye, expecting nothing in response. And now it was worse. Now I could see her face. Now she was the ache beneath my ribs, and I knew I would carry her with me always.

Even alone, I was ashamed of my sorrow. A punitive voice kept emerging to say, *It's not all about you.* But it was about me—my grief, my acknowledgement of Aviva, which left me so weak, I could not lift my cheek from that slab of wood.

My desktop was a cold hard mother. I know you well, I thought.

Then later: *Selfish! Wipe your foolish tears, pull yourself together and go to work!*

And so I did, just as I had been trained. At dawn I rose, showered, dressed. Before this trip to Israel, I had worn jeans to work unless we were scheduled to see clients. Now I dressed with inordinate care, but knew as I did so that I was crafting a veneer. Scrutinizing myself in the mirror, I thought of my mother, who loved fashion, though she would deny it, disguising her passion by speaking of cut and tailoring and the quality of cloth. Now, when I thought of her buttoning her mauve silk blouse, stepping into her slip with its lacy trim, adjusting the tweed wool skirt with its invisible zipper, and the jacket with its handmade button holes, when I thought of her choosing the lapel brooch, the tiny watch on a chain, when I saw her smoothing her sheer hose and slipping into her buttery Italian pumps, I saw how many layers it took to cover the soft, private self.

And then she steps outside. My father is warming up the car while classical music plays on the radio. She settles into the passenger seat for the short ride to work. What did they talk about? When she wanted him to pick her up; what needed to be purchased, repaired, renewed, or paid. They did not talk about Aviva. It would have been impossible. I knew this, though I had no proof. My father's job was to keep her steady, to buttress and protect her.

I chose an eggplant-colored shirt, a soft cotton knit, and buttoning it, wondered when they had entered into this silent accord. It must have taken considerable effort at first. What did they say to each other on the night they decided to give her up? And the night after that? Who held Aviva as they drove her to the institution? They did not yet own a clapboard house that needed to be furnished and painted, carpets steam-cleaned, shrubs trimmed, grass cut. They had no car with brake pads to replace and tires to have rotated and balanced, no retirement portfolios, accountant, or housecleaner. My mother had no conferences, my father no periodontal appointments, not then, not in Israel. I knew what it was like to have the hours surrounding my workday crammed with the chores that allowed me to function as a responsible citizen.

I arrived well before the others, unlocked the door, and sat on the sofa, studying the high ceilings and wood floor, grooved and marred with age. When Kayleigh switched on the lights some time later, she was so startled, she gasped, grabbed her chest, and said, "You scared me! How *are* you?"

Then she sank onto the cushion beside me. Her hair was piled up in a pretty, haphazard way. Gold rings lined the cartilage in both ears; on her feet were gold clogs.

"I'm fine," I said. And I really was, just then. "I'm okay. Those clogs are amazing."

She tapped her toes against each other, waited for me to speak, and said in a soft, hesitant voice, "Do you... look alike?"

I felt compelled to show some enthusiasm, though the only image I could muster was Aviva, limp in her wheelchair, chafed face, blank gaze. "Our hair is the same. And our nose."

Kayleigh touched her heart and said, "Awwww," and I said, "It's okay," to ease her discomfort.

When Les arrived and saw us sitting together, he shed his leather jacket, and said, "What's up?"

"I'm here!" I said and watched him shift his weight and cough into his fist. "It's okay. It's fine." Just what I'd always said when telling people my name. *Roxanne Garlick. It's okay, it's fine. You can laugh.* This time, I didn't say: You can laugh.

Then there was espresso, projects to review, tasks to delegate, and some silliness about their lunch with the new tenant in the space beside the yoga studio, an environmental not-for-profit run by a guy who was totally retro, with a little gray ponytail and wire-rimmed glasses. "So, so sweet," said Kayleigh, and Les said, "Total pothead." Listening to them lifted and delighted me, and then hours passed, and I did not think about Aviva even once.

Aviva was in the interstices. She appeared when I crossed the columned lobby of our building, when I called my mother, when I saw a possum split open like a ripe fruit, her shiny entrails on the asphalt beside her, when I stood in front of the mirror, absently brushing my teeth, when I saw four small roses leaning against the trellis outside my house, the buds just opening and I knew the frost would kill them that night or the night after. Her name rose from the darkness. *Aviva.* Like the rustle of trees. Tires on a wet pavement in the distance. *Sister.* A train chugging slowly on distant tracks. *Me, not me, me.* Nearly every night I dreamt of water.

I took the envelope with her medical records and drove to a cluster of stone buildings in Squirrel Hill that had been a Catholic church, school, and rectory until the 1990s, when a Jewish school bought the property. The summer before the crosses had been whittled from the tops of the buildings and the cornerstones sanded, the site was used as a movie set for an American remake of a classic French horror film. Every night the whole corner was lit up like a stadium. Neighbors wheeled their sleeping babies, toted their older kids, set up canvas chairs at the periphery to catch a glimpse of the movie stars.

I parked the car and waited for the crossing guard in her Day-Glo vest to wave me safely across the street. Approaching the complex, I saw that after all that whittling and sanding, after incantations and signage with bright blue Stars of David, the structures still looked like a Catholic school and church with the crosses mysteriously missing.

In the former rectory, I was given the name of a translator. I tucked the slip of paper in my wallet and went to work. On my way upstairs, I saw Les standing in the hall with a yoga mat beneath his arm. Nomi, as elegantly formed as a praying mantis, stood beside him, attentive, listening. There was a softness in Les's stance. He looked so vulnerable, though maybe in part it was because he'd shaved his little beard.

He seemed offended when I asked if he was going out with Nomi.

"She's my teacher," he said solemnly. "We're doing a private. I'm learning how to breathe."

"You didn't know how to breathe before?"

"Not in a healthful way."

"She's very pretty," I said.

He bristled. "I don't think of her that way. She's a wonderful person. Very wise. Look what she's done against all the odds, starting this beautiful school with all these classes? It was just voted best yoga studio in the city, not that she cares about these things. I'm just saying she's a remarkable woman."

I spent that Sunday working on a tiny lobster trap, an exact replica of the real thing, with coated metal sides and a mesh opening designed in such a way that the lobster is enticed to enter and then can never leave. It was a birthday gift for Les, whose greatest fear was that he'd take some woman's bait and get stuck forever in her house. It was so easy to chuckle at other peoples' fears and call them irrational. Just do it! I wanted to tell Les, in this time when I was living with such heaviness. Just ask her out!

To grow, a lobster must shed its entire exoskeleton. Beneath that carapace is a soft, vulnerable body. In the period before a new shell grows, when it is completely unprotected, it tries to hide beneath a ledge.

As for the untranslated files, every morning for the next month, I picked them up when I left for work and threw them in the back seat of the car. At the end of each day, I carried them back into my house. In the morning, I scooped them off the hall table and took them to work, threw them in the back of the car.

"Not this year," I told Mindy when she asked me about Thanksgiving.

When I tried to explain why I wouldn't drive to her house this year, though I always spent the holiday with her family, she said, "Oh, come on; the kids want to see you. And Mr. Suppowitz will be up from Florida."

This was a joke we shared. While Mindy's mother had always been "Muriel" to me, her father, a paunchy, introverted engineer, with an immaculate workshop in the basement, remained "Mr. Suppowitz." Three years ago, after he'd been widowed, he'd moved to West Palm Beach, met Doris in Century Village and reinvented himself so thoroughly he became Mr. Suppowitz to Mindy, too. It didn't pain her that he'd taken up with Doris, a nice enough woman.

Rather that he'd forgotten everything about their family life. "Gone," she'd said. "Irretrievable. And it's not dementia. The man is as sharp as ever."

"You don't want me at your table," I said, as if I were a nasty microbe.

"Rox," she said. "I always want you at my table."

"Not this year," I said. I was too much of a gloomster, unable to imagine going back to Chaverim, and yet tormented to think of Aviva living out her days with no family member looking out for her.

"You could round up people to visit her," Mindy said. "If you got six volunteers, and each person went twice a year, someone would be seeing Aviva once a month. People do these things, you know."

People like Mindy, who had a busy private practice, taught a course at the university, drove to the nursing home once a week to visit Stu's mother, brought food to an ailing neighbor. At her Thanksgiving table would be cranky in-laws and aged aunts with a greater number of dietary restrictions than I had friends. Because she lived this way, and caring for others was an essential, if exhausting, part of her life, she saw the world as full of others who did the same.

"I don't know that I could impose," I said.

"Maybe you wouldn't be imposing. For some people, helping out fills a need. They do it because they want to. You just have to ask. If you don't, you'll never know who might want to lend a hand."

When I hung up the phone I made a list. I put *Ronit* on top.

I crossed out her name.

Next I wrote *Dina*.

The dental surgeon she'd been seeing had taken Dina to meet his ancient Hungarian mother who lived not far from Chaverim. Mama complained about the man's former wife all through dinner, and at the end of the meal, when Dina excused herself from the table, Mama began to shout: "WHY DID YOU BRING THAT *SCHVARTZA* HERE?" Later, Mama escorted them to the double bed she'd made up then settled herself with a newspaper right outside their door.

I crossed out *Dina*.

It felt strange to put Baruch on my list, since he was already visiting my sister.

His card was still propped against the lamp on my desk. In the corner was his email address. I could see him when he said: "It's a different country." His blue eyes, full of sadness and irony. "You don't know the language, can't find your way around."

I wrote *Dear Baruch*, and deleted it. (Dear was so arcane!) *Shalom*, I wrote. It struck me as pretentious. I worked my way through *hello* and *hi* and *hola!* and *buenos días*, and *Baruch* and *remember me?* and *a belated thanks.* I tried *Greetings from Pittsburgh*, and *I hope this day finds you well.* If a day could find anything, I'd ask it to locate my slippers.

Hello, Baruch, I wrote at last. *How is Aviva? Have you seen her? I hope you're well and still enjoying your visits.*

I signed it *Roxanne/Vered.*

Pressing send was like pressing on the *okay* veneer, and I could feel the roiling layer of emotion beneath this jolly *okay.*

She is splendid, he wrote in return.

∿

All right, I'll go already.

This was my pretend attitude when I agreed to join Mindy's family for Thanksgiving. Really, I was afraid I'd be unpresentable. A downer, a dud. To work against that, I insisted on bringing several contributions: a favorite Rioja, dark chocolate, a walnut pate, which I was preparing on Tuesday evening when the phone rang, and a woman said, "You don't know me. My name is Tammy Schmidt, an old friend of Harley's. I don't mean to intrude, but I'm worried about Harley."

I'd never heard her name, didn't know that Harley had friends; though given how secretive he was, she could have been the mother of their infant son. Nothing would have surprised me.

"Harley's been talking a lot about killing himself. Every conversation it comes up. Maybe it's just talk, but I've always been told that when someone starts talking suicide, you should never brush it off. Nothing lifts his spirits. Not even when I ask about the boys. I worry that he's isolating. That he's started to drink. If I wasn't so alarmed, I wouldn't be calling you. Believe me, I'm not that kind of person."

"Is he seeing someone?" I could not guess her age or relationship to Harley. "Professionally."

"If he is, I don't think it's helping. That's why I'm reaching out to you, as his friend. Someone who cares about him. I was hoping you'd give him a call."

"Calling him would be a bad idea. A terrible idea."

"Just to help him over the hump."

"You don't understand." Just then it seemed as if I'd spent my whole life explaining, outlining, defending, justifying. It made me feel like an arcane piece of equipment no one knew how to use. "If I call him, he'll start believing we're getting back together again."

"He knows it's over. He isn't bitter about it either."

"He *doesn't* know. He's still calling me all the time. What about Byron? Or one of his sons?"

"Are you crazy? He'd never forgive me if I did that. Please. He speaks *so* highly of you. He's always telling me what a good person you are. Please help. I don't know what to do."

Mindy's voice was one of many in my head, the most benevolent for sure. *Don't answer his calls no matter what*, I heard her tell me. *It gives him hope, keeps him going.*

"I've been advised not to call him."

"You've been *advised*? He's threatening to kill himself and you're not going to call him because you've been advised? Oh. My. God," she said. "You *are* heartless." Then she hung up.

Heartless. I was heartless. My greatest fear articulated by this woman I'd never met.

In the courtroom in my head, where in off-hours I prosecuted myself, I brought out evidence in support of her allegation:

Exhibit A: the half-page ad from Smile Train in the back section of a magazine. Winsome big-eyed babies, their lower faces split in two. Ladies and gentlemen, Roxanne Garlick looked; she saw. But did she give money? She did not.

And further back: the big, handsome girl from my neighborhood I tormented in third grade. She was twice my size, a star student, so energetic in her desire to call out the answers in class that when her hand shot up, it lifted her whole body from the seat of the chair. Was this why I threatened to beat her up?

In seventh grade, two popular girls confronted me in the hall. "Is your father a math teacher at Solomon Schechter?"

"No."

"Then how come he smells of garlic like you?" said one. "'*Jzzoseph*, it is simple—*kh kh kh*,'"said her friend, as if my father's phlegm was in her throat.

I laughed to support my lie. Laughed at my own father.

I did not mock the children in the special-ed classes. I gave them a wide berth, as if they carried germs. Held my breath, did not think of them as human. I held my breath when mention was made of "Jesus" or "Christ" in the Christmas carols sung in school. (Fear, not heartlessness, I suppose.) And when the spastic boy got on our school bus, I stopped breathing until he was past my row. I remember a frigid January morning, shivering in my winter coat, the heaters blasting beneath the hard seats, scorching my legs but failing to radiate upward, the floor wet from the slush we'd tracked in, and this boy with his loose-limbed gait, arms grasping the metal seatbacks, legs that seemed to have extra joints, as he worked his way to the back of the bus, a journey that took so long I nearly passed out.

I was still that way, I thought, recalling the pale, skinny girl I often saw in our building, with a mass of auburn curls and big discolored teeth.

And now: Aviva's medical records tossed into the back of my car. Harley threatening suicide. Any way I turned I would be heartless. For refusing to call him—how could anyone be so cruel? For calling and giving him hope, "keeping him warm."

Harley's son Yanni lived with his girlfriend Julia in her parents' condo on a golf resort in Myrtle Beach. I dreaded calling him. When I finished tidying up the kitchen, I counted the reasons why.

There was the phone, which I hated.

And Yanni, who probably hated me.

Maybe no one called him "Yanni" anymore.

It made me sad. I didn't want to call.

My concern for Harley was greater. Or maybe it was the guilt I'd feel if he hurt himself.

After two rings I heard his familiar boyish voice.

"Hi, Yanni, it's Roxanne."

"Hey." His voice was toneless, as if we'd spoken an hour before.

"How are you?"

It was noisy wherever he was—blaring music, a shriek of laughter. Either he was in a room with a hundred people or the TV was turned up loud.

"I'm good."

"How's Julia?"

"She's good."

Exactly his words years back when I'd ask if he wanted something to eat. *I'm good.* A sandwich? *I'm good.* A glass of milk? *I'm good.*

Affection and regret welled in my chest.

I had wanted to be someone for Harley's sons, had believed if I were patient, it would happen. I could wait. I understood they were boys and not all touchy-feely, and also loyal to their mother. I'd tried to engage them in conversation, to win them over with home-cooked meals when these young men had no experience of sitting at a dinner table with their elders and preferred ordering pizza and scarfing it down from the box. After these mistakes, I downgraded my expectations and hoped they would tolerate me. Later, I downgraded another notch and wished for eye contact.

"Your father's friend Tammy called today to tell me your dad was having some problems. She said he sounded really depressed. She's worried he might do something to himself."

I listened to the party noises. "Are you there?" I asked.

"Yea," he said, as if casting a vote.

"Could you talk to him? I think it would help."

There was a siren, definitely not on TV. I waited. In the old days, I was always rambling on nervously, offering food or entertainment.

They'd look at me blankly, Harley's sons. *No, I'm good.* Never rude. No sons of Harley could be rude. Yanni, who'd rolled out of his frat house with all his frat boy ways intact, knew enough to position the knife and fork in the finished position when he was done eating. He might puke in a girl's bathtub, but he knew how to hold the door for her when they entered a room and shake hands with her dad.

"What do you say? Could you talk to him please? Let him know you care about him?"

"Isn't that part of your job description?" he said at last.

"The problem is I've resigned from that job."

Another long silence. In the background, shots, breaking glass, a screaming woman. Definitely TV.

"We don't live together. You know that, don't you?"

He didn't. It made me want to take back my words, expunge this phone call from his memory.

"You're in touch, though, right? I mean, he calls you, doesn't he?"

"Only like twenty times a night."

"And you don't talk?"

Silence.

"Okay then. Listen. I'm concerned. I don't want anything to happen to him. He's a good person."

"Really? I'm still waiting for those Penguins tickets he promised."

I couldn't tell if he was kidding. "Yanni. He's your father. I need to hear you promise you'll call him."

A long time passed before he said, "Ah, right."

That night I dreamt I was in a vast expanse of ocean. In the dream the water is like a mirror, flat and glistening. Skyscrapers rise from a distant point of land that I recognize as the Battery, in New York. Hannah is with me. She's afraid and begins to cry, and I experience how small I am in this flat smooth water, with only my fluttering arms to keep me from sinking. "I can't swim," Hannah cries, and though I know I am not strong enough to tow her to safety, I tell her not to worry. "I can save you," I say. There is no way I can get her to land, and yet in this dream, I know I will.

EIGHTEEN

Mindy's house was packed with guests when I arrived. Everyone was there except Mr. Suppowitz. In the kitchen, the women were snapping beans and washing lettuce. Mindy's aunt was arguing with the gravy maker who did not want to use the turkey bastings. In the family room, a football game was on a huge TV and the men were on couches and chairs, pecking away on their laptops, looking at spreadsheets and email. I picked up the remote, heard Mindy's aunt say, "I'm telling you, without fat, it will have no taste whatsoever."

"Anyone mind if I shut this off?" I asked.

The men snapped to attention. "Just kidding," I assured them.

I started downstairs to the finished basement to stow my overnight bag and heard two of Mindy's kids quarreling in a good-natured way. *You're such an asshole; oh fuck off, loser.* They desisted as soon as they saw me in the doorway. Hannah greeted me with a hug; her brother Adam accepted a kiss on his cheek.

I could not imagine having children this old; the sadness, when it rose, was for babies. I perched on the edge of the bed to ask Hannah how she was doing and the dream returned, that glassy water, the certainty that I could rescue Hannah.

She had made a deal with her parents and was living at home and working at Rutgers until the summer, when she would work on an organic farm with a friend in Chile or Peru. When I asked her how she was doing she said, "Living here..." Adam finished her sentence. "Sucks."

Hannah punched his arm and told me about her job at Rutgers. "It's kind of a nothing administrative assistant job, but it's in Philosophy and the grad students are great. I'm learning *so* much more than I ever did in my classes."

"Philosophy! Really?" I was excited. "Maybe you can help me find the true purpose of my life."

"No one talks about the meaning of life," Hannah said. "At all."

I feigned disappointment, though beneath the mock surprise, I realized I still believed there was an answer, a single one-lane road that would lead me to, not paradise, exactly, but some settled place.

A gorgeous holiday smell wafted upstairs. I excused myself and joined the women in the kitchen. The counters were covered in dishes—stuffing, sweet potatoes, brussels sprouts—and one of Mindy's cousins was saying, "Lemon zest on everything. That's my secret!" so I took the microplane and two lemons. In the family room, a huge cheer was followed by a groan, and Mindy appeared while I was grating the rind onto waxed paper. Usually unflappable, she said, "*Now* he tells me the daughter is coming? Adam? I need another chair."

She left. Distracted, I shaved the skin off my knuckle and while I was pulling off a sheet of paper towel, an elderly woman said, "And who is this?" Her thin hair was golden and her formidable bosom was packed inside the jacket of a Chanel suit.

"I'm Mindy's friend," I said, wrapping the paper towels around my bleeding knuckle. "From way back." The blood kept seeping through. "We've known each other forever." I pulled off another sheet of towel and the woman snapped her fingers. "What's that line about old friends being like gold?"

"Make new friends but keep the old..."

"That's right." Satisfied, she walked off. I picked the bloody gratings from the pale mound of zest and went back to work.

A decision was made to serve dinner before Mr. Suppowitz and his crew arrived. Mindy hustled everyone to the table and Hannah stood on a chair in the doorway. Glasses were raised and toasts were made, and she snapped photos until I talked her down, because I was the one who should have been taking pictures of this family. I was Mindy's friend and had known her *forever*, but in this picture, years from now, I would be *unidentified on left*. "Get in there," I told Hannah, reaching for the camera.

As I stood on the chair, I felt my sister inside me, and my mother, far away. On this holiday, which I had been invited to share, I felt the ways I'd been shaped by each of them. I loved these people. Why hadn't I doted on the kids and made myself an auntie, instead of standing to the side, ironic, elusive, reserved, that stance masking and reining in a desire to be with them always.

Two hours later Mindy's father arrived with his silver-haired girlfriend, both of them sporty and cheerful in fancy jeans, leather jackets, black boots, so much more youthful in demeanor than the woman's middle-aged daughter tagging along, with her stiff hairdo and her doughy, disappointed face.

When they settled into chairs at the empty table, Mindy said, "Dad, you remember Roxanne."

"Oh, *sure*," he said. "Nice to see you."

I was part of his forgotten life: He did not remember me at all.

Mindy raced off to the kitchen, and I said, "You brought me to Beach Haven for a week one summer."

Every afternoon he'd taken us into the ocean. Out beyond the breakers he roughhoused with Mindy, picking her up, whirling her around, pretending to throw her into the waves. I bobbed beside them, watched her climb onto his back, desperately wanting him to play that way with me, unable to ask. Mr. Suppowitz saw and hesitated. I was not his little girl. Maybe he was afraid it would be inappropriate to pick me up and whirl me around. Or maybe my raw need scared him. Then one day he relented, said, "You want a ride too?" then lifted and spun me in one quick loop.

Now, in an absent way, he said, "Right! Beach Haven. We sure had some good times back then."

The disgruntled daughter poked her index finger into the sweet potatoes and said, "These are like *ice*." Mindy took her plate back to the kitchen.

"Mindy tells me you were just in Israel," said Mr. Suppowitz's girlfriend. "Business or pleasure?"

"I have family there."

"Are they all right? It's such a shame, all those bombings. Marv and I were supposed to go last spring. The tour company swore up and down it was perfectly safe, but then you read in the paper about these fanatics blowing themselves up, even the women, and to be honest, I didn't see the point. So we're going to Prague."

"My mother lives in Tel Aviv," I said. "So does my twin sister." I hesitated, unsure how to describe Aviva or the place she lived. Something had shifted within me when I'd stood on that chair, snapping photos of this family I loved. Maybe it was seeing my connection to them and also the distance I'd kept. Or maybe Mr. Suppowitz's forgetting had pricked me, making me aware how easily the past could be dismissed. Or maybe it was the second glass of wine. "She's profoundly disabled and lives in a 'home for life' in the Galilee."

Mindy turned to me. The disgruntled daughter said, "Your sister is institutionalized?"

"It's not an institution, where she lives. It's beautiful. Before I went up there, I thought it would be a hellish place, a snake pit, and she'd be sitting in the dark, or stuck in bed." *My sister.* The heat rose in my cheeks. "Her days are full of activities." What a tender wound. I inhaled slowly.

"Huh," said the daughter, chewing.

She wasn't buying my description, so I went on, telling her about the images projected on the ceilings for all the residents positioned in such a way that their gaze was directed upwards, and the board beside the elevator, with textured panels glued to it, so during the wait, residents in wheelchairs could feel feathers and gravel and rubbery knobs. As I continued, I realized I'd seen aspects of Chaverim I hardly realized I'd absorbed. And still the woman seemed perturbed.

"I'm sure it's very beautiful."

Her tone put me on edge.

"Yes," I said, expecting a political objection. *Are Palestinians there too? Why not?* I didn't know the answer and said, "It really is."

"Be that as it may, it's still a step backwards."

"Why is that?"

"I'm sure I don't need to tell you all the years it took, all the effort from lawyers and family members, to get disabled individuals out of institutions and into their communities. It's been one of the great civil rights struggles of the twentieth century."

Mindy stepped behind me and rested her hands on my shoulders. "Rox didn't even know about Aviva until a few months ago. She didn't know she was a twin."

"A twin! Imagine that," said Doris.

Her disgruntled daughter eyed her. "I'm just saying there's no such thing as separate but equal. We all agree on that, don't we?"

I was the one who broke the uncomfortable silence. "Obviously."

"Can I get a cup of coffee, hon?" the daughter asked Mindy.

I excused myself and sat in the family room, where the TV blared on and the men once again were pecking away on their devices. Still stuffed from dinner, I reached for a bowl of mixed nuts and searched absently for broken cashews, as if to satisfy some primitive gathering instinct. I felt foolish and ignorant and angry with myself for having done such a poor job describing Chaverim. I should have told her about the concert by a visiting chamber music ensemble. I should have mentioned the new greenhouse, with its warm, earthy odors, and the fundraising plans for therapeutic horseback riding. Hardly an institution with doped-up inmates stuck in wards. I pushed the bowl of nuts across the table.

Mr. Suppowitz poked in his head, and seeing that Stu had vacated the lounge chair, rubbed his hands together in a gleeful way, settling in with a long, satisfied sigh, adjusting the level until he was perfectly positioned for a dental procedure. I thought of the images projected onto the ceiling in the music room at Chaverim, animals and birds that seemed to be part of an endless parade.

"Beach Haven," he said to the ceiling. "Yep."

The TV was tuned to ESPN, and footage was from a game that had been televised earlier in the day. Life on the huge screen was brighter and crisper than anything I'd ever seen.

"When I was a kid, being with your family was the best part of my life," I said. "I adored Muriel. She was so loving toward me." Like silk, she'd murmured, stroking my hair when I curled beside her.

"Ah, those were the days," said Mr. Suppowitz, with a long, musical sigh.

I'd visited Muriel shortly before she died. She'd been tethered to oxygen and could hardly get enough air to form her words. "Come. Sit down," she managed. "Tell me about your life."

I was married then, deeply in love, so unhappy.

"He treats you well?"

"Yes," I had lied, unable to tell her otherwise.

The couch rocked like a small boat as the disgruntled daughter settled herself beside me. "I missed your name," she said.

"Roxanne."

"Roxanne. Sue." She dragged the bowl of nuts toward us and grabbed a handful. "I've been a social worker for nearly thirty years, so I've seen firsthand what it's like when individuals get to live in their community."

"My sister has no community. My parents gave her up when she was a baby."

"That's not so uncommon. Many individuals have stories like that. Generations of individuals who never had the benefit of family life."

Individuals. Such a bureaucratic word, a social worker word, on the ugly list with *utilize* and *fungible*. Everything clenched inside me. What's wrong with *people*? I wanted to ask.

"You don't think she'd enjoy living in a neighborhood?"

"I have no idea," I said.

She popped the nuts into her mouth one at a time. "What's her functional level?"

"I don't know. Her medical records are in Hebrew."

"Is she verbal?"

"She's brain damaged and in a wheelchair. She doesn't speak. She doesn't do anything. Not by herself, at least."

"They don't do assessments in this place? They must."

"Maybe they do. I assume I'll find them when I get the records translated. I just haven't done that yet."

"So you don't *know* if she's had access to any kind of adaptive communication device?"

"I'll have to ask."

"First you need to make sure this facility does proper assessments, because these days, with the technology now available, the lives of so many individuals with communication disorders have been completely transformed. This one gentleman, Charlie, we moved several years back? Long history of institutionalization, where he was more or less shunted into a corner and dismissed as too low-functioning to profit from any training. No contact with the family. Transferred to an ICFMR when they shut the facility down. Then while we were looking for a placement for him in the community, we arranged for a proper assessment. Long story short: this young speech pathologist, a real determined gal, started working with Charlie. At first it was something simple, like a picture communicator, yes and no and some pictures of familiar objects and places. Food items. He really took off on it. We started to learn a whole lot more about our Charlie. He likes girls *a lot*. Chicken nuggets. Country music. He's got a *major* thing for Shania Twain. He's saving to go to Vegas."

She continued depositing nuts in her mouth, like coins in a meter.

"She's not shunted into a corner."

She—Aviva. Would I ever say her name without sorrow rising within me?

Sue looked at her salty hands, as if she didn't know exactly whose they were. "I was just saying, since Mindy told me your background."

"I think," I said, hoisting myself up from the couch. "I think I need to make myself useful."

I found Hannah in the kitchen. While she was emptying the dishwasher, I donned the yellow rubber gloves, got to work on the turkey pan. I worked the steel wool into the baked-in grease in each corner and listened to Hannah explain that she and her friend would be "woofing" in Chile—"woofing," what volunteers did when they were matched up with farmers through WWOOF, which she thought stood for "Willing Workers on Organic Farms." The old aunties came in to say goodbye. Then Adam and Stu wandered in, looking for drumsticks to gnaw, and praising the Steelers, as if I had a role in coaching the team. After that, the waves of conversation in different parts of the house grew softer, the TV was switched off, the rooms darkened.

I went downstairs to the finished basement where I'd sleep, sat on the old plaid couch, and waited for three a.m.—ten in Israel. On the half-empty bookshelves were paperback spy novels, old psychology texts, and a well-thumbed book called *Jokes for Your John*. Next to it was *More Jokes for Your John*. The jokes did not distract me from Charlie and Aviva, the enormity of what I did not know, and a desire for answers that was so fierce that I called Chaverim before I'd figured out what to say.

"A woman, a social worker, told me about a man." This is how I began when Mrs. Silk got on the line. "Everyone thought there was nothing inside him but they gave him this device. And now he can tell them who he is. He can say what he likes. It's like he's a person with opinions and dreams."

The story poured out of me, with its gaps and digressions. *Someone told me something and now I'm upset.* I was too agitated to be embarrassed.

I wanted Mrs. Silk to say, "Don't worry. Aviva is not Charlie," because I could not bear to think she had been locked in darkness for all these years, a thrumming, unexpressed self trapped inside her. It was too awful to think of her crying out in the dark and finding herself alone. Or worse, learning not to cry. *She is not Charlie. Please say she is not.* Just as fervently I wanted to hear that Aviva was someone, a real sister, just as I had pretended when I was young, whispering to my doll, lying to my classmates. Someone who could know me, who could share this puzzling life.

"The newer technology is marvelous," Mrs. Silk said. "Some of our residents have done very well with assistive communication devices."

"And Aviva? Could she profit from something like that?"

"I'm afraid not."

Mrs. Silk tried to explain the ways Aviva's brain had been damaged, but I was not relieved and I kept pushing. "Are you sure? How do you know? How can you tell what's inside her? Have you done any assessments?"

"Yes, of course. On a regular basis." Then without a glimmer of impatience: "Have you had the chance to look at the sensory checklist?"

"I have the name of a translator, but I've been really busy."

It was such a lame excuse I wished she would call me out. *Busy —give me a break!* But she would not do this because Mrs. Silk did not judge family members, even those who practically begged to be judged.

"Let me know when you're ready. We'll set up a time to go over Aviva's records, page by page. I can clarify whatever you don't understand. The medical terminology and technical language can be quite dense."

"I'm sorry to be so annoying," I said.

"You aren't annoying. It's natural for you to have questions. You're just getting to know us. You're just getting to know Aviva."

"I'm *not* getting to know her. I live thousands of miles away and I don't know how. I don't even know what it means to know her. Is it something I could learn? Seeing her was excruciating," I said, unable to hold back. "I understand why people turn away, but I can't. I've been trying, but I can't. I guess I don't want to."

Sitting on the edge of a foldout bed in that recreation room in New Jersey, I felt the weight of my own words. "She's my sister. I don't know what that means or why it matters, but it does."

"Why don't you start by reading the checklist. It might help make your visits more rewarding. I can't promise this, but I know your father enjoyed visiting Aviva."

"Then why did my cousin tell me how much he cried?"

"Leaving was very difficult for him. That he lived so far away. And all the secrets were a terrible torment. Even so, he got a great deal of pleasure from these visits."

"More than he got living with me," I said.

"No," she said with conviction. "That isn't so, Roxanne."

"How do you know?" I asked.

"Because I came to know your father very well over the years, and I knew how proud of you he was and how he ached for you, because he told me often."

I waited for her to go on, hardly breathing, and when she spoke again, it was as if a different person was on the other end, someone formal, who was encouraging me to call whenever I wanted, with any questions I might have, who assured me that the staff at Chaverim welcomed the involvement of family members.

When I got off the phone, I paced in the dank room, waiting for the sun to rise, then made myself wait a while longer.

The translator answered his phone. We made a date to meet in the back of the Coffee Tree in Squirrel Hill on Monday morning.

How would I know him?

"You'll know," he said.

Everyone was in the kitchen by the time I rose from the basement, toting my overnight bag. Hannah, in oversize plaid pajamas, was leafing absently through *Consumer Reports*, while Adam and Stu once again gnawed on turkey parts. Mindy, putting away the last of the serving dishes, demanded I eat *something* before the long drive home

While I sat with the others, Aviva, Charlie, and the untranslated documents expanded in my brain in such a way that I had no words to add to the easy conversation around me, no thoughts or opinions. Stuffed with the unspeakable, I thought.

What a lot of effort it took to squelch what I could not say. Is this what my father had done, distancing himself from those who could have loved him, withholding his truest feelings, blotting out himself? Is this what I had done too?

Mr. Suppowitz and his crew arrived and I started on my round of goodbyes. I slipped on my coat and Max, their old dog, hustled over with his leash. "I'm sorry, boy," I told him.

Baruch would have laughed if he'd seen my crouching before the dog, murmuring into his fur. "Sorry, boy. Sorry, sorry."

NINETEEN

The translator was right: On Monday morning, I walked right over to the pudgy young man in a small knitted yarmulke who sat alone at the back of the coffee shop. I said hello, placed Aviva's file on the table, and settled into the empty chair. He hefted the envelope, as if he charged by the pound. "So," he said. "You've brought me *War and Peace.*"

Such long, thick eyelashes. Like Aviva's. "It's not literature," I said. "I don't care about beautiful. Accurate is what I need."

The translator, raised in Philadelphia and Jerusalem, was in Pittsburgh while his wife was finishing her PhD. She was a happiness researcher.

"Is she happy?" I asked, though I suspected it was a tiresome question.

"She is studying too hard."

"Maybe after she gets her PhD?"

"She would say no. The PhD will only bring her transient happiness."

The translator picked up the envelope and bounced it in his palms. "So it's not a book of poems. Then what?"

"Medical records." I thought of Disgruntled Sue, going on about assessments, and said, "Assessments. A sensory checklist. And something else." Mrs. Silk's words came back. *Some of what you read will be disturbing.* "Something I shouldn't read alone."

I hadn't intended to say this, but the translator had that gift of benign stillness that drew me close, and I went on. "I was in Israel this fall and found out I had a disabled twin sister. I think this is her story, in a way, and after I read it, I'll understand her better."

And if she was a husk, a shell, with no soul, no awareness? How then would I build the next part of my life, now that I woke every morning and felt her inside me?

The wet, boundless grief rose. I pressed on my chest, and the translator hurriedly uncrumpled a napkin, trying to flatten it on the table before sliding it to me. "It's clean," he said.

I caught my breath and let myself be distracted by a woman who joined the man at the table beside ours. Forties, maybe. Long dark hair and dimples, fitted wool dress. A first date, or second. Then I returned to business. "There's so much here. Maybe you can skip the unnecessary sections and translate what's important."

"You want *me* to make that decision?" he asked.

"No," I said. "I guess I don't."

The translator asked when I expected the work to be finished.

"How about around Christmas. Do you go away for Christmas?" He tapped his yarmulke.

"What do I know? Maybe you're a Jew for Jesus," I said.

His eyes widened. He said, "Heaven forfend," and then informed me that Christmas was much too soon.

I felt light without those files and glided across the lobby of the lime-green schoolhouse, thinking about the couple at the next table, and remembering a time when men were like flies, always buzzing around me. How tempting to say it was my youth alone that had attracted them, but that wasn't the only thing. I was open, in those days, fearless, receptive, ready for a romp. I felt a yearning just then to unseal my lips, exhale all the unspeakable stuff, to lean across a small table and feel the flush of attraction. Yes, a date, I thought, so immersed in this vision that I did not see Harley slide into view from behind a column, dressed in a crisp shirt and gray crew-neck sweater, wool slacks, tie shoes. I hesitated then continued on. Harley blocked my path. His face was red and swollen. I stepped; he blocked, arms spread wide.

"Why would you call my son and humiliate me that way? Why? Didn't I look after you always? Didn't I love and respect you? Why would you repay me by ruining my relationship with my kids?"

The mail carrier stopped wheeling her cart to watch him block me at the base of the stairs. "You know what you've done? You've proven their mother right, given them an excuse to wash their hands of me. I can't even face my own kids, and I don't understand. When did you get so mean?"

"Come on, Harley. Please." I stepped to the side. He stepped with me. "You were talking about suicide. I was worried about you. And so was Tammy."

"Tammy is a stupid, nebby bitch."

"Whatever she is, she was trying to act responsibly, and so was I."

What seemed true before now felt like a sign that I lacked the milk of human kindness. *He's threatening to kill himself and you're not going to call him because you've been advised?* "Get some help, Harley. People struggle. They have bad patches. The world has changed. No one's going to think you're a wuss."

A pair of Nomi's yoga students with their rolled-up mats worked their way around us. Harley began to weep. His despair was so raw. I tried not to let it pierce me. "We weren't even *together* all that long. Check your calendar. We spent way more time breaking up than we ever spent being an actual couple. You need to accept that it's over and move on."

I lowered my head as if Les might not notice me on the way upstairs.

"I have accepted it. I live with it every day. What I don't understand is why you can't just talk to me once a week. You're the only friend I have. Please. Once a week. If I abuse the privilege, I swear you can cut me off."

I didn't want to call Harley. I wanted him to go away. Now, though, this fierce, futile desire for Harley to vanish brought to mind my untended mother and sister.

Then Mindy's voice, louder and more loving: *don't engage with him.*

"I can't, Harley. It doesn't work. It never has."

"I'm seeing a counselor. I've done everything you've asked. How about cutting me a break? Talking to me *once* a week. Would it kill you to take my call for five minutes once a week? Can you do that as a friend? Is that too much to ask?"

No, I thought. "Yes," I managed to say.

"Just tell me one thing: What have I done to deserve this?"

He dug into his pocket for a hankie. I raced upstairs.

Les swiveled slowly in his chair when I walked into the office.

"Am I mean? Tell me the truth, because I haven't been leading him on."

"You're a pushover, Rox."

"Really? I haven't talked to him, haven't taken his messages." I collapsed in my chair.

"Why didn't you just walk past him instead of stopping?"

"And you could do that after someone threatens suicide? Really?"

"He's playing you," Les said. "You can see it a mile away."

I thought of Harley, weeping in the lobby. Maybe he was playing me, but his despair was deep and real. "I called his son. That's why he's upset. But I'm still worried. Harley won't be honest with Yanni. His kids have no idea what he's really like. Maybe I should take his calls." I shrugged off my jacket. "If I do, the whole thing will start up again, but if I don't he really could do something terrible to himself."

"And you have the power to prevent him from hurting himself? No. You don't. And it's not your job. It's a job for a mental health professional."

The phone rang. We turned in unison, and listened to Kayleigh say, "Intelligent Designzzzzz."

Les said, "If you really want to be done with him, you know what you need to do?"

"Yes. I'm supposed to cut his underwear into squares and set his car on fire."

"How about for a start if you just walk on by? There's a lot of pain out there. You can't let all of it in. Sometimes you have to turn away and walk on by."

All day, I heard Dionne Warwick sing, "Walk on By" in that amazing voice, ragged with emotion, and while it was good to have her back with a song I'd thought I'd forgotten, it did not keep me from thinking about Harley *losing it* in the lobby—his expression—all the rules about voice tone and decorum *gone*. Nor did it stop me from wishing someone could give me some guidelines. How much of others' pain did a healthy person absorb? What was too much? What was too little? Why did everyone around me seem to instinctively understand?

☙

Each time I thought about the translator giving me his finished work, I imagined it the same way: We'd meet at the Coffee Tree, he'd slide the folder across the table and leave; I'd begin to read, and the question that had haunted me since Thanksgiving would be answered in these pages. She is Charlie; she is not Charlie. That's all I expected to read.

The sky stayed milky-looking day after day. Snow would have been nice, the kind of serious snow that starts as an inconvenience, and then brings everything to a halt. Snow that forces you to let go of all your plans. We'd had one of these storms not long after I'd moved to the city, and when I went outside on my little street, all my neighbors were there. The men who lived in the houses on either side of me couldn't shovel—bad back, bad heart—so three of us, all women, dug out a single car and shared it for the next few days. Now, though, in this period when Aviva's medical records were in someone else's hands, there was no snow, only the gray sky.

Les grew a beard then shaved it off while I was waiting for the translator. He let the stubble grow back. Shaved again. Left a soul patch, which looked good. I'd never wanted to be a man, never wished for a penis of my own, but the ability to change this way, to have a totally new look each week, was wildly appealing. A redesigned package: the contents *new* and *improved!* An updated Roxanne with a new E-Z opening, sweeter than the old formula. Less salty.

I did not shave my head, dye my hair, get plastic surgery. I called a realtor, though. New residence, different life. This seemed a good way to begin again. The evening she arrived at my house, she thrust a carton into my arms, saying, "Ooh, Saks Fifth Avenue—*someone's* a lucky girl!" I glanced at the box, which was addressed to me, and followed her through my rooms. She praised the assets of my lovely home, counseled me to repaint the walls a neutral color and "de-em-phasize" the contents of the upstairs rooms.

When she left I sliced the tape from the shipping carton, pulled out a satiny box, lifted a silver cashmere sweater nestled in tissue. Then the gift card. *With love from Harley.* I slid the box back into the carton, sealed up the sides, and propped it outside on my steps, hoping a burglar or mischievous kid would steal it. There were thieves around. The wheelbarrow in my yard had been stolen. It's valuable, the cops had explained when I'd reported the theft. Handy to transport stolen goods.

Whoever had swiped the wheelbarrow didn't return for the box. Nor was it taken by neighborhood kids, the mail carrier, the joy killer next door. The box was there when I left for work, and there when I returned.

I signed a contract with this woman and promised to ready the house for the spring market, which improbably began in February. I did not paint the walls. I did not call Harley, who owned the contents that needed to be de-emphasized.

On the first Friday in February, a For Sale sign was pounded into the hard earth outside my house, and the translator emailed; just as I'd imagined, he suggested we meet on Monday evening at six at the Coffee Tree, and when I confirmed, the rest of the scenario played out in my head: the folder pushed across the table, the translator leaving, the answers in the text. She is Charlie; she is not Charlie.

That same afternoon, Les said he was leaving work promptly at five to meet a guru from California, who was holding an introductory workshop in transformative breathing at Nomi's studio. Nomi said he was wonderful, so he'd signed up for the all-day sessions on Saturday and Sunday too.

"Nomi's the one who sounds wonderful," I said.

"She is," said Les, "an inspiration."

I followed him upstairs to catch a glimpse of the guru. The air smelled like burned sage. I perched on a bench beside Les as he took off his boots and his socks. It was strange to see his bare feet with their stubby white toes. After a few minutes the guru appeared from behind a rice paper screen. He looked like a rocker from the 80s— long layered hair, full beard, white T-shirt, drawstring pants. Bare feet—not strange. Nomi was a step behind, short wavy hair framing her pretty face, elongated limbs. Les rose, drawn by a force outside logic, and crossed the studio like a sleepwalker. It was something to see.

Baruch came to mind, sitting beside me, listening. Ridiculous, I thought, and stayed where I was while the others joined the guru, waiting for equilibrium to return.

On the way out of the studio, I heard the toneless voice of the odd girl with auburn curls and discolored teeth, and before I could back off, she pinched me. Her mother peeled the girl's fingers from my arm and said, "I'm Jill, Nomi's sister, and this is Jessie. We've met."

"Of course," I said. "I'm Roxanne from downstairs." I wanted to say Aviva's name, to say, what? *I have a sister who...* "Going home?" said the girl, reaching for me. Her mother stepped between us.

"Yes," I said. "I'm going to skip the breathing and go home."

Charlie, not Charlie, I thought on my way downstairs. It would not be so simple.

On Monday night, a parking spot opened up a few doors down from the Coffee Tree. I locked the car and walked to the café.

The Everything

TWENTY

The translator was sitting at the same square table in the back, tea in a mug, squeezed teabag in a saucer. He watched me unwind my scarf, watched as I unbuttoned my coat, then slid the folder to me, long-lashed eyes briefly meeting mine. There was no small talk this time. I gave him a check and he left.

I was not exactly alone when I unwound the striped string looped between the button closures and withdrew two packets. Two strangers sat nearby—a bundled-up old woman, doing a word search on a folded square of newspaper, and a young man with a laptop and a tower of library books. All of us wanting proximity to other humans, without interaction; reassuring sounds that did not demand our attention. Quiet, but not silence.

The Book of Aviva began with the medical records. My eye went right to "dislocated right hip" as if these words in the middle of the page were in bold. I made myself go back to the first line, to read the sentences in order.

The medical history was scant, with no fleshed-out narrative, only dots I had to connect myself: Full-term delivery without complications. Smaller at birth than a twin sister "of normal health." "Irritability reported" in the first weeks. Hospitalization at six months due to subdural hematoma. Surgery to remove the blood clot." It had been reported that she had a neurogenic dislocated right hip, which happened at time of injury as an infant."

It had been reported.

I looked up to place myself in this coffee shop I knew well, and heard Mrs. Silk's question: did I have someone to sit beside me when I read these papers? These strangers engaged in their own lives were not enough, not then or ever.

Irritability, dislocated right hip.

I closed the file, took in the dark green walls, the framed drawings of coffee cups by a local artist. Jars of biscotti on the counter. Pastries behind glass. I could feel my pounding heart. Ceramic mugs clinked on the tray a barista was carrying into the back; the strip of bells strung on the door tinkled when a man walked in, a gust of frigid air blowing in with him.

Dislocated right hip. Which happened at time of injury as an infant.

I recalled the shadow across Ronit's face when I asked about Aviva. My father's sorrowful breathing. The newspaper photo of the woman who'd grabbed her baby from a high chair and threw her against the wall. My sister, our history, the bitterness of our mother's milk.

Okay, I thought. I closed my eyes, put my hand over the translated pages. It was like pressing down on a powerful force of nature. A force of nature—what my mother had been called at the *festschrift* held in her honor.

It had been reported.

I saw my mother's warning gaze, the arched eyebrow that for so long kept me from knowing anything. There was no *who* in this report, no name or detail. Only my mother saying, "The mother is the villain. It's always the mother's fault."

This mother, whose parents had been taken—violently? While she watched? Who went on a train when she was very young, with the fake passport from a dead Aryan girl. Her mouth stuffed with chocolate so she would not speak, "safety" with cousins she loathed. Had someone in that family harmed her grievously? The father she despised? You learn not to ask. You learn it quickly. The look freezes everything inside you. Sometimes you can change the weather; not always, but sometimes. A dandelion bouquet, a clever caricature you've drawn, a silly song that might charm her, skills that become your armor, your only means. *I beg to disagree!*

But look, now in the coffee shop, waiting for the clamor to die down, who is in your head just now? What's happened to Aviva? Gone, because *her* story, Leona's story—from the time before your birth—extinguishes everything in its killing heat.

It had been reported. By whom?

Something primitive gripped me. Turn the page or Aviva will burrow inside you like a man in a basement. Turn the page or you will never know her, will never understand what knowing her might mean.

I began thumbing through the charts, dated entries, and health reports, until I found the sensory checklist Mrs. Silk had been urging me to read.

It had been designed to help therapists and aides identify the sensory needs of a person who could not directly express her likes and dislikes, could not speak, might be unable to signal what was relaxing, distressing, stimulating. It was long and detailed—134 questions about every activity in a person's day—sleeping, waking, eating, dressing. There were questions to assess Aviva's response to others and to the environment, to movement, to her own body, to sound, smell and light, questions about behaviors that were self-injurious or self-stimulating. Did Aviva resist assistance for feeding? Dislike having her face wiped? Gag or spit out certain foods? Did she resist having her hair washed or her teeth brushed? Is she difficult to rouse, lethargic during the day? Did she strip off clothing, dislike being barefoot? Refuse to touch certain textures, dislike being in groups? Did she withdraw from staff, lick inedible objects, seek having body parts rubbed or touched? Did she gag in response to certain smells, like to listen to music, prefer dim lights? Was she hesitant to move unless holding onto something or someone, become irritable when transported by vehicle, dislike lying on her stomach? Did she like to rock or swing for long periods of time, stare at shiny objects or mouth them? Did she grind her teeth, poke her eyes, pinch her skin, become frustrated easily? Was she hard to calm when upset?

Like me.

A young group arrived, crowding around the tables near the window and filling the space with laughter and conversation.

Sister, I thought. What did that entail? Had she bonded with anyone? With Baruch? With her therapists? Or Shelley, with her warm eyes and soft voice? And if they quit or retired? Would it make a difference to her? Did anything?

All the questions in the checklist were answered with a yes, no, or not applicable, then entered on a worksheet that listed six sensory categories—proprioceptive, tactile, vestibular, auditory, olfactory, visual. The responses were meant to understand in what ways Aviva was oversensitive and in what ways under-sensitive, so an environment could be created in which she was alert and comfortable, with activities that might give her the greatest pleasure. Aviva's immunizations were up to date; her health was stable. She liked the leaf swing, the vibrating snake upon her tray, hydrotherapy, music, movement, and touch.

I was still reading when half the lights were extinguished. It was after ten p.m. I could say, as I gathered my papers, that my sister got sleepy in a dim room and was alert in the greenhouse and in the water with the man named Baruch. I could let myself believe she was living in a place where her caregivers were sensitive to her needs, would know if she cried out in the dark, frightened to find herself alone. If there was something more—a secret love for chicken nuggets and Shania Twain—I could not tell.

I said good night to the barista, who stood by the door, waiting to lock up for the night. The bells tinkled, the lock clicked shut, and I was outside beneath the bare, lit-up trees.

Who would Aviva have been? The question I had never let myself ask now fell from the night air. An artist, a designer? Standing beside the bare trees with their lit-up limbs, I could see a woman, with children and dogs, long hair half gathered with ornaments made of bone, and her voice—I would know it anywhere. And is she a mathematician? That one egg cleaved in the middle, giving her one set of skills and me the other. Even-steven! And we live nearby, talk all the time, and she gets body-word of my mood from miles away, and so do I. *Hey, are you okay? Are you?* We carry tiny bottles of Tabasco to spike our food, love moody subtitled movies and comedies meant for adolescent boys; our laugh is the same. *You two are like twins!*

I got in my car. Could she laugh? The Aviva who lived in Chaverim. Was she able?

When I started the engine, those other words rose. *It had been reported.*

That night, Aviva laughed. In this dream, the first of many to come, we sat at a table, watching chickens peck the dust in the seams of the wooden floor, and her head was thrown back, neck arched, long, rippling hair, and when I woke, all I wanted was to hold onto the dream, as if there was something real in what I'd conjured, fragments from a life we'd shared, and if only I could recall the details I would have something of her always.

•

In the weeks before Dr. Berenbaum called to say my mother was dying, I faced head-on what I had read. I turned away from it, sickened. I thought, something is better than nothing. *Something* is mass, is clay, you can work with it, change its shape, build onto it. I tried to believe this and briefly succeeded; then, felt that what I'd read would rip me in two and did not know how to escape it. Every day it was different.

And still, I called mother every week, just as before, and listened to Sunny coax her to the phone, her tone gentle, playful, firm, and I said, "Hello, Ma? How are you, Mama?" And when Sunny told me she could no longer walk down the single flight of stairs and slept for much of the day, the words vanished, everything I'd read.

Sometimes, cheerfully, I thought of myself as the typically developed sister and narrated all I was able to do: retrieve a newspaper, design a logo, a T-shirt, a poster. The typically developed sister could draw but had never been able to learn by rote. She needed to take information into her cells. To know where her body was in space, she needed to feel the ground beneath her feet.

I'd underlined the words in the medical report I knew but did not fully understand—proprioception, vestibular, cortical, subdural, axonal—and when I set out for my run, I felt the slant of the road, the sun on my eyelids, whistle of an overhead plane, the wheeze and clank of a distant compactor crushing garbage and experienced the way this sensory information from my inner ear, joints, and muscles told me who and where I was.

Aviva did not get and use input from these systems because of damage to her brain; information from the other systems—vision, hearing, touch, taste, smell—was also impacted.

When I climbed the long diagonal path to an upper trail in the park, a memory might emerge—the samovar in Mindy's house; the taste of brass when I licked it, blindfolded, playing a game; the coins stamped onto the sides, Russian words. Running in the park, the metals returned to me: brass, copper, silver, gold, their hue and sheen, the taste of each. I recalled Muriel's husky voice—*tsatskeleh, come!*—her unmade bed, the smell of cigarettes, Mindy and I snuggling beneath the sheets like puppies, then *love*.

Aviva—when I wrote her name in big, blocky print, emotion filled me, like ink drawn into the reservoir of my pen.

Aviva, who walked beside me in my vivid, fractured dreams, sat in my desk chair, wearing nothing beneath her old-fashioned raincoat, who smoked a cigarette, and, oh, I was furious and lunged for it, and when I woke I was upset that I'd been so out of control, and at the same time hated to lose these moments that had felt so real.

I could dream (could she?), could read and write, could conceive of a three-dimensional object and hold that image in my mind, the way I could hold images of the man, Baruch, who sat on the bench beside me. In casual conversation, I could be rueful, ironic, snippy, demanding, flirtatious, droll, doleful, negative. I could allude, pun, digress. I could bring to mind a raccoon, looking up at me in a bold, belligerent way from his hollow in the park, where I had once seen such a creature. Symbols rang in my ears. Metaphors flowed like water.

I had no control over the dreams, but I resisted calling these emotions "Aviva" or "Baruch," and yet, I would not dismiss all this as nothing. This was what Ronit had said of Aviva—*nothing is left*. In this time, *nothing* had been cracked wide open, revealing a world of sensations, of pleasures and unhappiness, textures I'd lacked the sensitivity to understand.

And what of the warmth of his gaze? I could remember it, could feel it, could distrust it, could turn around and doubt my distrust. This typically developed twin was capable of so many high-order functions, and still she did not know. What was real? Who could I be to Aviva? Who had I been to my mother? To Harley?

She doesn't know me, I thought when I got off the phone with my mother.

He doesn't know me, I thought, reading the note Harley had enclosed with the silver sweater.

Maybe for him, I was the ticking clock, wrapped in a blanket.

Maybe for me, he'd been the terrycloth monkey.

When Dr. Berenbaum called, I was standing on my front lawn while prospective buyers wandered through my house with their realtor. The couple's car was on the driveway, and in the driver's seat, their large, anxious dog scratched at the window, as if with enough effort she could dig a hole in it. The kids across the street were hanging an inflatable buck-toothed bunny from the limb of a tree beside the one they'd decorated with Easter egg ornaments.

"Your mother has pneumonia and was taken to the hospital this afternoon," he said.

"How is she now?" I asked.

"At the moment, her condition is stable, but she's quite frail."

I listened to the rest of what he had to say about my mother's health, and then I said, "Do you remember her telling you she had another daughter, and that I'd known nothing about it? She did have another daughter. Her name is Aviva, and she lives in a place in the north called Chaverim. We're twins. If it hadn't been for you, I never would have known."

The dog's scratching grew more furious. She whimpered, drooled on the glass. *Let me out!*

I said, "That's not exactly true. I knew something. Just not that I had a sister. Or her name or the nature of her disabilities, or that my father visited her four times a year and my mother never did."

Dr. Berenbaum interrupted me. "Has your mother made her end-of-life wishes known?"

"Is she dying?"

"She's not actively dying, but she doesn't have long. You shouldn't delay your visit."

"No feeding tubes. No breathing tubes." The words were harder to speak than I had imagined. "I'm sure she wouldn't want that."

"Then I will continue with the antibiotics?"

"Yes, but no machines. No heroic measures."

"And I'll arrange for hospice to come to her apartment?"

"Yes," I said.

Then Dr. Berenbaum said, "Our attitudes have evolved considerably since the days when your sister was born. Your mother might very well have been following the advice of a doctor who told her to forget this child was ever born. This is the way it was done at the time. Parents with children like your sister were told to give them up for the sake of the family. There was a great deal of pressure put on mothers to do this."

"I know," I said. "But still..."

"Would you like me to have a *shomer* stay with your mother?" he asked.

Having a *shomer* in attendance when the soul departed the body was a custom among Orthodox Jews, he explained. Though he knew my mother wasn't religious, it wasn't uncommon for a person facing death or members of the family to have a change of heart. Being a *shomer,* a guard, was considered a mitzvah, so it would be no trouble finding someone to sit with her in these final hours to be sure she was not alone when she died. What did I think she might want?

The soul? I imagined my mother saying, "What you call the soul is billions of neurons firing."

"Have a *shomer* stay with her," I said.

The realtor walked outside, followed by the young couple—a giant, pregnant blonde in spike-heeled boots, her dark doe-eyed husband. After they pulled away, the little girl across the street hurried across the road, uncertain in fancy flip-flops. "It's going to snow," she said accusingly. She put her hand on her hips, and big, beaded bracelets clanked on her skinny wrists. "Are you *moving?*"

"Maybe not," I said.

"Then why do you have that sign?"

"I thought I would, but maybe I won't after all. Who told you it was going to snow?"

"It just *is*," she said.

No travel advisories were posted when I went online. I booked a flight to Newark that left late the next morning, and from there a connection to Ben Gurion Airport. As I threw some clothing into a bag, I wondered if I would flourish after my mother died, released at last, or crumple, as if my tormented relationship with her gave me the friction I needed, the spark that lit my fire. I took Baruch's business card off my desk, though I did not know if I'd call him after all this time. But Aviva—the desire to see her bloomed.

Branches from the giant ginkgo scratched my upstairs windows. When I finished packing, I stepped outside. The snow flurries were like dryer lint. Nothing stuck. But the wind had picked up. The buck-toothed bunny was blown upward, as if he were riding a magic carpet.

All night it snowed, and by morning I had to shovel the driveway so I could pull out my car. The magnolia had been stripped bare, and my neighbor's inflatable bunny had blown onto their driveway. I felt offended by the snow. Why now, of all times? The season was over. *Look, the flowers are out. You're wrecking them!* Who was I talking to?

Each time I checked, my flight was listed as "on time" so I set out for the airport. Now the snow was falling in thick diagonal sheets. Only a few cars were on the roads, fools, hardy souls, crawling forward, all of us. I knew it was pointless to drive to the airport and drove anyway, staying in the right lane, clutching the wheel. It was pointless to get a ticket for long-term parking: I got a ticket, parked in the half-empty lot. I knew it was ridiculous to wheel my bag through the snow and rush on the moving walkway, which did not move: I wheeled my bag through the snow and rushed on the moving walkway. After a journey that felt endless, I found myself in a terminal silent in a post-apocalyptic way. There were only two of us—a woman in a navy baseball cap and T-shirt, who walked past with a dustpan and broom, and me. All flights were cancelled.

All this is the downside of *not done,* I knew. The chicken without a head. The body, my body, moving in a senseless determined way. A nameless fear blazed in my heart as I stood alone in the airport, and then when I started off on the long scary voyage home.

I drove slowly through the slanting snow. A truck with flashing lights threw salt on my windshield. Like a faux-atheist in a foxhole, I prayed. *Oh, please, let me get home safely.* I tried to concentrate on the white lines that marked my lane, and when they vanished, *please* rose. My car swerved on a downhill stretch of the road. I tried to brake and there was only the grinding sound of the anti-lock brakes as the car slid. The tires had no traction. The car seemed to glide into the left lane, toward a truck that was barely moving. It skidded slowly and inexorably. This elastic moment stretched out, giving me time to relax my shoulders, loosen myself for the impact, knowing there was nothing I could do. As I slid closer to the back of the truck, a single thought slipped through. *I don't want her to be alone.* Then the tires grabbed hold and I steered slowly back into my lane.

I made it safely home. Parked the car. Rose from the driver's seat. The snow was thick and beautiful. I stood in my open garage and watched. I made myself believe my mother would wait for me, that she would not die until after I could reach her. Wait for me, I whispered.

But the *she*, the *her*, in my rawest moment was Aviva.

TWENTY-ONE

Candles are burning when I open the door to my mother's apartment, one near her bedside and the others on the windowsills and the bureau top. The *shomer*, a young man with a yarmulke and fuzzy cheeks, dozes in the corner, near a window left open a few inches so that the soul, upon leaving her body, can escape the room. When I step close to the bed, I hardly recognize the woman propped against pillows. Only the nightgown with the lace yoke and violet nosegays is familiar. She'd worn it on the mornings when she stood in my kitchen in Pittsburgh and cried "help!" as if she were wounded. "Where's my juice?" Now she is sleeping on her back, with her hands arranged on top of the sheet, one slightly crossing the other. Her pale skin looks unlined and her hair, completely white, has been combed straight back. It's wrong, not the way she's ever worn it, so it takes a moment before I can see that she's clean and well-tended. Someone has put lotion on her skin and moisturized her lips.

Someone has tidied her apartment. The kitchen gives off an unpleasant chemical tang of industrial cleaner, and the refrigerator door is covered with magnets—Benny the plumber, embracing a toilet; Avi the exterminator, bashing a huge googly-eyed waterbug with a rubber mallet. A baby animal calendar is on the wall, turned to April, which features seals, with their winsome doglike expressions. The bags are gone from the living room, and a blue canvas cot has been set out for me, with linens and a pillow folded neatly at the foot. When I open the wardrobe in the small bedroom, where the person on duty sleeps, the overflowing bags expand. I have to press my whole body against the door to get it to latch again. It's as if Sunny is now Leona's daughter, and I'm a stranger snooping through drawers.

I sit on the edge of the bed and listen to the motorbikes and cars on the highway outside. Strangers care for my mother, paid companions. The *shomer* rouses and begins to softly recite prayers, and my

199

mother opens her eyes and seems to take me in. When she begins to speak, I lean close to try to make out what she's saying. "What?" I ask, and hear cars shifting gears, the blare of horns, the fan clicking on, blowing heat into the chilly apartment until at last I realize it isn't English she speaks, but one of the household languages I never understood. "Ma?" I whisper. "Mama?"

I take my mother's hand and stroke the soft loose skin, and it is enough, all I need. Her eyes stay closed, so after a while I get up, move my suitcase into the corner of the living room, and stand out on the small balcony that faces the sea. When I close my eyes, I find myself walking through the rooms of my childhood home, feeling the nubby upholstery on the couch, the gold embossed titles on the leather-bound books on the shelves, my father balancing their check-book at the dining room table, carrying her purse, warming the car for her, buying cheap paper towels and the wrong kind of sardines, absorbing her anger, muttering when she was in ill temper, never flinching. The time she went to the hospital for gall bladder surgery, and when I stopped by my parents' house, I found my father, who'd managed the household all those years, so undone he'd been unable to open a can of soup for his lunch. "Your mother is a fireball!" he'd cried. "She's a fireball!" Only then had I seen how much he'd needed her. Now, on the balcony, I turn that moment over and over as if it will yield, and I will know something that's been withheld.

Sunny sits on the edge of the bed, washes my mother's face, puts lotion on her hands and feet, changes her position. Her morose sister tidies the house, does the wash, buys food. All of us move slowly around the apartment. We whisper. We drink tea and eat the *burekas* Dina brings, warm pastries filled with potatoes or cheese. The *shomrim* come in shifts from a service that provides them, all of them young and religious, with their yarmulkes, loose white shirts and *tzitzit*.

And then she rallies. When Dr. Berenbaum stops by the next morning, he says her respiration has improved. I ask if I can go home, and he looks at me blankly, as if nothing can surprise this man, and tells me she will not live much longer. It could be a week— maybe two—he cannot predict.

At the airport, I'd seen the kind of chocolate my mother loved—extra dark, Belgian—and I'd bought two boxes for the Sunnys. After Dr. Berenbaum leaves, I take one from my suitcase, slit open the plastic, and bring it into the bedroom. My mother seems to watch me slide a chair beside her bed.

"I brought you some chocolate," I say. "Would you like a piece?"

I turn her hand and put the small wrapped square in the center of her palm. At first she seems to be holding it, saving it for the perfect moment. After a while it seems as if the chocolate simply fits into the fold of her palm. She makes no effort to turn it over or unwrap the foil. I take the wrapper off the chocolate, and when she parts her lips, I slip it into her mouth. The chocolate melts and begins to seep from the corners of her lips. I blot her mouth and chin with a cloth.

I am grateful for these others who can do what I cannot—sit, wait, pray, knit. I am restless, sit beside my mother for short periods of time, get up, wander around the small apartment, wonder when I can rent a car and drive to Chaverim, when I will be able to go home.

Hello, this is Roxanne. Aviva's sister. I did not rent a cell phone and the only phone is beside my mother's bed. Nonetheless, several times a day, I imagine calling him. *Shalom, this is Vered.* Then late one night, I slip across the hall to return Dina's plate. She opens the door, looking glazed and unkempt, as if she's survived a terrible storm. "Roxanne, I am such a slut," she murmurs in a woozy voice. Behind her is a short, bald man, arms folded across his hairy chest.

The next morning, when Sunny arrives, I leave the apartment. Instead of crossing the street and heading down to the beach, I turn the corner onto Ben Yehuda and walk past the corner cafes, with their outdoor seats all taken, the salons and little shops with wedding gowns in the window, and the grocery stores, the bins of bright fruit visible from the street. I stop to look in the window of a shoe store, where flats in bright-colored perforated leather are displayed. Pretty summer shoes, one pair deep pink, another a rich yellow and blue. I step inside to see them up close and when a skinny young salesman approaches, I search for the words to tell him I don't speak Hebrew—*Anee lo medaberet ivreet*—and before I can get them out, he says, his English barely accented, "Can I show you something?" I can't read his smile, can't tell if it's dismissive or friendly.

My mother is dying and I want shoes. I look at my watch. "I better come back later," I tell him.

On the street, I wait for guilt to descend. When it doesn't, I think: Maybe this is the way you're supposed to live. Disaster looms, and you hold onto your desire for shoes.

Then Dina goes to work, and I do call, and he answers the phone on the second ring before I have time to hang up. "Hi, this is Roxanne Garlick, Aviva's sister. We met briefly at Chaverim. Some months back."

"Yes, of course," he says.

"So I'm here in Tel Aviv. On Nordau Street."

"Splendid," he says. "Are you free this evening?"

"Yes," I tell him.

He gives me the address of a nearby restaurant, "famous for cheese," and I walk back to my mother's apartment, where Sunny is knitting a tiny yellow sweater, and a fat redheaded *shomer* rocks in the corner. My mother is in bed, her eyes open, her mouth slack. There is no one to ask—would it be okay? But that's not it, not really. I don't want to ask. My desire to see this man has ignited in a fierce and adolescent way. I go over Dr. Berenbaum's words—a week, maybe two, maybe tomorrow. She is not alone. The *shomer* is here. Sunny, her sister. It's foolish to be sentimental when I know my presence means nothing to her, and anyhow, I won't be gone long.

I dress in the bathroom. Stand on the toilet lid to see how I look. Grim. Wow, I think, and smile at my reflection. Is *she* ever mirthless.

I imagine sitting across from him at this restaurant, famous for its cheese, saying, "Excuse me, I am not myself."

Really? Then who are you? Why did you call?

If he asks me, what will I say?

To spend an hour with someone who knows Aviva. The storm had loosened a voice inside me, and my mother's impending death brings to mind decisions I need to make, responsibilities that rest upon my

202

shoulders. I feel the weight of them and know I want to manage them. Maybe he can give me advice. He sees Aviva nearly every week, knows aspects of her not revealed in the Sensory Checklist.

That night, on the short walk to the restaurant on a street lined with old gnarled trees, I ask myself what I want from this man, and *knowledge* seems to be the answer. Information he might be willing to share, directions I can jot in my notebook. "I'm lost," I want to confess. As if he can tell me which road to take. As if he might turn over his paper placemat, take out a pen and draw a map for me—take this street, then that one. Past this house, the school, some railroad tracks, the cemetery where his forebears lay, ye olde swimming hole where we could face each other, link our arms to form a cradle, and dance.

I have not acknowledged all that I want.

There are no paper placemats.

He is a stranger.

I know nothing about him, cannot yet admit how much I want his eyes on me, how I want to sit across the table and feel his gaze. I have no Polish, no French, no Yiddish, no Hebrew, no numbers, no words to speak of my desires.

All the outdoor seats are taken, mostly by young people with children, and placid dogs curled between the tables. A pug looks up as I push open the door to the restaurant.

He is sitting across the room. Clouds of gray hair, long legs crossed, half-empty glass of wine at the table. As I come closer, I feel an overwhelming sense that I know him and know nothing at all about him. He is familiar in a mysterious way and yet bears no connection to the man I've been imagining all these months.

"Am I late?" He fastens those big, sad eyes on me, and I experience him as a man and feel my anxious heart. "I'm so sorry!"

"Ah yes," he says. "Roxanne who is always sorry."

TWENTY-TWO

Here's what I recall of our dinner: fresh, salty cheese made from sheep's milk, sweet goat cheese, a salad with roasted peppers, falafel-coated artichokes, pita with za'atar, wine from vineyards in the Galilee, enjoying his company. As we polished off a bottle of crisp white wine, we talked about home and family and work. I liked listening to him talk about all the information that was revealed in the face, found it fascinating to think of our emotions leaking through as micro-expressions, even when we think we've hidden our truest feelings. That night, he showed me the difference between the true smile (the Duchenne smile, which involved the *orbicularis oculi* muscle and the *zygomatic major* muscle), and the fake one, that used only the *zygomatic major*, the corners of the lips. He spoke of slowing down a recent TV clip of a politician, to see the millisecond flash of contempt that "leaked through" on his face.

I didn't confess that I'd stood on the toilet lid and seen my own fake smile or demand he tell me what he saw in my face just then. I did not ask, as another woman had, if Camus had been correct to say, *Après un certain âge tout homme est responsable de son visage?* My interest was in him, so I overrode my usual self-consciousness. Who was this man who swam with Aviva, sat beside me in the garden at Chaverim, and passed long afternoons at the same San Francisco bookstore where I'd spent so many hours? He spoke with an edge of sadness of his son in Minnesota, who'd become so remote since he'd moved, so inaccessible, and his stormy daughter, who lived with her partner not far from him, and after years of anger toward her father had become his mentor.

"How so?" I asked.

"She gives me fashion advice and sent me to her 'stylist' so I might be presentable after my wife left."

"For your hair?" I began to laugh, though I felt the somber side of these details, too: the long-married man suddenly on his own.

"Can't you tell?" He patted his frizzy gray hair, and I said, "Fabulous cut."

A toddler's scream cut through our conversation. We watched the little guy tromp between the tables, with a side-to-side gait, like Dina's parrot, brandishing a spoon and shrieking until his father scooped him up, pausing at our table, child dangling from his arms, to greet Baruch. My mood dipped. I did not want the evening to end.

"Tell me about Aviva. Tell me everything," I said when the father left. "I'm so moved that you visit her every week."

"But I told you I enjoy these visits."

"I know," I said. "But still, you look after her. She's not even someone you know."

"No, no," he said. "Don't begin to think I'm a selfless individual. I turn my back on suffering every day. I make these visits for myself. Because it's something I want to do."

Like paying the check? He was insistent.

Outside, I fell in step beside him, on this tranquil street, the white apartment buildings beautiful in the low, forgiving light. When we turned the corner, we passed the store with the colorful shoes I'd wanted, but I was now in some sealed-off place, separate from my mother, the *shomer*, Sunny, and not-Sunny. What I wanted most was to hear about his weekly trips to Chaverim, what he did when he arrived, from the moment he stepped out of his car. When he began, I could feel the effort he put into framing his story, making certain I did not see him as selfless or kind.

It began, as I knew, with his sister getting cancer and asking him to be her son's guardian, and Baruch saying yes, without much thought. Yes, of course. Her death felt remote, and there was no one else. "She'd let this boy take over her life completely, traveling all over, borrowing money to take him to a doctor who had a database of fifty-three other children with the same chromosomal abnormality but no treatment to offer. The father had left long before. He had another wife, a different family, a better one. And the older brother, who moved to Australia, far from his mother and this boy who had taken over his childhood. Yes, sure, of course. To me, Danny was a disaster. I will be frank and say I saw him as non-human. My sister, even before Danny, had always seemed weak, like a little mouse. Her devotion to this boy I saw as pathetic. But as she got sicker, I began to see that this promise I made meant everything to her. Toward the end, every time we sat together, she would say, 'At least you'll look after Danny.' It was all she wanted."

And?

"The drive is very long. Danny is a tormented soul. After a visit or two, I began to resent the hours I spent in a car. Lost hours. And for what reason, when my company was irrelevant to him. My sister was dead. I began to think, why not just call and speak to one of the workers? Visit now and then so at Chaverim they know someone watches. If I wanted someone to agree, to say sure, this is okay, it would have been simple. He has no value in the eyes of most people, even his family members. So it's very easy to stop. You miss a week and the sky does not fall. You miss two weeks. Life goes on. Three weeks. Everything is still the same."

"But you didn't stop. Why not?"

He brushed me off with a flick of his hand, and though I felt his irritability, I saw it was directed at this notion that he was morally elevated, these trips a sign of his essential goodness, a proof that he was *something special.*

"I made a promise, and I was soon reminded that willpower alone is never enough. It's human nature for our best intentions to fade unless we are motivated to continue on. To honor my promise, I had to come up with a solution. To find ways I might enjoy these visits to Danny. I could listen to music in the car. Fine. Okay. I could visit my mother or meet a companion to hike in the Banias or the Hulu Nature reserve. This has been very nice, but my problem was not solved until Shelley and I began thinking about which of Danny's colleagues might enjoy my company. This is how I met your Aviva."

My Aviva.

"Last time we met, you said I should stop thinking all or nothing, but what if Aviva senses I'm here, and then suddenly I vanish for months with no way to explain why? It seems so awful. But if she doesn't care and my visits mean nothing, then my wanting to be with her feels futile. I didn't make any promises."

"Do you want to see her?"

"I ache to see her," I said, and when the words were out, I felt the truth in them, and walking beside this man, felt no conflict in this desire.

"Then you're here when you're here, and over time you build a relationship that's good for you both. This isn't futile, it's life. It's the way things are."

The old people I saw during the day were not around when we walked toward the beach—the women in skirts and pumps who sat on the bench below my mother's window, the men playing handball behind the hotels. I supposed they were tucked into their beds, replaced this evening by young people. We passed the hair salon his daughter had recommended, and he tapped on the window. I stood beside him, cupping my hands around my face, as if I might see him inside.

"The first time I arrived, the stylist walked around the chair very slowly. One complete circle, every angle. Lifted a lock of my hair. Another circle. Then he said, 'So. Tell me your vision.'"

"What *was* your vision?"

"I had no vision. My wife had just left after twenty-five years of marriage. My daughter thought a good haircut would help. I thought it would discourage him to say this."

"So what did you say?"

"Short on the sides and in the back."

The traffic light was green. When I started across the street, he said, "Are you taking me someplace special?"

"I was following you," I said.

"So you just walk wherever I walk?"

"I guess that's what I'm doing," I said, a little embarrassed.

"Shall we continue walking then? Or shall we start home?"

"Do you *mind* if we keep walking?"

"If I minded walking, I would not have suggested it."

"Sorry." I folded into myself, laughed ruefully: Roxanne who was always sorry. The whole city seemed to be out on this warm spring night. The promenade that ran along the beach was packed, and the restaurants propped up on the sand were bright and noisy. I could imagine that life on the beachfront was ordinary, if I wanted. I could take a snapshot like a tourist and say, this is what Israel is like. Was this how I lived? Did I only see the narrow slice of life that met with my approval? I thought about the girl at Nomi's party, with her insistent question. *Home? We're going home?* How come I'd never seen anyone like her before? Was it possible that before I'd met Aviva, my state of not knowing was so wide and deep I'd filtered out whole swaths of humanity I cared not to see?

I asked Baruch about the people who worked at Chaverim. Who were they? What were they like?

"For some it is just a job. Others find great meaning taking care of people, like Ora, who's been at Chaverim since the start. She knows how to bond with everyone there, which takes the kind of patience that seems unimaginable and very close study, until she knows if tactile is best, or vision, and how best to connect, to reach the little flame inside each person. But even Ora, who is remarkable, isn't selfless, superior in some way. Need drives her too. Watch and you will learn a lot."

The walkway ended abruptly in a construction site, with scaffolding and a fence, and the whole crowd of us continued in single file for the next few minutes. The kids behind me were raucous, jostling each other and me, and the questions I had boiled within me. As soon as we worked our way through and were again side by side, I asked, "Do you love your nephew?"

He said, "No. I wouldn't say that."

"Do you feel anything for him?"

"Of course. I've become his guardian. I feel a great deal for him."

"What do you call the feeling, if it isn't love?"

It took him a moment to find the word. "Kinship," he said.

"And before your visits?"

"Before he was nothing to me."

Kinship. I liked this word and wondered if I could use it to describe the nameless sensation growing inside me.

"So you drive there on a Friday. You park the car. And then what?"

He laughed. "You'll figure this out for yourself once you start visiting. Not right away. It is something that will happen over time, the same as with any two people. You'll begin to form a relationship with Aviva. It will not be like anything you've ever known, but if you are quiet, if you let yourself soften into it, you will find out what it is."

"Even Danny?" I asked.

"My sister, when I drove her to Chaverim just before she died, saw Danny sitting in the sun on the patio, and she was very upset and said, 'Look how they leave him in the sun like that!', and through her eyes, I saw him blinking and grimacing and that it was different from the grimaces I'd seen before, that he was uncomfortable, in pain. As soon as she moved him, his face relaxed and the blinking slowed, and when she talked to him I could see that it brought him comfort. So did he think 'mother' or something of that sort? Did it matter when she was the one who brought him something good? Now that she is gone, on good days, we have the CDs she made for him. Music. Her voice. We have movement. A walk if his seizures are under control. He is extremely sensitive to sun and wind and changes in temperature."

"And Aviva?"

"Ahh," he said. "You can touch her face. Hold her hand. You can carry her in the water, of course."

This detail, his long exhalation. For a moment I could not move.

"You will go and you will let her feel your presence. You will make sure she is comfortable. Soon you'll see what she likes and what she does not like. She will not thank you. She will not look in your eyes and say, 'You are something else.' She is not a dog; she will not greet you ecstatically each time you open the door. If there is reciprocity, you will find it much later. Maybe you will find you are kindred souls. Whatever it is, it will not be as you imagined."

On the promenade further south, big Russian teenagers with elaborate hair and tight pants walked with their arms linked, creating a barricade we needed to break so we could pass. *Shall we continue? Yes.* So we walked toward Jaffa, where the old mosque rose above the modern hotels, and worked our way past the small restaurants filling alleys lined with old houses, the chairs taken by diners, the table tops covered with salads and dips in small white dishes. Somewhere near, bread was being baked, and when I paused to take it in, I was jostled, pushed against him, and the desire came over me to rise on my toes and kiss him.

It changed everything, this desire, turned Baruch into a man, a man I wanted to kiss. I held back. There was so much yet I wanted him to tell me. But now this desire to rise, wrap my arms around him, to stop his words with a kiss, kept playing on, distracting me, as we wove through crowds on the narrow street, trying not to be separated.

On the way back, I asked if we could walk on the sand, and he said, "Of course." Kids were gathered around a bonfire near the jetty, strumming guitars and singing. We made our way onto the beach and when I paused to take off my shoes, he held out a hand to help me balance. Seeing the kids reminded me how much of my life had been spent around water, the Jersey shore in my childhood and teens, San Francisco in my twenties. I wanted to hear about his life in the days when he was married and had children. Everything interested me; where they lived and ate, what his wife did, where his children went to school. When we recalled the bookshop both of us had frequented, I brushed back my hair, as if to transform myself into the person I had been all those years before.

"Do I look familiar?" I asked. "I'm standing beside you."

He scrutinized me somberly.

"Hey, I'm stealing a glance. Checking you out. Cute guy. Amazing eyes."

This seemed to embarrass him. "I was very preoccupied. I want to say I looked up and thought, that's a beautiful woman. More likely, I looked up and thought, I need a better data set before that paper can go out."

"Is that what kind of person you were?"

High up was a storybook crescent moon that seemed to float in the black sky. "Yes," he said after a pause. "I was very preoccupied."

I wondered if "preoccupied" was a euphemism for "married."
"Did you look at women in your married days?"

"I looked. I did not act."

"You *liked* being married," I said.

"You're telling me this?"

"I'm guessing," I said, because I felt myself in the presence of a man who liked the quiet predictability of domestic routine, someone both alive and settled. I tried to hold off on the kind of relentless questions one might ask of a tour guide in a foreign land, where the natives were monogamous and thrived, but I wanted to know what it was like to be happily married, having failed myself.

"It sounds like you and your wife had many good years."

"We had many good years. And then she'd had enough."

"How did you know?"

We stopped while he gathered his thoughts. I curled my toes in the sand and listened to the strum of the far-off guitar.

"I didn't know."

"She just one day left, *a propos* of nothing?"

For a long time, his wife seemed to like their peripatetic life, he said. She was flexible and outgoing, made friends wherever they went, gave Hebrew lessons, taught Israeli dancing at a JCC, got a Masters of Art in Family Therapy. Then a few years back, he had a chance to spend a semester at a university in Northern British Columbia. When he told her, she became furious and said she was tired of the way he no longer asked what she wanted but announced like a king. She had a job she liked and was no longer interested in following along. So he made new arrangements to stay for only a month.

"On my second morning home, I'd woken early and was sitting at my desk. How long, I couldn't say. Only that at some moment, I turned and saw her standing with her arms crossed and could tell she'd been standing like that for some minutes. On her face was a look of contempt. That tightening of the lip corners. *She's leaving me.* The thought was not even complete when she said those same words: 'I'm leaving you.'"

"Before that morning, you had no clue she was going to leave?"

"She'd been unhappy. For a while."

"You didn't know?"

"The clues were there. I hadn't been looking."

How can you not know? I wondered. How can you live with a person who radiates despair? How can you live with a woman who insists you forget your own child, a woman who... and here I closed my eyes, to block out what filled my head. How do you live with a man in your basement? How do you live in a city where the sky is always gray, or in a country, where a fence has been erected, a wall between *us* and *them*? How can you live, knowing death awaits?

"I knew she was unhappy, but since she never spoke of it, I believed it would pass. You've been married so you know there are times when you're very close to your mate and other times when you're disconnected, maybe for a while, until something brings you together again. Isn't that how it is?"

"I guess," I said, then backtracked. "I'm not sure I had that."

"My wife said it was my doing. I wanted to be married, but I no longer wanted her."

"Is that true?"

"I suppose it is, though it took me a very long time to recognize this."

"Do you know why?"

The smell of pot wafted toward us. "What do people say when this happens? 'We grew apart.' I suppose this is what happened. Raising children is a long collaboration. Maybe we didn't see what had changed between us until that project ended. I'll tell you a story, though. Six months before she left, my wife had minor surgery. I took her home from the clinic and helped her get settled. I asked her if she was comfortable and what could I do for her, and she said, 'go to work,' and shooed me out of the room. So I went."

"Oh, but she *didn't* want you to go," I said.

"That's right. She wanted me to stay and look after her."

"You're a face guy. How come you couldn't just look at her and see that?"

Baruch leaned over to slip off his shoes. "In the years before

computer vision, we used videotape to record mother-infant interactions, I spent countless hours advancing and rewinding videotape,
trying to see the micro-expressions I'd initially missed. After my wife
left, I found myself going over and over past events, trying to find
what I'd failed to see. And I realized I'd registered her discontent.
I'd taken it in. But at the time, I hadn't seen it. Maybe it was too
threatening. Or I was too self-absorbed. We're human beings; we
miss things. We forget."

"Maybe what we need is a checklist, like the ones at Chaverim.
Maybe it should be required, like a blood test. Before you get a marriage license, you have to answer two hundred questions that let your
partner know exactly what you like and don't like. And then there'd
be a second section, the next level, where you have to give details
like, 'When I say go, I mean stay.'"

The sea was very tranquil, unlike the ocean where I grew up, where
once at midnight, drunk and giddy, I swam into the waves with my
friends. The undertow dragged me out, flipped me around, spat me
back onto the sand, and left me breathless. It was crazy, dangerous,
intoxicating. I'd wanted to do it again, to let go, to be dragged and
spun, powerless.

And now I wanted to walk into the water. To strip off my clothes,
curl into a ball, and let the ocean carry me away.

⇛

Later that night, beneath the perfect moon, we walked on the sand
and worked on sensory checklists for ourselves. It was warm, nearly
windless. We were on a second loop and again passed the kids sitting
around the bonfire, two of them silently swaying.

"Do you *persistently seek* touching?" I asked.

"Is a woman doing the touching?"

"Yes," I said. "A woman."

"Then I like the touching very much."

"Touching where?" I asked. "More data are needed. For my
checklist."

He was shy, glanced at me, averted his eyes. "Face, arms, chest, back, body. Inner thighs. No knees, not the knees. No feet. They're very sensitive, my feet."

"Lips?"

"Of course."

"Kind of touch?"

"Loving."

"Oops—sorry," I said. "Loving is not on the list."

"Soft," he said. "Firm."

The kids at the bonfire were singing softly. I listened, arms crossed, hands cupped around my elbows and not on him. "When you sleep, what's your preference, regarding a woman's touch?"

Now he let his eyes linger. "Very close."

"And when you're upset?"

"Even closer. And you, Vered?"

"Everywhere. All the time. Except knees. Like you, no knees."

"How do you react to movement?"

"Hesitant to move unless holding onto someone. Loses balance easily. Does not catch self when falling. The waves are so gentle. Do you swim?"

"Of course," he said, and went back to the checklist. "What about clothing? Fabric against your skin. Does it distress you?"

"Prefers wearing as little as possible. Dislikes shoes." I unbuttoned my cotton sweater. "Persistently strips off clothing. That's one on the list that stopped me. What do you do when your mission is to make people comfortable and you have someone in your midst who can't stand wearing anything at all?"

I let my sweater fall onto the sand. His smile was inscrutable. I could not say what it signaled and grew anxious. "You need to go home, is that it? *Get me away from this nut job?*"

"So you're a mind reader?"

"No." I laughed nervously. "Just the opposite. I can't tell what you're thinking."

"Are you planning to swim?"

"I want to," I said. "Will you come in with me?"

"Of course." Then just the slightest gesture with his chin. "You'll want to take off your jeans. You'll be very uncomfortable if you wear them in the water."

I held onto him for balance while I slipped off my jeans. The night was so dark and still, only the distant singing. When I was down to my tank top and underpants, he touched the hem of my shirt disapprovingly. "Cotton is a bad choice for swimwear."

"Yes, I know. Cotton, the death fiber."

I wove my fingers between his. This simple gesture, exquisite, intimate, almost unbearably so. "Excuse me, what was your name again?"

"You're American? Then for you it's Barr-ook."

"So Barr-ook, are you the type who dives right in?"

"Never. And you?"

"Not at all."

"I don't know that I believe you. There is some wildness in you still." He took off his jacket and lowered it onto the sand as if to avoid getting it creased. "I can tell there is."

"Has trouble with transitions. Cannot shift well from one activity to the next."

He said nothing, his gaze deeper, more candid, overriding our game.

I put my hand against his face. "You're a very kind person. Not a saint; you've made that clear. Not selfless. I wouldn't dare call you selfless. Just decent. You're a decent man. I can tell."

He put his hand over mine. "Which name do I call you?"

"The one you like."

"Vered. It's an old-fashioned name, but it suits you."

"Say it again."

"Vered."

He unzipped his pants, held onto my shoulder as he worked his legs free. I lifted my tank top over my head and we walked down to the water's edge, like children, dressed only in briefs. In that short walk, we entered a place where there were no voices or music, no people, no moon. The tide was very low. We walked in soft sand until our feet were wet and then our ankles. "Their journey was epic," I said, in my narrator voice.

I shivered when the water reached my thighs, and when at last it was waist-high, I lowered myself to keep warm, and paddled out until my feet could not reach bottom. We bobbed to keep warm, and he put his arm around me and said, "Vered, I feel as if I am starting to know you."

"Oh, wow, no," I said. "I wish, but I'm afraid you aren't. At all." I bobbed and submerged myself, as if to wash off this sadness.

"So there will be surprises?"

"I'm not as evolved as you." We fluttered separately. "*Vered G. is a troubled child.*"

I bobbed close, wrapped my arms and legs around his waist, became aware of his fragility and mine—skin and blood, bones so easily broken.

"So what is your crime? You rob banks? Is that what you do?"

"What does my face tell you?"

"I like your face. It's a good face, a beautiful face."

I kept my legs around him and closed my eyes so I could not tell if it was Baruch or the sea that rocked me. His lips brushed against mine as we were pushed together.

The bobbing jostled us apart.

"Do you believe in the soul?" I asked.

"Do I believe that God must first breathe into one's nostrils? No. But every human has a soul. A life force."

"Even Danny?"

"Danny too."

"And Aviva?"

"Aviva, yes. Of course."

"Do you believe that the soul slips from the body at death?"

"Yes," he said. "In a manner of speaking."

Our kiss was deeper and the waves more determined to keep us apart. I drew him close and tried to reach beneath his knees so I could hold him in my arms the way he'd held Aviva, and when he resisted, worried he would hurt me, I said, "Don't you remember what you said to me? 'In the water, we're very light.' Why is that? Do we leave our history on land?"

He worked his way free and in a quick move, cradled me in his arms. "We always have our history, Vered. It's like gravity, you cannot separate yourself from it."

I had been separated from my history, I thought. This is what had happened to me.

After a while he said, "You're shivering. My jacket is on the sand. Come. We'll get you warm."

I didn't want to leave, but I paddled with him toward the water's edge. When we reached the sand, he hurried ahead to retrieve my sweater and his jacket, to layer them across my shoulders. The air had cooled. Now I could hear the loud, frenetic music that had been inaudible to me before. "You need that jacket more than I do," I said.

"I live nearby. Come back with me. You can shower and change into something dry."

These words weakened my knees. I wanted to take off my clothes and make love to him, but to get to his apartment meant dressing and walking on sidewalks; it meant the jingling of keys, doors unlocked, lights switched on. It meant being plunged back into the bright un-avoidable world. I kissed him for a long time.

"Vered. You are something else," he said.

"Something. But what?"

"Something very special."

"No, you are," I said, and some time later, "Oh, wait. I'm not supposed to suggest you're nice because you aren't at all. You have no moral compass. You're just a selfish man."

"So I've been told."

"And a good lover. I bet you've been told that, too."

He did not say, "Yes, of course." But I could tell by his kisses, by his straightforward gaze and broad, loose, youthful stride. If I were young, I would have pulled on him until we sank to our knees. That's what I would have done. Nothing would have stopped me. "I'd like to stay all night with you," I said.

"What stops you?"

I listened to the faraway kids laughing. "Fear," I said and could not explain. Fear that it would not be enough, that I would never be able to leave.

He took my hand and we walked up a narrow path from the beach through a small, unlit park, until with every step, the long urban hum of traffic got louder. Then we were in the city again, in ordinary life, with streetlights and cars. He sensed the change in my mood and said, "What is it?"

"Life. I hate to leave."

A boy with a boogie board balanced on his head swerved past on a bike. Baruch put his arms around me and pressed me against the cool white wall of my mother's building. My legs were trembling, and I said, "Hold me up," and he pressed harder.

"So. Shall we drive to Chaverim together tomorrow?"

"Yes."

"You'll bring your bathing suit and some good shoes. *B'seder?*" He kissed me again. I pulled back, thought, *bathing suit*, and tried to regain my balance.

I found my key and clumsily worked it into the lock on the outside door. Before I entered, I turned back. He was still standing, waiting until I was safely inside. I held up my hand, and he put his fingers to his lips. The look on his face—I thought it would melt my bones.

TWENTY-THREE

As soon as the door closed, I was hit, as if by a club. I took a step, and the light flickered on, barely illuminating the dim hallway. I took another step, shivering hard. My hair was ropy from salt, my clothes were clammy. My mother dying in her room, my mother dead. It was three a.m. I was stunned by the way I had pushed this aside, deeply ashamed. I thought of the evening decades back when I'd brought Ronit home late and felt like that same heartless teenager.

My mother's apartment was dark and still. When my eyes adjusted, I tiptoed through the kitchen, past the canvas cot in the living room where Not-Sunny slept, covered with a sheet. Then further. I could see the flickering candles through the half-closed door. My mother was breathing. The *shomer* was folded over, his forehead on his knees.

I stumbled and he sprang up and the prayer book slid from his lap. "I'm allowed to sleep!" he whispered. He picked up the book and kissed the binding. "It's permitted. The rabbi will tell you."

It was hard to imagine this young plump man able to guard anything, least of all something as insubstantial as a soul. And still—while I had eaten dinner, walked on the promenade, took in the world around me and lost the world completely, while I met Baruch's eyes and while I avoided them, while I faced him fully clothed and then disrobed, while I stepped into the water so he could hold me and when I walked out—this young man was the one who sat beside my mother.

"Rest," I said. "It's very late."

I washed my face and changed into a nightgown. I could not go to Chaverim with Baruch. As soon as it was morning, I'd call. *It's me, Vered. I'm sorry, but I can't go.* I brushed my teeth and imagined floating to his apartment in my thin nightgown and bare feet, and Baruch, opening the door, taking me in his arms. Forgetting everything, making love, never leaving. The candles flickered and the building breathed and the s*homer* sat beside mother, so she would not be alone in her dying.

I tried to sleep, drifted, and could not sink. Images floated in the air. Squares of torn-up postcards. The curly-haired twins I'd seen at Chaverim, one pushing her sister's wheelchair, their identical, freckled faces. How it might have been for us, had we not been separated. The newspaper photo of Amber Chatsworth. The blunt, deadened look on her face. The s*homer's* reverent kiss.

Sister, I thought, and wondered what night was like for Aviva, if it was peaceful, pleasurable. And waking? Did morning signal expectation? Did she open her eyes and know something good was on its way—sunshine, voices, a transfer from her bed? Or was it waiting, uncomfortable, untended; her needs unanswered, hour after hour. Hadn't it seemed that way for me, able-bodied, alone in the house, waiting. How did she soothe herself?

Vered. His tender voice had cracked the shell, exposing a raw wound. What I wanted, what I could not have.

In the dark room, I felt the waves push me toward him, then sweep me away. Maybe I would go with him after all. The s*homer* was here. Sunny. Dr. Berenbaum. My presence didn't matter to my mother. Once it had, I suppose: when I cried and tugged on her, looking for attention, surely I reminded her of the one whose name could not be mentioned, the sister who'd been buried alive. What effort it must have taken, if not for her, then for my father, for all those years until he lost people's names, and the promises he'd made, until all that remained was a dim, persistent ache—Aviva. Now that I could say there'd really been no space for me in their house, I found myself asking, "Don't I deserve a chance at happiness?"

You deserve bupkis!

I deserved more than *bupkis*, but I couldn't go to Chaverim with my mother so close to death. I needed to call Baruch and tell him. I'd have to edge past the s*homer* to reach it. *It's Vered; it's Roxanne.* I imagined his eyes on me. *I'm so sorry.* What could I say? *I'll see you next time I'm here.* And when would that be? What could I say next? Hey, don't fall in love with anyone while I'm gone! It was so pointless, all of it. The night before, the days ahead, anything I might imagine. Thinking, wait for me.

Then a key turned in the lock, and half awake I heard someone enter. Sunny? The room was hot and my arms were folded across my chest like a giant bandage. Light came through the pinholes in the shutters, and in a dreamy state, the two of us in the water. The waves pushing us together, pushing us apart. Our lips touching.

Boker tov, Aviva! My sister's shades drawn, the morning sun flooding her room. Familiar voices. The smell of food. *Boker tov!*

The sound of water running in the kitchen, the kettle being filled. Then suddenly I was plunged into consciousness. What time was it? Had I missed him? I uncrossed my arms and sat up, pushing off the sheet. Holy shit, what time? I slipped into the sandy clothes I'd dropped on the floor. Had he gotten his car from the garage beside his building, backed out of the space, locking the cement pole so no one could take his spot? Had he pulled up to the curb to wait, turned off the engine when I did not appear? Checked his watch. He had no number, wouldn't buzz every apartment. What time was it?

Sunny was ministering to my mother, cooing, speaking softly. She looked up when she saw me. I took in the digital numbers on the clock radio and my mother, breathing, and said, "How is she?" I still had time. Sunny put a splayed hand across her chest and breathed very deeply. All those hours of conversation and never once had I mentioned my mother dying. I splashed water on my face and after a few minutes I went downstairs.

I stood on the street, bedraggled and salty. The air was still cool, and the crisp morning light made everything looked beautiful, the stumpy palms and peeling apartment buildings. On the strip of land that divided the street, a dog with ropy hair like mine trotted ahead of a woman with a newborn swaddled on her chest, and someone's horn root-tooted discreetly. I didn't know what kind of car Baruch had and failed to see him drive past until a white car pulled up to the curb beside me, and he stepped out, wiry hair, long legs, sunglasses, which he took off, as if to get a better view of me, standing on the sidewalk, barefoot and disheveled. "What's wrong?"

His kindness pierced me. "I can't go," I said.

He put his hands around my arms and held me tightly, so close to me. Then softly, "Haven't you slept at all? Did something happen?"

It seemed, just then, that I had waited my whole life for someone to speak to me with such tenderness. "My mother's very ill," I said. "I can't go."

I did not say that she would die, and there'd be a funeral and the dismantling of her apartment, and then I would need to go home.

"Last night was like an amazing dream," I said.

"Not like life?" he asked, lightening for a moment.

"None that I've known," I said.

"I'm sorry to hear about your mother. You've called a doctor?"

"The doctor knows," I said. "She's very old." Then after a long exhale: "Oh, why do you live here? It's so inconvenient. I mean, really, you want a woman who goes to sleep with you and wakes up beside you, someone who lives here."

"You're a mind reader? You *know* what I want?"

"It's not like that," I said.

"So you're telling me what *you* want?"

"In my life," I said. "Before now, before this, I've been trying really hard to make good decisions. And right now I'm just overwhelmed with a sense of futility."

We stood for a few minutes and watched the street come alive, a metal shutter pulled back, a store opening. One story up, laundry arranged on a drying rack. A cluster of children pushing against each other. It took effort to keep from reaching out, touching his face and chest. I clutched my elbows, averted my eyes, thought of my mother upstairs, dying. "And it isn't easy. I've never met anyone as kind as you. Ever."

"Kind." He seemed offended by these words.

He waited for me to say more, and I shook my head, confused, unable to string together anything coherent. He turned away and got into his car, and even then, I just stood. He drove to the intersection and waited for the light to change. I wondered numbly if he'd taken what I'd said as a flip goodbye, like a lover saying "let's be friends" while breaking up. I raised my hand, just as he turned onto Ha'Yarkon. And then he was out of view. I wondered if he would still swim with Aviva when he got to Chaverim, or if I had stolen him like a jealous sister, grabbed what I wanted, and thrown the rest away.

After I showered I sat beside my mother. Her breathing stopped and then startled, and it wasn't so much a rattle as a kind of gargling that Sunny told me not to fear. I put my hand over hers, then brought it to my lips and kissed her cool, loose skin, and she did not flinch, was no longer able. What had they done to her? What had happened to her long before we were born? "Is it better now, Mommy?" I asked, not caring if I was too old to call her Mommy.

She was so pale, her gaze as soft and unknowable as Aviva's. Her skin smelled like roses from the lotion Sunny had used. Now that I did not want anything from her anymore, I could sit beside her. Once she roused, as if startled, and then she slept. Her breathing slowed, and there was the dreadful gargle as if she was drowning. And then it resumed.

On the way to the living room, I heard an argument across the hall, two women, a slammed door, then silence. I had done the right thing, hadn't I? It didn't feel that way, but it would, wouldn't it? At conferences I'd met men from distant cities, lovely men, perfect, *if only…* The sadness I'd felt at parting was deep, the ache lingered, and then my vivid emotions grew hazy and disappeared into the soup of memory.

A different *shomer* sat in the corner while the hours passed.

Late that afternoon, I went out to the market across the street. The buildings looked crisp in the low light. I felt hung-over. What have I done? I asked myself. Our evening rushed back, intimate and otherworldly. The moon, the smell of pot, the briny sea, his lips against mine, his somber eyes, his flesh, the bones beneath it. My silence.

The fruit in the bins was old and bruised. I considered buying a freckled banana, then reconsidered. Two blocks away was a better market. I stood in front of the tilted boxes of produce and looked at the offerings the way one looked at art. The rosy rat-tailed radishes, cucumbers with prickly skins, smooth green peppers with their womanly curves and clefts. I could not believe what I had done, could not remember any hunger apart from what I'd felt for Baruch and purchased what was beautiful—tomatoes, lemons, fresh figs.

Sunny met me at the door when I returned, eyes brimming with tears. She took my hand and squeezed it. I put down my shopping bag, took in the playful seals on the calendar and Sunny's swollen face and went into my mother's room. Her hair had been freshly combed, and her hands again placed on top of the blanket. Her skin was still warm. She was so beautiful, my mother. Everyone spoke of this when she was younger, and now at death it was again true. I sat beside her.

Before this moment, I'd never understood why people said, after a death, "At last she's at peace." In my imagination, death was violent and tragic. When my mother died, I looked at her blue-veined eyelids and smooth skin and thought, at last she is at peace.

❧

I, too, felt at peace after my mother's death. It was so unexpected that I half awaited for the enormity of her passing to catch up with me. Maybe I'd be walking down the street when it would split me like an axe. Or at the funeral service, I'd be brought to my knees. I wanted to be able to cry as the casket was lowered into the ground. The others would expect this of me, since I was her daughter.

"My mother is dead," I told Kotovsky, the landlord, to practice saying it. I bought the pale pink shoes and set them in the small bedroom. Then I emailed Les. *My mother is dead.* It seemed attention-seeking, as if I were still pirouetting down the stairs, singing loudly and waiting for applause.

She died this morning. I studied the words, said them aloud. I felt no bolt of grief.

I need to stay through next week to take care of business. I didn't write to Harley, though his affection for my mother had been genuine. I didn't try to explain her death to Baruch, though I felt him holding my arms on Nordau Street, then felt his grasp loosen. It was as if my mother's death was in my brain and he was lodged in my body.

The funeral was held at a kibbutz north of Tel Aviv, where land had been set aside as a resting place for secular Jews and non-Jews.

My mother had planned for this civil service. The documents that stated these wishes were in an envelope Sunny had given me. While extremely helpful, I was reminded that she'd been of sound mind when she'd left New Jersey. She *really* didn't like me, I thought, when I finished perusing the instructions. It was hardly a revelation. I wished Mindy were with me, so we could name a couple of miscreants and petty criminals from our high school class who'd been blessed by their mother's unconditional love. Then I could say, "I wasn't so bad, was I?" and Mindy would tell me what I knew but did not yet fully feel: "You weren't bad at all."

Dina drove us to the kibbutz in her banged-up white car, restless behind the wheel, glancing out the side window, answering calls on a cell phone mounted on the dashboard, now and then *Pitts-boorg* lodged like a pebble inside a Hebrew sentence. She went on for a few minutes about my mother's greatness, then moved on to her newest boyfriend, the bare-chested man I'd seen in her doorway.

"I met this man who swims with Aviva every week," I said. "This totally lovely person. He has a nephew who lives a Chaverim and—"

Dina turned, alarmed. "This man, he swim with Aviva?"

"Yes, it's how we met. The last time I was here, he found me a bathing suit so I could join them in the pool, but—"

"Roxanne! You should not be doing this. These people, they must respect you. If they don't, they will not take such good care of Aviva."

"He doesn't work there," I said. "I thought he did, but—"

"No. It is different here. You *must* have a distance. Tomorrow, I'll take you."

"For now, I need to go alone," I said. "I'm still self-conscious when I'm there."

She lifted her chin and squeezed the steering wheel.

"Dina, you're wonderful. I don't know how I would have managed without you." Now it was worse. She curled her lip in disgust. "Can you tell me why you're offended when I say thanks?"

"Roxanne!" She turned to face me. "What have I done wrong?"

The car swerved. This argument would kill us both if I didn't stop talking. We drove the rest of the way in silence.

When we arrived at the kibbutz, Ronit and Meir were standing in a dirt lot, where a half-dozen cars were parked. I said, "My cousins are here," and Dina got out of the car, paused to smooth her skirt and introduced herself. She and Ronit were more like twins than Aviva and me, same height and shape, both dressed in loose jackets and short, straight skirts. As they walked ahead, I could see how enlivened they were by Dina's vitality, her unthreatening flirtatiousness, and wished I could be like her.

Sunny arrived, and then, in separate cars, three men she'd notified about my mother's death, physicists whose names and numbers were in the envelope. During the service, Dina and Ronit stood together. Dina wept. Ronit took a tissue from her purse and dabbed at her eyes. I stood dry-eyed, scanning the small group in attendance, their heads bowed, feeling stunted, damaged.

When I got back to her apartment, I opened her wardrobe, as if the smell of mothballs would make her death real. I moved the garbage bags and touched her slacks, hung neatly by the cuffs and her skirts on hangers. Then I knelt and went through her shoes. A dozen pairs of flats all the same style, with a crisscross elastic front. Full slips with darts and V-neck tops, trimmed with lace, delicate straps; half-slips with lacy hems in cream, ecru, oyster, sand, bone, eggshell, corn silk, vanilla, ivory, flax. Did these garments even exist anymore? I remembered her tweezing her eyebrows and penciling them. The face she made when she put on her lipstick. The smell of her perfume and cigarettes. Her disdain. The way she flinched from my touch. The template for what I'd recognized as "love." Someone who could not know me, who remained achingly out of reach. I hated it, knew it well. Baruch came to mind. The thought that I'd turned him into what I'd known best.

I wondered if my mother had thought of Aviva the way I thought of Baruch, if ghostly sensual memories flitted through her head. I slipped her wedding band and opal ring, her lapel pins and gold chains, into a small drawstring sack, then I slid shut the wardrobe door. Maybe this is it, I thought. Maybe it's already hit me.

TWENTY-FOUR

Aviva was out when I arrived at Chaverim, so I sat on the patio to wait for her return. Nearby was a woman wrapped in layers of mauve and gray, in her arms a tiny, curled man with a receding hairline. She was feeding him bits of something sweet, rocking him, humming in an airy, peaceful way. It was the strangest sight, his middle-aged face, like that of a scholar, the working of his tongue, his clenched hands, her blissful crooning. Strange, unsettling, but not a nightmare. Dear Baruch, I thought, thank you for giving me a passport into this country.

When the willowy caregiver wheeled Aviva onto the patio, I saw that my sister's head was supported with foam blocks and she was bundled in red fleece. Her hair was in a long braid, and her cheeks were flushed. Curled hands, chunky slipper-socks to keep her feet warm. A bouquet of lavender and thyme across her lap.

Seeing her was different than thinking about her. The smooth face, with its gaze I could not read, and long, thick lashes. The slack mouth. "Hello," I said. "Hi." My greeting was small and tight. Miserly. The caregiver showed me how to use the wheelchair brakes and when she left, I wheeled Aviva down the broad winding road that circled Chaverim, down past the gardens and chicken coops and barns, and when we had made a long loop, I returned to the patio and positioned myself so we could face each other. The old woman was still there, humming and rocking her tiny, middle-aged son. Aviva did not seem to see me. I could not want this from her. But she would not withhold her affection, would not lie or manipulate me. She made no promises. I uncurled her fingers, long like mine.

Her nails had been nicely cut. Someone had taken the time to clip them evenly and trim the edges. Aviva, with her hollow cheeks, the soft unlined skin of someone who had never laughed or scowled or played in the sun. Blinking. I said her name, pressed my hands against her cheeks. I remembered the list of sensations that pleased her and thought she might like this.

I thought of the story Baruch had told me about visiting Danny with his sister, just before she'd died. The CDs she'd brought of all they'd listened to over the years—classical music, folk, disco, Afro-pop, crashing waves and wind in the trees, recordings of her singing and talking so he'd always have her voice. It wasn't a sly maneuver to fool him into thinking she was alive. Comfort, that's what she'd intended.

I held her hand against my cheek and waited for the noise from the big thrumming world to recede.

I thought, what is it you like? Then I made myself say it aloud, "What do you like, Aviva?"

I looked out at the perfect line of cypress trees and the low stone walls that lined the road. Dina would have been better at this. She would have had a bright, shiny voice and no inhibitions.

I splayed my hands and said, "This is who I am. It's just who I am."

Her eyes, dark like mine, regarded me. We were fish in the same sea, I thought.

Then in a murmur, "We were fish in the same sea."

Wounded fish, I thought, left to flap on our sides.

Her skin was so soft. I lifted the lavender, held it to my nose and then to hers, and to myself I sang, "Parsley, sage, rosemary, and thyme."

And aloud, in my not-so-good voice I sang, "Parsley, sage, rosemary, and thyme."

She blinked and softened, and I thought, I can learn to do this. "Give me time, sister," I said.

I put her foot on my lap and eased off her slipper. The soft sole was hers alone. The high arch and narrow foot and bulbous oversized toe. I rolled my eyes and laughed—she had that same crazy toe.

And I said, "Poor you, with that same ridiculous toe. A lollipop toe, Mindy calls it."

We, I thought. *Us.*

Our start, curled together in our mother's womb. Our birth, when I cried and she did not. The months that followed, when she cried ceaselessly and I learned to be silent. It was just the two of us now, with our long fingers and lollipop toes.

I worked Aviva's socks back onto her feet. Then I knelt and grasped her feet and kissed her goodbye.

Later that day, on the long drive south, I thought I would write to Baruch, to tell him about this visit. Then I thought about Aviva. She had a life story too. I'd been slow to recognize this because it did not progress in a conventional way—childhood, schooling, occupation, marital status. I could not lose myself wondering who she might have been had fate been kinder. What mattered was that she was someone who was knowable, and someone I would get to know.

⁂

On the way back from Chaverim, I stopped at Ronit and Meir's. My cousin knew I loved her patio, so she loaned me a shawl and put on a bulky cardigan so we could sit outside after dinner. While Meir was clanking around in the kitchen, we talked easily—of Galia's travel plans, and Ronit's new job. Then I told her about my visit with Aviva, and what I'd read in her medical records. I said that I loved getting to know her again, that it meant everything to me, the way she welcomed me into the family. If every visit was about Aviva, and who knew what, it would create a wedge between us. "Please help me out," I said. My voice was shaking. "We've inherited a lot of hard history."

The night was cool. I drew the soft shawl around my shoulders, and Ronit buttoned her cardigan. She'd gotten her hair cut very short and in the dim light it was like a silver helmet. I knew I was making it hard for her and regretted it. Still, I waited.

"After your father stopped coming to see us, we forgot about Aviva. I know it sounds very cold-hearted, but this is the truth."

It was what Galia had said at my house. I understood. Aviva was not a person to them, alive or dead. She was not someone, not part of the family. I would have felt that way too.

Ronit shifted in her chair. "There was no internet then. It wasn't so easy to get answers. We were upset that no one bothered to tell us your father had died."

"I've read a lot about trauma in infants—from papers I found online, and some recent cases. What I read in Aviva's medical record are classic signs of abuse. Subdural hematoma—that's bleeding in the brain. Diffuse axonal injury happens when the head gets whipped back and forth, like in a car accident, or when a baby is shaken. Broken hip."

Ronit put her hand up. She covered her face.

"They're all gone," I said after a while. "Everyone in that generation. We're the ones who get to make the rules. Please. Let's not live with all these secrets anymore."

Inside the house, the phone rang. Ronit waited until Meir picked it up. "Your father begged me to stay silent, because to him, what *Savtah* and my mother talked about was a lie. Every visit, he would sit with me and take my hands. And he would squeeze them hard and ask what good it would be to whisper these stories, to spread them, after all this time. It would only make things worse."

We listened to Meir laugh then to his voice trailing off.

"He saw it as a very big sacrifice. You never got to know *Savtah*, or my parents. Or me, really." Ronit sighed. "You would have loved *Savtah*. She was very emotional, you know? She loved in a very big way and hated just as big. Between her and your mother, there was so much bitterness. Yes, I heard those terrible stories from *Savtah*. Were they true, when everyone said she and Leona could not be in the same room for even five minutes? What kind of person would I be to tell you what *Savtah* whispered when your father swore it was a lie?"

"Just tell me what you heard and let me take it from there."

"She was never healthy," Ronit said of Aviva. "She didn't feed well, and she cried all the time, and there was something with a doctor who said she would never be normal, they should send her away. Your father would not hear of that, but two babies, one who screamed day and night, was too much, so he asked *Savtah* to move in to help. She was very good with babies and loved them more than anything, but even she couldn't stop the crying. Your father told me about these nights, how terrible they were. And then what happened, I was too young to know. The way *Savtah* tells, one night she is feeding one baby, and the other is crying and crying without stop, and before *Savtah* realizes, Leona has taken the baby from the crib and is shaking her and screaming at her to stop and hitting her against the wall."

My body ached all over. I closed my eyes and listened to Ronit's chair scrape against the stones and when I looked up, we were sitting the way I'd sat with Aviva earlier that afternoon, our knees nearly touching. "I did not think this was something you should hear, especially because your father swore on his life the baby fell."

"She didn't fall," I said.

"Vered," Ronit said. "You cannot be sure."

"If it was an accident, why would he have hidden everything and everyone from me, not just Aviva?"

"He thought it was the right thing to do, that he could protect you. He didn't want another generation to live and breathe so much tragedy."

"I grew up with nothing," I said. "I never lit a candle or celebrated a holiday. I have no memory of our grandmother, didn't get to know my cousins. Even the ones in the U.S., like the Gorelicks in New Jersey, are total strangers."

"He worried about you," Ronit said. "Try to understand."

Sitting with Ronit, I felt like I was at the very beginning of a long journey to what was so blithely called "understanding." To understand meant having a firm, insistent "I," a road to the heart "I," while mine had been like a trapped bird, flying against a glass door.

"Understanding takes a lot of time. In this regard, I'm just an infant," I said. "A *tee-nok*."

"This is wrong," said Ronit.

"It's how it feels trying to grow into this life I hardly know. You don't know what it's like."

Ronit patted my knee. "But I do know you'll never be a baby boy."

TWENTY-FIVE

I asked Sunny to take whatever furniture, household items, and clothing she wanted, and Dina put me in contact with an agency that would donate the rest to immigrants. While I was waiting for the truck to arrive, I opened the door to the small balcony. For a long time, I stood looking at the sea.

By the time the taxi dropped me off in front of my house in Pittsburgh, the apartment on Nordau Street was clean and empty, ready for the next tenants. It had been an exhausting few days that left no time to mull over the past or the future.

The driver carried my bags to my door and drove away, and I walked through the damp grass to see what had bloomed in my absence. The hostas had spread their broad leaves, and the iris were purple and attentive. The long stems of the peonies were bowed and their big tender heads were weeping petals. I'd never had a garden before I'd bought this house and had imagined gardening as going out in a straw hat and waterproof clogs and clipping beautiful flowers. Never did I foresee there'd be such violence in the endeavor; that I'd be yanking out weeds, raging against the bunnies, throwing poison into mole holes.

My street was quiet. The children were still in school and no dog-walkers passed, so I picked up my bags and stepped into my house. I went down to the basement to make sure I was alone. So now I was more than a stick figure on a blank sheet of paper, I thought. There was a background, lightly sketched, and a foreground, incomplete. On my way back upstairs, I knew there was a lot left to learn to create what I called my history. Just then, though, all I really wanted was to have a life in the place I resided, a small, ordinary life, free of unnecessary drama.

Mindy had planned to spend the weekend with me in Pittsburgh. But my cousin, Mark Gorelick, had invited me to his house, which was not far from Mindy's. So I drove to New Jersey instead. Mindy and I stayed in our pajamas until noon, took long walks in the park near her house, chopped, diced, and sautéed for the dinner we cooked together. She'd framed a photo of the two of us from seventh grade, in which she is stern, big-bosomed, and matronly looking, and I'm little and bedraggled, hairband drooping, wrinkled blouse. Stu picked it up, said, "Mother and Motherless Child," and disappeared. All weekend, it made us giggle.

We talked about her kids, our childhood, how far we'd go to preserve a youthful veneer, and Baruch; I kept circling back to Baruch, the sound of his voice, this sense of connectedness I'd felt when we were together, each time asking her: Was I right to say goodbye? And each time, Mindy saying yes. It was too hard; he lived too far away. She was sure I could find somebody wonderful in my city.

Before I left for the Gorelicks' we sat on her living room sofa, just as we had planned. I'd brought the accordion envelope containing The Book of Aviva. She unwound the string, rolled off the rubber band, read the first pages of the medical records, which by then I knew by heart.

The soft leaves rustled. I'd told her about Aviva's medical history, but reading the actual words shook her, and she murmured, "So terrible," and looked up at me. I smiled and shrugged and said, in the kind of light tone I used to deflect and put others at ease, "It's awful, isn't it?"

Mindy would not avert her eyes, and the warmth of her steady gaze broke me, and before I could cover my face, I began to cry. "I don't know how to love!" Then I put my head on my knees and wept until I thought it would rip me in two. I hated this ugly story, felt it would twist my life forever, become the whole of me, all that I'd ever have. I tried to bring to mind the pleasure of this weekend, and the women sitting on the bench outside my mother's apartment, but all I could think was that I'd never again lose myself in laughter, never recognize love, never know how to love in return.

"Oh, sweetie, you *do* know how to love," Mindy said. "You love me, don't you?"

"That doesn't count," I said, sobbing, then laughing, then lowering my head to sob some more, because it did count, I knew it did, but even so, I could not stop thinking, "*Why* had I let him leave?"

⩢

My cousins lived in a tidy new house that was easy to find because of the truck on the driveway with *Gorelick Heating & Cooling* on the side. I hadn't even rung the bell when the door opened, and Mark, small, balding, and olive-skinned, wrapped me in a hug. His wife Marilyn stood to one side in a pink sweatshirt and jeans. She and I did a little ballet, starting to shake hands, then abandoning the formality to embrace. Inside, everything was cream: the carpet, the sofas, the Wheaten Terrier playing Frisbee outside with their kids.

"You two are like twins," said Marilyn.

Mark patted his head. "She has more hair," he said.

Marilyn knocked on the glass doors that led to the patio and Galia trotted over, barefoot and flushed. She kissed me on each cheek and then said, "So, Vered, you're angry with me?" Before I could respond, she turned to Mark. "She was very nice to me and my friend when we were in Pittsburgh, working at the mall. I don't know what happened, not answering the emails."

"You missed out on some free dinners," I said. I'd forgotten those emails and was pleased to see her.

Galia was staying with the Gorelicks, helping with their kids, and commuting into the city to take bartending courses. She'd finished the basic course, had three more classes in mixology, and then would work toward her wine certification. She was hoping to get a job that paid enough for her to share an apartment in New York, and after that, she wasn't sure.

"Where's Yael?" I asked, and Galia made a sweeping motion in her hand. "In Rio."

"You have cousins in Rio," Marilyn called from across the room.

"Yael doesn't," said Galia.

Marilyn had spent months constructing family trees for her side and ours. After lunch she showed me how complete the family tree was on Mark's side of the family. In some ways it had been easier to reconstruct our family than her own because of the detailed records the Nazis had kept—"Death Books"—with the names of seventeen million people, who'd entered a concentration camp, were forced into labor, or executed. She knew how most of our uncles, aunts, and cousins had died, and had names of many of the surviving remnants of our once large family, including several people in Lima, Peru, and Brazil. "Your cousin, Florencia Bursztein, is a well-known watercolorist who lives in Sao Paulo. You should see her beautiful website."

"Florencia," I said, drawing out the syllables.

And Marilyn said, "I'll call in the kids and we can eat."

Then the kids barreled in and the dog followed them to the bathroom, barking and jumping. The children sat on either side of Galia, while Mark and I reminisced. He had fond memories of his dormer bedroom, with its window to the eaves of the roof, but didn't recall that we'd sat there together, shooting spitballs at the guests. Nor could he recall when my father had started to visit, only that he was always alone.

"He was into puzzles and brain teasers, like the one with the missionaries and cannibals crossing the river, where the cannibals couldn't outnumber the missionaries or they'd eat them. And those little metal pieces you were supposed to untangle. He was a smart guy, your dad. Not someone you could picture going into the yard and throwing the ball around."

"Not much ball throwing in our house."

Just then, I remembered how thrilled my father had been by the Rubik's Cube I'd gotten him when they first came on the market.

"Did anyone ever say why he was always alone?" I asked.

"Your mom thought she was too good for the rest of us."

"That wasn't it at all," said Marilyn. "The split happened because your grandmother told everyone it was Leona's fault the baby was brain damaged, and that's why they moved."

"How did you know this?" Mark asked his wife.

"Because *I* listen," she said. Then, with affection: "He is so ADD he never pays attention to anything."

I said, "The *baby* is all grown up. Like me. Her name is Aviva."

I looked at the faces of these cousins, who waited for me to go on. They didn't know what to say—neither did I, really. But it seemed that the words I chose didn't matter. It was speaking of her, so she would be part of our family. I tried to describe Chaverim and say something about her daily life. Then I turned to Mark. "She looks like you," I said. "Like us."

I drove back to Pennsylvania after that and got busy, trying to create the ordinary life I'd so badly wanted. I cut my hair short, bought a dress to wear with the pink shoes, chose the paper to use for my letter to Baruch—ecru, deckled-edged, acid-free, with a handsome matching envelope. Sitting at my drafting table, I began to write. But I started to cry and the ink smeared and the paper got splotchy, so I put it aside and designed an insulated shopping bag, light, foldable, with as many Velcroed pockets as a photographer's vest. It was the blue of glacial ice, with a snowstorm of tiny, horned creatures with fat bodies, long arms, and short bowed legs. When Dina called, I set this creature on long journeys down winding streets with flights of steps cut into the steep hills, holding the insulated bag with his image. Her accent and rushed way of speaking made it hard for me to understand her on the phone and it helped me focus.

The realtor called to say the young couple with the dog wanted to buy my house. I countered their lowball offer and waited dispassionately. It felt like a game. When I thought I'd lose, I decided I could make a home in this house and let the beautiful garden go wild. But this big Slavic woman and her small Colombian husband were sweet. Winning meant they'd fill the rooms with love, set a dog bed in the corner of their bedroom, use the guest room for the child they'd have. I could stop hating bunnies, stop poisoning moles, and stop worrying that Harley was hiding in a room. When at last we made a deal, I felt a surge of energy. I would box my possessions, put everything in storage—my old life, my old self. Then, like a dormant plant, I would emerge when the seasons changed.

One Saturday, just after the papers were signed, I joined a group of volunteers planting saplings in Frick Park. While standing with a dozen others, waiting for the truck that carried the trees, their fragile roots wrapped in burlap, I saw Baruch in the distance, hurrying toward me with that familiar loping gait, and my heart began to pound.

It was a lanky boy, rushing toward the crew. I turned from him, put on my work gloves, and kneeled in the dirt. After a few minutes of digging, I pulled off my gloves so I could feel the cool soil between my fingers. I tossed the stones from the hole, yanked out the bigger rocks, deeply satisfied by the effort. Later, taking a break, I looked at the lanky boy who was not Baruch and felt like a fool for my error, for holding onto what I could not have.

I was bone tired from tree planting, and when Dina called to tell me about a new man she was seeing—Shmuel, Shuki?—I struggled to stay awake. As soon we I hung up, I fell into bed. I dreamt that Baruch and I were walking along Ha'Yarkon with our arms linked, the sea to one side. He was complaining about a traffic jam when I stepped in something sticky. I lifted my shoe to see what was stuck to my sole and cried, "Ugh! I've gotten *shmulik* all over my shoe!"

I laughed so hard in the dream that I woke myself up.

It made everything seem possible.

Dear Baruch,

Apart from sorry and thank you, which I mean sincerely, I wanted to tell you that my mother died the day I didn't go with you to Chaverim. After the funeral, I drove there myself. It was a weekday so I knew you wouldn't be there, but I kept looking anyhow. It's still hard to see Aviva and harder to leave, and I miss her now that I'm home, though it's impossible to explain this to anyone except you. One of the aides told me she ate pureed food and the next time I go up, I could try to feed her. Bananas are an obvious choice, but I love a good latte myself, iced or warm, so maybe she will too. I have so much else to say, but maybe for now I'll just ask why you were offended when I called you kind. That's how it seemed, and it puzzles me. I hate the way things ended between us, and hope, truly, that life has been sweet.

With love, Roxanne

The weather got steamy. Baruch replied, saying, "Thank you for your splendid letter. Let me know when you return." There are only so many ways two sentences can be interpreted, and I worked at them all, until the effort wore me out. I needed a place to live. That's where I had to put my energy.

Les took on my search for a home, making it one of the many projects on his virtual drawing board, along with a bottle that would appeal to mature consumers and a logo for a brokerage house. He fancied himself immovable in the Federal house he'd bought years back in the Mexican War Streets and presented his quest to find me a perfect neighborhood as a vicarious pleasure. Every few days he showed me listings of spaces in converted factory buildings, some within walking distance from our office—the Cork Factory, the Cigar Factory, Otto Milk. The city had begun to evolve since I'd moved here, and so had I.

"You need to choose a place that works best for the person you are right now," Les said.

"The person I am right now is sad. Should I buy a sad, dark house? Something with bricked-in windows and a rusted fence? Because that's the kind of house that fits the person I am right now." I'd seen that house exactly. Listing toward an empty lot, across from a burned-down building.

I was touched by Les's interest, though it made me feel porous, an empty vessel. So I let him take me to see a loft in a partly renovated factory building a few blocks from work. On the way back, as we were crossing our lobby, I heard the echo of laughter and footsteps, and my mother's words returned to me—anechoic, impedance—and a memory of her taking me into an anechoic chamber at Bell Labs, a weird, padded room, where sound was flat, free of all echo, and her delight as I cried out, "The quick brown fox!" and "Four score and twenty years ago!" Not a monster, and my sadness just then the ordinary feeling of loss. As we approached the steps, Les's shoulders dropped, and his posture softened, and there she was: Yogi Descending Stairs.

She was so pretty, with her small, pale face. *Oh*, I thought, when she reached us. It was an exhalation, an awareness of loss and love.

She took my hand in both of hers and said, "I'm sorry to hear about your mother."

"Thank you," I said and told her I was glad to be home, or would be if I had an actual home.

Nomi looked at Les. It was almost too charged, too intimate standing between them, like hearing lovers in another room. As if to whisk away this unseen charge, Les waved the floor plans for this loft I did not want, with its broad open space, which he saw as a blank canvas on which I could *become*. Nomi sensed my dismay, and so I confessed. "I can't see myself there."

"My sister owns a duplex in Squirrel Hill," she said. "Her upstairs tenant is leaving at the end of next month. I bet she'd be okay with giving you a month to month lease while you're looking."

"She doesn't want to live in Squirrel Hill," Les said. "It's all families and old people."

Nomi regarded him with bemused acceptance. Oh, people, with their different ways! she seemed to be saying.

A breeze fluttered the hem of my dress. I wanted to put a hand on his shoulder and hers and push them into each other's arms. Stop squandering your good fortune, I wanted to shout. Instead, I walked off. I knew they were not alike, that she was tender and spiritual, while Les was bristly, rough around the edges, filled with unquenchable ambition.

I glanced back and saw them standing at a slight distance, already molding. Were their differences really unbridgeable?

Oh, I thought, as I slid into my car. I imagined Les could hear me whisper in his ear, *She is your bashert. Go for it.*

His *bashert*: his intended. The single person meant for him.

Was there such a thing? One single person of all the beings on earth? It seemed absurd, sentimental. Also foolish. Self-defeating.

I considered Baruch. We'd sat together at a time when grief had stripped me of my defenses and he was open and unencumbered. Months later, we had dinner together—crisp, dry wine, more than I'm used to imbibing. Candles flickered on our table. We walked for hours, stripped off our clothes and submerged ourselves in the sea. His kisses were salty. He rocked me in his arms. A bright crescent moon shone in a clear sky. In the distance young people strummed their guitars, serenading us. The sweet smell of pot wafted our way, giving us a contact high. His eyes, strange and beautiful, acknowledged sorrow and carried the expectation of pleasure. He knew Aviva, better than I did. Maybe these factors together created the illusion that he was my *bashert*.

I had loved madly before, been defenseless, was married in a friend's apartment weeks after we'd met by a judge who'd biked uptown from arraignment court. After our "I do's" my new husband and I fell into each other's arms and wept from happiness. Friends chipped in and bought us matching yellow waterproof jackets and overalls for sailing—foul weather gear.

He had not been my *bashert*. If anything, he had been my unintended, the worst person on earth for me.

He left. I got the foul weather gear. It hadn't helped.

Then soft-spoken, silver-haired Harley, with his blurry gaze and cashmere sweaters and sons who might grow to love me. Different in every possible way from my wild, faithless husband. I thought about our first date, how over dinner, while the tea lights flickered at our banquette, he told me everything, and even so all I saw was Harley's graciousness and old-fashioned manners.

Then the perfect chair, where he spent his nights, clutching his cell phone, unable to call these premonitions of disaster anxiety, unable to perceive me as human. Harley, like the still-faced mother of my youth. When I thought of all the ways they were alike it made me feel as if the only men who attracted me were either wild or deeply wounded.

Sitting in the car, I sifted through my memory of Baruch, searching for troubling signs I'd missed, so I could let go of my feelings for him.

Suppose we'd met at the salon where the stylist had held a lock of his hair and asked, "What is your vision?" We're sitting beside each other, our capes snapped tight at the neck. My mother is not dying. He does not know Aviva. I swivel in my chair, then he does. His eyes draw me in.

Hello!

No moonlight, no sea, no serenading guitars or salty kisses.

Beautiful weather.

Of course!

Do you come here often?

Of course!

Was it possible to take away time, place, and situation? Or was that like going back to the way I had lived my early life when I'd stood on nothing?

What if Aviva was back, but not the wine or moonlight? What if I restored my mother's dying, which left me puzzled, unsure what to mourn?

It was impossible. I tried to tell myself that holding onto my feelings for him meant that the steady love I claimed to want would forever be out of reach. And still, no matter what I subtracted, or how often I told myself I was being absurd, adolescent, in the deepest, truest part of my being, I still felt he was the one.

Twenty-Six

Before work one morning I drove to the hilly street where Nomi's sister lived with her daughter. Their apartment was the top floor of one of the dark brick duplexes that lined the street. "I need to warn you that mornings around here are very rough," Jill said, on the stairway to the second level. "There's a lot of screaming going on. A *lot* of screaming. But…" She tightened the sash of her yukata and smiled ruefully. "The evenings are quiet. No loud music. No wild parties."

The vacant apartment was shabby, with flattened beige carpet and textured walls, but there was an alcove off the living room for my desk, and a dry basement where I could store the furniture that did not fit. I liked Jill's matter-of-fact manner, and that I could walk to the movies and to stores. This is what I told Les, and what I believed, not yet able to articulate that I'd also wanted to be near Jill and Jessie. To live in their country for a while.

I let Kayleigh from our office talk me into having a yard sale, which she and her friends would run. "It'll be so fun!" she promised.

"Fun" didn't seem like a possibility, but there was a lot I wanted to leave behind, much of it tangible.

I emailed Harley to tell him about the yard sale and move. "You can come whenever it's convenient, as long as everything is cleared out by Saturday," I wrote. "Whatever you leave behind, I'll donate to charity." At the end of the message I told him of my mother's death.

Minutes later, Harley called to offer condolences and make arrangements to pack up his possessions. "How about eight on Friday morning? Unless that's too early?"

"Eight o'clock would be perfect," I said.

"Because I could come at eight-thirty if that would be better."

"Eight is fine," I said. "It's good. It's actually great."

"Or nine. I don't want to inconvenience you. I know you have a lot on your plate."

My plates were already packed. "Eight works for me," I said. "You've got a lot to sort through. Let's go with his first offer. Eight o'clock! Sold!"

"I'm not getting you up too early?"

"Harley. You lived with me. Am I asleep at eight a.m.?"

"You like to sleep in," Harley said, "with that Lone Ranger mask."

His wife Tina was the one who'd liked to sleep late, wearing a padded black mask, but I no longer needed to point that out. I no longer cared what he remembered. I could be like that tree in a forest. If I forgot along with him, then who was there to say that anything happened after all?

At exactly eight a.m. on the morning before the yard sale, my doorbell rang, and there he was, leaning against the brick, feet crossed at the ankles, navy polo shirt, crisp khakis, boat shoes that would never see the deck of a boat. He looked like a fashion model in an ad for senior living. Smooth skin, silver hair. Healthy.

"You look *good*," I said.

A smile flickered across his face in an out-of-synch way, odd, if familiar. "Can I come in?"

He wiped his feet on the doormat and stood uneasily near the door until I coaxed him into the kitchen, with its bare shelves and nearly empty cabinets. He seemed relaxed, well past whatever had stirred him up for so long. I ground beans for coffee and he gave me the family update: older son pursuing his interest in craft beer in Boulder, younger son working in the pro shop at a golf course in Myrtle Beach.

"Everyone at Byron's has joined AA. Even the dog is twelve-stepping it. Any day you should expect Mackie to call and apologize for the ways he's wronged you."

He took my hand, turned it to see the raised scar that ran down my thumb. It felt so tender in this time when I felt so untouched, and in my darker moments, untouchable.

"Everyone misses you," he said.

"Everyone who?" I asked.

"The boys."

"*No.*" They'd been so guarded when I'd been around, had always seemed to view me as some alien being. A Rox-anne, dug up from foreign soil.

"They looked up to you," he said.

"I don't think so." I said this gently. "What about you? Where are you living anyway?"

Again that chuckle. *Heh.* "At an Embassy Suites near the airport."

I hated that "heh," knew it meant I'd get two answers or no answer. "Really?"

"No."

"*Are* you?"

"Yes." He picked up my hand again. "No, of course not. You're so gullible. I'm sorry to hear about your mother. She was a great lady. I was very fond of her."

I didn't tell him about the *shomrim* or the pink shoes or that I'd bobbed in the tranquil sea with a man named Baruch. I said nothing about the money I'd inherited, money that made me feel that my mother's dislike of me was less about my flaws and more about what she could not forget when she saw me. I did not tell him about my plans to give part of that money to Chaverim.

I just said, "I know. You were very kind to her."

"It's quite a loss."

"Well," I said. "It's a loss."

"This must be a very difficult time for you."

"Yep," I said.

I left Harley alone in the sleeping porch he'd used as an office when we'd lived together. While he sorted through his belongings, I finished packing my own. How strange to look at objects that had been at the center of bitter fights with my former husband—a vase, a lamp—and find they had no charge, were no longer invested with our passions and rage and had reverted to their natural inert state. There was so little I wanted.

Later that afternoon, I went upstairs with spare unassembled cartons and found Harley sitting at the desk, facing the ginkgo. His stuff was scattered everywhere—shirts, books, shoes, hanging files, photo albums, golf clubs and lamps. I propped the cartons against the wall, relieved none of this mess was mine. "It looks like you can use these," I said.

Outside, a squirrel scrabbled along the gutter. "I hate those squirrels," Harley said. "If I had Yanni's pellet gun, I'd blow that critter away." He turned to me. "You need to cut down that tree."

"That's crazy. It's a beautiful tree. Look at that strong trunk. And those elegant leaves? Ginkgoes are related to ferns, you know. They're very ancient and propagate by spores. Anyhow, it's not mine to cut down."

I'd started out of the room when Harley said, "You're so beautiful, Rox."

I turned back. "At seven a.m. my crew is coming, and a whole lot of people will be trekking through the house, so you'll want to step up the action here."

"Your crew? Does this include your so-called partner?"

"He *is* my partner, and, yes, it does."

"I've got to be honest with you, Rox. Les Sheldon does not have your best interests at heart—"

"Don't," I said. "Whatever it is, don't say it, please. We've been doing well so far. We're moving right along. Let's not get distracted by old quarrels."

"Ah, Rox. You think of yourself as this sophisticated woman, but you're so naïve the way you live in this narrow world with your artsy friends. When was the last time you interacted with a normal person?"

"Harley," I said. "The clock is ticking."

He looked at me in a blurry way. "You have no idea how much I miss you."

How easily I'd been hooked before—flattered, charmed, defensive, annoyed. I did not care anymore and did not care that I did not care. I left the room, my mind on all the *stuff* that needed to be priced and tagged before my crew arrived to set up folding tables in the garage and the living room. My mind was on *my crew*, out stapling Day-Glo signs to poles at major intersections. I had to care for my crew, to feed them when they returned.

Les arrived first with wine and Nomi with sparkling water. Her sister Jill—dark-haired and unadorned, so different from her ethereal, strangely beautiful sibling—brought brownies. When the others arrived, I went upstairs to ask if Harley wanted to join us. The collapsed boxes were propped against the wall and the floor was still completely covered. "You don't want to do this," I said. "If you don't pack up your stuff, it'll be carted away on Monday."

The handsome man who'd stood at my door this morning had vanished. Harley looked haggard. "I can't make any decisions, Rox. Everything's a blur, a mess. Give me until morning when I can function."

"Strangers are going to be sniffing around all the rooms. You're going to be really unhappy hanging out here when they arrive. Even with the door shut."

"Strangers?"

"For the yard sale. Kayleigh and her fiancée posted signs all over this part of the city, and the weather looks good. I have a feeling a lot of people will show up. They're not supposed to come until nine, but I bet a few will get here earlier. You write 'no earlybirds' and the earlybirds fly in anyhow."

"A yard sale? Good lord!" Harley laughed. "With blouses hanging from the trees?"

"That's a thought," I said.

"You're joking. You must be. You never said anything about a yard sale."

"Really? Then why are you here?" I asked.

"You're selling our house."

"My house," I said.

"I just can't wrap my mind around this. It's just…beneath you. Why didn't you tell me you were having a yard sale?"

"I did tell you."

"No." He pressed his temples. "No. You never said a thing. Never. And now, I'm finding it hard. This news is hard to process. You're telling me I have to pack up everything. Tonight. I don't see how that's possible."

"You have a truck coming for the heavy stuff. At least that's what you told me. Wow," I said.

Harley leaned back in his office chair, pressing his eyelids.

"We talked about this. We emailed. I can show you our correspondence. Don't do this. Please."

"You never told me," he said.

"Harley."

Hadn't I been here before? Yes, I had been here. I had been here many times. I wasn't going to rush off and find the email. "There's food downstairs. You want some coffee, I'll make it. That's it."

I went back downstairs and sat in the dining room with my crew. I tried to shift, to join the conversation, but after a few minutes I excused myself and logged onto my email, seeking proof of what I knew was true. It made me angry that I still needed confirmation, as though I could not trust my eyes or intuition or memory. Harley had come to the house on Friday morning because I'd told him the yard sale was on Saturday. How could he so easily crush my certainty? Why did I need someone to agree that my bedroom wall was green? Wasn't it enough that I saw it as green? I wanted to believe I could change, but right then I had to say: I am a woman who has trouble trusting what I feel, who cannot hold in my heart what I know is true. I believe and doubt and believe and doubt in a constant dizzying way.

Crows woke me early. On the way downstairs, I passed Harley, perched on the radiator, his possessions scattered everywhere.

Outside a man with a giant gut and broad red suspenders was drinking takeout coffee and chatting to a stout older woman in shorts. Two rows of butterfly barrettes held back her gray hair. Her skinny legs were very white.

"Why are you doing this to me, babe?" he asked when I set a mug of coffee on his desk. "I've done everything you've asked. Why would you turn around and sell our house? Take what we owned and lay it out on the lawn like an Okie?"

It wasn't *our* house. I wasn't selling anything of his. Even so, his distress was upsetting to witness. "Listen, Harley. I've moved on," I said. "I met someone else." I hadn't planned to say this, and yet it was true. I had met someone else.

My words instantly sobered Harley. "You have *not.*"

"What makes you so sure?

"Because you love *me*. That's why. Because *I'm* the one. Why do you think I've stuck it out? I'm not a wuss, like you think. Haven't I proved I can tough it out? Haven't I shown I can do what it takes to win your heart?"

My heart: like a big blue dog he might win on the boardwalk. Misshapen and stuffed with broken shells.

Before I could answer, the back doorbell rang and I let in Nomi, her sister Jill, and their two little girls. Nomi's daughter stepped inside and looked around, silent and big-eyed, and Jill's daughter said, "Home? In a car?" Les arrived a few minutes later. Then Kayleigh in a Pirates cap, ponytail sprouting out the back, and her boyfriend Ryan, a sweet young man with square black glasses and an arm tattooed with the first line from *The Metamorphosis*, starting at the wrist with "Gregor Samsa awoke one morning," and ending mid-bicep with "giant insect." We hung clothes in the trees and set tables in the open garage, finishing just as waves of people showed up. First, the dreaded earlybirds, then the professionals, with their beat-up pickup trucks. Next came recent immigrants—Russians, Chinese—in need of basic furnishings. Then graduate students, one of whom questioned the translation Ryan had chosen for his tattoo and wanted to know why he'd gone with "uneasy dreams," and "giant insect" and not "unsettling dreams," and monstrous vermin," or "anxious dreams," and "verminous bug."

Mothers came later in the morning with little kids disappointed there were no toys. I let the girl from across the street who'd been outraged by my defection pick out a few beaded bracelets for herself, and as she tried them on, the world seemed to brighten, along with her opinion of me. Nomi sat at the cash box, and Les stood at a distance, watching her, useless in this state of love and resistance, and Jessie wandered on the driveway and lawn, clutching shoppers' arms and asking, "Home?" *Oh, I don't know, it's too nice to be stuck inside.* "Going home?" *I've been ready for an hour.* "In a car?" *As soon as my wife stops dickering over those placemats.*

Watching people recoil, I found myself wondering: Why are we afraid? Was it her difference, her foreignness? Her impenetrability? The intensity of her grasp? Did her question trigger a longing for home in its deepest way? But still, why fear? She was so small and skinny, with wild auburn hair, budding breasts, knock-knees.

When noon approached, I headed back to the garage to tell Ryan and Kayleigh they could cut the price on anything left, heard from above the scratch of metal against wood, and saw the casement window facing the beautiful gingko swing open. By then, it was less about business and more a chance to socialize. Kayleigh was gesturing with a ceramic lamp; our letter carrier, distracted from the swift completion of her appointed rounds by a velvet cloche, was showing Ryan the dolphin tattoo on her ankle. An old man with a long white beard and a belt so tightly buckled his trousers looked like a grocery bag was studying a piece of amber someone had given me years before. He held it up to the light, and I looked too, and heard the voices of strangers and neighbors, Jessie's plaintive "home?" and it made me feel part of a web. I wondered if I could hold onto this feeling, bank it, build on it, use it as a bridge to a future.

"Take it," I said to the white-bearded man. "You can have it!" I called out to a mother admiring a bronze candleholder, while her chubby son rolled down the driveway on a plastic trike, his father shuffling protectively beside him.

My next-door neighbor pulled up at the curb and was getting out of her black sedan. I'd left a note for her, saying we'd clear out by noon, and now at twelve-thirty, a few stragglers remained—the white bearded man, the chubby boy, his parents, my crew. I started down the driveway to apologize, and just as I reached her, saw a branch of the gingko tree tremble. Both casement windows in the sleeping porch were open wide. We shielded our eyes against the sun. "Look!" she cried. It was a squirrel getting ready to catapult himself to her window.

We watched the squirrel bear down on the branch, get it rocking, then leap. "It's so *clever* how they do that."

What happened next was sudden and unexpected. Harley's leg on the ledge. His other leg. I grabbed onto my neighbor's sleeve. Below the window were air conditioning units. A cement pad. I went very still, unable to speak.

"What's he doing?" she asked, peeved rather than alarmed. "He shouldn't horse around like that. It's dangerous!"

Harley, perched on the window ledge, began to howl. The people milling on the driveway turned. For a moment, we all froze, as if afraid a sudden move or barked command would unbalance him, and he would fall to the unforgiving ground. Harley covered his face, but the grief escaped with such force he swayed on the ledge, his neatly-tied boat shoes dangling. "Home?" Jessie called, in a plaintive voice. I clutched my neighbor's arm, the way Jessie had clutched mine, not knowing if it was worse for Harley to see me, or worse if he thought I was not there.

Nomi stepped out of this tableau, reed-thin and calm. She looked upward, blinking in the sun. Her daughter hurried forward, and Nomi said, "Harley?" and scooped her close. "Harley, I'm Nomi. And this is Alix, my little girl. I want you to hold on, Harley. Just hold on. You have friends down here. And children. Alix and Jessie. And a little boy."

Harley was weeping hard, swaying.

"You're a father, aren't you, Harley? You would never hurt your children. You would never want them to see something awful. Something that would trouble them for all their days and nights. Listen to me. Please. I want you to take a deep breath. Will you do that for me? Will you breathe with me for just one moment? It will calm your aching heart. Just breathe. Hold on and take a very slow deep breath, because sometimes, Harley, we have these moments of pain that seem so unbearable we forget they'll pass. I want you to breathe with me, Harley."

I loosened my grip on my neighbor's arm and stepped away from her, breathing deeply, aware of the stillness. No wind, no motion, only Nomi's firm, reassuring voice. "You aren't alone, Harley. Alix will breathe with you. And Jill. We'll all breathe together, along with you. Everyone here. Will you do that with us, Harley? Will you do this? Together, starting with *puraka*. A single long inhalation. Let's do this together. Good. Beautiful. Yes, that's okay, you can pause. It's called a broken *puraka*. Harley, we will get to the exhalations, but for now, I want you to stay with me. To feel the way we are all breathing together, everyone here, the men, the women, the children. We're going to share your inhalation, your lovely, deep, calming inhalation that relaxes your entire body. Harley, okay, *abhyantara kumbhaka*. Pause, you will be motionless. Don't make your lungs work. Ease your shoulders. We are pausing with you. We have reached *rechaka* and will exhale, all of us here. We are all with you—*puraka*. Look around at your friends, at the kind faces below. *Abhyantara kumbhaka rechaka*. Harley, a smooth, continuous exhalation. All around, we are exhaling with you. Can we do that again? Can we all breathe with Harley?"

The old man in suspenders breathed deeply and paused. The boy, motionless on his trike. Ryan, who'd tattooed the first lines of *The Metamorphosis* on his arm—I could feel his *puraka* as I slipped into my house. And Kayleigh, who loved Ryan, I could feel her exhale with Harley as I worked my way up the stairs, stepping over the hangers and clothes and books on the sleeping porch floor. While my neighbors were breathing with Harley, I stepped up to the wide-open windows, leaned as far as I could safely stretch, feet planted firmly, in those moments not thinking or worrying or grieving, not guilty or regretful. Only my arms extending until I could embrace from behind this man I had once loved—this aching, wounded being, still breathing with Nomi, still following her so closely I could pull him safely inside.

TWENTY-SEVEN

Harley's brother Byron drove him to a "retreat" in Western Massachusetts, and I moved into the top floor of the duplex where I would live until I figured out what I wanted next. When I called Byron to find out how Harley was doing, he made the retreat sound like a vacation destination. Everything I said made him uncomfortable. There's no shame in this, I wanted to say, because I knew he was ashamed of Harley, and knew well this unbearable emotion.

The website was just as evasive. There were many photographs of Sunnyledge's "gracious environment" and "elegantly appointed rooms" that made it the perfect setting for an "intermediate length of stay." You had to look hard to see the fine print saying insurance was not accepted. Byron didn't want to talk to me. He did not want to know me. "Little Bro has always been a problem child," he said, and hurried off.

The moving truck had not yet arrived, and in the morning light the empty apartment looked bleak and shabby, with a living room carpet stamped flat by prior tenants and a permanent gray crust where the carpet met the molding. The walls had been freshly, if hastily, painted a yellowish beige gloss that showed off the drips, each one ending in a tip as thick as a match head that marked the place where the paint had simply stopped moving. On the kitchen counter was a box of chocolates and a welcome note from Jill.

A charitable organization had picked up whatever I hadn't sold, and the movers carried so little upstairs it only took a couple of hours for me to set up. After flattening the last carton, I stood in the middle of the living room and imagined myself congealing right here like a drop of wet paint. Then I found my backpack and walked "upstreet" to buy some food.

The dark brick duplexes that lined both side of my street were softened by flowers in window boxes, planters and garden beds—pansies, nasturtium, zinnias. Tall sunflowers rose against the walls, their heads drooping as if in sorrow.

It was late afternoon and hot. Early September. School had just started. I didn't know this neighborhood well and felt an edge of discomfort as I walked—single, childless, in my shabby digs. As I reached the stores I saw a long line snaking down the street and around the corner. Closer, I saw that the line began outside a store that sold ices. The girls wore tiny shorts and flip-flops and boys were in T-shirts and droopy shorts, and they were bouncing and giggling and pushing against each other, their exuberance contagious, and when I passed, I thought with some excitement: Of course you feel a little uneasy. You're creating your own story. Right now.

The person I am now is walking into the supermarket.

It seemed, then, that the discomfort I felt was intensified by how new this was, not merely the apartment in an unfamiliar neighborhood, but the story, my story. I was stopping at the post office as a twin, wheeling my grocery cart as one of two, with a sister who was in me and far away. I didn't know the end. That day, though, alone as I felt, I understood that part of the reason I'd cast off so much of what I'd owned was that these trappings had belonged to the hollow old self, the fake self, and this was new.

This was the year she took a modest apartment.

Her landlord left her chocolate and a card that said: May your days be sweet.

At the front of the checkout line, I smiled, thinking of this welcome gift. The cashier eyed me warily. "Do you have your Giant Eagle Advantage card?"

"Somewhere," I said. "Give me a second while I check."

Harley was at a retreat in Western Massachusetts; the young couple and their dog were moving into my house, and I was searching my wallet for a Giant Eagle Advantage card to get ten cents off on cottage cheese.

I lowered my backpack slowly onto the table. I did not arise from a spore, like a ginkgo, did not invent myself, was not a citizen of the world. I was a single woman, born in Israel, raised in New Jersey, living in Pittsburgh, Pennsylvania. I lowered my backpack slowly onto the table. My mother was dead. Like millions of others, I had ties in more than one country. I put the groceries away and saw in the fridge a bottle of sparkling wine with a curled ribbon around the neck. I felt energized, full of possibility.

That night I found the sheets and pillowcases I'd packed and made up my bed. These familiar linens made me feel at home, and I fell right to sleep.

Then light, and raw, ragged screaming that jolts me awake, cutting through my chest like a knife. I try to sit up and catch my breath, but the screaming is stuck inside me, and it is Aviva, my mother, Amber Chatsworth, *frustrated that she was difficult to feed,* it is a baby, it is me, it is someone screaming, *Stop it, stop!,* and I am sobbing and want it to go away, the screaming, the life, this history. Then quiet, and I take in the shiny, unfamiliar walls and wait for fragments of reality to reassemble. My mother is dead. Aviva is at Chaverim. Harley has not jumped. I've sold my house. It's Jessie from downstairs. It's only Jessie.

By the time I get myself outside, Jessie is already standing on the steps.

"Home?" she asks me. Her lush auburn curls are tied in a ponytail, and her pale face is smooth and untroubled. We watch a wizened Chinese couple push a baby stroller up our short hill. "Home?" Jessie calls, flapping her arms as they pass. It's impossible to believe she is the same raging being I'd heard only minutes before.

Later that fall, after the clocks changed, Jessie's raw, primal screaming reached me in the darkness and unearthed what I will call memory—vivid, wordless. It seemed to bring me back to that small flat where my parents had lived with their unexpected babies, children my mother had not wanted and could not nurture, one healthy, the other impaired, one consolable, the other red-faced, wide eyes wet with tears, impossible to calm, her skin-piercing wail breaking my mother as Jessie's wail broke me.

Trembling in bed, with the light barely rising, this is what I wished I could have told Baruch: I was raised by a mother who had been damaged in her youth and had motherhood thrust upon her, that I'd never know what was in her heart that night or years later, only that she had been as impossible to comfort as a wailing baby. Whatever accommodation I made with the facts of my own life, which I was only now, slowly, beginning to assemble, it would not be as simple as "blame" or "forgiveness," but something else I could not yet name, some still undetermined path of my own making.

In the weeks that followed, I got to know Jessie. I saw her walking to school with her arm linked through her mother's, or breaking into a flat-out run, arms flapping, backpack flopping, laughing in the same unrestrained way she screamed. On Sundays I sometimes sat on the brick patio out back, paging through the *Times* while she and her mother sat at the round glass table, an antiquated boom box covering the hole where an umbrella might stand, listening to "Under the Boardwalk" or "The Sloop John B." I learned that Jessie was *tactile-defensive,* so distressed by certain sensations, that Jill had to detach all the labels from Jessie's clothes or she'd rip them off her body, but that she'd let her mother brush her lustrous curls with an old-fashioned boar bristle brush.

I no longer thought *she,* as I had with Aviva. *Her.* This life Jessie had with her mother, the school she attended with other children who rolled and walked down the sidewalk on outings. I no longer thought *they.* I thought of the way my mother had spoken about Arabs, or what Harley's mother, "the most unprejudiced person in the world," thought about "Jewish people," those loud, pushy others, and I was reminded that my world was narrow, not in the way Harley thought it was—long on "artsy" friends and short on MBAs—but ignorant thus far on the ways of Jessie and of Aviva.

I would never get used to the screaming.

&

The afternoon Dina called to tell me about her new beau, I was again sitting on a wrought-iron chair in the small yard behind our duplex, the Sunday *Times* spread across my lap. Pots of burgundy and gold chrysanthemums had been set out on the brick patio, and the last red leaves fluttered from the maple beside my rickety chair. Otis Redding was singing "Dock of the Bay," all that emotion squeezed and distorted through the puny speakers in the boom box, and even so, it pierced my heart. I'd booked a flight to Israel, and now, watching Jill brush Jessie's hair, I could feel in my chest and arms the desire to sit beside Aviva, to hold her hand, and if she liked it, to loosen her hair from its braid and brush it, gather it, divide the locks in three and make a new braid. I was eager to see Shelley Silk, too. We'd been in regular contact these last months, regarding the therapeutic horseback riding that was being planned for Chaverim. Money my parents had left me would cover the cost of the stables.

I tried not to moon over Baruch and in daytime succeeded, though at night, I still felt myself in the sea with him, the waves bringing us close, pushing us apart. I did not cultivate these memories and even went out on a couple of dates with an energetic thrice-divorced man named Fred, about whom I could say: not Tom, not Harley. So the sea inside me, so often churned up, was as still as glass.

Dina had a long update on the renovation in my mother's apartment, the young oboist who lived there with her husband, and the fantastic new man in her life, and in the background Otis sang, "I can't turn you loose." I wondered, too, what it must be like to have something so raw and pure inside, to be able to open your throat and let it out, and Fred came to mind, his place in my life, it seemed just then, was to give me something to tell Dina, whose sentences were in a little boat on the still sea inside me.

Jessie lifted her chin high in the air, and Otis, who died at twenty-six, began singing, *Fa fa fa fa fa fa fa fa*, and when I asked myself whose life was hardest and lined up all the people I knew, it was not Aviva, who'd win the popular vote, not Jessie, who did not perceive herself as different, had no angst, was not "challenged," the way her mother often was.

Harley. Handsome, affluent, father of sons.

A name rocked the boat. I covered my free ear and my chair wobbled on the bricks.

Then a detail about the profession of Dina's fantastic new beau. *He studies faces! It is the most interesting work.*

"Wait a second," I said. "What's his name?"

"Baruch," she said.

"That's crazy!" I said, standing so suddenly the chair fell backward and Jessie shrieked.

"We saw him together."

"Yes!" Dina said. "You said 'go out with him,' and you were so right, Roxanne, he is the most intelligent man."

I walked between the duplex apartments, away from Otis and Jessie and Jill, and by the time I reached the street, I remembered seeing his photo on JDate and the profile I could not read, and Dina trying to get me to contact him, and that I'd said, "You like him, you go out with him." You take him, as if he were an object at yard sale. You can have him.

I lowered myself to the stoop, listened, and did not listen. Across the street, a neighbor was raking her small lawn. Her dog rolled over, scratching his back in the pile of leaves, scattering them. Dina laughed, asked how far Minneapolis was from Pittsburgh, and the neighbor, admonishing her dog, said, "Bernie. *Bad!*" It all seemed so absurd—Dina and Baruch, that I lived in this duplex, that the woman across the street was castigating her dog in a loving voice.

When I got off the phone, I unlocked the outer door of the building. The staircase smelled of mildew. I climbed slowly, entered my shabby apartment, with its bare walls and flattened carpet, the broken burro on the windowsill. I had no reason to be upset, I thought, as waves of sadness washed over me. No way would I see them together when I was there.

But I would, of course. At Chaverim.

Twenty-Eight

I arrived at my cousin's house in Ra'anana late at night and Meir showed me to Galia's old room. Unused to such dark, silent nights, I slept so deeply I did not know when I woke if it was late afternoon, or two days later, until I opened the shutters and saw the white morning sun and my rental car. I dressed and followed Ronit's voice out into the garden. Breakfast had been laid out on the patio table—salads, soft cheeses, and bread.

Meir, small and polite, stood when I arrived, and Ronit said, "Meir thanks you for the gifts. He says you have a very optimistic nature. You'd like coffee?"

"Yes, thank you," I said. I'd never been called optimistic and was puzzled by this comment.

I'd brought my cousins iPods and mag lights, and as an afterthought, I threw in a couple of my insulated bags. Meir brought me a cup of hot water and a jar of Nescafe and sat back down. While Ronit and I caught up, he lifted the flap of the bag, pressed the Velcro together, and ripped it apart again. He wiggled his fingers inside, quietly exploring the interior.

Ronit had visited Aviva, once with Meir and once alone. It was difficult to be there, she confessed. It pulled at her insides. Meir could not go anymore. Better to die quickly by whatever means than to suffer the way these poor people did.

"You don't have to go," I told her. "I hadn't suggested visiting as a punishment. But please tell Meir that Aviva isn't suffering. She doesn't have a 'before.' Her way of being is what she knows. It's her life."

Ronit watched Meir stick his whole fist into the bag to assess its capacity and said, "Your father also brought very nice gifts."

"Did you know what he used to do at Chaverim? Shelley said he brought presents for everyone and had catered lunches set on the patio and hired a klezmer band and a string quartet."

"And for the girls, too," Ronit said.

"What did he bring them?"

Ronit got up from the table, and Meir patted the insulated bag.

"Yes," I said. "I had fun with that one." I gestured to the table and grape arbor, the beautiful garden, with bougainvillea and green lemons dangling like ornaments from a pair of trees, and said, "*Yafe? Yafa?*"—unsure of the gender of this lovely tableau. After that we waited in amiable silence.

Ronit returned with a Parcheesi set and two big picture books. *Wonders of the Natural World* and *Manmade Wonders*. Everything had been extensively repaired with duct tape, the corners of the Parcheesi box, the spines of the books. I recognized my father's handwriting when I opened the first book and saw the inscriptions in Hebrew and in English. On the flyleaf he had written, "To Galia and Maya." In the second book he had written, "To Maya and Galia." It was as if I were learning about his secret family, with grateful girls who did their homework eagerly. It cut deep.

I had to leave for Chaverim in an hour. I showered and dressed, checked the mirror, and saw a portrait of despair. Not good, I said to my reflection. Not good at all.

Some women, this one at least, have moments of feeling that perfect attire can vanquish despair. Thus motivated, I pulled my shirt over my head, slid off my jeans, and perched on the bed, intending to reconsider my options. I studied the inadequate rental car map instead—the only places of interest seemed to be rental car locations—then reached for one of the picture books my father had given Ronit's daughters. Flipping through the pages, past the Grand Canyon and Victoria Falls, I thought once again what a waste it had been, all those nights we'd sat in the dining room, my math homework spread across the table. There was no way to tell him that the look on my face was hopelessness, not scorn or disrespect as he'd believed.

I put the book aside, slipped on a dress, a long-sleeved black jersey that, like my insulated bag, could fold into a little square. I put lotion on my legs, moisturized my heels and then each toe, and when I stood, I slid in my sandals. I imagined sliding toward Baruch, arms extended, and Baruch stepping back and letting me fall.

I'd freeze up there in the mountains. I changed back into jeans, chose a long-sleeved shirt, packed a bathing suit and jacket, and slipped on boots. By then it was one-thirty.

Here's why I was late to meet Baruch and Dina, why I am often late. Living alone, I had no one to push me from the gunwales of the boat, backward into the unknown.

❧

The two of them were sitting on the patio when I approached. Dina saw me first, cried, "Roxanne!" and shuffled toward me in her mules, her arms outstretched. I embraced her, taking in her scent of sandalwood and cloves.

Baruch rose slowly. Pale, thin, distracted, his odd, luminous eyes looking elsewhere. He seemed to occupy a different plane, high above his small, voluble companion. Six months had passed since he had rocked me in the cool sea. I don't know this man in his zip-front sweater and khakis, I thought.

Dina kissed both my cheeks. "You are looking like a movie star, so beautiful, wow! Baruch, this is my very good friend, Roxanne."

My body could not be fooled. My heart was racing. "Hey," I said, friendly, questioning, wishing someone would fill me in on who knew what.

Baruch extended his hand and glanced at me briefly, and when I felt his leathery palm and the shape of his hand, I did know him and wanted to say, "What are you doing?" I wanted to say, "It makes no sense, the two of you together."

"I'm sorry I'm late," I said.

"This is so fantastic, the two of you with me. And now we will get Dan and Aviva and we will all take our walk through the beautiful garden, and later, Roxanne, we have so many special places to show you."

I followed Baruch and Dina on the broad winding paths beyond the patio, past lush plantings and sculpture gardens. Dina's enthusiasm was a relief and a distraction and kept me from sinking into pointless, bitter feelings. I didn't need to return to the evening when I'd leaned over Dina's computer to study his photo and said with irritation, "You like him? Fine, you take him." As if he were an object at a yard sale, gently used.

It was chilly. I dug around in my bag for my jacket. *You go out with him. He's not my taste.*

Dina paused, putting a hand over her heart. "To be in this beautiful place with you and Baruch? This is a dream, Roxanne. The most special day." She moved to the side to let a father wheel his son past us, the heavy, dark-haired man and spastic, skeletal son in matching yarmulkes. "It is fantastic," she said.

My heart could still ache and did.

Baruch fell back a step so Dina could take his arm. At the bottom of a long hill, Dina stopped. "This is where they'll have the horses. You know about this, yes?" She gestured toward a flat, rocky stretch of land where soon there would be stables and a therapeutic horse-back-riding program.

"Yes," I said. "Tomorrow Mrs. Silk is showing me the plans."

"I am trying to bring Etti here, so she can see it is so fantastic and tell her father." Etti was the oboist who'd moved into my mother's apartment, whose father owned hotels in Greece. "He don't know what to do with his money, he has so much. And he is a very good man, Roxanne. Very generous. He get a job for my Tali at one of his hotels and this has been fantastic for her; you can't believe. Roxanne, you're in love?" Dina gestured with her chin. "I call her, she tells me nothing on the phone!" she said to Baruch.

I stole a glance at him and the night in Dina's apartment again flashed through my mind, how drawn I'd been to his photograph. *What?* I'd thought when his face appeared on her computer screen. *Tell me, what is it?* His straightforward gaze had been so compelling I kept returning to his photo. Now I found myself wondering if it was simply the expression of a man who was not paying attention.

"No," I said. "Not really."

Dina slowed, so we could all walk together. "We will find someone for you."

Baruch flashed what even I knew was a fake smile, just the corners of his mouth raised.

The doors opened for us and we entered the building together, approaching the warbling birds Dina seemed to dislike. As soon as she moved beyond them, she was comfortable, greeting therapists, family members, maintenance workers. I followed along, and the familiar sense of being stuffed with the unspeakable rose within me. Baruch slipped his phone from his pocket and checked it as he walked. I had to make something of this visit. Isn't that what he'd advised? Learn what pleased Aviva, and be with her in a way that would hasten my return?

I couldn't spend my time pushing Aviva in her wheelchair and talking to Dina. I'd traveled too far to settle for this. So when we reached the greenhouse, where Dan and three other residents in wheelchairs sat with an aide, enjoying the rich, loamy scent, I said, "I'm going to swim with Aviva."

"Tomorrow you swim; that will be very good," Dina said. "Today we will walk with Dan and Aviva and then we will take you to Akko. You've never been there, Roxanne, it is the most ancient city, so full of history and also the most fantastic restaurant, with a chef who is a brilliant man, all over he is famous. You have never had such delicious food."

"That sounds perfect. I've never been to Akko. Why don't you two walk with Dan while I swim with Aviva, and we can meet in the lobby in two hours. We'll have the whole rest of the day together. Would that be okay?"

It was not okay. Dina looked as if she would cry.

Baruch put his hand on Dina's arm and spoke softly to her. She nodded in a resigned way. I continued ahead, hoping I could cast off the familiar sense of having disappointed someone yet again. Dina for certain—I was always letting her down. Baruch didn't seem to care, about this or anything else.

At least I was doing what I needed to do, I thought, as I changed into my bathing suit.

My pride was short-lived. I walked into the natatorium, took in the still blue water in the pool, the walkers and mechanical lift, and realized I'd forgotten to ask that Aviva be brought here to swim with me.

The natatorium was annexed to the main building and on this afternoon felt as quiet, as sealed-off, as a bunker. I wandered barefoot, towel wrapped around my waist, accosting everyone I met, calling "Anglais?" my language a useless currency down here, where everyone was Russian. "Anglais?" I tried, tightening my towel.

I dressed and made my way to the main office where a young office worker, fluent in English, told me I'd find Aviva in the "Quiet Room." An aide escorted me down the corridor, and I stepped inside the room where the lights were dim and New Age music played. On the wall was a bubble column with real-looking fish swimming in the bubbles, while the background color changed. I looked for Aviva. Not in the waterbed, gazing at a segmented mirror, not near the bubble column. It took me a moment to find her, swaying in a leaf chair that cradled her body, a sparkly net drawn over her. The air had a faint floral scent. Was that why she was here? I knelt in front of her, lowered my shoulders, then slipped my hand through the mesh net and placed it over hers. *I'm here*, I thought.

"I'm here," I said aloud. "Vered, your sister, a.k.a Roxanne."

I worked the soft shoe from her foot, felt the shape of her arch, and each toe. While music played softly and the water bubbled in the tubes, I took off her other shoe, and while she swayed in the chair, massaged her feet, with their soft soles that had never touched the ground. I pushed the chair gently so it swayed and wished there were room for me beside her. Maybe I could ask if there was a leaf chair for two. Or if not, I could design one. I rested my head on her lap and imagined a checklist for myself: brings objects to nose, enjoys being naked, likes to spoon with a man in bed, seeks out having body parts rubbed or touched, withdraws from peers, avoids sustained eye contact, hard to calm when upset.

I had the same visceral response, seeing them in the lobby two hours later. *Wrong.* On the way to the parking lot, the word rang in my head like a chime. *Wrong.* All the other men she'd liked had been lumpy and distracted.

I volunteered to sit in the back of the car. Dina moved the pile of folders, newspapers, and empty water bottles to make room. I climbed in and sat with my knees pressed together. At the start of the drive to Akko, I craned forward, trying to hear above the road noise. Dina spoke to Baruch in Hebrew, but there was also a brief narrative for me, an accounting of all the people who'd stirred up the dust in Akko: the Canaanites, the Israelites, the Greeks, the Persians, the Egyptians, the Romans, the Byzantine empire, the Christians, Arabs, Baha'i, the Crusaders, the Druze, the Ottomans, the British, the Jews. I couldn't get the gist of their conversation, only understood that they weren't chatting about history.

I leaned back, pretending to be drowsy until I became drowsy, and entered a dreamy state from which I was shaken when Dina turned sharply onto a traffic circle. I peeled off the newspapers and water bottles that had slid onto my lap, took in the drab apartment blocks on the outskirts of town, the laundry on racks, and nearly empty streets.

Just outside the old city Dina pulled into a dusty lot. I'll wait in the car! I imagined saying, as I had when Ronit had visited my family all those years before. Or I could be like Hannah, who refused to go to Vermont with her parents the summer she turned fifteen. "But it's so beautiful," Mindy had tried to explain to her sullen daughter. And Hannah, voice dripping with disdain: "I did beautiful last year."

Dina said a few cheerful words and slid out of the car. Baruch got out next. I pushed the front seat forward, thinking, "I'll wait in the car! I did beautiful last year!" as I scuttled awkwardly to my feet. Then Dina wove her arm through Baruch's. *He's great!* I'd have to tell her that. *I'm so pleased you've found someone you like.* I'd have to tell Baruch. Or maybe the truth would slide out, and I'd say, "You've got to be kidding." It was brutal seeing them together.

We walked on the stone path toward the harbor, where fishing boats were anchored. Ancient Turkish houses opened to the sea. I made a half-hearted attempt to take in the stone walls and mosques, the boats with their clanging halyards, the blue sky and crisp breeze, if only to file away these sights for a time when they might interest me. I asked occasional polite questions. Dina answered and digressed. Baruch walked beside her, silent, chin raised, as if busy smelling the air. All I wanted was to go home, to get to that elusive non-place, instead of strolling beside the two of them, making admiring noises, feigning pleasure, bilious with despair.

It was still early when we arrived at the restaurant. A few diners sat inside, but all the tables on the patio were empty. We sat at one, listened to the gulls, praised the light wind. A small swarthy waiter brought us a wine list. Dina talked to him for five minutes and then turned to me. "What the chef is making they will bring to us."

This is how it would go. We would be offered one course after the next until we'd had enough. I fished around in my bag for a scarf to wind around my neck and suggested they choose the wine.

"Baruch is just home from Minnesota," Dina said. "That's near Pitts-boorg?"

Closer than Winnipeg. I imagined saying this. I imagined running off, and then, what—standing at the traffic circle, trying to hitch a ride back to my rental car in the lot at Chaverim? "Not particularly," I said. "Were you there for a conference?"

This was the first question I'd asked Baruch directly. He looked up. Dina said, "His son live there. *Lives* there."

"Really!" Of course he'd told me this. "We're all so scattered. It's another diaspora, everyone travelling to the land of best opportunities. That's how I ended up in Pittsburgh. It's not like I'd ever been there. I hadn't even known what it was, Pitts-boorg. But it's not so dramatic when you think of the journeys other people make on rafts or in trucks to cold unfriendly places." My bracelet got stuck in my sleeve. I busied myself, working to free the clasp from an invisible thread. An unforgettable image came to mind: two Somali boys sitting in a bare room in North Dakota. "I think about this a lot."

Dina didn't, at least not then. "You're going to move to Israel." She squeezed my wrist. "Everyone is here. Your cousin Ronit, such a wonderful woman; we have become very good friends, and you know, we love you so much, Roxanne. We will take such good care of you."

"I know you would." I turned to Baruch. "Do *you* get to thank her? I'm not allowed to say I appreciate everything she's done for me, so I won't try to tell her anymore. But it's true, what she says. Almost everyone is here. I have a friend in New Jersey who's like a sister, and I've just reacquainted with some cousins, also in New Jersey, and there's my business, my little company, in Pittsburgh. And my partner. That's kind of it, which I guess is pathetic, but maybe not. It's a life."

The waiter brought us a plate of grilled red peppers, feta, and olives. Dina arranged some on a hunk of bread and held it to Baruch's mouth. He protested weakly, opened wide, then gently moved her hand. I turned away from this awkward interaction and watched a steady stream of visitors ambling past. Couples. A foursome of nuns in white habits.

"Nuns!" I cried.

Baruch's phone rang. He took it from his pocket, then rose, and walked off. Dina listened for a moment, before providing me with a subtitle: "From all over the world they work with him."

"Yes," I said.

"He is *very* important in his field, so respected, and with me, Roxanne? He is such a good person!"

"I know," I said.

"You cannot take Aviva from this beautiful place where they look after her with such love."

I knew that too. I'd never uproot her. "I'll do what my father did and see her four times a year. That's the way it is for a lot of families these days, isn't it? His son in Minnesota, your daughter in Greece. How often do you get to see her?"

"My daughter. *Fff.* She is happy with her low-class job." Dina waved her hand, then rejected the beets. When Baruch returned, we both watched him settle into his seat. "I know a very nice man, a history professor. You'll like him very much," Dina said to me.

"Dina is always trying to fix me up," I told Baruch.

At home, in my imagination, we understood each other. Here, beside Dina, he seemed completely closed off. I clasped the edge of the table and shook it lightly. Once I'd seen someone tip over one of these and send all the dishes clattering. It was very dramatic.

"Everyone should have a chance to be happy!" Dina said.

"You can be happy and single," I said. "People do it all the time, women better than men, according to studies. Women have friends; we know how to take care of ourselves."

"You turn me down every time, and look!" She elbowed Baruch gently and laughed. "See what you can find?"

"A big fish," I said.

Really, it was a pan of calamari the waiter brought to our table.

As we were dividing it, a woman in a billowing muslin dress paused beside our table and said, "That looks utterly delicious. What is it?"

"Calamari," Baruch said. "Squid."

"Squid isn't Kosher!" The woman and her husband backed off, then stopped in the middle of the stone walkway to consult their guidebook, blocking the path of other tourists. The man had on a terry porkpie hat. Yards of wrinkled muslin went into the woman's dress, and beneath all the layers, thick-soled Mary Janes. Nothing good was going on there.

"What's that supposed to be, homeless chic?" I said. "The paper-bag look? You want to be cool, there are other ways."

Baruch looked at me, his expression unreadable. My cheeks burned. "*Comfortable* cool. It probably seems shallow for me to go on this way, but I think about these things, the way you think about faces. Maybe."

The American couple backtracked, taking the table beside us.

"Dina tells me your mother was a physicist," Baruch said.

"She was," I said. "Did she also tell you I was a negligent daughter?"

Dina laughed. "She told me nothing," Baruch said.

"She worked in psychoacoustics," I said. In high school, I'd tried to impress a boy by saying my mother's field was psychoacoustics. Thereafter, whenever he saw me in the hall he danced around me in a googly-eyed circle, crying, "Psycho!" and flapping his hands. "Have you ever heard of Bell Labs?"

"Of course."

Of course. For an instant it was as if nothing had come between us.

"Did she know Penzias and Wilson?"

"Sure. She adored Arno Penzias. He was a Hungarian Jew, an émigré, like her. After he and Wilson won the Nobel Prize, she brought home a red T-shirt with little 3ks dancing all over for it for three degrees Kelvin—three degrees above absolute zero, the temperature of the cosmic microwave background radiation at the time of the Big Bang, which I guess you know. Then below all the dancing 3ks, it said, 'This is the way the world began, not with a whimper but a bang.' Penzias and Wilson were awarded the Nobel Prize and all I got was this lousy T-shirt," I said. It was an obscure joke, which I hurried past.

I'd loved that T-shirt. I knew the temperature of cosmic background radiation and the original line from "The Hollow Men" because I wore that shirt all the time and got to explain what it meant. "It's not like I actually understand the Big Bang. It's not like I understand anything. Obviously."

Baruch met my eyes, bored, interested, I couldn't tell.

"Here's a story my mother loved," I said, propelled by nervous energy. "Penzias and Wilson came to Bell Labs to do radio astronomy, because radio waves are important for all kinds of things, including communication, and they were trying to get rid of all the noise in radio amplifiers, trying and failing, because *something* kept coming in from outer space. There was this other guy, an engineer, who also noticed this low noise. The engineer was set on solving the problem of how to make the best amplifier ever, but Penzias and Wilson were physicists like my mother and interested in the fundamental nature of the universe, and they started asking bigger questions that led to their accidental discovery of background radiation. For my mother, the greatest thing in the world was to be a real scientist who asks big questions and not just a technician."

This was a life lesson I actually loved: that you were supposed to look up. To ask big questions. How strange and disturbing that the scientist who believed this forgot her own daughter.

Dina's eyes filled. "She was a very great woman."

"A great scientist, maybe, but a terrible mother," I said.

The waiter lowered a plate on which was a small sizzling fish. Dina made space on the table, and the woman in the billowing muslin dress leaned over and inhaled deeply. "That smells divine. What is it?"

"St. Peter's fish," Baruch said. "It's Kosher."

Baruch took his fork and worked the skin and flesh cleanly from the bones.

My mother was gone, but there were still unanswered questions, dancing around like those little 3ks. I handed Baruch my plate. I hadn't seen that T-shirt in ages.

The tables on the patio began to fill. Dina spoke to Baruch and then got up. I watched her walk into the restaurant, kept watching until she was no longer in view. When I turned back to the table, he was sitting across from me.

"Hi," I said.

He gave away nothing, just took me in with those big, pale eyes.

"I get to thank you at least, don't I?" I asked.

The breeze blew a hank of his hair straight up.

"Baruch…" His name an exhalation, a question.

"Vered." He said my name with such tenderness.

"Listen," I said, then hesitated, searching for words. I closed my eyes to blot out the voices of tourists and diners, the plaintive cry of gulls, and sizzling from the nearby kitchen, the scent of olive oil, garlic, brine, the scrape of chairs against stone, the Americans at the table beside us, with their grating, familiar voices. All that came to me were images, sensual ones in the sea, where we had rocked together, his lips, his body against mine, the tacky feeling of dried salt, the pitch and tenor of his beautiful voice. The chocolate seeping from my mother's lips, the loose skin on the back of her hand, my sister in the leaf chair, her fists turned inward, her need, I feared, like mine, to have someone curled in my arms. Not someone, no, a man; not any man…

"Is this serious?" I managed.

"You mean Dina?"

Easing back into her chair. "The smell from what they are cooking! What do you think, Roxanne, is this fantastic? I speak to the man who owns this place and he is going to bring us something special, like you never had before. You wait." She pulled her napkin off the table with a flourish.

"I'm totally stuffed."

"Roxanne, you must have what he bring. I ask him to make it special for you."

"Ai!" I cried.

"Take a bite already," said the husband in the porkpie hat. "It'll make her happy."

In the parking lot, Dina began to make plans for us for the following day. She was upset when I told her I'd be spending the afternoon with Aviva. I kissed Dina and promised we'd get together on Sunday, then stood on my toes and pecked Baruch chastely on the cheek.

On the long drive to Ronit's, I was drunk with fatigue. The thought of falling into Galia's bed kept me focused on the road. But first I had to email Shelley Silk, so she'd know when I would arrive. As soon as I got back to Ronit's I wrote the message. I reread it to make sure it was coherent and then went to sleep. The next day, I saw I had requested some *intruction* so the too of us could be in the pool together. *The too of us.* I had written that.

Ronit and Meir were already gone when I woke; it was just me and my bad spelling in their house. Then me—my grammar toasted by lack of sleep—punching radio buttons, seeking a distraction on the drive north. Israeli pop music, a talk show with angry Israelis, a BBC reporter with her plummy voice and depressing news, my own interior voice: *The too of us. The too of them.*

TWENTY-NINE

When the mild, imperturbable Shelley Silk saw me in the doorway of her office the next day, she rose, hugged me briskly, and said, "We are over the moon! Leave your things here, and let's go down to the site."

I put the bag with my bathing suit and towel on a chair, and we left the building together. On the broad path toward the parking area, Shelley took my arm, and I slowed my pace to match hers. The sun was blazing in the bright sky, and the wind whipped my hair across my face. In the distance was the large, flat expanse of land, already cleared of stones and scrub. Modest plans for a stable had been in the works before I'd talked to Shelley about the money I'd inherited from my parents. Now, though, we could have a full-time instructor and four horses for the residents of Chaverim, as well as space to board privately owned horses and future plans for adaptive riding classes for nonresidents, which would defray the costs of the residential riding program that would bear my father's name.

"I wish your father could have seen this," she said, pointing to where the stables and riding ring would be. He would have been thrilled. But I was here, and it was marvelous. "You remind me so much of him," she said with surprising affection.

"Really?" No one had ever said this. "In what way?"

"He was a little sparrow, like you. And his hair was very dark. Mine was, too, in those days. We grew old together, your father and I."

I shielded my eyes and looked out into the field, imagining what might be in the future.

"He really loved it here, didn't he?"

Shelley paused, sensing, it seemed, the bitter sense of loss I still felt. "He felt a great deal of guilt about Aviva and about you, but when he was here, he was able to let it go. He had a home here. Everyone adored him. We were like children, waiting for him to arrive."

"What did he tell you about me?"

271

"That you were a wonderful artist, and beautiful and good—you were a good person. He brought photos of you and newspaper clippings about a show you were in."

"I wasn't so good," I said. "I wish I could be like you and take comfort thinking I did the best I could and he did the best he could, but I can't. I'm still wishing I could go back in time, knowing what I know now. It would have changed everything. I was so scornful."

Something between us had shifted. It wasn't just the money for the stables, I thought, but that I was invested in Chaverim and would keep returning, as my father had. Or maybe, like my father, the burden of holding onto secrets had worn her down.

"I sat with someone when I read her medical records," I said. "Not the first time, but later. Is Aviva the only one with such an awful history?"

"I'm afraid not. Years back, the details were scant so we could only surmise."

"*It was reported*," I said.

"Yes, that's how it was. Now, though, physicians are alert to these kinds of injuries, and there are CT scans and MRIs. The records are much more thorough, so you see this. Not often, but you do."

"Was my father candid with you?" I asked.

She seemed relieved to say yes. "He had no one else, did he?"

"He had no one."

We turned and headed back to the main building. On the steep upgrade, Mrs. Silk paused to catch her breath, and I took in the cloudless blue sky. The air was crisp and fresh and full of contradictions. A community, where all humans were treated with dignity, set in this most contested land.

"Shelley," I said. She'd been asking me to call her Shelley since we'd met, but this was the first time I'd complied. "Did my father see what happened to Aviva?"

"Yes," she said.

I had needed so much to hear that. It hurt but it was what I needed to hear.

She went on, "He could never forgive himself for failing to

understand how sick your mother was. Not that he was alone. Back then, even the so-called experts dismissed postpartum depression. You read childcare books from that era, where it's called the 'baby blues,' as if it's a little mood swing that will pass. Sometimes it does— it did for me. But not always. From what I understand, your mother was unstable even before."

"And after," I said.

She put her arm through mine and after a few steps, stopped again. "It was very hard, your growing up, wasn't it?"

Even then, standing outside Chaverim, where my sister had been placed—battered, broken, deleted from the family—my parents' history retained its power, and I said, "Harder for them."

"Oh, I don't know. Your mother had her work, and your father had Chaverim and Aviva. Who did you have?"

I was searching for an answer when she asked again, "Who did you have in that house?"

The main doors of the building parted for us, and the sound of bird song filled the space. A family caught sight of Mrs. Silk and converged on her, and I sat on a bench and studied my trembling hands, replaying the end of the sentence. *That house.* She greeted them tenderly, the parents and able-bodied boys, the rigid, pigtailed sister in a wheelchair, her gaze fixed upward. *That house,* where everything was in place, and I was alone, and the long stretches of silence that were pierced by my mother's episodes, where my father could not meet my eye. *That house,* where I flailed and kicked, shadow-boxing the nothing, the everything, believing the only way to "find myself" meant brushing off the tiniest dust of history that still clung to my shoulders. Wasn't this what I wanted—a name, a reason, a story to frame and color in the blankness of my history? Wasn't this what I needed to give me proof, yet again, that however good or bad I was hardly mattered? Yes, my father saw what happened.

Another family stopped to talk to Shelley, and I listened from the bench. Even in Hebrew, with its harsh sounds, her voice had a soothing effect. I turned my hands palm up and asked them to be still, and they would not obey. It was so sad and complicated, this past that lived inside me.

When Shelley was back beside me, we talked about a timeline for the stables, a date for groundbreaking, publicity for the opening. We talked about getting Aviva on a horse. The heaviness remained. Then she looked at her watch and said, "I'm pleased that you and Baruch have become friends."

"He's amazing," I said, in a weary way. "Too bad he lives here."

"When I was a girl, 'love' was a man and a woman, living in the same house, day after day. There was no other way, except in books, where love bloomed through letters, which, frankly, I never fully understood. If I've learned anything after all these years at Chaverim, it's what a 'relationship' can mean, and all the shapes and satisfactions of 'love.' Go enjoy your visit with Aviva," she said, rising slowly. "Don't worry about transferring her from the wheelchair to the lift. It isn't something family members ever do. I'll get Ofir to bring her to the pool."

I followed her to her office, where I'd left my canvas bag and rested in her chair, looking at the cacti on her windowsill and the *lithrops,* the living stone, and thinking about Shelley and my father, turning it over, wondering if they had been more than just friends. It was difficult to contemplate just then—impossible, probable, hurtful, reassuring, in the past, like everything except Aviva, who was just then being dressed and transported to the pool.

I put on my suit in the changing area and entered the natatorium, with its thick air and chemical tang. A dark thin man with a missing tooth greeted me with a nod, and a moment later Aviva was wheeled in by Ofir, a burly tattooed aide I recognized.

My stomach knotted when I saw my pale sister, with her slack mouth and fisted hands, her long braid, with its strands of gray, and her red swimsuit, baggy on her skinny frame. I'd been so philosophical with Ronit the day before, and made it sound, even to myself, as if I was completely at ease here, in a place beyond sorrow. And I was not.

I stood near Ofir and watched closely. Aviva seemed to like his firm, gentle support as he eased her onto the hydraulic lift. Her gaze was untroubled, her body relaxed as he began to secure her in the seat.

I watched, aware of voices behind me, the familiar, inscrutable sound of Hebrew. I took in the language, the way I took in the smell of chlorine, the light in the bubble columns, the neon wands in the basket, absorbing these sounds and scents as if I were Aviva: echo of indecipherable voices, soft mechanical hum from the pump, one voice rising above the others, its familiarity piquing my interest. The pitch said *listen*. And even then, the gentle tone was such that I did not turn to see the speaker, merely noted it among the other voices, as I watched my sister slowly settle.

The water changed, the surface no longer glassy. There was a slight chop, and when I turned, Baruch was walking toward the lift, the water halfway to his chest. Not the man from the day before, but the slender, sad-eyed one I'd seen five months earlier, with that rabbit-tail tuft in the middle of his chest.

"Hi," I said. *Avoids making sustained eye contact.*

"Shalom." Even though the water was shallow, he made those little paddling motions, as if that were the only way he could propel himself forward. "So today you will join us," he said, noting my bathing suit.

I turned and stepped down the ladder. The water felt like a liquid extension of my own body. It really was something else.

I worked my way over to Baruch, awkward, relieved to see him, and when we stood facing each other, I said, "I was worried you'd stop swimming with Aviva."

"Why would I? It's something both of us enjoy."

"But yesterday you seemed so angry with me."

He lowered himself in the water and then rose slowly. I said, "I'm pleased that things have worked out for you and Dina. You deserve to be happy."

"You *know* what I deserve?"

Startled by this brief flash of anger, I said, "I guess not."

The lift began to descend. Aviva was slowly lowered into the pool, and I moved past this uneasy exchange and said, "This is my first time. I've never done this by myself."

"It's not so hard." Baruch walked toward the lift, making those little paddling motions. Ofir unclasped the belts and Baruch eased his arms beneath Aviva. The echoing voices that had provided a pleasant background a moment before now made my ears throb. Baruch was cradling Aviva when he turned. She was so limp in his arms, head thrown back, limbs loose, that I felt a surge of panic and said, "I'm not as strong as you are."

"Don't you remember? In the water, she is light. Don't be afraid. It's very nice."

Standing beside Baruch, I saw no glimmer of impatience on his face. I could not say then or years later how much time passed before I was cradling my sister, my other, my twin. It was true: in the water, Aviva was so light it was as though her history had floated free and left us with no story of what might have been, only the pleasure of this moment. She made a sound I could not interpret, a yawn or yowl, and he laughed and said, "Very nice, Aviva." He put his arms around me and said, "Now we will dance," and drew us close so we bobbed in the water together, weightless as moon men.

He gave Aviva a slow whirl through the water, then held out his arms so I could hold my sister, and I did, though with far less grace, since I was new at separating myself from the fraught world on land. I couldn't say when all the voices vanished, the instructive one, the punitive one, the one that urged caution, only that they did, and there were no rules to follow, just our bodies moving in the warm water. I was surprised when the thin man with a missing tooth returned, and I realized an hour had passed and we had to stop our dancing and leave the pool. I watched as Aviva was transferred back onto the lift, staying focused on my sister and on the aides, with their sure hands. Then I grasped the ladder, took the three steps slowly and stepped onto the tile.

I felt swollen from all that was unspoken between us, stuffed with the unspeakable, like my father had been with me. It was exhausting. I padded over to the bench to get my towel and tried to tuck it tightly around my waist. Baruch walked beside me and the two of us watched Aviva being wheeled from the room as if it were the end of a fabulous performance. Then we were alone, and I could feel him breathing, could sense the blood in his veins, his steady heartbeat, his life force, fierce and vulnerable and human.

"You're right that I don't know what you deserve," I said. "I was just trying to say I wished the best for you."

"Do you?" he said.

"Yes," I said. "It's strange to see the two of you together. It shouldn't be, since I was the one who told her to go out with you. I saw you first. Your picture, that is. The one where you're standing against a wall by yourself. It's an amazing photo, the way you're totally unguarded, looking straight into the camera. Not protecting yourself. I was so taken by it. Why did you walk away when I said you were kind? I wasn't blowing you off," I said. "I'd really wanted to come here with you."

"But it was futile," he said.

"What was?" I asked.

"That's what you said. That it was futile."

"I said what was futile?"

We listened to voices echoing in the distance and the murmuring of a pump. Then we tightened our towels. Baruch, with a subtle gesture that meant *whatever*, said, "I misjudged how you felt. It happens."

"That night? In what way? I never felt so connected to anyone."

"You said it was futile."

I covered my face and tried to remember standing on the sidewalk, stringy-haired, sandy, barefoot. "Couldn't you tell how much I wanted to be with you? I thought you did that kind of thing. Professionally."

"We hadn't finished our checklist," he said. "And you never called."

"I did once," I said.

"But never again, because it was futile."

"At that particular moment, it felt futile," I said.

We laughed. It was so ridiculous. Then we inhaled and tightened our towels again, and Baruch, with a chin gesture like Dina's, said,

"So, Vered. The world ends not with a bang but a whimper?" He looked at me in that frank, open way of his, not the faraway gaze of a distracted man, though in time I would get to know that look, too. "It's splendid to see me with your good friend Dina?"

"Right," I said. "Okay. So for me, personally, it's not so splendid, but since the two of you are together, I'm going to work toward thinking it's splendid."

"What do you know of my time with Dina?"

"'You are the most wonderful man in the world.' That's the report."

He closed his eyes and shrugged.

"It doesn't count that I wrote?"

"Thank you for everything. You're very kind."

"I don't know," I said. "To me, kindness is a virtue."

"Tell me something. What do you want for yourself when you're not so busy wishing I have everlasting joy with your good friend Dina?"

"To be an honorable person."

"That's a very noble sentiment."

"What do you want me to say, that it kills me to see you and Dina together? Okay, fine, for what it's worth, it kills me. But, what the hell, I'm like a cat and will go on with my next life, where I'll pursue my dreams and…go to Sicily. Get myself a nice place to live. Meet a man who is whole and healthy and tender and intelligent and sexy. And kind. You think that's asking for too much?"

I laughed. It really did seem like I was asking for too much.

I untucked my towel and used a corner to wipe my face, and when I was done, he extended his hand as if we would part with a brief businesslike handshake. I reached out and he took my hand in both of his and held it until the door to the natatorium opened, and a skinny man with a frail neck and thick curls was wheeled in. I thought of the peonies in my yard, with their bowed heads.

"For you, for your sake, I hope you and Dina are happy. But if it doesn't work out, let me know. Or be practical, and don't let me know, though I'd like to spend more time with you."

He kissed my hand in a princely way and looked up, his expression so piercing and inscrutable that I said, "Oh, what will happen to me?"

He turned my hand palm up and said, "You will live for many years, Vered. And then on your one hundredth birthday, your friends will bring you a cake with one hundred candles, which you'll insist upon blowing out yourself."

"And then I'll die in the process, face first in the cake."

He turned my hand back over and said, "Yes. But it's a long time until then."

He let go and walked off. I watched him leave the natatorium and thought, this is not over. I was surprised to feel so confident. We had parted with no word about the future.

Trust what you see, I told myself. Trust what you feel in the air, what you read in someone's eyes. Trust what you take in when there are no reassuring words.

Then I was home and the days passed and I did not hear from Baruch. I grew shaky, and doubt rushed in, and the foolishness of falling in love with someone so far away. It was harder then, and I had to keep reminding myself: Hadn't he called Shelley to find out when I'd be seeing Aviva? Hadn't he waited for me in the pool? Hadn't he put his hand to my cheek and waited for me to meet his eyes? Each time I recalled these moments, I told myself he'd call.

THIRTY

Rosh Hashanah, the Jewish New Year, fell on the same date as Kayleigh and Ryan's wedding in Ohio, so I missed Dina's call, wishing me *"l'shana tova,"* and got only her cheerful voice and nothing about a new beau, which was what I'd been waiting to hear. By then, nineteen days had passed since Baruch had held my hand in the natatorium and looked at me in such a way that I was certain he would call. The certainty changed as often as the weather, but I was not entirely ready to say I had misread our last moment together.

Les picked me up on the morning of the wedding in his handsome German sedan, with its purring engine and tan leather seats. He was clean-shaven, his suit on a hanger in the back. When I hooked my dress beside it, I saw a family walking to one of the half-dozen synagogues near my apartment. The interior of the car was so pristine I took off my shoes after I was buckled in. Pairs of men walked ahead of mothers pushing strollers. Grandparents with toddlers, older children zigzagging ahead, little girls with drooping headbands and patterned tights, their brothers with crisp collared shirts partly hanging out of their khakis. It was strange driving past them, as if I'd been left out of a party everyone else was attending. The culture in which I was raised had been Jewish, but the box had been empty.

Though nothing inside a sanctuary could quench the left-out feeling, the desire to mark the new year took hold, and while we drove, I told Les about a Rosh Hashanah tradition called *tashlikh*, in which observers threw bread in the water, as a symbolic casting off of sins. As I talked, I thought of our city, with its three rivers and sandy trails.

"Sins?" said Les. "Isn't it a little fire and brimstone to be worrying about sins?"

"Forget the sins and think of it as a time to reflect on your life. To go down to the river and symbolically cast off your regrets and sorrows. I bet you have a regret or two you'd like to send downstream."

"You bet. I've got a bushel." He pressed a button overhead and light flooded into the car from the moon roof, and I closed my eyes and settled in for the rest of the ride.

It was nearly five when the valet at the country club waved us over to the gravel lot where the wedding guests would park. The blue sky I'd seen from the car's open moon roof had been replaced by charcoal-colored storm clouds. After a delay, the reception was held outdoors, as planned. The guests huddled on folding chairs, the women with shawls or men's suit jackets across their shoulders. The minister appeared. Then at last the groom and his family walked on the papery runner covering the grass. They waited, and we did, for the bride to appear. Time passed, and the clouds darkened. Les put his arm around me, and I rested my head against his chest. The music changed, and the first chords of the Beach Boys "God Only Knows" began to play, and Kayleigh appeared. Ryan's face crumpled as he watched her walk down the papery aisle. Les squeezed my shoulder. Hold on, you two, I thought, almost fiercely. Do not forget this moment ever.

When fat cold drops of rain came, we scooted under the huge tent with clear plastic cutouts for windows. The women's heels sank deep into the wet grass, and the wind came with such force that the musicians couldn't plug in and the tent shook, its canvas luffing, its stakes squeaking and rattling. It died down during dinner, and by the time the toasts were made, and embarrassing stories unearthed by half-drunk fraternity brothers, the weather became a convenient metaphor. Les and I danced a few slow dances, and I joined some women I didn't know for the fast ones, and then we drove home.

In the morning, I put a hunk of frozen bread in my backpack and rode my bike through Squirrel Hill, where the sidewalks were again enlivened by strolling families, and then through Polish Hill, past the stately Immaculate Heart of Mary church, with its copper domes, and tolling bells on this Sunday afternoon. Les was standing outside when I arrived at the lime green schoolhouse, his bike against the wall, and we rode out to the trail together. At an agreeable spot we propped our bikes against the guardrail. The hunk of bread I'd carried had defrosted and broke nicely in two.

I threw the first crumbs. The wind carried them horizontally, in an unsatisfying way. At the edges of the sandy trail were jagged little stones. I scooped up a handful. The first one I threw into the river fell with the satisfying, substantial plop of a cast-off regret. I threw another pebble and listened to it hit the water. Sorrow. That was what I wanted to leave behind. The sorrow that I'd never said to my father: *Yes, there was another one.* It didn't matter that I hadn't known about Aviva. There was still the sorrow that I hadn't said "yes." *Yes, Daddy, there was another one.* The sorrow that I'd never said, *What about me? Why can't you love me, the child in your household?* The sorrow of never knowing what might have come of such a conversation, if he'd needed me to speak these words before he could reveal his own heart.

Mom, Mama, Mommy. A pebble for each forbidden name, for what had been done to her. For the way she'd harmed Aviva. Another one when I thought of Harley standing outside my house, that genial, gentlemanly veneer his downfall. Standing on the cinder trail, looking out at the water, there was the sorrow that for so long I kept expecting him to become someone else. The sorrow I'd been angry when he didn't. The sorrow recalling him sitting on my window ledge, his despair so dark and deep. (Had it been that way for my mother that night? Had it been that way for her forever after?) I felt such sorrow to think of the effort they expended masking their despair. Harley had to pay out of pocket for his stay at the "retreat" where Byron had taken him. I imagined this as a source of sorrow for him.

Les had walked a few feet up the trail and was standing with his arms crossed. I stepped beside him. A nearby sign said, "These waters receive sewage from sewer overflows as a result of rain, snow-melt, and other events."

I threw another pebble. Oh, such sorrow I felt that environmental restrictions had been eased and the river received sewage. Sorrow that the earth was warming.

I was sorry that years before, I had thrown that puppy, tossed him mindlessly to the ground while gabbing to friends. The puppy had screamed in a most human way, then rose, trotted off, and lived until he was sixteen, which made him, in human years, roughly the age of those yogurt-eating Georgians. Though as far as I could tell, he'd been unscathed by my carelessness, I continued to hear the puppy's scream, for which I was sorry.

Standing on the riverbank, contemplating water that received sewage, it seemed as if the reason I was the sorriest person was that I'd been unable to discharge any sorrow. I threw a pebble, wished I had a pipe from which *sorrow overflow* was released. I closed my eyes, imagined all the wounded animals, the homeless and disenfranchised and victims of war that lived inside me, crawling, limping, rolling, walking down a ramp in twos, departing from my brain. This left me with the sorrow that I'd never had the chance to care for someone else before now, and the fear that I might not know how.

I stopped. I was already doing it, wasn't I? Or beginning to?

I threw a pebble long distance and listened to it plop. The sorrows life dealt were different from the ones of our own making. I didn't want to look back and say, "if only" or "I wish," and said, "I need to go to Israel sometime soon."

I was sorry there was no two-state solution, no peace on the horizon, and sorry when I thought, as Dina had said, that too much wrong had been done on both sides.

"I have to work these visits into my life in such a way that they aren't a big deal. People do it, a lot of them. You have to admit that travel seems to loosen me up. Or maybe it's nerves, though historically I've done good work when I'm gone. Don't you think?"

"Historically." Les nodded.

"Did you know that ladybugs are a symbol of good luck all over the world? Every day I find dozens of them dead on the windowsill. I try not to impart any meaning to this, but it troubles me to see them upside down on their shells. It makes me feel cold, heartless, to quote Harley's friend. And it's so far from the truth, which is more that it's hard for me to follow my heart, when that's only gotten me in trouble, and now I don't know if this one time I should trust my heart and go for this man, this really wonderful man, when Dina spits him out, which for sure she will, since the expiration date on that union has passed, and he's definitely not her type. He lives thousands of miles away, which makes the whole thing insane. And maybe it isn't really what he wants, but still, I can't help thinking that the last thing I want to do is spend the rest of my life regretting that I didn't—"

"Rox." Les cut me off. On his face was an expression of such bald despair that I stopped apologizing for having gone on that way and said, "What? Are you okay?"

We hugged the guardrail to avoid being crushed by a family on wheels. The youngest rolled in a closed cart attached to his father's bike, a little pasha.

"Nomi," he said.

I held my breath. Waited. Life could be so cruel.

"I'm in love with her. Like *totally*." He threw a pebble into the water.

"Of course, you are. Why do you sound so stricken? She's not married, is she?"

"Oh no, oh no. Not at all. Not married at all. It's just that she's amazing."

"I know that," I said. "We all do."

"It's intense, Rox. And my track record. As you know, my track record is dismal. It really sucks, my track record. I don't know what she's doing with me. And the kid. I've already fucked up one kid, and hers, her little girl, is the nicest kid I've ever met, smart and *open*, like her mother. She's a remarkable child."

I squeezed his shoulder, as if to console him for his loss. "You were practically a teenager when you had your son. Don't you think maybe you've matured?"

"Me?"

Our mood lightened after this exchange. We threw the rest of our stones in the water at once. It was like the last blast of fireworks on Fourth of July—every single sorrow exploding in the water.

It was time to head back. We put our helmets back on and buckled them beneath our chins. "Do you love me in a platonic way as a partner and friend?" I asked.

"Why do you ask these ridiculous questions?"

"Does it matter why I ask? Isn't it enough that I'm asking?"

"Yes. What the fuck. We practically live together. You know everything about me. Can't you tell?"

"So? You think it's a personality flaw that once every five or so years I need a little reassurance? I'm supposed to buck up? Be a man? I don't want to be a man. Maybe *you* need some practice before you try out for the major leagues."

"I like you," he said.

"Oh, jeez. I'm touched."

"Rox," he said. "You're my closest friend. What's your problem?"

"I'm overwrought," I said.

Les put his arms around me and gave me a squeeze. Our bike helmets collided.

It was dark when I got home. I stowed my bike in the basement and made a cup of peppermint tea. I thought about the wedding, the look on Ryan's face when Kayleigh walked down the aisle, then Les, when he said, "Nomi." I sipped my tea, opened my sketchbook, and sent my creature down to the river, where he climbed on a steamboat and traveled to a faraway place where he might find another creature, whose jagged edges fit perfectly with his own. Then I got up and emailed Baruch to tell him I was coming to Chaverim to see Aviva and him.

I was still sitting at my desk when I got his terse reply. "Splendid," it said. "Send me your travel plans."

Everything Else

THIRTY-ONE

I tried not to think about him on the flight to Ben Gurion Airport, but when the plane began its descent, and the wheels stuttered and took hold, jostling us in our seats, *he* came to mind, and I thought, *yikes!* like a cartoon character. I let the other passengers rise and reach for their bags, while I stayed in my window seat and released all the nervous questions that had been unformed until then.

I let the others work their way down the aisle, let them push ahead through customs, while I lollygagged, used the restroom, splashed water on my face, squeezed toothpaste from a tube the size of my pinkie nail and brushed my teeth. Eventually, I finished with the minor grooming, went through customs and found myself outside of security, facing a horde pushing against the barrier, limo drivers with signs, family members with helium balloons and elaborate bouquets, parents and children and lovers. A young woman rammed into me on her way through the crowd, crying, "Oh!" and her beaming parents extended their arms, reaching out as she sank to her knees so her small dog could lick her face, neither getting enough of it.

I thought I saw Baruch, a head taller than the others, and expected to be wrong, since I'd seen him in Pittsburgh and New York. Though he knew my itinerary, he'd never actually said he'd meet me at the airport, and I made my way through without being certain he'd be there. When it was him, and he stepped toward me, I let go of everything—suitcase, resolve, worried self—and rose on my toes to embrace him and stayed long enough to feel his ribs beneath his jacket, looked up, kissed his warm neck in error, found his lips, and then, "Hello, hi, shalom, I can't believe you're here."

Taken aback for a moment, he said, "Where did you think I'd be?"

He took my bags to the car, and when I slid into the passenger seat, I leaned over and said, "So you've forgiven me."

"Not completely," he said, and we made out like teenagers with nowhere else to go, no bed, no privacy. Then finally: Was I going to tell him where I was staying?

When I said "Paradise," he said, "Alone?" and I got to say, "It wouldn't be paradise without you."

I knew what I wanted in that cool, spare room with its tile floor and the photo of the German doctor in wire-rimmed glasses, posed with his associates, but I was no longer a girl who was looking for thrills. What I needed was more complicated and nerve-wracking, something I hadn't really known.

We checked in. He carried my bag down the dim corridor, and I worked the key with the plastic oval that said "Paradise" into the lock, rattled the door, turned the key this way and that before the lock snapped open. Though it was not the same room as before, it was as spartan as I recalled, and I began to say something about its austerity when he put down my bag. I turned and was in his arms in a single fluid move, and we began the clumsy, comical business of unclothing, a bra that would not unfasten, cuffs around ankles. There would be no popped buttons, no sex slammed against the wall: this was a man who liked to see what the clothes covered, flushed skin, bones softening, breath rising, *look at me,* his long torso, puff of white chest hair, the surprise of his erect penis (why a surprise? Hadn't I expected this greeting?) Then merging and sinking onto the bed, the two thin pillows tossed to the ground. And the distance forgotten, the barriers and complications. His flesh was cool, his cheeks rougher than I imagined, soft mouth, and when he entered me, relief and pleasure and the desire, stronger than anything, to stay where we were, to never leave his arms, this bed, this room, this place.

Later, he said, "Vered, have you found someone to love?"

And I said, "I went out with a factory owner named Fred," and then, "No. No one."

And I asked, "What about you? Aside from Dina."

And he said: "There was a widow awhile back, an architect. An unpleasant woman."

The next day, sun peeping around the edges of the shutters,

"Wouldn't you rather be with a person who lives here? It would be so much easier."

And he said, "Yes, of course it would. Much easier." Though he said this in a teasing way, it was true, and it upset me.

Later I learned that he'd planned side trips for us, none of which we took. We did not see the antiquities at Caesarea or dine in Jerusalem or visit Safed at dusk. We missed dinners and breakfasts and rose only to go to Chaverim. Then we stumbled back to Paradise, shuttering the windows, drifting into sleep, until the cock crowed, and we woke in each other's arms, made love, fell asleep again, woke, made love.

Then the last day: Getting up, showering together a final time, our own slippery bodies slapping together. Clothes packed, toiletries. Power cords. He finished first, and while I nervously rearranged the contents of my suitcase, he answered some emails, which struck me as reassuringly ordinary, and strange, given how imminent our separation.

I zipped my bag and waited by the door. "And now what?" I asked as we wheeled our bags down the corridor. I had not meant to say this.

"We will be apart and then we'll be together," he said.

"So we'll just see how it goes?"

"Yes," he said. "We'll see how it goes."

Then the long, gloomy drive to the airport. All that was left of our togetherness was my hand on his thigh.

He cursed at other drivers. *That* was a surprise.

I had wept when I left Aviva. I hated walking away without being able to explain to her that I'd return. It was so incomplete.

In the car beside Baruch, I was dry-eyed, and when I saw the terminal in the distance, I said, "You can just drop me off at departures."

"I should just deposit you on the sidewalk and drive off?"

"Well—" I said as we approached the parking area.

"Because it's not so good for you to tell me to do what you *don't* want me to do. I thought we'd figured out this one."

"You're right," I said. "Come home with me and never leave. That's what I want."

He could not come home with me. Instead, we had Skype as our bridge. Endless, endless calls on Skype.

You tell stories when you fall in love. We did, too, night after night, the hunger for the details of each other's past lives as insatiable as our physical ardor. We filled the gaps between our lovemaking with stories and continued when we were apart and all I had was his voice. I loved our flow and fluency, the way we rarely overlapped or ran out of things to say. These long, tender conversations bridged our distance.

Though Baruch did not see our storytelling as serious business, as I did, he let me coax tales from him, knowing how important it was for me to construct his past, at this time when I was working to construct my own. Some of my questions led him into rooms he had forgotten. His earliest memory (peeing into a milk bottle); his first sexual experience (in a Danish hostel). Others came easily: His wife, standing and waiting for him to turn from his desk on his second day home from Canada; the night, after she'd moved out, when he was walking alone and failed to see the barrier around the broken-up sidewalk, fallen in the rubble, and wrecked his knee. He could not walk up the steps to his apartment so his daughter and her partner cared for him. It was the lowest moment of his life (literally), that gave him a taste of dependence and frailty that was bitter until he gave into it at his daughter's flat, where he sat by the window, listening to the world awaken, and watching with pleasure his daughter and her partner's comfortable domestic rhythm.

I learned to stitch together sentences from separate stories until I could see the shy young man I'd never know, with an outgoing wife who brought him into the world. For years, it only took the slightest tug, as with a cord dangling from an overhead fixture, and he'd get up from his desk and join the others. The story of why he'd begun to resist was as complex as his lengthy marriage, and he would speak of it, when I asked. But the despair he felt after his wife left and his fall on the sidewalk at night, he continued to dismiss as trivial, for Baruch regarded himself as a fortunate man, a witness to much heartache, a man who'd been brushed by disaster and never really tasted it. Through all that he said and did not say, he remained the man I'd first seen with Aviva in his arms, with his luminous eyes. *Come in, it is something else.*

Sometimes talking too long of the past made me melancholy. If only we could wake every morning together; if only we could have had a child together; if only we'd been lovers before we became, each of us, so tied to the countries where we lived. Oh, if I had only known you then, we often said.

But then it could not have worked, I knew. I had to be the woman I was right then. If I had met him when I was younger, I would have found him mysterious and attractive, would have pursued him, and burned my way through and left, because he was not elusive, did not withhold his affection, shaking me to the core, which in those days I mistook for love. But I was no longer that woman: not fresh and young. Nor was he. We were both a little worn, a little battle-scarred.

During one of our long conversations, when I'd been lying on the spongy carpet in my rented apartment, we'd pledged to speak to each other of our hurts and desires, to confess to our vulnerabilities, and I told him about a newspaper story I'd read about war correspondents that included a Hemingway line that I'd often heard quoted: "The world breaks everyone and afterward many are strong at the broken places." I'd found myself turning that line over and over, because I didn't think it was true. "I think those of us life breaks are weaker in the broken places," I said.

"Maybe. I can see you might feel that way." But he disagreed, citing broken bones, no weaker after they knit, and thinking of the long period after his wife left, how after that break he was stronger, more fully human. I thought of broken bowls, the mended seam always vulnerable. And I thought of myself, still asking, "Are you glad I'm here? Are you pleased to see me?" and Baruch saying, as Les had, "Do you need to ask?"

Yes, I did need to ask. I needed him to say these words and mean them. I needed the directness of his gaze and his soft, warm voice to keep me from falling into an anxious, questioning state, then deeper, into a state of *wanting* that left me frozen with fear, unable to ask for what I needed most. I tried to explain to Baruch that the broken place was still there. I didn't feel it, and he didn't see it, so I said, "Look, we disagree!" But it was there.

On our second visit, we stayed at the spa where the guests meandered through the lobby wrapped in thick terry robes, like patients in a sanatorium. We studied the menu of massages, and he chose Shiatsu while I decided on hot stones. When it was time to make our appointments, he said, "I don't need a stranger's hands," and neither did I. Later, through the gap in the curtains, we saw the sky grow dark, and he said, "If you want to eat, we better go now," but I was hungry only for him, so we stayed in bed. It was thrilling to separate ourselves from the world and learn every inch of each other's bodies, to let the conversation continue this way.

We roused ourselves and drove to Chaverim, and I thought about the massage menu and wondered how much training I'd need to work with Aviva. When I arrived, she was in the art room, secured upright in an EasyStand—weight-bearing was important and helped to keep her strong. I kissed her hello and touched her cheek and hair, and asked Ora, the curly-haired therapist arranging a sandy substance on her tray, what kind of training I'd need to work with Aviva.

She laughed and said, "We do the work. You do what's nice."

I stood, awkwardly. Ora took my hand and brought it to her nose. "Almond. So nice." Had I tried other scents with Aviva? Had I noticed how much she loved warm towels? "And look," she said, putting Aviva's hands in the sandy stuff on the tray. "If she did not like this, she would pull way, or get stiff, or shake her head like this. Don't be shy!"

Shy. It was true. In this time when I'd been so avid with Baruch, when our body conversation began to evolve, and we became sensitive to gentle touch and rough play, I was still reserved with Aviva. I knew the importance of eye contact for Baruch but had not thought how much I could learn by looking into Aviva's eyes, hadn't known until I saw her react to the texture of the sand that she could smile, hadn't thought to interpret her vocalizations.

Our bond deepened when I began to attend, to feel the way she took in the scent of me and relaxed in my arms, to see her open her mouth for the pureed banana, spit out the yogurt, a clear sign of displeasure, move close to sip the café au lait avidly, vocalize for the vanilla ice cream, even letting me help her use the spoon to scoop.

By the time the stables were built, I began talking to Aviva when she and I were alone. The voice rose naturally, as if it had always been inside me, waiting for release. It was a tender voice, like mothers use with children, but not baby talk, though the register was softer, higher pitched. I don't believe what I said made a difference to her. Perhaps it was like music. Human music that settled her when we were together, that settled me. I took off her slipper socks, massaged her feet and the voice came from inside me, along with songs and pet names. Vivi. Avivi. Sweetie. Honey. I'd disliked pet names meant to placate and manipulate. Softened by Baruch's love, the names that came out unbidden, when I was with Aviva—sweetpea, sweetheart, sweetie pie, honey pie, peanut—were more like the twittering of a bird, calling to its mate. I stopped being self-conscious, stopped worrying who might hear.

I never told Baruch how surprised I'd been that this voice was inside me—for Aviva, for him. I didn't tell him what it was like to see I could take care of someone who loved me in return, and someone who liked my tending and touching.

And then: saying goodbye to Aviva in a cheerful way. Pausing on my way out to greet residents or staff, amiable, composed, fine as I stepped through the double doors. Then outside, weeping.

When I teared up with Baruch, he embraced and kissed me. "Don't be sad, my love. It won't be long." Aviva could not tell me she was sad, could not say, "We will count the days together, love." There could be no final embrace to carry me through the next weeks. I could not tell her, "Soon I will be back, love," and promise to sing to her, massage her fingers and toes and tuck her into bed. Now when I read accounts of parents who stopped visiting, saying it was too wrenching to leave, I understood something of what they felt. I was not grateful for the pain. It did not bring me wisdom, make me a better person, or prepare me for the later anguish. I bore it because I wanted to see my sister: in this way, it was about me. When I was home, I worried about her wellbeing because she could not tell me if someone had harmed her.

Once, filled with the determination to bring Aviva home, I asked Jill to explain the way families got funds for children with disabilities, and she went on at length about county money and federal money, funding streams and waiting lists and people I might contact. By daylight, all the cracks in my sentimental picture were illuminated. Would Aviva's life be better with me? What if I bought a new house with big windows and was home with her each night? I could get aides to come in when I went to work. But the pool, the greenhouse, the fragrant gardens, the voices of others she'd long known, the horses for her to ride? How would it better her life to take her away from her home? How could I bring her all that she had at present?

It took me a long time to agree with the disgruntled daughter I'd met at Thanksgiving. The old model of institutions should not be restored any more than the old model of dictators, no matter how benign. Aviva, my sister, had suffered misfortune twice, at birth and at my mother's hands, but she had landed in an unusual place, as I had; so I, who could travel, flew to Israel, swam with Aviva, massaged her calves and feet with warm towels, brought ice cream and café au lait, surprised myself by hearing all the endearments that were inside me, and all the music lodged there—show tunes, folksongs, arias, songs by crooners, rockers, and divas. "Doe a deer," and "Lean on Me," "I Feel Pretty," "Day-O," "Born to Run." Then swimming, the three of us, and afterwards Baruch and I checking into the spa, where we made love in the king-sized bed, showered and dressed in the thick robes, made cups of tea with fresh spearmint or peppermint leaves and wandered in the lobby like the other patients.

Vinnie, I called him. Vincent the Robe.

Then Skype with Baruch. And later, with Aviva. Endless, endless Skype.

Here I am at six months: Standing outside security at the airport in Pittsburgh, bouncing at the knees like a kid. Waving when I spot him. Hurrying forward. Baruch, letting his bag drop. Embracing in the midst of the stream of travelers in a way I had witnessed, envied, and never fully understood. Embracing again, separating. My hand on his cheek, the intangible feelings brought to life. Kissing, embracing—real, it is real. The flesh of my loved one is just divine. His scent, the roughness of his cheek, unshaven for a day, the smell of his shirt. My hand at his waist. "Oh, Chubby, don't you eat when I'm not around?"

Chubby or Fat Man, that's what I called him. Or Chub, as if he really was a fish that Dina reeled in first. (Dina, who claimed to be delighted by our liaison, took credit for it, married a retired chemist in Haifa, called me less often, then not at all.)

On the drive home, he observed this city where I lived, this young place, with streams cut deeply into the shale and jagged mountains. No Crusaders had tromped down these roads, no Romans, Ottomans, or Greeks, no Bedouin or Druze. Scant evidence of Native Americans remained, only a couple of forts from Revolutionary times, some grand edifices left behind by robber barons, such recent history compared to his.

I'd planned a post-industrial tour, beginning high up on Mount Washington, where he could see where the Monongahela and Allegheny Rivers merged to form the Ohio, and picture the era when factories and mills lined those river banks. Then later, before taking the incline down the mountain, we could see photographs from those smoky, prosperous years, and maybe on our last day drive to the Laurel Highlands to Falling Water, the Frank Lloyd Wright house. While planning this tour, I was surprised to find myself telling a story about the emergence of love. I hadn't realized until then how fond I'd grown of my city.

On Baruch's first morning with me, Jessie did not scream, and we slept until the crows woke us with their harsh squawking. Still in bed in Pittsburgh, we had our first serious talk about the need to balance work and love. It was still hypothetical, but we knew it would be crucial. Others who'd managed love at a distance spoke of the necessity of figuring this out.

When we got up, I showed him the alcove in my apartment where I'd set up my desk and urged him to make it his own. "Now," I said. "Just try it out. See if you like the chair." It would be necessary. We were adults and knew that much. We could hold each other for hours, swear we'd never tire of our kisses, look up and know that we would.

We knew everything. We were smart and experienced. Baruch had even read the Book of Love, my name for Dorothy Tennov's research on limerence, that crazy, weak-in-the-knees period at the start of love affairs. We were amused to think that we were closing in on the expiration date for the limerent stage; we were amused by everything. In those days, he could quote from Tennov's research, read passages, and joke about how we were nearing the end. You can know it's a stage and still be deliriously in it. You can say, "Tick tock, baby," while doing a striptease, as I did, because the end, while inevitable, feels unreal. Something that happened to others.

I'd seen his imperfections, his humanness, and knew he was no prince, and even so, we approached the end of the limerent stage and still raced into each other's arms as if we could outrun time. We acted as if what we had together was somehow different, better than what others called "love," and at the same time we were old enough—bruised, savvy, jaded enough—to laugh at ourselves, to acknowledge the inevitability of change.

We did not believe it. Not really.

Tick tock. Dina faded, and he did not, because he was my *bashert*, my intended, and we were walking toward his car, toward my car, toward his plans, towards mine, which we might keep or might not, it hardly mattered.

Time was different for us. At some point, after a year had passed, I attempted to calculate what our twelve months together would have equaled if we'd seen each other every night, but I failed, and it was okay. What we had instead was a year of seeing each other whenever we could, on each visit stepping out of our ordinary lives. Maybe that was why we did not hear the bell toll.

THIRTY-TWO

Baruch's mother, a small, round woman with hair dyed the color of pomegranates, dressed in a sleeveless orange shift the day we met. It was two months before his second visit to Pittsburgh, the terrible one. Baruch had told me she'd had many miscarriages before his birth and had regarded him as a miracle. When she opened her arms to hug him, I saw that she'd never altered her view. I'd always known he'd been loved, could feel it in the unapologetic way he carried himself. Now, though, when she released him, she opened her arms again and embraced me, then gestured to the seat beside her. When I sat she took my hand and squeezed it.

"Her parents are alive?" she asked Baruch in Hebrew. "She has children? Sisters and brothers?"

After he answered, her voice became stern.

"She's worried I won't know how to take care of you," he said.

"Tell her you're doing fine, that you've made me very happy."

Later, his daughter arrived with her partner, Natalia, and some family from his father's side. I watched them joke and argue, doze in the corner, eat with their fingers, perch on a kitchen counter, and I thought, as I had at Mindy's, that this was what it was like to have a family, a *we*, an *us*. Once, I'd asked Baruch why my feelings for Aviva had emerged as soon as I knew she was alive. Why had I wanted to care for her? Why did it matter that my cousin's wife had found some of the surviving remnants from my father's once-large family, in Lima, Peru, and Sao Paolo, Brazil, where a cousin, Florencia Bursztein, was a watercolorist of some renown? Why did it matter that in a photo of my paternal grandparents—a bosomy, solemn-faced woman, standing with a palm on the shoulder of her tiny, seated spouse—their two olive-skinned girls, dressed in fancy white blouses, had narrow faces and almond-shaped eyes like mine?

As a species, we lived in small groups, he'd said. "We recognize our own and distrust the other; this tendency is encoded in our genes. We'd no longer exist if not for this behavioral adaptation."

This earlier conversation distressed me the afternoon I met his family, reminding me that what was good—kin, us, family—had a deadly flip side. Not us, them. Once again, I did not know what sadness to take on, what inequity to accept. I left Israel, this tormented land I'd tried not to love, and went home to my country, engaged in its own long, heartrending war in the Middle East.

The terrible visit began this way: Baruch had a conference in Arizona and a collaborator arriving at his lab in Tel Aviv a week later. He'd looked at a map of the U.S., saw that Phoenix was two inches from Pittsburgh, and shrank the distance. It was still a time when everything seemed possible. I suggested he postpone, and he said, "You don't want to see me?"

I did want to see him. I always wanted to see him.

It was the end of August, and hot air blanketed the city. I arrived at the airport ridiculously early, bounced at the knees, raced toward him the second I caught a glimpse. He dropped his bag when he reached me, and we embraced in the midst of the stream of travelers just as before. I touched his face, hugged him, touched his face again, as if I still needed proof he was real. *What?* I pinched his waist and felt his uneasiness. *Oh Chubby.* It was like swallowing a bristly little seed.

That seed went down hard and lodged in my gut. I did not say, "You seem anxious! Distracted." Because I had no words for this bristly discomfort, could not articulate my fear that something was wrong when there was no evidence. In the car he confessed to feeling pressured by work, and so as soon as we got back to the apartment, I led him to the alcove, patted my desk, and reassured him. "Do what you have to do," I said. "Take whatever time you need."

I unzipped his laptop sleeve, opened his computer, made him set out his work. I could not see myself slipping into the good-girl dance of my childhood, could not sense how uneasy this dance was making him.

The tomatoes in the salad I made were mealy, the couscous

over-salted. We picked at dinner, made love, woke to Jessie's screams. Baruch wrapped a pillow over his head, and I sat with my hand on his back, and waited for my heart to slow. While Baruch was still beneath his pillow, I got up to shower. By the time I was out of the bathroom, he was sitting in the alcove with his back to me.

"Hey!" I called softly. "Yo!"

When he failed to turn, a voice, detached from my discomfort, piped up. *Let the man work in peace!*

My ability to cooperate was limitless; I was a most compliant girl. I slipped on a T-shirt and shorts, left a note on the table, tiptoed out. *Went out for bread. Call when you're up for company.*

I'd signed it with *x*'s and *o*'s, picked up a loaf of olive sourdough bread, stopped at my office. An instructor in Nomi's studio was leading a group of older women in Gentle Yoga. She enunciated each word, her voice full of syrupy cheer.

I turned on the lights, my computer, the radio, hoping to drown her out, wishing I could fall into my work, the way he fell into his, and lose this sense of foreboding. Nothing has happened, I told myself. Nothing at all. I recalled the Fridays when I stayed late to call my mother. The way I had braced myself. *Ask for nothing.* All these months, he had quenched my fear so completely I'd forgotten the old terror of *wanting.* Alone and unsettled in my office, that wanting made me feel boneless and vulnerable.

He did not answer my call. After an hour, I went home.

He turned slowly in the desk chair, annoyed. "Where were you?"

I lifted the bag of bread. "I didn't want to disturb you. Did you see my note?"

He studied me in a slow, critical way. "No." Drawn out. Dubious.

"I was trying to give you a break." I picked up the note, showed the *x*'s on the bottom. "Those are the kisses. The *o*'s are the hugs." I felt foolish trying to explain this. "Hey, are you upset about something?"

"That girl." He pointed below. "How can you live here?"

"It's just for a while. I didn't want to rush into buying just any house. I'm looking for a place I can make into a home." For us, I was thinking. "A place you could feel comfortable. You know?"

Maybe not, since he said nothing. I asked if he was feeling caught up. If he wanted some bread and cheese. Not that either.

Love withdrawn—that's how I would describe what I felt when I took in his expression. "If you're feeling pressured, just keep going," I said. "You have all day and night if you need it."

He stood, arched his back. "Don't we have plans with your friends?"

"Sure, but I could go alone if you're busy."

This suggestion displeased him. "I thought you wanted me to meet your partner?"

"I do," I said.

"Then why would you go alone?"

"I just thought. I wanted to make sure..."

All these jagged stops and starts.

"Then I'll finish what I'm working on, and we'll go as planned. *B'seder?*"

He turned away before I could agree, yes, *b'seder.* There was only his blue shirt and the curls at the back of his head, and my desire to step behind him, kiss the nape of his neck, slip my fingers into his hair, have what we'd shared for all these months, that now felt like a soap bubble.

I stepped into the bedroom instead, felt the clock, each bruising tick digging into me, reminding me how little time we had together. What would I do if I felt this unsettled when he left? How would I get through the weeks? I wanted to walk over to him, to call his name, and didn't, because it would break the rules we'd set ourselves.

I did not see myself sinking, too vulnerable to ask that small, essential question I would always need to ask. *Do you love me still?*

Until it was late. And then later, in a tentative way, "Am I interrupting?"

"No, no." He checked his watch. "We should go. Your friends are expecting us."

My *friends.* I draped myself across his lap, felt his ribs and knees, kissed his rough cheek, wishing we could drop everything and be where we'd been before.

"Yes," I said. "I need to prove to Les that you exist. He's convinced I invented you, that all the nice things I report are part of a marketing campaign to change the public perception of Israeli men."

"Should I prove him wrong?"

"You wouldn't know how," I said.

"I could skip my shower." He held onto his chair arms and hoisted himself up and I spilled from his lap, surprised to find myself on my feet.

"Hey, are you okay?"

"Vered, *why* do you keep asking?"

He took a long shower. I waited, knocked, feeling needy, childish, asking to come in. He said, "Of course," and I sat on the edge of the tub, watching this man with a white, shaving-cream beard make faces in a misty mirror. No one I knew.

Les still owned a Federal house in the Mexican War Streets, even now that he lived with Nomi. He still needed that residence as an emergency exit, would not rent it or put it up for sale. I wasn't surprised Les loved Nomi, since I'd watched it emerge, and I'd expected his transition from tolerating her daughter to falling for her. That he loved Nomi's old farmhouse "in the boondocks," with its slanting pine floors and low ceilings was as unexpected to me as the voice that had emerged when I was with Aviva. Les redesigned Nomi's kitchen. During the renovation, contractors found a hearth inside a wall. They had it restored and turned it back into a working oven.

When Baruch and I arrived, the oven was fired up for pizza, and all the guests had brought the ingredients for their favorite pies. They came with custom semolina flour, porcini, pesto, fontina, sundried tomatoes, homemade sauce. I hadn't known how broad and deep was the world of pizza or how I'd overlooked this part of the invitation and had showed up with only a bottle of wine, in attire that was all wrong. My tunic, too sparkly for this crowd in aprons and jeans, with bell-shaped sleeves that would drip in sauce.

While I was being embarrassed, the guests, mostly strangers, were busy rolling their crusts, assembling their toppings, exchanging arcane information about artisanal flours and cheeses and their sources for these ingredients. By the time I steadied myself enough to introduce Baruch to the few people I knew, he was talking contentedly to a woman whose hair hung in long, gray spirals.

I was standing alone in the pantry when Nomi found me. "He's just *lovely*," she said, after brief kisses, one per cheek.

"Yes," I agreed. The ache rose in my chest, bruising my ribs. "He really is."

"You must laugh when you hear Les complain about this commute."

He and Nomi had grown up in the same city, worked in the same building, spoke the same language. They woke in the same bed each morning, renovated a kitchen, spent time with a child, became part of a community. "We're doing okay with the distance," I said. "When we're together, it's just so great."

Standing there, the reality of what I'd never have by choosing someone who lived so far away hit hard. I looked for Baruch, hoping he might nudge me out of my funk, but where was my Fat Man, my *bashert?* Talking to a pizza maker with platinum blonde hair, crimson lipstick, and boots. "The thin crust is splendid," he was saying. "And the mushrooms, what are they?"

"Shiitake and porcini. I use a mix of whatever I can get."

"From the fields?"

"The *fields!* Ah ha ha!" She laughed, got a bit wobbly. Clutched his arm for support.

At last we could leave. On the drive home, he said, "You have interesting friends. The woman with the blonde hair..."

"No idea who that was. Whatsoever. Never laid eyes on that chick."

Did I actually say that? I did.

We did not make love that night. It was the first time we'd switched off the lights and turned away.

I felt him prop his hands behind his head, as awake as I was. "Can't you sleep?" I asked after a while.

"All that cheese. My stomach is upset."

"There's a twenty-four-hour drugstore nearby. I could run out and get you something."

"Stop *running* and go to sleep," he said sharply.

"Why are you so testy?" I asked.

"I need some sleep before that girl will wake us up."

The clock confirmed this. In five hours, Jessie could start scream-ing. My head already ached.

&

When I woke, I was alone. Loss was like the engine of a train that had taken me into a long dark tunnel. Gone. So was the second, more reasonable voice. All I felt was the fear that *it*, our bond, our love, had been severed. There was no *shomer*, sitting in a corner of the room, waiting to catch it. Gone.

Outside the sky had brightened, though no sun shone in that milky sky. He was not at my desk in the alcove. I waited for him to return, so far down it was as if I had returned to the dark room of my childhood, a place of no solace.

I clutched my phone, ready to call. Then footsteps. The front door opening. He'd been standing outside. His face was puffy. "Every day is like this? So dreary."

"I know," I said. "It's not like in the land of eternal conflict, where the sun always shines."

He took in my tart words without comment. "I checked the flight board. Both flights are still listed as on time."

He wasn't scheduled to leave until late that afternoon. "Someone's in a rush," I said.

Breakfast? Neither of us wanted to eat.

The coffee was bitter. "Terrible coffee," I said, pouring what was in my mug down the drain.

He checked his watch, returned to the desk I'd set up for him, my desk at other times.

In the shower, a voice of reason rose. *Get a grip!* His stomach ached from all that cheese. Deadlines pressed on him. He'd never been de-ceitful, never withdrawn his love. Nothing foreshadowed a change of heart. Unless seeing Nomi and Les in their remodeled kitchen, in the same house, same city, same country, had shaken him the way it had shaken me. Maybe he'd felt it before he'd arrived and intended to tell me now. Couples parted all the time. Breakups were as common as dirt.

I dressed, making myself recall the promises we'd made to always speak of what upset us. Couldn't I say, "I'm afraid"? Couldn't I say, "Something feels different"? Couldn't we talk, as we always had? We'd been so intimate, had confessed to so much, but never of our doubts or hesitations, the constricted quality of our time together.

I stepped into the living room, pausing, in awe of his *sitzfleisch*, his ability to concentrate, for indeed it was easy to imagine him sitting undisturbed in a burning building, easy to picture him pecking away at the keyboard, while outside the wailing fire engines pulled up, and the fireman broke down walls. I stood, searching for words, turning over these thoughts.

I can't say how long I waited, admiring his focus, willing myself to interrupt, only that when he turned and saw me with my arms folded, his eyes widened and he rose from his chair and snapped shut his laptop. "I can leave. I'm all packed."

Stunned, I said, "I don't want you to leave, but you are, anyhow, and then what? It's not like we can build anything together. So go ahead and get an early start."

His look chilled me.

"It's true. You've been so distant, so obviously unhappy. Go home. It's what you want." And still that cold look. "Isn't it?"

"What do you want me to say?"

"What you feel," I said.

"That it's hard? Is that what you want to hear? That it feels too hard. Look," he said. "Let's just stop this. I can call a taxi."

"I can drive you," I said. He turned, began stuffing papers into a folder. The apartment could not contain the two of us. "I need to get gas. *Don't* call a taxi. I'm just getting gas."

I brushed the keys off the table and hurried outside. My car was at the curb in front of the building. I slid into the driver's seat and turned the air conditioning to its highest setting.

Don't crash, I thought, as I pulled into the road. I'd read that car accidents skyrocketed for couples getting divorced. I gripped the steering wheel and drove carefully and kept thinking: *don't crash,* because I wanted to drive into a wall. I wanted to accelerate and ram into something—a parked car, a garbage truck.

On the way to a gas station in Oakland, I passed the universities. Everywhere, students were hauling lamps and comforters, laptops slung across their shoulders; freshmen, I assumed, since weary parents trekked behind carrying open cartons piled high with rolled-up posters, pillows and shoes. So many tan, ponytailed girls in shorts and flip-flops, discreet little tattoos on their ankles.

The pumps were all busy; the other cars were packed with kids and pulsated with music. I got out of the car when it was my turn and thought about Hemingway and the broken place within him that could not be fixed. When my tank was full, I pulled up to the vacuums. I popped my quarters in the slot, uncoiled the hose and vacuumed the floor mats and the crevices in the seat until the prickly urge to ram into something began to dissipate.

Okay, I thought. I'm okay.

I cut carefully into traffic on Forbes Avenue, drove slowly and sanely past the coffee shops, Mexican chains, the local diner, with its cluster of customers lined up on the sidewalk, waiting for tables. But I wasn't okay and pulled into an empty spot beside a hydrant, put my forehead against the steering wheel, and began to cry. Baruch was back at my apartment, waiting for me to take him to the airport, and I was parked at the curb, heartsick, feeling that I lacked the stamina to go on. All my life I'd wanted to be fully and deeply loved and to prove I could love in return. Now I felt that I did not have the strength to do it.

A tall, ponytailed boy walked past, his parents trudging along behind on this major day, this turning point in their lives. I could believe that what had come between us was a misunderstanding, a series of missed cues. A first quarrel that could be resolved. I could believe that. But he would still be leaving when I got home, and there would be weeks apart, other quarrels that would leave me at the side of the road feeling as if I had turned myself inside out from crying.

A girl in a tank top walked by, a teddy bear under her arm, its head nestled against her enormous breasts. I dried my face with an old napkin, and saw myself standing, searching for words, desperate for reassurance, and the look on his face when he turned, the way he gathered his papers.

Why had he been so angry? What micro-expression did he detect on my face? When he turned, what had he seen?

His wife, surprising him like this the morning she said she was leaving? Approaching him from behind, waiting with infinite patience, her arms crossed. He had turned, had seen her scornful expression, had known before she spoke that it was over between them. After all the stories he'd told, I'd never thought of him as a man who knew that loss was just around the corner. Never once had I imagined how he might feel losing me.

I put the car into gear and continued home. My parking space was still free. I pulled to the curb just as the old Chinese couple was pushing their carriage up the hill. The little boy inside sat upright from the bumpy ride, his mouth an *O*, as if delighted by the sidewalks buckled by the roots of old trees, by the trees themselves, or the dog stretched out like a rug while the gardener pulled weeds. He grasped the padded bar and took it all in, wide-eyed.

The outside door was unlocked. I imagined the empty apartment, how unbearable it would be if he had left, and how I'd be forced to bear it. Then I opened the door and saw him standing in the middle of the room. I meant to tell him about this fissure in me, that it would always be there, but when he stepped toward me, I saw I was not alone in feeling broken and crossed the room to slip into his arms. "You're home," I said, and he said, "What are we doing?" with such tenderness. "What?" he said again.

He was my home, and in his embrace, I forgot what I could not do, forgot that I was broken, forgot the distance between us. We were loving each other, that's what we were doing. We two adults, bruised by life, frayed at the edges, a little slow to learn, but lucky, both of us, able to love each other.

His question then, his question now, all these years later, was easy to answer.

ACKNOWLEDGMENTS

Heather Sellers read a very early version of this novel and urged me to carry on. Thank you, Heather, for your wisdom and encouragement. Thanks to Jane McCafferty and Jane Shapiro for reading drafts more than once, to Julie Baretz in Jerusalem, for filling in some blanks, and to my other wonderful readers, Carol Ardman, Jen Bannon, Kathleen George, and Mary Morris.

I'm fortunate to have a home in the English Department at Carnegie Mellon University. Thanks to our head, Andreea Ritivoi, who supports and appreciates creative writing, and to my friends in the Creative Writing Program. We are small but mighty because of their dedication as writers and teachers.

My inspiration for Chaverim came from Kishorit in the Western Galilee. Here I first saw a community where men and women with disabilities could live, work, and create meaningful lives. Kishorit's founders, Yael Shilo and Shuki Levinger, are true visionaries.

I am indebted to the staff and individuals who welcomed me at the Merakey Allegheny Valley School. Thanks to Staff Development Executive Carol Erzen, and Executive Director, Development & Communications Dorothy Gordon, for giving me access to the Merakey AVS Sensory Development Program & Sensory Checklist. Visit avs.merakey.org for more information.

Monthlong residences at the Tyrone Guthrie Centre in Monaghan, Ireland, and Brush Creek Foundation for the Arts in Saratoga, Wyoming, gave me the time to write and think. I am grateful to the staff and administration of these beautiful retreats.

Thanks to Jaynie Royal, Elizabeth Lowenstein, and Pam Van Dyk at Regal House Publishing for their diligence and care.

To my daughters, Charlotte and Rachel Glynn, who continue to teach and delight me, and to Jeff, for his love, patience, good humor, and perfect espresso—thank you a million times.

CPSIA information can be obtained
at www.ICGtesting.com
Printed in the USA
FSHW011206190919
62161FS